NOVELS BY JOYCE CAROL OATES

Butcher

Butcher

[FATHER OF MODERN GYNO-PSYCHIATRY]

Joyce Carol Oates

 ALFRED A. KNOPF · NEW YORK · 2024

THIS IS A BORZOI BOOK
PUBLISHED BY ALFRED A. KNOPF

www.aaknopf.com

Knopf, Borzoi Books, and the colophon
are registered trademarks of Penguin Random House LLC.

Library of Congress Cataloging-in-Publication Data
Names: Oates, Joyce Carol, [date] author.
Title: Butcher : father of modern gyno-psychiatry :
a novel / Joyce Carol Oates.
Description: First edition. | New York : Alfred A. Knopf, 2024. |
This is a work of fiction incorporating episodes from the lives of the historic
J. Marion Sims, M.D. (1813–1883), "The Father of Modern Gynecology";
Silas Weir Mitchell, M.D. (1829–1914), "The Father of Medical Neurology";
and Henry Cotton, M.D. (1876–1933),
Director of the New Jersey Lunatic Asylum, 1907–1930.
Identifiers: LCCN 2023018108 | ISBN 9780593537770 (hardcover) |
ISBN 9780593537787 (ebook) | ISBN 9781524712662 (open market)
Subjects: LCGFT: Medical fiction. | Novels.
Classification: LCC PS3565.A8 B88 2024 | DDC 813/.54—dc23/eng/20230622
LC record available at https://lccn.loc.gov/2023018108

Jacket image: Tetyana Afanasyeva/Shutterstock
Jacket design by Kelly Blair

Manufactured in the United States of America
First Edition

For all the Brigits—the unnamed as well as the named,
the muted as well as those whose voices were heard,
the forgotten as well as those enshrined in history

As Columbus gazed upon the *New World* in wonderment,
as Copernicus & Galileo gazed upon the *Heavens,* so I,
Silas Aloysius Weir, M.D., have *gazed into the dark enigma
of the female vagina*—alone of all men, until this time.

SILAS ALOYSIUS WEIR, M.D.

A surgeon must have the brain of an Apollo, the heart of a
lion, & the hand of a woman.

SIR JOHN BELL

Joy there was, amid sorrow.
Amid sorrow, joy.
For sorrow-joy more
sharp to us
than mere/merest
Joy.

BRIGIT AGNES KINEALY,
Lost Girl, Found: An Orphan's True Story Told by Herself

Butcher

Editor's Note

HEREWITH, a biography comprised of divers voices, primarily that of my late father, Silas Aloysius Weir, M.D. (1812–1888), for thirty-five years Director of the New Jersey State Asylum for Female Lunatics at Trenton, New Jersey: by consensus among his fellow physicians, surgeons, & psychiatrists, the "Father of Gyno-Psychiatry"—that is, psychiatry with specialization in the female. But Silas Aloysius Weir also pioneered in other aspects of medical science, as this biography will reveal.

Originally, it had been my intention, as the executor of my father's estate, to gather together a compendium of testimonies from his professional colleagues pertaining to the pioneering work of Silas Aloysius Weir, in commemoration of the (tenth) anniversary of his death; much of this original intention remains, of course, though it has been amplified by other documents, from unexpected sources, as well as my own commentary.

I have discovered that a fair representation of the life & career of Silas Aloysius Weir has been all but impossible to obtain. As a courageous if sometimes headstrong pioneer in his field, my father naturally stirred much resentment, rivalry, & censure during his lifetime; following his death, positions regarding his reputation have hardened, falling generally into two camps, of *support* & *denunciation*.

My own position, as executor, but also as my father's eldest son, is nonetheless, I hope, *objective*.

It must be said, however, that Silas Weir was a most unusual scientific researcher, a pioneer not only in the field of psychiatry but of Gyno-Psychiatry, a controversial area of specialization to this day; along with his kinsman Medrick Weir, Father was a co-founder of this entire area of specialization, still but sparsely followed in the profession. In some quarters, Father was reviled as a physician who preyed upon his (helpless) patients, to advance his career as well as for more personal, prurient motives; yet, the fact remains, none of the more orthodox physicians of his time would have wished to examine Father's typical (female) patient, let alone attempt to "cure" her of her maladies. For at the Trenton hospital, Father's patients were often indigent persons, the "flotsam & jetsam of the Earth," as Father called them. Though he had, for some time, a flourishing private practice in Trenton as well, among well-to-do patients, his greatest responsibilities were to the afflicted of the New Jersey State Asylum for Female Lunatics. This he believed to be a sacred trust placed upon him by the Governor of the State, the New Jersey Public Health Commission, the taxpayers of the State of New Jersey, & Providence itself, in which he never ceased to have faith.

(Indeed, it is a much-iterated theme of Silas Weir's autobiography that he seemed to have been convinced that whatever he did, *Providence was guiding his hand.* The smallest tasks, Father believed to be essential to his destiny; what those of us of a younger generation would likely attribute to mere chance, if not the whimsicality of fate, Father interpreted as the will of God.)

I will allow that salacious rumors were circulated of Silas Weir, by persons who knew little of him; even among his Cleff in-laws, my mother's relatives, from whom I must acknowledge I have become estranged, for reasons that will become clear in this biography.

So it is, testimonies from Father's cohort of physician-associates have proved disappointing, over all, & would make for very dull reading in any case: hagiography, from his closest associates & defenders; or, incensed indignation, disgust, & disapprobation from his detractors. As I do not intend to elicit testimonies from Father's relatives, from whom I am also estranged, there is a dearth of biographical material herein except for that supplied by Father himself, in excerpts from his (posthumously published) autobiography, *The Chronicle of a Physician's Life,* which I have edited for inclusion here.

(In the interest of full disclosure, I should note that the *authenticity* & *accuracy* of Father's autobiography have been called into question by some historians. In particular, it has been charged against Silas Weir that he much exaggerated his surgical "successes" & deliberately failed to record his most egregious failures, as a physician is ethically bound to do. Following a devastating fire, in March 1861, in Silas Weir's Laboratory in the Asylum at Trenton, records of his most controversial experimentation have been lost; all that is known of these accomplishments is what Father wished to preserve in the *Chronicle*.)

What I have amassed, finally, is, I hope, a convincing & authentic portrait of my father, Silas Aloysius Weir, M.D., comprised of a chorus of witnesses: some clearly biased & others more objective. The most unexpected, as it is the most unsparing, is Part V, excerpts from the best-selling memoir of Silas Weir's most renowned former patient, Brigit Agnes Kinealy, provocatively titled *Lost Girl, Found: An Orphan's True Story Told by Herself* (Matthew Carey Publishers, 1868), providing testimony regarding my father's practices & personality impossible to acquire from other sources, & differing from my father's accounts in most striking ways.

Thus, a document of inestimable value in the troubled history of Gyno-Psychiatry in which, all too rarely, the objects of the science, i.e., *females,* were allowed to have a voice.

That my eclectic biography is likely to be "controversial"—indeed, "scandalous"—to many readers is an inevitability which I must accept, as Silas Weir's eldest son, at once a disappointment to the man, yet his most crusading chronicler & heir.

Jonathan Franklin Weir
Boston, Massachusetts
October 1898

PROLOGUE

. . . we had not begun murdering the Red-Handed Butcher before it was over. He had fallen at once to the filthy floor like a dumb beast smote by the hand of God slip-sliding piteously in his own blood. Weeping like a whipt child bereft of all hope & shamed & his clothing torn & yanked from him, in his nakedness mangled genitals bleeding between sallow old-man thighs we screamed with laughter to see. Hallelujah!—the cry of the wrathful Jehovah God of the Israelites pushing forward in the fury of joy like flood-waters overspilling the riverbank, the boldest of us were bent on murder, the joy of murder, our knives were hungry for the soft-fleshy chest of the Red-Handed Butcher who had kept us captive, the heart of the Red-Handed Butcher who had tortured us, the belly of the Red-Handed Butcher who had sodomized us even as the wisest of us cried—No! No, we must not!—it will be our doom, if we murder the Butcher-doctor.

Hid my eyes for I could not look upon it, what we had wrought.

I

YOUNG DOCTOR WEIR

THE SUITOR (1835)
MRS. ELIAS ROLLINS, NÉE TABITHA TYNDALE
CHESTNUT HILL, PENNSYLVANIA

GOD FORGIVE US!—we failed to recognize the young genius who appeared out of nowhere in our midst, in the autumn of 1835; indeed, like the silly geese we were, so blinded by our own vanity, & the puffery of our feathers, we mistook this inauspicious apprentice-doctor for something of a fool, though shy-seeming & clumsy & said to be of a "very respectable" family in his hometown of Concord, Massachusetts.

Indeed, we *laughed* at him, for imagining himself a *suitor*!—of any of *us*.

Calling himself "Silas Weir, M.D."—in a gravely solemn voice that could not escape boastfulness. Surely, the least attractive bachelor in Chestnut Hill that season!

The first thing you noticed about Silas Weir: His skin was unhealthily sallow, the very hue of *earnest*. The face of a young doctor who has kept himself indoors for too long, immersed in medical textbooks, airless operating theaters, & those dread places called "morgues," where cadavers are cruelly dissected. A face both boyish & careworn, with worry-lines in the (high, bony) forehead like lines made by a fork in dough, & a squinting look about the eyes as of unease, guilt.

He was of moderate height. His head was overlarge upon his stooped & spindly shoulders; his stiff-tufted hair of no discernible hue, neither dark nor fair, needed a more expert trimming; his eyes rather deep-set in their sockets, like a rodent's eyes, damp & quick-shifting. His ears were curiously white, protruding somewhat from his head. Yet there was an awkward sort of dignity in his bearing, as in one masquerading as someone he is not.

His clothing of lightweight dark wool was of good quality (so sharp-eyed Mother observed) but somewhat rumpled, as if he had been sleeping in it. His linen might have been fresh when he'd set out from his lodgings on the farther, downside of town, but after a few minutes in our over-warm drawing room it began to dampen; his stiff-starched collar began to wilt. In our brightly hued silks & satins, tight-laced inside our whalebone corsets, we *young ladies* were white-powdered with talcum, most densely in our armpits & in the nether-world between our legs, which had no name & was thus unnameable; if it was, for any of us, *that time of month,* we were buttressed between our thighs with thick gauze-bandages that soon became heavy with brackish blood that dried & chafed against our tender skin like the coarsest sandpaper; this, also liberally powdered with talcum, for it was, of all things, including even heinous sins & crimes, the worst possible fate, that *that time of month* might become evident to any others, & of these most particularly men; & of men, those designated *eligible bachelors.* In a panic of being discovered, *sniffed-at, smelt, detected* by (male) nostrils, we were perpetually on alert, which made us skittish & (occasionally) cruel, & certainly sharp-eyed, for we did not wish to be taken unaware.

Thus we took note of Silas Weir with some condescension, & relief, since clearly here was an *eligible bachelor* whose opinion did not matter to us in the slightest. Our Chestnut Hill suitors were known to us since childhood, & even the least handsome of them was handsome to us, like relatives; in truth, young Dr. Weir was not so much ugly as simply *too ordinary,* & lacking social graces.

Those impressive likenesses of the older *Silas Aloysius Weir, M.D.,* which have appeared in newspapers, & recently in *Harper's Weekly*—so stern & assured, with a jutting jaw, & frowning eyes, revered as an award-winning research scientist & honored in the White House—are not at all how I remember sallow-skinned young Dr. Weir.

In our drawing room in Chestnut Hill in the fall of 1835, Silas Weir was a curious sight. He smiled when he should have been somber-faced, & he was somber-faced when he should have been smiling. His mouth was soft-seeming as putty & worm-colored; the prospect of such a mouth *daring to kiss* you would make you howl with laughter like a banshee. (None of us ever got that far in imagining, I am quick to reassure you!) He had the demeanor of a forty-year-old but was said to be only twenty-three!

His accent struck our ears as very—odd. You did hear people from Boston speaking like this, as if they had head colds; Silas Weir's accent was even more pronounced. Though he could enunciate fancy-sounding words—(*Aristotle, Galen, contagion, exsanguination*)—the effect was comical. We'd have dissolved into giggles if we dared to exchange glances with each other as we'd done many a time in school & at church, except we weren't children any longer but *young ladies.*

Every now & then like a snake flicking its tongue Silas Weir's small damp eyes would glance in my direction: swiftly traveling from the toe of my slipper peeking from beneath my heavy skirt & petticoats to my cinched-in waist, to the lacy brocade of my bodice, lifting to my pale throat & pale-powdered face while not daring to actually meet my eyes.

Of course, it was not Silas Weir's fault that he'd become a weekly, barely tolerated guest for tea at our house in Chestnut Hill—he had not invited himself. My great-uncle Clarence Tyndale was a deacon at our church, the First Episcopal Church of Chestnut Hill, where Silas Weir had joined the congregation; out of Christian charity, with every good intention, Uncle Clarence encouraged "young Dr. Weir" (as he called him) to "pay a visit" to our household. Silas Weir knew no one in Chestnut Hill, or so it was said. He'd just graduated from the Philadelphia College of Medicine & was an apprentice to our local physician, Ambrose Strether, who maintained a diminished practice as he neared retirement age (sixty); this was not a very promising start to a career in medicine for a young doctor.

(Only later would we learn that Silas Weir had been "exiled"—in a manner of speaking—by his own family, having failed to maintain the high standards of excellence expected of the Weirs of Concord, Mass.; performing with little distinction academically, thus failing to be admitted to Harvard College, which every male Weir had attended in the history of the family.)

No doubt, Uncle Clarence hoped to help the young Christian gentleman. Jesus's admonition *Love thy neighbor as thyself* had burrowed into Uncle's head like the ash borer into our stately ash trees, & made him a nuisance to his relatives.

An eligible young Christian bachelor who has studied to be a doctor. Who knows what his future will be. You young ladies will be kind to him, I know. You will make him feel welcome in Chestnut Hill, where, I fear, there is a history of "class snobbery."

So long ago, makes my head swim.

I was just eighteen, having graduated from the Chestnut Hill Academy for Girls. My dearest closest friend, Fiona Fox, had graduated with me. Also in our circle was my (older) sister Katherine, a grave-faced beauty, & our lively cousins June & Jetta. And Belinda Prescott, the judge's daughter. Have to say, without wanting to boast, that those years, in Chestnut Hill, our circle was *the* circle. Girls from the best families vied to be our friends just as their brothers & cousins vied to "court" us, but we were young & spoiled & choosy, which made us cruel.

Yes, I will acknowledge: We were *pretty*. All of us!

And very prettily dressed in our frilly flowery lacy ribbon-bedecked dresses with tight bodices & sprawling skirts to the floor, hiding our (slender, white-stockinged) ankles; inside our fine clothing we were obliged to sit very straight indeed, posture-perfect, laced into whalebone corsets so that, just barely, we could breathe.

My twenty-four-inch waist reduced to a sylphine nineteen inches, between the satiny glisten of the bodice & the flounce of the skirt, designed to entice a young gentleman's eye.

That sick drowning look in Silas Weir's face when he first saw the array of us like gladioli in a lush garden made us feel sorry for him—almost . . .

Holding his hat in both hands as Lettie escorted him to the doorway of the drawing room. Staring & blinking as if a blazing light were blinding his eyes. Quickly Momma put the awkward visitor at his ease, or tried to: Poor Dr. Weir stumbled over his own feet taking a seat beside the hearth, fiercely blushing. He had never been in such genteel company before, it seemed!

He had never gazed upon *young ladies* like us before, obviously.

How many times in that year, & part of the year to follow, Silas Weir returned to our house, I cannot recall. We did not take him seriously when there were certain others, far more attractive young men, of "good" Philadelphia families, vying with him for our attention; of all the "eligible bachelors," Silas Weir was the runt of the litter. But he did not know that—of course.

After the first awkward visit, Dr. Weir never failed to bring flowers to present to Momma: often, coarse flowers like hydrangeas in full bloom, even hollyhocks & tiger lilies! (These flowers Dr. Weir very likely discovered growing wild in fields & ditches, as if we wouldn't have suspected.) Momma had not the heart to discourage him. No other house in Chestnut Hill was open to him. It was not our fine-steeped English tea or our cook's delicious tea-sandwiches & crumpets that drew the awkward young man, for he had scarcely any appetite in our presence; if he lifted a delicate teacup to his mouth, in his quivering hand, he was likely to spill the contents on his ill-fitting trousers. Politely we put questions to him which, all eagerly, with smiles exposing odd-shaped teeth & damp gums, he stammered to answer, as if we were genuinely interested, & not being merely polite; or, worse yet, at times, & I confess that I was one of those guilty of such cruelty, teasing him as one might tease a clumsy dog.

What did the young physician, one day to become so famous, tell us in our drawing room in Chestnut Hill, so long ago? I seem to recall a certain shy boastfulness as Silas Weir prattled of his plan to advance human knowledge & "make a name for himself" in the field of medical research, as well as achieving a career as a clinician & surgeon; he spoke of "experimental surgery" he was planning, with the hope of correcting "congenital malformations" in children & even infants. We winced to hear such vulgarisms as *cleft-palate, club-foot, cross-eyed*—crude expressions never uttered in mixed company. The dread word *consumption* the young physician dared speak; such obscene words as *cadaver, confinement,* even *womb.* (But perhaps it was not "womb" that was uttered by Silas Weir, this being a word we would not have recognized, as it was, literally, unspeakable; possibly in his nasal New England accent the awkward young doctor had actually uttered "whilom," a most peculiar but poetical expression reminiscent of the poetry of Edgar Allan Poe.)

Amid the decorous murmur of subdued voices, there would come a sudden stark silence as Silas Weir's voice was exposed, overloud & foolish; the young doctor blushing fiercely & glancing about the room like one who has inadvertently appeared in public disheveled & in disarray, hoping that no one has noticed.

My friends teased me mercilessly that "silly Silas" was *in love* with me! My cousins June & Jetta were the worst.

Judging from Silas Weir's manner if I merely glanced in his direction, let alone exchanged a few words with him, or smiled at him, this appeared to be so; when he dared to utter my name—"M-Miss Tabith-a"—it was in such a cracked, croaking voice we nearly forgot ourselves & burst into gales of laughter.

In turn, I took care never to call the young doctor anything other than "Dr. Weir." I certainly never called him "Silas." Despite what others thought, I *did not encourage* him even as a whim.

So, eventually, Silas Weir came to realize that Tabitha Tyndale was not attracted to him, & he turned, somewhat desperately, to dear Fiona, whose kindness of heart could not allow her to be rude to anyone, however clumsy, though neither did Fiona encourage Weir; & shortly thereafter, when Fiona's attentions were dominated by her dashing suitor Rufus Clark, Silas Weir turned, with yet more desperation, to my flirtatious cousin Jetta.

Of all the girls in our circle, *Jetta*! Avid to toy with the naïve young man's heart as a cat will toy with a mouse, initially an entire, living mouse, but eventually with just the remains of the mouse, its innards, its tiny skull, & last of all its rubbery little heart.

For Jetta was inclined to be something of a performer, provoking laughter at the expense of the (unknowing, unwitting) "mouse"—poor Weir so deluded as to think that the vivacious red-haired Jetta, aged seventeen, could be, for a fleeting instant, interested in *him*.

How we laughed at the fool, in the privacy of my bedroom afterward! So very hard, the tight-cinched laces binding my torso, waist, hips, & buttocks caused me such great pain, I nearly fainted & had to be *unlaced*.

"You girls! That is very cruel of you, & not at all Christian. The poor young man adores you all. Is this a gracious way to repay him?"—so Momma scolded us, sighing.

Of such antics in the drawing room at our Friday afternoon teas, Papa knew nothing—fortunately! Never did Papa step a foot inside these gatherings, which interested him, a Calvinist businessman, for whom genteel conversation had little allure, not at all.

In the end, his daughters would marry young men of whom he approved, because he knew & respected their fathers, as they respected him; all the rest was mere banter & flirtation, & harmless.

But next time Silas Weir came to our house, presenting Momma with an untidy bouquet of black-eyed Susans & daisies, Jetta's pretense of interest in the young doctor had waned, for there were other, more interesting young men at the gathering; nor did Fiona pay more than stiffly polite attention to him, leaving him quite forlorn. By this time also, Elias Rollins had returned to Chestnut Hill, in his West Point cadet's dress uniform, so ravishing a sight I could hardly look elsewhere; in an instant, though my perfect posture, predicated by the invisible corsetry, did not allow any suggestion of it, all my coquettish defenses *melted*.

For here was a handsome young man whose father my father respected, as he did business with him in the city; here was a young man who was indeed a *suitor*.

Yet awkwardly, with no idea of how foolish he was being, & how futile his behavior, Silas Weir dared to tug a chair in my direction, in an attempt to join the conversation between Elias & me, like a donkey trying to frolic in a meadow with two Thoroughbred colts. Coldly I stared at the ill-favored young man with the absurd Boston accent, as if I had never seen him before; I did not introduce him to Elias, for I saw no purpose to it; each stammering word he uttered to us, I did not seem to hear.

At last Momma noticed, & took pity on Weir, & came to slip her arm through his, & led him to one of our older relatives to be introduced as a "most promising young physician, new to Chestnut Hill."

The look on the morose horse-face! The deep flush, the narrowed rodent-eyes & hurt mouth—you don't expect a fool to be so *wounded*.

It was that afternoon, as Momma bade Silas Weir farewell in the foyer of our house, that she murmured, in a tone of deep regret, "I think we will not be home next Friday, Dr. Weir. We are all going away, you see. I am so sorry."

"Oh. *I* am sorry." Weir could not have been more stunned if someone had struck him over his thick head with a poker. "W-where?"

" 'Where'—?"

"—are you going?"

So naïvely Silas Weir asked this rude question, with such a look of boyish innocence, Momma did not cut him dead as she might have wished, but murmured something about a death in the family, a funeral, a period of mourning . . .

"Ah, I see! I am so, so sorry. May I offer my condolences, Mrs. Tyndale?"

"You may, Dr. Weir. You may."

Even as our Irish girl escorted him out of the house, & out of our lives forever, with a barely suppressed smirk of derision.

Rid of the pest at last! We all rejoiced, for we would not miss Silas Weir.

Yet, I did feel some semblance of guilt, amid my buoyant happiness at my own thrilling future.

At least one further time, to our surprise, Silas Weir appeared at our house, at a large Christmas gathering. It was probable that Uncle Clarence had invited him, though Uncle Clarence denied it afterward; but we did not put it past the desperate "suitor" to be spying on our household, noting the occasion of a large gathering & simply following guests inside, knowing that in such gracious surroundings he would hardly be turned away at the door.

Lovesick, with damp rodent-eyes, gazing about the drawing room, fastening onto *me*.

But this time, I was determined to discourage him. Making it a point to approach Silas Weir as I had never approached him before, gaily lifting my hand to him—"My news, Dr. Weir, is—I am engaged!"—in triumph showing him the beautiful heirloom engagement ring, a square-cut diamond edged with rubies, that had once belonged to Elias Rollins's great-grandmother.

His eyes, which had brightened at my approach, were sicklied over with a look of pond scum, & his mouth went slack in dismay. I am not proud to confess, I was heartless. I am sure, my eyes shone with triumph. Like stepping on a moth you didn't mean to step on, didn't mean to injure, but now the pathetic thing is flapping & fluttering in the grass & you just feel unaccountably *annoyed*.

Despite his shock, Dr. Weir managed to stammer congratulations. Fortunately, my dashing fiancé Elias was not present, which made the encounter somewhat less of a strain for Weir, who did his valiant best to recover, & not to take his leave immediately. Indeed, the entire drawing room had gone quiet, for my cruelty to Silas Weir registered as a kind of *frisson* in the hearts of Fiona, & Katherine, & Belinda, & June, & Jetta, who, long in states of apprehension & anxiety regarding the more suitable young men of our acquaintance, could rejoice in our unalloyed collected contempt for the interloper.

Following this, young Dr. Weir departed from our lives. We had so little interest in him, we never inquired after him, nor even remembered him, until Uncle Clarence happened to inform us months later that Silas Weir had "somewhat abruptly" left Chestnut Hill, & his apprenticeship with Ambrose Strether, to take up a position in New Jersey.

.

"Tabitha! Is this Dr. 'Weir'—'Silas Aloysius'—*our* Dr. Weir?"

Though grown elderly, Momma was nearly as sharp-eyed as ever, having caught sight of a familiar likeness in the latest issue of *Harper's Weekly,* which she held out to me with a commanding expression.

"Why, I think—yes—I think it *is.* 'Silas Aloysius Weir' he calls himself now, it seems . . ."

I stared at the drawing, of a most dignified middle-aged gentleman with a bristling mustache. I was feeling quite abashed. And Momma's sardonic smile was not a great comfort.

No one in Chestnut Hill had given "Silas Weir, M.D." a thought in decades. He had passed out of our minds with no more trace than one or another of our Irish indentured servants who toiled in our households, came to the end of their contracts, & were released from servitude with a small fee & Father's blessing, sent on their way & forgotten. Until, years later, Dr. Weir was noted as having received a distinguished award from the National Society of Medical Science for his "profound innovations" in surgery involving the "female anatomy"; & came to be called, most astonishingly, the "Father of Modern Gyno-Psychiatry."

Gyno-Psychiatry! A word scarcely to be murmured aloud, it has so ugly & alarming a sound.

Only vaguely did we suspect what *Gyno-Psychiatry* might mean— a "mental" medical specialty involving women, it seemed. But a very rare sort of specialty, with no physician in Chestnut Hill trained in such a field.

What Dr. Weir's medical innovations are, I do not know. I only glanced at the article in *Harper's Weekly.* It would make me faint to be informed in detail about such matters of the *female body,* I am sure; my nerves are so frayed, certain words have the power to upset me.

Still more, unwanted memories of a long-vanished girlhood when I was so beautiful I could laugh cruelly at a "suitor" . . .

Ah, Dr. Weir! After twelve pregnancies, seven stillbirths, & five births, blessed with two surviving children, both now adult men, & seven (surviving) grandchildren, you would not recognize your kittenish Tabitha, I'm afraid.

My nerves are not so steady as they once were, nor my thoughts so playful & sparkling. My swollen ankles & varicose-vein-riddled legs can barely support my girth. My udder-breasts that would sink like sandbags into my lap, if they were not severely restrained by sturdy undergarments.

Indeed, I find it very taxing just to *think,* let alone *regret*—I know not what . . .

And here is Momma bringing up the subject of Dr. Weir to chide me, as if I were not a very middle-aged woman with a permanently flushed skin & thinning hair but a headstrong young girl with a nineteen-inch waist.

"*I* thought that young doctor showed much promise, as you recall— *you* & your sisters were very silly, to have thought otherwise. If your head hadn't been turned by the Rollins clan, & you'd married dashing young Silas Weir instead—this very hour *you* would be the wife of the Father of Gyno-Psychiatry . . ."

THE APPRENTICE (1835–1836)
MILTON THORPE, M.D.
CHESTNUT HILL, PENNSYLVANIA

*H*IM! Not likely I'd forget "Silas Aloysius Weir"—as he came to call himself.

Fact is, while we knew him in Chestnut Hill he was "Silas Weir"— nothing fancy about him or his degree from the Philadelphia College of Medicine, where the full course of instruction was but *four months*.

My reminiscences of Silas Weir date back to the turbulent year we spent in each other's company in Dr. Strether's surgery, as apprentices to the senior physician; I, the elder by two years, with my medical certificate (like his) from the Philadelphia College, & Weir only just graduated in 1834, & very young & inexperienced for a twenty-three-year-old.

Indeed, Silas Weir was not a promising physician, still less a promising surgeon. He allowed me to know that there were several "distinguished" physicians in the Weir family of Massachusetts, & that one of his uncles was a renowned astronomer, at Harvard; which made me very curious, of course, as to why Silas had gone to so inferior a medical school, & not rather to Harvard or the University of Pennsylvania, though I was not so rude as to inquire.

Weir exhibited an actual fear of confronting a patient in Strether's examination room—invariably, he would urge me to "go first" & he would follow me into the room.

Unless Strether turned to him, to challenge him to hazard an opinion, Weir would remain tongue-tied through an entire examination, staring with fearful eyes at the afflicted person, if male; if female, scarcely daring to look at her at all.

At times, I could discern Weir visibly *trembling,* as with cold.

(And indeed, Weir seemed often cold. His fingernails were bluish, frequently his lips, in cold weather. His ears, which were somewhat larger than normal ears, & slightly pointed at the tips, were a curious waxen-white as if frostbitten.)

Thus, I was obliged to assist Dr. Strether most of the time, which I did not mind since I learned, in this way, a good deal of old-fashioned "hands-on" doctoring, while Weir cowered in a corner like the coward he was.

For it soon became evident that Weir was very ill-at-ease with the *physical*—a considerable handicap for a doctor! Clearly he'd had no intimate experience with any female, & certainly he had never gazed upon the female body unclothed. The sight of a naked woman, or even a partly clothed woman, was frightful to many Christian youths of that time, & Weir was one of these; indeed, girls from good Christian families had no idea what their own unclothed bodies looked like, having been taught that their private parts were sinful to behold, if not demonic. Of course, they were totally innocent of any knowledge of the physiological mechanisms of *procreation* & entered into marriage in profound ignorance.

In addition to ordinary unease, Weir seems to have felt, like many men & boys of his time, a particular repugnance for female "private parts"; an undeniable attraction, in the way that one is attracted to the forbidden & obscene, but over all, a visceral dislike, mounting to outright disgust.

In time, as it will be revealed in his autobiography, Silas Weir would have little difficulty treating females of the *lower classes,* in particular indentured servants & Irish immigrants whom he considered "animalistic"; but he was struck dumb in the presence of women of "good family."

The more genteel, the more well-to-do, Weir shrank from as if they were goddesses, as they resembled the women of his own family, & their neighbors in Concord. As he was somewhat *déclassé* himself, as a younger son, not likely to be a major heir of his father's estate, Weir had become obsessed with the hope of marrying well, through an (unlikely) alliance with one of the young heiresses of Chestnut Hill.

As Dr. Strether was approaching retirement, & younger physicians abounded in the wealthy Philadelphia suburb of Chestnut Hill, he had lost his richest patients; most of the women in his practice were the wives & daughters of local tradesmen, working-men & laborers, underpaid teachers, & the like, with a sprinkling of servants & farm hands, sent to him by their employers. Some of the immigrant women, of the poorer sort, were startling to behold, uncorseted, their mammalian bodies distended & grotesque from multiple pregnancies, & likely to give off a most repugnant odor; such females are a challenge for any doctor to examine close-up, even a seasoned physician like Strether.

"You will have to learn to hold your breath, Silas," Strether would remark, with a pitying smile for Weir, & a glance of bemused complicity with me, "if you want to be a physician. Our brethren in the clergy have much the best of it, dealing with vaporous souls that emit no odors."

Weir tried to laugh, feebly. One might almost feel sorry for the man, that sick, sinking look in the morose horse-face.

"Yes. I tell myself: 'Jesus loves us *all.*'" But the expression on Weir's face told another story.

Do you wonder how we'd come to be certified as physicians, with so little experience with patients? At the Philadelphia College of Medicine the primary course of instruction was lectures, usually of a dull, friable nature, delivered by an elder physician-instructor in a monotonous voice that soon put us into a drowse. Unlike medical students at more reputable schools like the School of Medicine at the University of Pennsylvania, we did not encounter patients; we did not visit hospitals; we had no official experience of sickness. Our lectures dwelt upon human anatomy, with much emphasis upon memorization of the parts of the body, as well as the myriad bones of the human skeleton. The practicing physician had no real reason to recall such information since he was likely to have, like Dr. Strether, medical books & charts in his surgery, to consult. The reigning wisdom of the day was *When in doubt, bleed*—the patient, that is; but we had little firsthand experience with the actual drainage of blood from veins, a messy procedure we would learn as apprentices to elder physicians.

We were made to witness dissections but were not allowed to participate, to our relief. There was a shortage of corpses available to the school, & these the most decayed & derelict of paupers' corpses, after the more prestigious university medical school had had its pick of superior specimens.

For "clinical examinations" we practiced on mannequins designed to mimic male & female anatomies. Though these were not very life-like, with blank, blind eyes & a poreless, sand-colored epidermis, they seemed distressingly realistic to the more impressionable among us who were but young men, scarcely more than boys, & quite inexperienced; even a rudimentary representation of *human genitalia* was shocking to our eyes. Yet more upsetting were the "pregnant" female mannequins with swollen bellies that, hideously opened, revealed "fetuses" secured inside; these, to be expelled from the mannequin's womb through a uterine track, of a repulsive flesh-colored hue . . . Medical students as naïve as Silas Weir were likely to feel faint, or nauseated, seeing such a ghastly sight.

As most babies were delivered not by physicians but by midwives, childbirth was not taken seriously within the medical community. Only if there was an unusually difficult labor involving a woman from a good family, a physician might be summoned & would attend as a personal favor to the head of the household; otherwise it was accepted that a number of infants died at birth, or shortly after. A healthy mother might bleed to death in childbirth, or acquire a high fever & die, for some mysterious cause no one could determine. ("Infection" was evident—but how was it caused? And how was it to be treated? Bleeding a female patient who has already lost a good deal of blood did not seem practical. Aristotle had not discussed this medical problem, but if he had, surely in women it would have been ascribed to a kind of *hysteria* of the blood, related to the uterus. But how was *that* to be treated?)

The problem was, mannequins are inert, indifferent to "pain," & do not suddenly begin to hemorrhage while laboring to give birth. So, we young physicians were ill-prepared for an actual, difficult childbirth. It was believed that a young physician would learn all that he needed to know in his apprenticeship with an established physician, as any young apprentice learned from an elder, in any trade; for medicine was, in those days, a trade & not a respected profession. Rote memorization of the parts of the body was expected of the medical student but not knowledge of *how* the living body actually worked; the model body was a (white) male in his prime, with women & children of secondary interest.

Silas Weir's first encounter with a pregnant female was cataclysmic—for him: The mere sight of the (fully clothed) woman in Dr. Strether's surgery with her swollen belly, awkwardly seated, & displaying, for the physician's frowning scrutiny, fleshy white legs grotesquely varicose-vein-riddled, which she'd bared by pulling down her thick stockings, caused him to fall into a dead faint!

It was I who revived Weir, with smelling salts. In a quavering voice he told me he'd had glimpses of his sisters' bare legs when they were children, but he'd never in his life seen the *naked legs* of any adult woman & had had no idea how "coarse, ugly, & hairy" they were—not so different from his own.

Fortunately, female patients were examined more or less fully clothed, & male patients, partially unclothed. If he saw the need, Strether might "lay hands on" a (male) patient but did not touch female patients if he could avoid it. His apprentices were yet more diffident. Indeed, we'd never listened to an actual heartbeat with a stethoscope, until Strether foisted it upon us roguishly—"Here! See if there's anything beating inside."

The elder doctor's humor could be a bit strained, at times. Once while examining an elderly (male) patient Strether passed the stethoscope to Weir, to listen to the heartbeat, while gripping the instrument with his fingers in such a way that the sound was cut off; Weir turned very pale as he listened in vain, at last blurting out: "My God! His heart has stopped!"—even as Strether winked at me & began laughing with much zest.

More mirthful yet was Weir's fright at the sight of blood. At times, at *the mere prospect of the sight of blood.*

It would be revealed in time that Silas Weir had insisted upon attending medical school over his father's objections, for Percival Weir did not, evidently, hold his youngest son in much esteem; his fear of the sight of blood, as of other natural phenomena, was known within the family, & ridiculed. There was an older brother named Franklin, much the favorite, who'd graduated with honors from Harvard Medical School, & had embarked upon a very promising career as a surgeon in Boston. Even a younger brother, only just graduated from Harvard

College, had a promising career as a research chemist. Anything that Silas attempted was in sharp contrast to this brother's achievements & found wanting.

Reluctantly, Weir's father agreed to pay his tuition at the Philadelphia College of Medicine only because Silas demonstrated no other skills or aptitudes—for the law, for education, even for the ministry; he was certainly not likely to marry a wealthy Boston heiress, nor find a lucrative position in business or finance. Doctors whose practice did not include the affluent, particularly doctors in rural areas, were considered not so very different from itinerant handymen summoned for repairs, & were poorly paid, if at all: It looked as if Silas Weir was destined for such a debased life, to the disgust of the Weirs of Concord, Massachusetts.

When I asked Weir how he hoped to keep Dr. Strether from discovering that he was terrified of blood, Weir begged: "Can you help me, Milton? I am *trying*."

When a young laborer was brought into the surgery with a near-severed foot following an accident with an ax, Weir stood apart helpless & trembling as Strether & I tried valiantly (if futilely) to save the man from hemorrhaging to death before our eyes; another time, Weir (weakly) assisted me as I dealt, in some frantic haste, with a badly bleeding head injury suffered when a woman fell down a flight of stone steps outside a Chestnut Hill church, striking her head on every step & lacerating the scalp so that it was nearly torn from the skull—& this woman, of stout middle age, was of a very distinguished local family.

Another time, Weir fainted dead away as I assisted Strether in the removal of gangrenous, badly rotted toes on the foot of a (diabetic) patient who'd had to be strapped down so that we could "operate"—that is, amputate with a saw.

Of childbirth labors lasting as long as three days, requiring that the blood-splattered physician insert a forceps into the gaping womb of the mother & haul out the infant living or, more likely, dead, or, bloodier yet, executing a clumsy Cesarean with no anesthesia—Weir had to shut his eyes, & murmur prayers to himself, lest he fall into a faint.

On one occasion, painfully swollen hemorrhoids afflicting a corpulent (male) patient required the strenuous procedure known as *écraseur*—shutting off the blood flow to the hemorrhoid by the deployment of an instrument resembling a garrot. As this procedure, too, was executed without anesthesia, the patient had to be shackled to a table, to insure his safety; for the pain was such, he would have assaulted Strether in his kicking & flailing about, as Strether wielded the instrument with an expression of intense concentration, if distaste, before turning it over to me, as his apprentice; & then to Weir, whose fingers but weakly grasped it, as it was slippery with blood.

Strether spoke harshly to Weir: "Take this, Silas, & use it properly—or you are finished here in Chestnut Hill."

So Weir tried, manipulating the device with clumsy hands; fortunately for him, the screaming patient had fainted by this time, & presented no resistance. But even so, Weir fumbled the procedure, actually dropping the *écraseur* instrument to the floor, where it became somewhat begrimed.

Patiently, Strether commanded Weir to continue, for but one swollen hemorrhoid remained, & this, the tremulous young doctor managed to shrink, after some awkward minutes.

"You see, Silas—you have only to persevere. Who knows, you may one day grow to enjoy these rougher moments."

Afterward, as we were washing up, an ashen-faced Weir asked me if I had known that such horrors existed in God's creation—*he* had certainly not known.

Coolly I replied, "To God, all sights are equal, I would guess."

"*All sights*—'equal'? I cannot believe that."

Weir stared at me uncomprehending. His God was the God of John Calvin, fiercely contemptuous of human weakness, all too willing to see some sights as hellish, even damned.

I must concede, when a patient did not present an emergency, & there was relative calm in the surgery, Silas Weir was a competent enough apprentice. By degrees he acquired a somewhat pompous air of authority, at least when Strether was not present, in dealing with commonplace ailments—bunions, rashes, (normal-sized) hemorrhoids, cysts & boils, stomach upsets, headaches, joint aches, constipation, wheezing lungs, fevers & chills, flu, "ringing in ears," "nerves," etcetera; for these ailments, as for virtually any other, we learned to follow the practice of the day prescribing a limited repertoire of medications: laudanum, foxglove, mercury, belladonna, echinacea, ginkgo biloba, hawthorn, garlic, black cohosh, Saint-John's-wort, small quantities of arsenic, & cocaine drops.

As I have mentioned, the most popular medical procedure was *phlebotomy,* or bloodletting, prescribed for most ailments as it was believed that most illnesses were caused by an overabundance of blood, or "heated" blood. This, a tradition dating back to ancient times, was one in which Strether firmly believed: *When in doubt, bleed.* But it was a disagreeable, messy procedure which the elder physician preferred to delegate to his apprentices.

For this, surprisingly, Weir discovered a peculiar talent, as his panic at the sight of blood was apparently mitigated when *he* was the agent of the bloodletting, & not a mere witness.

With the passage of time, indeed I detected a curious glisten in Weir's deep-set damp eyes as he took up the bloodletting knife to open a vein in a patient, whether the ailment was fever or a cold, clammy skin; throbbing headache or wheezing lungs; chest pains & palpitations, spinal injury, severe constipation or diarrhea, nausea, tumorous growths—so skilled did Weir become in the art of *phlebotomy,* he was soon able to bleed even female patients, provided they were not from "good" families, were fully clothed, & not young or attractive. More than once I had glimpsed Weir regarding his own red-gleaming hands, before washing them, with a look of startled admiration.

"At last, something our young friend can do," Strether observed dryly to me, "—without falling into a faint himself, only just causing the patient to faint."

Of course, phlebotomy is an uncertain science, like phrenology, & it sometimes happened that when we bled weak, pale patients, they grew weaker, & more pale, & lapsed into a faint, & occasionally *passed away* before our eyes as their blood drained into a bucket on the floor; this happenstance, dismaying & infuriating to Strether, who, in irascible old age, did not like to be embarrassed by his apprentices.

"What, you fool, you have done it again?—let another breathe his last?"—so Strether would fume at Weir, whose habit of shutting his eyes tightly, & murmuring prayers under his breath that put him into a kind of trance, was not helpful in these circumstances.

Such deaths in the physician's surgery were considered *acts of God.* A Christian would understand—*It was his time.*

Taking heart from his success as a *phlebotomist,* Weir began to fancy himself an *experimental surgeon.*

There could be no future in mere clinical medicine, Weir realized. If he wanted to compete with his brothers, & with other (male) Weir relatives who were "making names for themselves," he would have to pioneer in new fields, & take risks, & publish his findings in the most prestigious medical journals.

After the office was closed in the early evening Weir would remain to peruse medical journals, by candlelight, as late as midnight. Ah, to be one of the celebrated of American physicians! Physicians who had mastered medical procedures, radical new surgeries! Seductive fantasies came to Silas Weir of pioneering in the repair of common maladies (club-feet, cleft-palates, crossed eyes)—this alone could assure success, & a place in medical history. A notion came to him of curing "mental illness" as a variant of "fever"; he fell under the spell of phrenology, a new science that linked areas of the skull to human activities & emotions, determined by the shape of the skull-bone, which taught that such conditions as epilepsy, mental retardation, insanity, & "oscillations of mood" could be treated through surgical intervention.

Many of these maladies, it was believed, were caused at birth, by the actions of ignorant midwives; this was commonly taught in medical schools. That midwives were *female* guaranteed a good deal of error on their part, causing disastrous injuries to women giving birth, & to babies; yet, so shunned was the delivery of babies as a medical procedure, literally the most filthy & abhorred of all procedures, it was not likely that reputable physicians would lower themselves to assist with births except in special circumstances.

It was at this time that, through the good intentions of a deacon in the church Silas Weir attended, he began to be invited to Friday tea at the home of the Tyndale family, one of Chestnut Hill's leading families—about which Weir couldn't resist boasting to me, like the vain fool he was. (As if I could be jealous of *him.*) Naïvely confiding in me that he hoped to "make a name for himself" with which to impress the youngest Tyndale daughter, Tabitha, an "angelic beauty" who would one day be a Tyndale heiress; indeed, Weir seemed to think that Mrs. Tyndale was partial to him, & appeared to be encouraging him to "court" Tabitha, who was only eighteen years old.

So boastful was Weir in his crude, callow way, I had to tell him finally that I did not want to hear any more about the Tyndales; when he was affianced to Tabitha would be soon enough for him to boast.

"True! You are correct," Weir said, blushing, more out of anger than chagrin, "—that day is not yet here. But—we will see."

In such ways the colossal egotism of the man was revealed. In his person not at all impressive, rather slight of build, with prematurely stooped shoulders & a lined brow, & a manner that was "fussy," like a dog scratching compulsively in the dirt—yet he thought highly of himself.

No doubt, *delusions* are commonplace to those who aspire to greatness without the requisite integrity, insight, & genius required for it.

Soon then a particularly unfortunate infant came into Weir's hands, that were greedy for *experimental surgery.*

This infant, a little girl but five months old, was the ninth child born to a woman who lived not in Chestnut Hill but in an adjacent rural settlement of working-men, laborers, & ne'er-do-wells, many of them unemployed for divers reasons—age, illness, injuries, alcohol. The woman, whose surname was Brush, cohabited with a motley succession of men, all of them inclined to drink, & was said to be of a very low intelligence, like her progeny; a sprawling family of dubious pedigree, clearly of mixed blood whose "feeblemindedness" was evident to the discerning eye.

With Christian sentiment so opposed to sinful living outside wedlock, & medical care so little available to impoverished persons, there was a scarcity of charitable aid for such a derelict mother & her children. Even Dr. Strether, not by nature self-righteous or judgmental, often said, with a pitying shake of his head, that the one blessing such creatures had was *short lives.* It was not expected that such afflicted children would live beyond the age of six or seven; yet, as it happened, as if perversely, the feebleminded Brush family seemed to grow, if not prosper, in a run-down hovel at the edge of town.

Exactly how Weir came into contact with the slatternly mother of the five-month-old girl—how the Brush infant happened to be brought to him, after hours, when Dr. Strether would have assumed that his surgery was closed—I never knew, though in the wake of the catastrophe, rumors were rife.

Perhaps, as some speculated, the ambitious young doctor had made inquiries among the poorer residents of the area, offering cash payments for volunteers for his surgical experiments; it is possible that he'd "leased" the infant for his use.

Initially, Weir was evidently pleased with the infant—indeed, inspired. For here was a specimen badly in need of repair, as anyone could acknowledge simply by glancing at it.

The fretful, feverish infant had a misshapen skull, like a melon that has grown asymmetrically. A bulbous bone-growth above the right eye, a shallow ridge running across the crown of the head, like nothing the novice doctor had seen outside of a medical textbook. With his fingers he could trace this ridge, & with his fingers he could *almost* reshape the deformed skull, for the cranial bones of an infant's skull grow together gradually during the first year of life & are malleable, to a degree, before then. In this case, Weir noted that the infant's scalp felt heated—though admittedly, he did not know how warm an infant's scalp should be. Was this fever? The skin tone was certainly unhealthy, a jaundiced yellow, unlike the more natural rosy glow of a normal infant, & the eyes appeared to be asymmetrically focused—that is, each eye appeared to be "seeing" at dissimilar angles. (Or was the poor creature *blind*? Weir waved his fingers in front of the eyes but could not determine.)

By examining the infant's skull in relationship to the phrenological chart on the wall of Strether's examination room, Weir concluded that the area in the brain believed to be the seat of "moral & religious sentiments" had been unnaturally flattened, while those areas of the brain related to "destructiveness," "secrecy," & "duplicity" were disproportionately developed.

The Brush infant, then, if allowed to mature unchecked, would likely grow into an amoral creature like its mother. *He* would remedy the condition.

With the strong impress of his fingers, even as the infant kicked, thrashed, & screamed, red-faced as a demon, Weir attempted to reshape the infant's skull. So loud & lusty were the infant's cries, Weir had to resort to inserting a wad of cotton into its mouth, to muffle the sound, which seemed to suffice, to a degree. Soon then, Weir gave up on a manual application of the skull, which required more strength in his hands than he possessed, & began working with a surgical instrument from Strether's surgery resembling a (sharp) pliers, to reposition the infant's (soft) cranial plates; then, a shoemaker's awl discovered in a drawer, which allowed of more leverage.

Unexpectedly, rivulets of blood began to stream from wounds in the infant's scalp.

Weir swiped at the infant's blood with swaths of cotton gauze. Ah, he must not succumb to panic! He'd forgotten, if he had ever known, that veins in the scalp are particularly fragile, & that scalp wounds bleed most spectacularly, even (evidently) in an infant.

"Stop! For God's sake, no one is hurting you . . ."

For some painful minutes the struggle consisted, as Weir attempted to wield the awl to correct the (obvious) misalignment, & the infant resisted, kicking & thrashing for its life.

"I said—*stop*. You are a little *demon*."

Abruptly then, to Weir's horror, the infant ceased struggling, & a moment later ceased breathing altogether.

Weir removed the gag from the infant's mouth, & for some frenzied minutes attempted to revive the infant by palpitating its tiny rib cage, & praying to God for help, & for mercy. As if to mock the grandeur of the young doctor's dream, the little lungs had ceased to breathe, & the little heart to beat. A hot-skinned but lifeless *doll*—Weir recoiled from it on the operating table, sickened.

How could this have happened?—the little demon had been so intensely, combatively *alive*, beneath his hands; then, *lifeless*.

Before he'd been given sufficient time to correct the misshapen skull, Providence had thwarted his efforts—but *why*? Was it some sort of violation of God's will, that a physician-surgeon might attempt to *correct* such an affliction?

Weir so readily believed in his Creator, & in Jesus Christ his Savior, he could not comprehend how, with such good intentions, *God had allowed him to fail at the first experiment of his career.*

For some minutes he stood unmoving, struck dumb in the presence of the bloodied little body. The silence in the room was deafening: Not even his father's disgust with him was voiced, just yet.

Until by degrees Weir came to realize: The Brush infant had obviously been defective, & had not been destined to survive.

Very likely the infant had been injured at birth by an ignorant midwife, thereafter carelessly nursed by the slattern-mother. This being the case, the death was assuredly *not his fault*.

Still, Weir was agitated at the sight of the small body. So much smaller now that it was unmoving than it had seemed to him when struggling for its life. He had never seen a dead infant before, nor indeed a dead body apart from corpses at the medical school, & these mangled specimens he had only just dared to peer at through his fingers.

"It is not my *fault*. Yet—I suppose I must bear some responsibility."

Weir sent word to the mother to come fetch the infant at once. He tried to speak calmly in the face of the woman's distress, & the sickening smell of gin on her breath; he did not wish to blame her, nor to cast reproach upon anyone, yet he had to reiterate that the infant *had been defective* when it was delivered to him.

Weir paid the mother in full, as he had promised, despite his conviction that the infant had been damaged goods foisted upon him, & that very likely, the woman had played him for a fool, perhaps instigated by a cynical male companion.

It did strike the young doctor's heart as a sight of pathos, that the flush-faced woman so resignedly took up her lifeless infant in her arms, wrapped in the stained shawl in which it had been brought to him, weeping as an animal might weep, if a brute animal could weep; yet more pathetically, the woman humbly muttered, *Thank you, Doctor,* for the several bills he had pressed into her hand.

So certain was Silas Weir that he would one day become a celebrated man of medical science, he maintained a physician's log through these apprentice years. An obvious reference to this botched procedure occurs in the first of the eleven journals, though there is no date given:

What a blow! I could not grasp the justice, that Providence had been so cruel as to allow me to lose the first patient wholly mine, in a small community like Chestnut Hill, in which all might gossip about it, the only blessing being it was to be a feebleminded child, of a feebleminded & diseased mother, who would accept the modest payment given her & make no trouble for me, I was sure.

As a good deal of blood had been shed in Dr. Strether's examination room, & Weir was not confident that in his agitated state he had managed to wipe it all away, the young doctor thought it wisest to arrive early the next morning, to do more cleaning, & to confront the elder physician at the outset, to "make a clean breast" of the unfortunate incident.

At first, Strether stared at him in disbelief, & glanced about the surgery, as if he expected to see the maimed infant somewhere in a corner. Then, as Weir fumbled an apology, Strether interrupted irritably: "Silas, I hope you didn't apologize so cravenly to the Brush woman! It was a very stupid thing you did, but do not forget: *You are the doctor.*"

"But—"

"No, no! None of that wheedling tone. *You are the doctor.*"

"I—*I am the doctor* . . ."

"If the woman accepted money from you, that should be the end of it. An accident—or rather, *not an accident:* an 'act of God.'"

These words of wisdom, Weir tried to absorb; yet still, in a tremulous voice, for he had had very little sleep the night before, Weir tried again to apologize, whereupon Strether lost patience: "See here, Silas. You may be a blundering fool but you were well-intentioned. I hope you have learned your lesson & will not attempt such tomfoolery again. Certainly not on these premises! But you must not go around apologizing, or even speaking of this to anyone—it must remain our secret. Certainly you don't want to apologize to the Brush family— whoever the wretches are. Doing so only acknowledges your guilt."

"But, I—I believe that I am guilty, Doctor . . ."

"*You are not guilty*—a physician is never 'guilty.' Wretches come to us for help, & we provide what help we can, with God's grace; if God does not behave charitably with His grace, that is hardly our fault. We do what we can, more than that we cannot do. You were trying to help an indigent family. Like a good Christian, you were volunteering your time. You were attempting 'good works.' Correcting a malformation of the skull of a pauper's child—that is quite admirable, in intention at least. I have experienced similar incidents, over the years—not involving infants, of course; I would not have attempted anything so absurd as 'repairing' an infant skull, but I have had patients die on me, quite suddenly, & unexpectedly. Or rather, it is to be *expected,* that a patient will die. As you say, this infant was defective, destined to be feebleminded like its mother; it is a mercy that its life has ended. I am quite sure, if we knew the family intimately, we would learn that there is relief that the infant has died, if the mother has had many others, & they are poor. They are no strangers to infant deaths—not unlikely, the mother has helped an infant or two into the next world, along the way. May I ask what you paid the woman?"

With some embarrassment, Weir told the elder physician the sum, which did not seem very generous now, so bluntly stated, in the light of the death.

"Well—you might have given the grieving mother a little more, you know, Silas. I would suggest that you offer to pay for a coffin, & for a funeral. That will seem to the Brush family very generous of you."

"But—what would an infant's coffin cost? And a funeral?—I have no idea."

Strether laughed, as if Weir had said something very witty.

"Silas, don't be absurd. They will bury the wretched infant in the backyard, in a box or wrapped in a sheet, & spend the money on gin. But you are not to know this. *You* will be generous—give the woman again what you'd given her last night, & she will be overwhelmed with gratitude."

"I—I see. I will—"

"And tell her that you are praying for the infant's soul, that it will be taken up by God to Heaven, & not cast down into Hell like the rest of the Brushes. That will make an impression on her, for she will naturally be in awe of a young physician like yourself, apprenticed to *me*."

Quickly Weir said that yes, he had been praying. Of course. He'd begun praying immediately, when the infant was first stricken.

"And I've been praying through the night, on my knees, for the infant's soul, & also for the grieving mother."

"Well, tell her. When you pay for the coffin & the funeral, be sure to tell her. What good is praying for the soul of a dead infant if no one knows about it?"

Weir protested: "God knows about it . . ."

Strether laughed impatiently.

"God is not a resident of Chestnut Hill, Dr. Weir. God is not going to do your reputation here any good."

•

Despite Dr. Strether's excellent advice, & the alacrity with which Weir gave the Brush woman money for a coffin & a funeral, with money borrowed (in secret) from his mother, fortune did not smile upon the naïve young physician. Within a week, a coarse-minded male companion of the Brush woman, claiming to be the father of the "murdered" infant, insisted upon further payments from Weir, with a threat of going to the authorities. In a state of great distress, Weir was forced to borrow money (in secret) from his elderly grandmother, with whom he had always been close; this, he was foolish enough to hand over to the brute blackmailer, with the result that, as he should have known, a third payment was demanded the following week, which he despaired of making.

"God help me. For I cannot seem to help myself."

Weir pondered whether he should appeal to Strether for an advance on his (very modest) salary, which barely covered his expenses at his boardinghouse; so desperate was the fool, he even appealed to me, out of some strange delusion that a fellow apprentice might have money to lend him, for a purpose he was reluctant to disclose.

(In time, I would discover the lurid tale behind Silas Weir's distraught state, & his agitation at needing to borrow money; but not just yet.)

Though the brute blackmailer never went to authorities, no doubt out of a fear of law enforcement, disquieting rumors began to spread through Chestnut Hill like surging waves of filthy water, that cannot be ignored, or denied; & soon many in the village were speaking openly, with much alarm, of the young physician apprenticed to Dr. Strether, who had caused an infant to die through "demonic experimentation."

When at last these rumors made their way to Strether, he had no recourse except to profess total surprise, disapproval, & condemnation. A negligible infant death that might have been dealt with summarily, in the elder doctor's practice, had festered out of control, having been caused by a young apprentice acting without his elder's knowledge.

"And using my instruments! Committing such butchery!"—so Strether muttered, working himself up to indignation. "At the very least, a breach of ethics. *Trust.*"

No, it did not matter, Strether pointed out irritably to his apprentice, that the Brush infant was of enfeebled stock, surely of "mixed" blood; the fact remained, Weir had tried to keep the infant's death a secret, & might be said to have bribed the parents into silence, sure signs of criminality, & guilt.

"Don't even try to defend yourself," Strether said, interrupting Weir as he began to speak, "—your career is over in Chestnut Hill."

Without Weir directly involved in the negotiations Strether met with Chestnut Hill authorities, to work out an agreement that, if the guilty apprentice left the area at once, with a promise never to return to the State of Pennsylvania, no charges would be brought against him, & none against Strether.

Hurriedly, some sort of arrangement was made, by relatives of Weir's mother living in New Jersey, that Weir might come to board with them in Morristown, where the only local doctor had recently died of cholera.

"Exiled—to New Jersey! God help me, Father must never know."

So humiliated, Weir began to speak more openly to me, as to a comrade, though I held myself at a distance from him, in contempt of his callow ways & thoughtless cruelty to the "experimental subject" he had killed, to which he alluded now as if it had been a foolish blunder, & not a heinous act.

As Strether had "washed his hands" of Weir, in his own words, it fell to me to help him pack his few possessions into a trunk, & arrange for him to travel by coach out of town; with his certificate of medicine from the Philadelphia College of Medicine, Weir reasoned that he could establish a practice of some sort in rural New Jersey, where standards were not so high as in the more civilized Philadelphia area. For there, doctors were in demand to tend to farm-laborers, many of whom were indentured servants, often as ill-treated by their Masters as Black slaves to the south.

This being the lowest form of doctoring, hardly a step above nursing & midwifery, no one was likely to look closely into Silas Weir's background.

Instead of expressing gratitude for being let off so lightly by Chestnut Hill authorities, Weir complained pettishly to me: "I was not given a fair chance! The old man—" (by which he meant Dr. Strether; it was like Weir to speak critically of the very person who had protected him)

"—did not give me a chance to explain: The infant was damaged past repair! And diseased! Skull surgery will be the salvation of humankind in the future & might have had its origin in Chestnut Hill but now—Chestnut Hill will remain a backwater forever."

"And what of your fiancée, Miss Tabitha Tyndale—what will you tell her?"—I could not resist teasing Weir, who drew himself up like an affronted snake rising on its tail, & said, tears of disgust in his deep-set eyes: "*She* has been unfaithful, too. I am through with all of you here."

Editor's Note

*T*HOUGH FATHER *regarded the female vagina as a "hell-hole of filth & corruption" & the female genitals as "loathsome in design, function, & aesthetics," yet somehow it happened by God's interdiction that there were nine of us borne of his loins & the womb of dear Mother, the first & eldest, myself, having been born on the eve of Christmas 1838.*

(As Father took virtually no interest in his offspring, my eight siblings will play no role in this Life.)

As the firstborn child of Silas Weir, as well as the executor & principal heir to his estate, including the physician's journal to be titled The Chronicle of a Physician's Life *(several thousand pages in ledgers kept intermittently through decades), I can claim a unique perspective: I am the only individual who has read all of Silas Weir's private journal, with the prerogative to quote from it; & I am also in a position to remember Silas Weir in a familial, not merely a professional, manner.*

Learning of my relationship to Silas Weir, many an individual has said to me, "But what was your father like?"—a query very difficult to answer, as the child of any prominent father would understand.

Thus, let me declare forthrightly that Father expressed disappointment with me as one "too timorous" to take up the mantle of experimental Gyno-Psychiatry which he believed to be his legacy; indeed, the reason that Providence had created him. Pressed to help Father with his experiments when he ascended to the Directorship of the New Jersey State Asylum for Female Lunatics in Trenton, in 1853, I could scarcely

*bear to step into the airless, feculent atmosphere of the experimental
Laboratory on the topmost floor of North Hall; many a night, like my
siblings, I had to press pillows over my head, to muffle cries ensuing
from that hellish place, that penetrated our household on the grounds of
the Asylum, when the wind blew from that direction; I failed utterly to
take up the mantle, i.e., the scalpel & the curette, which Silas Weir had
wished to will to me, to assure his legacy in the field of Gyno-Psychiatry.*

*Entrusted just once with disciplining a misbehaving indentured ser-
vant of Father's with a whipping, I failed Father another time, fortunately without his knowledge.*

*My political views, tending toward Abolitionism, were not radical for
the time, in Philadelphia, New York, & Boston, but somewhat out of
place in New Jersey, where I grew up, in Father's household; as Father
himself inclined to a moral disapproval of slavery, like all of the Weirs
of New England, he did not disagree with me on principle; but he did
object, indeed he became most agitated, if I spoke out too vociferously
against slavery in the presence of certain of his associates who were, if
not slaveholders themselves, indifferent to the morality of slaveholding.*

*Like many Northerners, indeed like Abraham Lincoln himself, the
Weirs did not believe that Black men & women were the "equals" of
white persons, but they did not, as Christians, believe in chattel slavery.
It was a heated topic of the era, scarcely to be laid to rest even by the Civil
War, whether the wealthy Southern slaveholders should receive repara-
tions for their losses, or not; & whether Black slaves should be encouraged to "return" to Africa, or be made citizens of the United States &
granted voting rights (Black males, that is). Such subjects never failed to
rouse angry debate, often within families, & certainly between fathers
& sons; & my relationship with my father was very much characterized
by such disagreements, never entirely resolved.*

*Yet, Father had no recourse except to forgive me, for a firstborn son
& heir is priceless to a Christian who has imagined himself one in a long
lineage of patriarchs descended from Moses himself. Indeed, none of my
five brothers has chosen to follow our father into medicine, still less into
Gyno-Psychiatry; nor has even one of our three sisters married a physician, despite a plethora of young physician-suitors who courted them as
the daughters of the renowned (if controversial) Silas Weir.*

Some of you will be highly critical of my decision to excerpt passages from Father's journal that might be characterized as obscene, if not sala-cious; & for other passages in this biography that some might find offen-sive. It has been my intention, however, to present a fully shaped portrait of Silas Aloysius Weir for the historical record, & not a partial, conde-scending hagiography of the sort that has already appeared in multiple obituaries.

Jonathan Franklin Weir

Exile: Morris County, New Jersey

1837

FROM *THE CHRONICLE OF A PHYSICIAN'S LIFE*
BY SILAS ALOYSIUS WEIR, M.D.

*F*OR THE FIRST SHALL BE LAST, *& the last shall be first. Blessed is the name of the Lord.*

These thrilling words of Jesus, my salvation. How many times murmured aloud during my months of exile in Morris County, New Jersey.

Plunged into the depths of Shame, as into the depths of Hell— the humid marshlands & pestilent bogs of this rural wilderness as a *despised poor relation* living in cramped quarters in a great-uncle's farmhouse north of Morristown; in such a state of penury, barely eking out a living as a physician-for-hire lacking an office or a surgery of my own but forced, like an itinerant salesman, to make my way by horse & wagon along badly rutted country roads amid swarms of mosquitoes trailing after me like a plague of ancient Egypt.

So exiled, so humbled, only Mother knew of my whereabouts, my father & family being encouraged to continue to believe that I was apprenticed to a respectable elder physician in Chestnut Hill, Pennsylvania.

The injustice! My heart beat hard, in dismay & resentment. For Providence had suggested to me a very different fate: acclaim & honor for having corrected a malformation of an infant's skull, an effort undertaken in the hope of advancing medical science, for charity's sake, & not a penny earned. At the very least, publication in a medical journal—an article by Silas Weir, M.D., in *The Boston Journal of Medicine.*

How impressed Father would be, & all of the family—*if only* . . .

Yet my fate must be borne, I came to realize. With the model of Jesus before me.

Misunderstood, reviled, betrayed—*crucified.*

And now this interim in Hell, from which I can only pray, with Mother, that I will be delivered.

Who can foresee when these faltering words of mine will be read? By whom? As I am almost too broken & humiliated to take up this pen, to express what is in my heart.

Banished from Chestnut Hill & from the Tyndale household. Banished from civilization.

Very likely never to glimpse Tabitha again; no doubt, already forgotten by the fickle girl, flaunting her engagement ring in my face, in needless cruelty.

The female, the preying mantis. Beneath their finery, & beneath the corsetry, what devils!

I am sure that I was not mistaken: There had been an understanding between us, a *rapport.*

And the mother, Mrs. Tyndale, seemingly so kind, urging me into the drawing room, to be seated by the hearth, & take tea with her & the others *as if indeed we were equals.*

I did not boast of my New England forebears except very sparingly, in recounting the early arrival of the Weirs at Boston Harbor in 1679. I did not boast of my ancestor Thaddeus Leiden, who was a high-ranking official in the Dutch West India Company, nor of my great-grandfather Demetrius Weir, who was an aide to General Washington in the War for Independence; I did not speak of my father, Percival Weir, except to note, in a murmured aside to Mrs. Tyndale, when the reference seemed appropriate, that Father is a founder of the Bank of Concord, & that my eldest brother, Franklin, is, like me, a young physician, just embarking upon his career. For I understood that the Tyndales, grown wealthy through the family ownership of a granary on the Delaware River, were of relatively recent stock in America, & not nearly so distinguished as the Weirs. If there were to be a wedding, if our families were to be united, that would be an appropriate time for such revelations; & how much more laudable, to hold such information in check.

Silas is so very modest! We had no idea, his background is so impressive.

His family! So very impressive.

My (naïve) hope had been that I would soon be announcing to the world the success of my first experiment in *cranial surgery*. With the caution of a research scientist, I intended to operate on one or two more infants with misshapen skulls, to perfect the procedure.

This, I had no doubt, would impress the Tyndale family greatly, & raise me in their estimation—for I had yet to meet Tabitha's father, Robert, one of the prominent citizens of Chestnut Hill.

Many a feverish night in the spring of 1835 I had lain awake imagining a light breaking in Tabitha's eyes, at the awareness of *who Silas Weir is*—a figure one day to bestride the globe, not limited merely to Chestnut Hill & a local clinical practice. The understanding would pass between us scarcely requiring words—that *she* would be *mine*; & all that is *hers* by lineage & inheritance, would become *mine*.

A beautiful dream rudely thwarted when, one day, Tabitha lifted her hand to me, to show me a ring on her finger—stating that she was *engaged*; but allowing me to know by a demure gaze & an intonation in her voice, that should circumstances alter, she would consider breaking this *engagement*, to pursue another life with Silas Weir, M.D.

I am sure that I did not imagine this. My senses were overwhelmed, a faintness rose in my breast—the realization came to me that *I must hurry*.

In this matter of achieving public success, I must *hurry at once*.

And so, the alacrity with which I undertook my experiments—there being *no time to waste*.

Knowing my position as a humble apprentice, I meant to reveal the success of my cranial experiment first to Dr. Strether, showing him the repaired infant skull, with its phrenological explanation—which he was sure to applaud, I had thought; the infant now "normal" through my effort. The vain old man whom in my naïveté I had meant to flatter by acknowledging how much I owed to *him*, for having taken me on as a fledgling physician, & displaying faith in me from the start; even offering to share with him, to a degree, the success of the surgery.

And yet—how did it happen!—the procedure failed; & I was not allowed to repeat it, with another infant specimen.

Granted, even, that the Brush infant was of very poor stock, virtually subhuman, & clearly damaged by ignorant midwifery; yet, the fact was, it had been *alive* when brought to me, & was *deceased,* when carried away by its grieving mother—this, I could not refute.

And so it was, he who should have been *first* was relegated to *last.*

Forced to flee from Chestnut Hill under cover of darkness, a single trunk filled with my earthly possessions, like a common criminal hurriedly packing my few articles of clothing, my medical books & journals, & my Bible; my bloodletting tools, & divers quantities of medicines purloined from Strether's slovenly shelves, which were not likely to be missed; & the shoemaker's awl which I had employed in the cranial procedure, but inexpertly, & hoped to employ again more fruitfully in the wilds of New Jersey.

The Hermitage, Ho-Ho-Kus, New Jersey

1839

FROM *THE CHRONICLE OF A PHYSICIAN'S LIFE*
BY SILAS ALOYSIUS WEIR, M.D.

D R. WEIR!—you must come with me at once, my Master begs you."
The astonishment of my life—the very day to determine my
Future—at last!

A sweltering day in June in hot-humid Morris County, New Jersey,
where my spirits had begun to melt, & to rot, like festering brains in a
bucket, & there seemed little hope for me beyond a lifetime of squalid
bachelor servitude in the countryside north of Morristown of small
threadbare farms & settlements, no more than bleak crossroads, where
payment to a physician was likely to be in bartered goods—decapitated
chickens, bushels of unshucked corn, stacks of firewood—when there
was payment at all; on this day when my hope of pioneering as a medical researcher was all but crushed beneath the burden of mere brute
existence as a *poor relation* of little more stature on my great-uncle's
farm than his ill-sorted staff of servants & laborers; on this day when
by noon I'd arrived back at my cramped quarters dazed with exhaustion & humiliation having been summoned to attend to a patient who
turned out to be, when at last I located him, an obese stroke victim in
his late seventies in the very throes of death, whom Our Savior Himself could not have saved: on this day summoned to the Hermitage at
Ho-Ho-Kus, in Bergen Township, the home of the Rosencrantz family,

owners of several cotton mills on the Ho-Ho-Kus Brook whose wealth was already legendary by 1846.

The Hermitage!—the relatives with whom I was boarding, who rarely expressed much enthusiasm for my meager news, still less for my presence, were indeed impressed with this prospect, & bade me excitedly on my way.

Indeed, the patriarch, Elijah Rosencrantz, had sent his own buggy, with a matched team of horses & uniformed driver, to bring me to Ho-Ho-Kus as quickly as possible. For once I would not have to drive myself, with a horse & wagon, like an itinerant salesman!

Jolting along country roads, teeth rattling in my head. Gripping my valise on my knees.

I will confess—I was trembling badly. I could not afford to fail again; such an opportunity was not likely to come another time.

"God help me! This will be my final plea to You, I promise."

In my feverish fantasy imagining that I'd been summoned to the Hermitage to attend to a member of the Rosencrantz family—the elder Elijah, himself?

Or—his wife? Daughter?

Though it should have seemed unlikely to me that a wealthy family would not have its own physician, or physicians, living close to them, & not depend upon the emergency recruiting of a stranger, yet the feverish fantasy gripped my mind that the patient might be a female member of the family, & could I treat such a patient? Could I summon the courage?

How hard it had been not to stammer & blush in Tabitha's presence. The thought of treating a female patient of good family left me feeling faint . . .

Trying to console myself: If the patient were a Rosencrantz woman or girl, certainly another female relative would be present at the examination. A male physician would not be allowed to be alone with any female, thus I would be spared. Surely another woman would chaperon. A mediator. Or a male relative. *Someone.*

During the jolting hour-long ride to Ho-Ho-Kus a kind of madness came over my brain: what I might say to whoever greeted me, how I might speak, how I must remember to keep my shoulders *back & up* as Mother would urge me, & *not slouch.*

Must try not to swallow nervously, lick my (dry, parched) lips. Try not to clear my throat as I did, evidently without knowing, as it was frequently complained in my great-uncle's household that I had developed an "insufferable" habit of doing, a most unpleasant sound that carried to the ears of others & annoyed them greatly.

Though I was most uneasy, yet it did not fail to fill me with a rapturous sort of pride that Elijah Rosencrantz had summoned *me.*

Indeed, how had the mill-owner even heard of me? My "successes" in Morris County among my humble patients scarcely outnumbered my "failures"—indeed, in some cases, "success" & "failure" were scarcely distinguishable.

Elijah Rosencrantz was celebrated as one of the most successful tradesmen in northern New Jersey, & much feared & resented by those obliged to do business with him. As an ambitious young man in his early thirties, a recent settler in New Jersey, he had already made a small fortune in dealings with Southern cotton plantations; though staunchly against slavery himself, Rosencrantz nonetheless did business with slave-owners & their associates, at great profit. With his acquired fortune he had purchased the property known as the Hermitage at Ho-Ho-Kus, a fourteen-room Dutch-American stone manor house in which, during the War for Independence, General Washington & his aides had lodged; & not long afterward, Aaron Burr had resided on the property with his wife, before moving to Manhattan, & entering the most notorious phase of this ambitious & controversial politician's career.

It was acknowledged even by his business rivals that Elijah Rosencrantz was "harsh but fair"—though sympathetic with Abolitionism, & likely to look the other way if runaway slaves passed through the Hermitage on their way to freedom in Ontario, nonetheless a sizable number of Rosencrantz employees were indentured servants, contracted to work long hours for no pay, just food & lodging, for periods as long as seven years.

In Concord, Massachusetts, there were no Black slaves—of course. Virtually the entire town was Abolitionist. Nor did the Weir family employ indentured servants—Father did not believe in such servitude, which was, under the law, virtually identical to slavery, as the indentured did not have any rights as American citizens, & might be worked, or whipped to death, with little punishment for their Master. An essential difference was that indentured servants tended to be of the white race & were not chattel—that is, their offspring did not belong to their Masters but to them.

In my heart, as a Christian, I did not "believe" in slavery, nor in such servitude, which was often contracted for the young by their fathers in Europe, to pay for their transportation to America, & seemed a particular sort of cruelty, of fathers selling their own children for profit. A further danger was, as the indentured entered the final months of their servitude, their Masters had no great reason to continue to feed them, or seek medical treatment for them, but might "cast them to the wind" as their contract was voided.

Though the indentured were not chattel slaves, like the cruelly enslaved Africans, the fact that their children would not belong to their Masters, but would be free Americans unbeholden to anyone, could be a danger to them; for, while the slave-owner naturally wished to keep his pregnant female slaves reasonably well-fed, that they might give birth to a new generation of slaves, & increase his wealth, the Master of the indentured had no interest in the well-being of a new generation, nor in any pregnant female. (Indeed, it was likely that a female indentured servant unfortunate enough to become impregnated was in danger of being starved, or kicked, or made to swallow certain medications, to insure miscarriage, as I was soon to discover.)

As my great-uncle's household had several indentured servants, I was not in a position to be overtly critical of the practice. My great-uncle was not a cruel Master, as he was a well-to-do gentleman farmer, with a sizable property. It did seem to me, from a philosophical perspective, that those (of us) who had to work for a pittance were, in a sense, "enslaved"; we were free, yes, but free to starve. Yet I vowed that I would not appeal to Mother another time for money, but only for understanding & sympathy, & for her prayers; for, after more than twelve months, it was still not revealed to Father that I had been so rudely dismissed from Chestnut Hill, indeed so shamefully loathed, *exiled from the State of Pennsylvania.*

Other physicians had been summoned to the Hermitage, I could assume; others must have been dismissed when they failed to please the Master. With Providence guiding me, *I would not fail.*

"Dr. Weir—this way, please."

As it happened, to my disappointment I would have no more than a glimpse, at a distance of some fifty feet, of the austere old stone house built on a knoll above the Ho-Ho-Kus Brook: a forbidding vision in shimmering sun, amid lush greenery & red climber roses as vivid as exposed hearts.

Later visits to the Hermitage would allow me to admire, at closer quarters, the construction of the large house, of fieldstone & mortar, with steep wood-shingled roofs & prominent chimneys, & somewhat narrow windows, originally built in 1750; an appearance reminiscent of a fortress, rather than a domestic dwelling, but over all very imposing, larger than any residence in Chestnut Hill.

(As to *Ho-Ho-Kus:* The curious name is said to be Lenape Indian in origin, evoking the sound of *wind whistling through trees.* Appropriate for the dense stand of deciduous trees & firs above the Ho-Ho-Kus Brook that surrounded the Hermitage as well.)

Upon my arrival it was soon revealed that I had been summoned not to the manor house, nor even to a smaller residence nearby, but rather to crowded rowhouses at the rear, out of sight behind farm buildings; where workers lived in cramped quarters, & a powerful odor of infected & unwashed flesh pinched my nostrils & brought tears to my eyes.

Ah!—was this not a descent to Hades, a shameful descent for a physician from an upstanding Concord, Massachusetts, family!

Told, by one of Mr. Rosencrantz's administrative staff, that a farm-laborer had "met with an unfortunate accident"—(this information given to me in a tone shockingly lacking in respect)—I found myself staring down at a most piteous sight, for which, I must admit, I was totally unprepared, having so intensely imagined a female patient of a genteel sort, & not this: a young bare-chested man lying in the dirt, on his side, seemingly in a fever delirium, insensible from his wounds, his broad muscled back shining with blood, & buzzing with flies; his face contorted with pain & beaded with sweat. Apart from his injuries, a fine physical specimen of manhood, of an age near my own.

"An 'accident'? What kind of 'accident'?"—in my naïveté, I could not resist asking; but the steward walked away with but a glance of contempt in my direction.

Standing about, a little distance from the stricken man on the ground, were half a dozen of his comrades, who stared at me with expressions of distrust.

Ah, I saw: This was a *whipping*. It was stunning to see, for the first time in my life, the terrible effect of a whip on a man's bare skin, transforming it into raw festering flesh upon which flies were alighting, to torment him further.

I asked the onlookers what on earth the poor wretch had done, to merit such punishment, & was met with purposefully blank expressions, as if I had asked a very foolish question no one wished to dignify by answering.

At last a stout-bodied woman of about forty years of age, with large glaring eyes, flushed cheeks, & muscled shoulders, her hair a pale frizz about her coarse-skinned face, laughed harshly at me. In heavily accented English saying scornfully: " 'Merit'? What is 'merit,' Doctor? There is no 'merit' here."

As in a fever delirium, the bare-chested young laborer stared at me with eyes widened in alarm as if, in my dark physician's garb, valise in hand, I were a figure in a nightmare, summoned to do him further harm. Quickly I thought to console him: "I am Silas Weir, M.D. I am here to take care of you. Do not fear!"

These inspired words, coming of their own volition, appeared to appease the young man, who looked upon me now with a glimmer of childlike hope.

A wild sort of happiness coursed through me. *No one had ever required my comfort before*—not like this.

That I—Silas Weir, M.D.—scorned in certain quarters, & made to feel an outcast—might *be of use*.

Most surprisingly, I did not feel my usual trepidation at treating a patient, but rather pity & compassion; for the young man was one of a number of indentured servants contracted to Mr. Rosencrantz for labor on the farm, & not a U.S. citizen. In their eyes I was invested with an aura of authority, invested in me by their Master.

Indeed it would transpire, from this Day of Miracles forward, as one aligned with the authority of the Hermitage, I would be more self-assured as a physician, in treating patients of the working-class, or lower; particularly such miserable wretches as this bare-chested, badly whipped young laborer.

So it was, in my Christian magnanimity I surprised the onlookers, & dispelled their suspicion of me, by treating the patient with such care; bathing his wounds with my own hands, if a bit clumsily; not only those wounds fresh that morning from a beating, but older wounds that had not healed & had opened anew with the whipping, a network of wounds festering & maggot-infected—terrible to see.

Winning the grudging respect, I believed, even of the stout-bodied woman, who offered to assist me when she saw how sincere I was, though (somewhat) inexperienced.

While treating the patient, I took care to remain reticent. I did not inquire into the identity of the whipper, nor further into the circumstances of the whipping. Such punishments are, it might be said, *Acts of God*. It was not my role—it would never be my role—as one hired by the Master of the Hermitage, to cast blame on any of his staff; for this would be, if but indirectly, to cast blame upon *him*.

Indeed, I had no way of knowing what the young laborer might have done to provoke such punishment, being a vigorous-looking brute, very likely hotheaded, like all such youths, impatient with taking orders from their elders.

However, it did not fail to touch my heart that the patient wept in gratitude for my physician's care, when at last he was capable of speech; he, too, spoke in heavily accented English, identified for me as *Slavic*. I was in a position to speculate that sensitivity to pain, like sensitivity to any discomfort or injustice, has much to do with the social standing of the patient: The more impoverished, like the wretched Brush woman, the hardier they were, not feeling pain as more educated & affluent persons do. It was not a matter of sex, primarily—a muscled brute of a woman would be less vulnerable to pain than a gentleman of a higher class.

Not only did I succeed in bathing, stitching, & dressing severe wounds, such as I had never done previously, but Providence provided me with a nurse—the stout, coarse-skinned woman who had laughed at my question—revealed as the "most skilled midwife" for workers at the Hermitage; one of the staff of indentured servants, from

Amsterdam, named Betje, who would assist me on future visits to the Hermitage, over a period of years.

What a blessing! Without Betje, this *chronicle of a physician's life* would be very different indeed.

When I acted hesitantly, or seemed to have no idea what I was doing, Betje wordlessly came to my rescue, without being asked. Where, in Strether's surgery, his longtime nurse was often impertinent to me as a lowly apprentice, Betje always knew *her place;* for I was the physician summoned by her Master, & she was but a lowly indentured servant not (yet) an American citizen. And of course, Betje had been a skilled midwife for many more years than I had been a certified physician.

On that sweltering-hot day in June, having brought with me to the Hermitage my valise of medications, I administered to my patient liberal doses of belladonna, Saint-John's-wort, & laudanum, all of which hasten healing as well as suppress pain & induce sleep; this, with Betje's approval, for, as a mere midwife, Betje had no access to such medications for her patients, but had to rely upon what she could harvest in the field at any given time.

Seeing that I had fared unexpectedly well with the young laborer— (who, it was revealed, had been declared "past mending" by a previous physician summoned to the Hermitage)—I was brought by the steward to attend more of the injured or ailing, including mill-workers as well as farm hands, several children, & young persons; women of divers ages, including pregnant women, women who had recently given birth & had not recovered, or had suffered miscarriages. Over all, there were many more patients than I could see in a single day, & so it was requested that I return to the Hermitage later that week; & following this, the next week. You can imagine my gratification, that Mr. Rosencrantz was pleased with my work, & paid me generously!— that is, through his steward.

Over all, my patients at the Hermitage were a heterogeneous lot, indeed, as they were divers in their nationalities—Dutch, German, Norwegian, Scots, Irish. Some suffered from badly infected wounds (some of these clearly from lashings on bare backs); sunstroke, from working in blazing sunshine, in acres of corn, beans, cabbages, & other crops; every sort of accident amid clattering mill machinery & farm equipment. Sprained & broken bones, shattered kneecaps &

vertebrae; boils, festering sores; bunions, hernias, cysts, & tumorous growths; ingrown toenails; fevers & chills; intestinal flu, constipation, diarrhea; dropsy, gout, wheezing lungs, & shortness of breath; arthritis; rapid heartbeat, chest pains; every sort of female malady & misbegotten pregnancy. Among these were individuals obviously very ill but beyond my capacity to diagnose, of whom many had been "given up for dead" but revived, to a degree, following my ministrations, with the able assistance of Betje; & were able to return to work.

Of course, if an indentured servant contracted to work for seven years was incapacitated for weeks, or months, this period of time would be added to the contract, under the law. The more frequently ill or injured, the longer the period of indenture, which might prevail through an entire lifetime, as the indentured did not live long lives, on the whole. In her Dutch-inflected English, sounding to the ear as if the woman's tongue was too large for her mouth, Betje explained to me that she should have been given her "freedom dues" years before, but, due to illnesses, & pregnancies, she had been unable to work steadily; & so, her contract with the Rosencrantzes had been extended several times.

"It is a joke by now, Doctor: I will 'never' be free—they will make me work until the day I die, & on the morning of that day, they will make me dig my own grave."

Betje's laughter was shrill, & not very feminine; her clumsy speech grated against my sensitive ears, but I made every effort to listen to her with sympathy. It was all I could do not to recoil from the rank animal odor of the woman's body, which was not bathed nearly so often as it should have been; for Betje was a farm-worker, whose province was the milking & care of cows in a large cow-barn. Her shoulders had become stooped, in the long effort of *milking*; & her hands stank of rancid milk, which could not be washed away.

As few patients had ever thanked me in the past, & some had expressed outright criticism of me, I was greatly moved at the Hermitage, to be so respected. Not only did the young, badly whipped laborer thank me, but others as well, whom I had not treated but who were grateful that I had treated their family members & comrades; most gratifying to me, I would learn at the Hermitage to proceed with calm & authority, & not hesitation. Soon, I was not timorous at the prospect of examining & treating females of this lowly station, whether young

& shapely, or older & disfigured; whether beauteous, or very plain, or even repulsive.

Why was this?—I have given it much thought, & have written about it at length in my journals.

It is unmistakable that the female body is, in certain respects, repulsive to examine too closely, a curse of the flesh which the wisest females accept as a debt inherited from Eve; not so much the mammalian aspects of the body, which can be sightly, if properly corseted & clothed, as the nether parts, between the thighs & upward, a veritable hell-hole of filth, though strangely identical to the birth canal with its sacred mission.

Yet, with the women at the Hermitage, as with the men, I did not feel as if I were trespassing in a forbidden place but rather that, as a physician of a higher social station, it was my privilege to do as I wished, without regard for any judgment. Of course, as a Christian *I was obliged to do good.*

We have been taught that tincture of skin is everything, & that there are "superior" races & "inferior" races. My own conclusion is more complicated, & does not rest upon tincture of skin or breeding merely, but rather, along with these, a consideration of *social station*.

For I have no doubt, if I were required to examine Black nobility, of some ancient African lineage, I should find myself abashed, as if confronted with white nobility; whereas, with the classes of laborers, there is no reason for hesitation, for they are likely to be grateful for any services we proffer them, of our own magnanimity.

Soon then, Silas Weir, M.D., became something of a savior to patients at the Hermitage; they learned not to fear me, as they feared other physicians, who treated them by crudely bleeding them, no matter if, as a result of whippings or accidents, they had already lost much blood. (Of course, when *bloodletting* was an obvious remedy, I did not hesitate to *bleed*.) When the overseer's whip lacerated their bodies, it was I who treated them by staunching their bleeding wounds, & cleaning their infections, with the help of Betje; if there was no hope, & it was *their time*, it was I who gave them a final dose of laudanum to deaden their pain & quell their turbulent hearts. As one might speak to children, I spoke calmly to them, showing only patience, kindness, & Christian fortitude.

Even when I could not save a gangrenous limb from amputation, or remove with a forceps a stillborn baby impacted in its (often very young) mother's womb, nor successfully staunch the hemorrhaging that followed like a geyser—it was evident that my presence made some difference, at least; where in the past, as it was told to me, a very high percentage of the ill & injured had died, or had been allowed to starve to death as they were useless for work.

Instead, as a result of my diligence, an impressive number of the afflicted soon recovered sufficiently to return to work; so much so, the Master himself began to take note, & one day requested that I be brought to meet him, to be thanked in person by Elijah Rosencrantz!

Despite all that I had been told of Mr. Rosencrantz, whom many on his staff seemed to fear, I was not prepared for his *gentlemanly* manner, & the graciousness with which he received me, if not inside the great stone house, on a shaded veranda of the house. Indeed, Mr. Rosencrantz saw fit to pay me with his own hand, & not through the usual intermediary, in excess of what had been promised me.

Gravely, I thanked him. This generosity moved me deeply.

In my awe of the man, I found it difficult to raise my eyes to his face. My impression was that Elijah Rosencrantz exuded strength without effort—a slight figure, with a dignified bearing & recessed eyes like a turtle's.

"You have saved me a considerable sum of money, Dr. Weir! These 'indentured servants' have been dying like flies. I pay for their transportation from Europe—I pay for every damned morsel they eat, & they eat like horses—they thank me by dying. The Irish are the worst! The Irish are *always* the worst! They make themselves drunk & get tangled up in machinery to spite *me*. I hope that folly will come to a stop, now."

Mr. Rosencrantz laughed, not harshly but with an air of incredulity, as if he could not believe how poorly he was treated, & how crudely.

His age was difficult to determine, perhaps an advanced age—in his late sixties, or early seventies? Or was he much younger, but had suffered some sort of affliction, had lost weight & most of his hair? His skin appeared to be pocked, if mildly; his left eyelid, to sag.

I had thought that perhaps I would be invited to remain at the Hermitage for the evening meal, at which occasion I would be introduced to the ladies of the Rosencrantz family; but this did not come to pass.

Nor did Mr. Rosencrantz inquire after my family, as I imagined he might do, out of politeness. (For I had rehearsed how I would speak of the Weirs of Concord, Massachusetts—what I would select to say, of Father's many accomplishments, while maintaining an air of modesty & proportion, considering the great fortune & reputation of my host.)

Abruptly, it seemed that our conversation was ending.

"You will return to us again, Dr. Weir? A pestilent season is close upon us—'yellow fever'—they will use any excuse they can, to drop like flies. *You* will keep them on their feet, eh?"—with a wink at me where I might have expected a brisk handshake; as a steward appeared beside me, to escort me from the veranda to the waiting buggy.

Writing that night to Mother—*Today I shook the hand of a most illustrious gentleman—Elijah Rosencrantz himself. My fortunes have turned, at last!*

Early Years as a Practitioner

1846-1851

FROM *THE CHRONICLE OF A PHYSICIAN'S LIFE*
BY SILAS ALOYSIUS WEIR, M.D.

FOLLOWING THIS, through the patronage of Elijah Rosencrantz & his family, & my move to modest quarters in the village of Ho-Ho-Kus, a forty-minute ferry ride from Manhattan, my life was changed utterly.

Lifted from the fate of a most debased *country doctor,* whom everyone scorned, to another plateau entirely, in my skill at ministering to the sick & injured, of whom there were a countless supply; for, as Mr. Rosencrantz had said, the indentured had a way of arriving at our shores, contracted to work for seven years, soon taken ill or injured or keeling over dead as if to spite the very persons who had paid for their transportation.

Of these mill- & farm-workers likely to speak in a babble of foreign speech, or in such mangled English one could scarcely comprehend them, only a hardy few would survive to become full citizens of the United States. Of babies born among them, only a very few would survive—no doubt, a blessing.

Most strikingly, for me, my fear of patients, in particular my fear of women of a genteel class, began to lessen, as I gained confidence with patients of the lower classes; my fear had been that of a young novice, shrinking from the judgment of others, where it was made clear to me, with these patients, that I had little or nothing to fear from *them.*

A young doctor must learn to maintain an air of self-assurance & never betray anxiety, dread, or despair. It is not the Hippocratic oath that guides the physician—*Do no harm;* but, rather—*Do not falter in your decision, whether you do harm or no.*

By far the most challenging task for the young physician is what might be called the *female problem.*

That the female, in her most exalted spiritual mode, Mother, Wife, Beloved, is yet *female* in her bodily being, inescapably.

The physical repulsiveness of the female body is not a matter of race, ethnic identity, or tincture of skin; rather, an inheritance from Eve accepted as such by the wisest females. Indeed, genteel women have not the vaguest idea what their *nether regions* look like, no more than a husband does, for the marital act among married couples is performed in darkness, as in pained silence. (In my early years as a physician I was, of course, not yet married; until my wedding night, as much a *virgin* as my dear bride.) Never would I be fully at ease in examining women of my own station or higher, as I was with women of the lower classes. With the female mill-workers, farm-laborers, & household staff in the employ of the Rosencrantzes, I learned an ease, almost a jocularity, which would aid me in later years, when my practice broadened to include more affluent patients, as the experimental surgery I performed upon these early patients would prove invaluable, in time.

Most significantly, I took care never to be alone in an examination room, or indeed in any room, with a female patient. Usually, a male relative would be present; if not, Betje would assist me. Discreetly I would "listen" to a pulsebeat (at a wrist) with my fingers or lay my hand against a fevered forehead, but such touch was never prolonged. If a woman suffered from a rash, cyst, lump, or tumorous growth in a "private" part of her body, she would not ordinarily wish to speak of it to a (male) physician but would have confided in a relative who then reported to me, to determine how best to proceed. Most of my consultations with the better class of women were a matter of careful inquiry, my questions & their replies, a listing of symptoms, of which many were very familiar: breathlessness, fainting spells, no appetite, an excess of appetite, rapid heartbeat, slow heartbeat, night-terrors, motiveless weeping, excitation, extreme fatigue as did not allow them to rise from bed on some mornings and lace themselves into their whalebone corsets, etcetera; usually then, I would treat the patient with a healthy dose of *bloodletting*, to quell the tremors of the nervous womb. The earliest mode of what would become, in my practice, the renowned *Chair of Tranquility*, was explored in Ho-Ho-Kus, with dampened towels tightly wrapped about the nervous woman, with a dosage of laudanum, to induce sleep. (Quite the reverse was advised for men, who require an excitation of the musculature, not a tranquilizing.) If there appeared to be a swelling of the patient's gums, with a sharpened lancet I cut the gum back to the teeth, following up with extract of echinacea, quinine tablets, & tincture of arsenic—a prefiguring of the procedures I would perfect some years later, in my quest to cure madness through the removal of infection.

A novelty treatment, taken up after my move to Ho-Ho-Kus, & suggested by Elijah Rosencrantz himself for the treatment of divers ailments, was *mustard plaster.*

(Smelling most loathsomely!—but good for the morale of the female patient who associates strong smells with potency, & is soothed by aggressive measures into an agreeable sort of *female passivity*.)

When convalescing, the patient was prescribed medicines appropriate to her condition, usually drops of morphine, or laudanum, which proved agreeable with genteel ladies who need not exert themselves through the day, unlike mill- or farm-workers who had not that luxury; for these hardier specimens, a solution of nicotine extract or cocaine drops would trigger a more rapid heartbeat, & a rush of strength in their limbs, so much more hardened with muscle than the limbs of genteel women, whose upper arms were scarcely larger than their wrists when young, & piteously flaccid & loose by middle age.

It was rare that I did not closely consult with a husband, a father, or a brother after having examined a female patient of a genteel background, before revealing my diagnosis to the patient; where coarser females seemed to wish to be confronted with the truth, more genteel females shrank from it, as from a blinding light. Every detail of the genteel woman's treatment was with the approval of a husband or a male relative, of course, for it would be he who would be paying my fee, & it would be his satisfaction I would have to provide, particularly in the case of certain "controversial" surgeries with which I began to be entrusted: requests by husbands of women concerned for their well-being, whether extreme agitation in the woman, or lassitude; manic laughter, or helpless tears; "frigidity" of the lower body inhibiting conjugal relations, or, perversely, an unnatural "avidity" of the lower body during conjugal relations—all these, forms of *hysteria*.

Encouraged by a plethora of such requests, & perusing medical journals for instruction, I began to explore a new area of medical treatment, for me, involving the *female organs*. Of these, we were taught virtually nothing in medical school; to compensate, I attempted some surgical explorations of animals, namely dogs & cats; though very messy, & of necessity executed in secret, with the remains removed from my quarters by night, & buried at the foot of a garden, these surgical explorations would prove infinitely helpful to me.

More fruitfully, I was able to acquire the bodies of several recently deceased females, including one, by her swarthy complexion & low brow likely an immigrant from southern Europe, in age no more than twenty, with a swollen belly—a *pregnancy*. This unexpected boon allowing me, once my nerves were sufficiently steeled, to learn much about the female *private parts* unknown to me previously, & astonishing.

(I could not help but feel a thrill of gratification, that the very disadvantages of my early career, that I was obliged to treat such lowly patients, would turn out to be distinct advantages, of a kind unavailable to my brother Franklin, associated with a prominent surgery on Beacon Street, Boston.)

Over all, it was enormously beneficial for me to treat female patients at the Hermitage, that my skills might be honed for a wider practice. Removal of the ovaries was frequently prescribed in medical journals for the cure of *neurasthesia;* in more extreme cases, the removal of the entire uterus (thus, "hysterectomy") was advised; in other cases, the surgical removal of the vaginal "clitoris," like the appendix a functionless part of the female body described in Galen as hypersensitive to any touch, with a propensity to exacerbate excitation, anemia, sleepwalking, hyperventilation, overeating, anorexia, morbid thoughts, migraine, insomnia, atheistical tendencies, madness, & certain unspeakable habits of a degenerate nature more often associated with the adolescent male of the species.

As it evolved in my practice in Ho-Ho-Kus, the course of treatment was: The (unwitting) patient was brought by relatives to the physician's surgery, where she would be put at ease by conversing with the physician on such topics as the weather, poetry, or upcoming holidays while provided with a hot liquid, usually tea, containing a strong soporific, usually laudanum, that would soon cause her to fall heavily asleep, without the slightest suspicion; when, hours later, the patient was capable of being roused, the surgical intervention in the nether region of her body would have been completed, & apart from minimal pain, & bleeding, & occasional complications requiring further treatment, the patient would be carried home to heal in quiet, sequestered circumstances for as long as was required.

Rest assured that these surgeries were carefully executed to protect the modesty of the patient: the head & torso of the comatose woman chastely draped in a white cloth, to render the circumstances impersonal, as in an anatomy lesson, while the thighs were propped up, & spread, exposing to the surgeon's clinical eye the nether regions of the woman, i.e., the vagina, labial lips, birth canal, etcetera. Steely nerves were required of any surgeon who ventured into such territory, which presented a hellish spectacle to the eye. According to my carefully maintained physician's log for these years, however, in no cases did one of my female patients complain of the purifying transformation of her body; rather, the removal of ovaries, uterus, clitoris, was scarcely registered in those who survived, most of whom continued on a daily regimen of laudanum.

Younger women, however—"girls"—were not always so tractable. A rebellious spirit is a handicap of youth, long quenched in married women, even those still fairly young. It is said that some wickedly curious girls, in adolescence, are driven to hold a mirror to the forbidden part of their body, between their legs, to peer in astonishment & dismay at precisely *what,* they have no clear view, & are likely to drop the mirror in fright, & never pick it up to try again.

For the dread of the young, virginal girl is that the *hole* that is the core of her being, between her thighs, is *so very small,* it is a vexing puzzle to imagine how on earth an infant might be "delivered" through it; such circumstances a mystery even to those of us trained in human anatomy, beyond our ability to fathom. As medical students at the Philadelphia College of Medicine we were naïvely misled by the *rigidity* of the mannequins with which we were taught female anatomy, that could be manipulated to expel "fetuses" with little effort; in actual life, the flesh of the woman, the birth canal, uterus, etcetera, is *soft & giving,* not rigid. And of course, there is likely to be a geyser of blood accompanying the delivery.

Of the young girls who came into my surgery at Ho-Ho-Kus, or rather, who were brought into my surgery, one case stands out, disturbingly: Mr. Rosencrantz's seventeen-year-old granddaughter Bettina, the daughter of his eldest son, Joseph, described to me as a "difficult, willful, headstrong, & contrary girl," suspected by her father of an unclean personal habit as well as a propensity for disobedience & insolence in church—all expressions of *defiance.*

When Joseph Rosencrantz brought his sulky daughter to me, the ginger-haired girl was immediately suspicious, & declined to smile at my playful banter; declined to drink the sweetened cocoa we offered her; & insisted that there was "not a thing wrong" with her; & would not cooperate when I attempted to bleed her, though it was evident that her blood was pathologically hot, & needed cooling.

"Daughter, *you will* obey the doctor," Joseph Rosencrantz said in a voice quavering with indignation; while Bettina continued to behave in her *coquettish contrary fashion,* which, one could see, had been indulged in her, by her family, for too long, likely because Bettina was very pretty, with milky skin, pale eyebrows, & dark green eyes.

Eventually, after rational persuasion by both physician & father failed, headstrong Bettina had to be forcibly restrained, by servants brought by Joseph Rosencrantz from his household for just such a purpose; strapped screaming to a table & sedated by a forced ingestion of morphine drops; that I might examine a most shocking sight in one so young & (presumably) virginal, the offensive little organ at the mouth of the vagina being erect & inflamed, like a miniature male organ, with an obscene fire lit from within.

By this time, the room had been cleared of Joseph Rosencrantz & the others, that I might summon all my strength to act decisively; with a prayer to God our Father, & to Jesus Christ our Savior, that my hand would not quaver in this surgical debridement, the first of its kind, in my experience as a young doctor & novice surgeon.

And soon then, the obscene fire was quenched—the slight bit of flesh swiftly cut out & tossed away like garbage amid medical waste, & the bleeding wound staunched, stitched with tough black twine to be removed after a fortnight.

Still unconscious, headstrong young Bettina was carried out of my surgery, & back to her home at the Hermitage. If I felt a twinge of pity for her, I felt a stronger sense of righteous relief, that the girl, still so young, may have been spared a most unhappy life as a harridan; & would make now a most ideal wife & mother, for some suitable man.

For this single surgery, I was handsomely paid; & quick to assent to Joseph Rosencrantz's urgent wish, that I tell no one about the transaction, for few within the family knew, including Bettina's mother.

As it happened, though I fully expected to be summoned to the Hermitage, to look after the convalescing girl, & remove the stitches, I did not see her again; nor did anyone inform me of the distressing fact that, only just a few days after the procedure, when the surgical wound was still most raw, ginger-haired Bettina slipped from the house by night; & under cover of darkness took her life by drowning in a mosquito-infested marsh bordering the Ho-Ho-Kus Brook, hardly a mile from my dwelling in the village.

This shocking news made its way to me circuitously, after some weeks. I recall that I was struck dumb for some minutes when I heard, & sank to my knees, to pray for the girl's soul, that it might not fester in Hell; I could not help but torment myself that, if only Joseph Rosencrantz had brought his daughter to me earlier, & I had had the opportunity to execute the procedure when she was younger, thus less rebellious & habituated in her ways, her life might have been spared, & her soul—but it is fruitless to contemplate what might have been.

·

Soon then, with the blessing of Providence, & the continued patronage of the Rosencrantz family, my medical practice, once so humble, began to flourish. Within several years devoted to ceaseless industry I would accumulate sufficient savings to marry an exemplary Christian woman from a family of some substance in South Jersey; a bride perhaps not so comely as Tabitha Tyndale, nor as wealthy, but a helpmeet who would prove devoted to me, unquestioning in her loyalty & to the demands of our family—in all, nine blessed children.

Summons to Trenton

1851

FROM *THE CHRONICLE OF A PHYSICIAN'S LIFE*
BY SILAS ALOYSIUS WEIR, M.D.

DR. WEIR? Silas Weir? Please come with me, there is a dire medical emergency & you are wanted urgently in Trenton!"

Another time, like a bolt of lightning out of a clear sky, Providence intervened to alter the course of my life, utterly; & this time, most unexpectedly, as an intervention of Percival Weir—I would have imagined, of all persons, the least expected to favor *me*.

This, on a rainy September morning in my surgery when, by happenstance, I had no appointments awaiting me through the day; & thus was grateful to be summoned to Trenton by a dark-clad individual whose name, so taken by surprise, I failed to hear clearly; except to understand that circumstances were grim, & *my services desperately needed*.

Barely, I had time to fetch my valise, & bid a hurried goodbye to my dear wife, Theresa, in another part of our residence, with a vague promise of being back home before midnight; though admittedly perplexed that no other physician in the vicinity of Trenton, the capital city of New Jersey, was available to attend to a *dire emergency*. For Trenton was eighty-five miles from Ho-Ho-Kus, & would involve a harried drive in a buggy in pelting rain.

However, such challenges never failed to stir in me a sensation of great excitement, commingled with panic: the hope that my medical skills would be adequate to the occasion, yet dread that I might fail most ignominiously.

On the jolting ride to Trenton, it was explained to me by the dark-clad individual seated beside me that my *expert knowledge of female anatomy* as well as my *surgical skills* were much needed, there being a particularly difficult delivery at the State Asylum for Female Lunatics in Trenton, & a dearth of qualified physicians on the staff.

"'Asylum for Female Lunatics!'—ah, I see."

It registered with me now, with something like chagrin, yet with even more apprehension, that a distant relative of my father had been appointed Director of the New Jersey State Asylum for Female Lunatics in Trenton several years before: Like a key fitting into a lock, I surmised that some contact had been made between Father & this relative, with the intention of advancing my career.

So far as I could recall, Father's relative—very likely, a cousin—was also named *Weir;* I felt a quickening of the pulse, that, like a young person in an adventure tale, though (indeed) I was no longer *young,* I was setting off to realize my destiny, at last.

"Is it very large, this Asylum?"—I could not resist inquiring of my companion, who seemed altogether affable, yet little inclined to conversation; & was told by him, "Yes, it *is*"—with teasingly little embellishment.

"And is the Director a 'Dr. Weir'—?"

"Yes, he *is.* 'Medrick Weir.'"

At this, I laughed nervously. For it seemed redundant of me to remark that the Director of the renowned Asylum was a kinsman of mine, as well as boastful. Yet, my black-clad companion made no further comment, but turned to stare gloomily out a window, at pelting rain like a scrim, ever shifting as the wagon plunged forward along a muddy roadway.

It had been some time now since Father had been informed, by Mother, of my unfortunate banishment from Chestnut Hill, indeed from the entire State of Pennsylvania; he knew of my present circumstances in Ho-Ho-Kus in service to the wealthy Rosencrantz family; that I was married, & had a brood of children (of whom he had met but three). In Father's eyes I was no longer a *young practitioner*—indeed, no longer *promising;* as my older brother, Franklin, had soared ahead, in terms of a successful career as a physician for the well-to-do of Beacon Hill, Boston. He may have been satisfied, to a degree, that I could support, however minimally, a wife & a growing family; but could no longer have seriously entertained any notion of my being renowned in any field of medicine.

In all of the world, only my dear mother & my dear wife retained faith in me, though perhaps Mother more than my wife, over all.

For, by this time, my wife & I had endured a good deal of financial strain, with our brood to feed & clothe on my meager salary, & with a wavering sort of financial support from my in-laws, who were large property-owners in South Jersey, & regarded with a degree of skepticism their daughter's impetuosity, in marrying an *aspiring medical researcher,* in the guise of a *country doctor.*

Thus, I was as excited at the prospect of the *dire emergency* as a doctor ten years my junior might have been; & prayed to God most fervently, that He would not allow me to fail when so much depended upon my succeeding.

This Day of Miracles, when I first cast my eyes upon Brigit Kinealy.

Of course, I did not know the girl's name at this time, nor could have guessed that this piteous, misshapen creature, writhing in agony amid bloodstained sheets, could survive her ordeal of labor, let alone feature so prominently in my life.

"Doctor!—thank God *you are here.*"

A flush-faced female attendant at the delivery whom I took to be a midwife explained to me, in a jarringly excitable voice that the young mother had been in labor for eighteen hours, steadily weakening & losing blood. One of the Asylum doctors had been assigned to the birth, but had not remained in the delivery room more than a few minutes, being overcome by the sight & smells; another staff doctor had been ordered by the Director to oversee the birth, but had never appeared at all.

The young mother (Brigit) was an "orphan"—a "deaf-mute"—who worked at the hospital in a lowly position, for her mother, a kitchen worker, had contracted her to the institution, not long before she died; by the terms of Brigit's contract, she would not be released from servitude until the age of twenty-one. It was believed that Brigit had "gotten into trouble" with someone on the staff, one or more of the (male) orderlies, who had taken advantage of her naïve & child-like nature.

After so many hours of horrific labor, it seemed that no one expected the young mother to live; but it was known that the Director of the Asylum wanted the infant to be spared—at least.

It was shocking to me, that such a very young-looking girl, hardly more than a child in her physical development, & possessed of an angelic sort of radiance, should be *pregnant* at all; & in such agony, at a renowned mental institution headed by my father's kinsman Medrick Weir! Of course, the girl was of Irish descent, which would account for a certain degree of dissolution; I recalled that our household servants in Concord, & those of our neighbors, tended to be Irish females who were forever getting themselves pregnant by the young men of the household, & having to be summarily dismissed.

Women give birth in sorrow, it is said, as a consequence of Eve's sin, yet how sad this seemed, for surely this girl was innocent of (conscious) wrongdoing; & most peculiarly pale as if all the blood had drained out of her body. Her skin was waxen-white, her eyes so pale they appeared translucent, her lashes & eyebrows colorless, & her hair such a pale blond, it appeared almost white.

Was this an *albino?*—a freak of nature, as I recalled from medical school; said to be short-lived, & with very poor vision.

Yet, though an *albino,* & so strangely pale, Brigit possessed an eerie, angelic beauty quite unlike any I had ever seen, far surpassing the more robust beauty of Tabitha Tyndale.

Newly arrived in this chamber of horrors—a *delivery room,* as it was called—(for we had nothing like this at the Hermitage, but only just used one of the farm outbuildings for such emergencies)—I stood staring down at the hellish sight. Halfway I wondered if my cruel father & his kinsman had conspired, not to advance my career but to humiliate me further, indeed to unman me. I felt a numbness in my limbs, & my thoughts came in a swarm. Of all medical situations, it is the horror of childbirth that physicians dread for sheer disgust: the hugely swollen belly of the pregnant female streaked with blood, the strained, stretched blood-glistening vagina rawly exposed, in normal conditions an obscene sight but the more hideous when turned inside out as during childbirth; the beauty of the young mother defaced, & scarcely feminine, which might have lent some charm to the gruesome spectacle.

(Of the head of the infant impacted between blood-smeared thighs, seemingly clamped within the straining vagina, a mere glimpse of which so shook me that I feared fainting, I cannot bring myself to speak; words fail me, I must be silent.)

So agitated was the pregnant girl, she seemed but scarcely aware of me, as I tried in a hesitant way to comfort her, with the assistance of the midwife; the pale eyes were terrifying to behold, as I half feared I might be gazing into another's very soul, yet seeing nothing human there.

As in workers' quarters at the Hermitage, there was a buzz of flies, & a very foul stench; though this was the State Asylum for Female Lunatics, at Trenton, a compound of impressive red-brick buildings said to have been designed by a notable architect, & not a makeshift hospital, yet conditions in the delivery room were nearly as deplorable.

Except for a vow to make my father proud of me at last, I would have fled the scene as previous doctors had done.

Though the young albino Irish girl was said to be a deaf-mute, this did not impede her ability to scream, most heartrendingly, as a child might scream, in helpless agony. For it was clear that the slender girl lacked the pelvic girth for childbirth; & the baby, sired by who knew what brute, appeared to be too large for the birth canal. How, & why, had our Creator designed the female body so *ineptly*, I had to wonder, not for the first time. At the Hermitage, Betje & other midwives dealt with difficult births, for it was not considered worthwhile for the Rosencrantz family to pay a physician's fee, to summon me to the premises; if it happened that I was at the Hermitage for other, more pressing reasons, involving valuable male workers, I might be engaged to oversee the delivery; but Betje or another midwife participated in the actual birth while I merely stood by, often with my eyes shut so that I had no actual memory of what maneuvers the midwife performed with her bare, bloody hands. I recall that Betje shouted encouragement to the straining mother-to-be in a jarringly loud voice; such excitable behavior I did not feel that I could mimic, nor did I wish to, for I am a gentleman, & not a *shouting type*. Still more, I had no idea what to say, & worried that the midwife at the Asylum, & others in attendance, who stood gawking in the doorway of the delivery room, might identify me as a fraud, & laugh at me.

Here, too, the midwife, whose name was Gretel, was calling out encouragement to the straining young mother, shaping her mouth expressly so that she might "see" the words even if she could not hear them.

In all, a very noisy scene, upsetting to my nerves. Female shouts & screams—for which we were ill-prepared in medical school!

I saw no recourse except to explain frankly to Gretel that I had little idea what to do, for I had never "delivered" an actual baby myself, only a mannequin-baby in medical school, with several other medical students, & that years ago; my dear wife's labors & deliveries were dealt with most capably by a midwife of her choosing who could be trusted not to fall into a dead faint, as a husband/father might—(for of course, I would have been banished from the bedroom, even if I had been home for the births). My dissection of the pregnant corpse I chose not to mention, for I had botched that surgery, too, I am sure—afterward hastily scraping together the remains & burying them at the farthest end of a cornfield near our house with the other postmorten specimens upon which I had experimented, human & animal. *No, I was not proud of myself, for my cowardice.*

"A 'Cesarean' "—I heard myself say, with surprising authority. "I am here to perform a 'Cesarean.' "

For it came over me, I had been summoned to Trenton because of my skill as a surgeon; that was the reason I stood here! Clearly it was no accident or whim, but the hand of Providence.

Fortunately, in idle hours in my home surgery I often perused medical texts, which described such procedures, including graphic drawings of the female reproductive organs, which I believed I could envision with some concentration. If only I had been told the specific nature of my mission in Trenton, I might have torn out the relevant pages to bring with me!

Like Betje, this midwife, a stranger to me, was behaving with surprising competence, yet deference, out of respect for my authority. It is indeed wondrous how a doctor & a female subordinate can work together, though they have never glimpsed each other before.

In my distraction I had forgotten that I was holding my physician's valise, gripped tight in my hand, & this Gretel gently detached from my fingers, & opened to discover therein the ugly instrument known as a *forceps*—which I recalled having used, or having tried to use, often with half-shut eyes, as Betje urged me, in one or another difficult birth at the Hermitage.

All this while, Gretel was fitting me with a protective cloth like a sheet, to cover my clothing; for I was wearing, on this warm September day, my formal physician's attire—a somber dark suit of a light woolen fabric, with a white cotton shirt with a starched collar & a proper tie, impractical in these circumstances.

"Doctor, here. We can begin."

With gratifying calm Gretel prepared the patient for me, helping to hold her down, & spread her legs; taking up the forceps, to press into my hand, & guiding me, that I might maneuver the forceps inside the straining vagina, urging me to close the forceps (gently) about the head of the impacted infant, & to give it a tug—gently at first—then more forcefully. By this time I was crouched between the young mother's thighs, in a most abject position; scarcely daring to breathe while moving the baby's head very slightly from side to side to loosen the grip of the vagina, even as the mother screamed, & Gretel shouted hearty encouragement to her—"Push! *Push!*"—in such a loud voice, even the deaf might hear.

How long this nightmare struggle persisted I would not recall afterward. As a woman gives birth in sorrow, so God in His mercy erases such memory; in such oblivion, the race of humans continues, as it would not, most likely, if the male of the species & not the female were impregnated, & made to *give birth*.

In this hellish place in the Asylum at Trenton, God must have given me strength to prevail, as a fine red mist came over my brain, & my heart pounded in desperation; for the damned baby refused to budge—*It did not want to be born*. Canny Gretel slipped into my hand a knife with a long, sharp blade, not a surgical instrument (it seemed) but rather a butcher knife, & told me that I must use it, to free both the mother & the baby, else both would die. Somehow, I did this; for

I had no choice; cutting in the pelvic region somewhat haphazardly, with half-shut eyes, willing that God would guide my hand, which it seemed God did, until at last the oversized head slid forward, an expression of surprise & chagrin on its small flat fish-face.

Following this, the entire body of the baby, slippery with blood, like a miniature seal, emerged from the mother's body, to cries of relief & rejoicing amid onlookers. Both in the delivery room & in the corridor outside was a rowdy gathering of Asylum workers, it seemed, identified by their green uniforms; with here & there disheveled females in dark brown clothing, inmates of the Asylum. Later, I would marvel at the general interest in the delivery of Brigit Kinealy's baby *as if its paternity were of more than ordinary significance,* but at the time, I must confess that I did not.

Ah!—in triumph the wizened little creature was lifted aloft like a rare prize, by Gretel; but almost at once taken from her hands, presumably to be washed, leaving Gretel & me to attend to the feverish young mother lying amid filthy sheets, still losing a good deal of dark blood.

"There, there!—you will be all right now, dear. You, & your baby. No need to cry, no need to *fear.* We will take care of you"—so the midwife assured the young mother, gesticulating with her hands and face in a most exaggerated manner, at which the exhausted young mother stared in some sort of dazed comprehension.

Ah! Even in the confusion of the moment I was aware, the brute baby was indeed a *he.* Filling his tiny lungs with air & crying lustily, like one entitled not only to life but to attention; borne hurriedly out of the rank-smelling delivery room & out of our sight.

•

"Doctor?"—the concerned voice of Gretel hovered above me.

Had I *fainted*? Only dimly was I aware of being lifted, & carried into another room; revived, or part-revived, & left to lie on a couch, too dazed to open my eyes. The back of my head ached where it had struck something hard.

So long had I been breathing the foul air of the delivery room, & so long the strain of the bestial labor, like no other experience in my life, a sudden darkness swooped upon me like a beating of dark-feathered wings, & I had fallen senseless to the filthy floor.

"We must stitch up the wound," I said, agitated, "—we have not finished with the young mother . . ."

"It has been done, Doctor!" Gretel assured me. "It is all accomplished."

Very carefully then, I sat up, blinking as the unfamiliar room spun about me.

"You are sure, Gretel? The suture has been done?"

"Yes, Doctor."

"But—who has done it?"

"I took the liberty, Doctor. I hope you do not object."

"*You!* Daring to stitch up a surgical wound?"

This was quite a surprise: a mere midwife, suturing the wound of a Cesarean! But I supposed such a female has had experience, & knows what she is doing.

"But the young mother will need more care, she has been losing much blood . . ."

"Oh, we will care for her, Doctor!"

With a kind of forced brightness Gretel spoke, as if she believed that there might be someone overhearing our conversation.

Managing to recover, I inquired if Dr. Weir—that is, Medrick Weir—knew that I was on the premises, & that the difficult delivery had turned out well.

"I am sure that Director Weir knows all there is to know," Gretel said, with a covert meaning which I did not comprehend, "—& that he is very grateful for you, Doctor, for your expert attention."

As I had journeyed to Trenton primarily in the hope of shaking hands with my renowned kinsman I was quite disappointed, for, instead of meeting Medrick Weir, I was met by his assistant, Pell, a sallow-skinned, porcine individual of about my age, who thanked me coolly for my services, & informed me that the Director of the Asylum had been called away—"Unavoidably."

"Called away?—where?"

But this was an impertinent query, I understood. Pell fixed me with a rudely blank expression; yet, I could discern a smirk of a sort playing about his thin lips.

"Here is your payment, Doctor. Your services are not further required at the present time."

This was a blow to my pride. Was I to be dismissed by my own kinsman, without having met him?

Embarrassing, too, to be given cash payment, so openly. As I if I had come all the way to Trenton for only this: fresh-minted bills, in the palm of my hand.

Though I thanked Pell for this payment, yet I hesitated to leave, just yet. For it seemed to me, as the physician who had delivered the albino girl's baby, I should examine the patient at least quickly, before departing.

"No need, Doctor. She will be well cared for."

"Such a young, malnourished mother will die, I'm afraid, if—"

"We will take care of her, Doctor. We are all M.D.s here. You have your fee which is quite generous, I think."

But now Pell spoke forcefully. I had no choice but to retreat.

Hurriedly, I stuffed the wad of bills into a pocket. I would count them later, indeed recount them, on the jolting buggy ride home.

Though not yet fully recovered from my fainting spell, I was urged to my feet by Pell, & led briskly to the waiting buggy. At the curbside Gretel lingered, uncertainly. It was clear that the midwife had more to say, but could not speak in such circumstances; for Pell glared at her, & waved her away with a motion of his hand.

The young mother is expected to die. They have no further care for her. They want you out of the way, your usefulness is over.

As if Pell could read my thoughts, he bade me farewell with a kind of mock jovialness. Reassuring me that Director Weir was "very sorry to miss you"—"hopes to hire you again soon when your skills are needed." To my surprise, he pressed into my hand a hefty object— a good-sized bottle of Scotch whiskey—"Courtesy of the Director."

In a faltering voice I tried to explain that I did not drink spirits, but Pell paid no heed.

I had no choice but to climb inside the buggy. At the window, leaning out, to protest another time, weakly: "But—you know—my work here is not really done . . ."

No one paid the slightest heed. The horse leapt into motion, hooves loud on the pavement.

"Good night, Doctor! Have a safe journey back to Ho-Ho-Kus."

It seemed to me, the name *Ho-Ho-Kus* was pronounced by Pell in a jeering manner.

The buggy moved off into the darkness of rural New Jersey. A rough journey, along rutted roads, with but lanterns rattling from the buggy's sides, to awkwardly shine light upon our way. Worrisome thoughts assailed me: Would the infant be returned to its mother, to nurse; or would a wet nurse be found, to care for it in her place?—assuming that the very young mother would not long survive.

Visions of the girl—*Brigit*—came to me unbidden: angelic beauty, innocence befouled, cruelly contorted in agony . . .

You must content yourself with knowing: You saved her from an immediate death.

Beyond that, you are not to blame.

Very tired from my ordeal, & weak from lack of food, I managed to open the bottle of Scotch whiskey, releasing sharp fumes like wires lifting into my brain. I dared to taste the liquid—which burnt my tongue, & seared my throat, like liquid flame. I dared to drink—just a swallow. A muted joy began to take shape in my heart. For it seemed, I might have the "gift of healing" that is a kind of grace, bestowed upon few in the medical profession. That, though deemed a failure elsewhere, & held in contempt by my own father, I might be viewed as something of a success at Trenton, performing a Cesarean procedure in emergency circumstances & saving the life of both mother & infant.

Hopes to hire you again soon when your services are needed—these words echoing in my ears as I sank into an exhausted sleep in the jolting buggy bearing me away into the sweet oblivion of a New Jersey night.

II

New Jersey State Asylum
for Female Lunatics

Destiny

FROM *THE CHRONICLE OF A PHYSICIAN'S LIFE*
BY SILAS ALOYSIUS WEIR, M.D.

As providence has guided my career, often without my comprehending the course laid out before me, but trusting in God, that my choices will be His bidding, so it happened that, within a few months of my first visit, the Director of the New Jersey State Asylum for Female Lunatics at Trenton contacted me a second time, with an urgent appeal to hurry to the Asylum, where there was again a *dire situation.*

In the interim, I had frequently succumbed to the most mesmerizing of dreams, of reuniting with the young mother Brigit, whose radiant beauty & innocence were clearer to me in my imagination, than in the brute actuality of the delivery room; if I had dared, I would have made inquiries at the Asylum, as to the well-being of the girl; but saw no way of doing this that would not involve unwanted attention upon me, that might even make its way back to my family in Concord, with disagreeable results. *You are a happily married Christian husband & a father many times over: That is your lot, & it is a blessed one. Rejoice!*

Usually, forgetfulness like torrential rain washed away all memory of my patients, no matter if my involvement with them had been a success or a failure; as a grievously overworked country doctor, I could not be expected to remember most of my patients, even if I had tried. At the Hermitage, tending to indentured servants & laborers as often victims of accidents in the Rosencrantz mills or on the farm, as natural illnesses, I had learned not to question *causes* but to deal only with *results*. Bloodied backs & heads, broken & crushed limbs, heat exhaustion, cardiac arrest, respiratory collapse, impaired vision, gastrointestinal hemorrhage, mania—all were equal to me, as a skilled practitioner, paid not to "cure" but to "restore" the worker to fitfulness, to enable him to *earn his keep*.

Yet, I seemed to know that something of a higher destiny could still be mine: My early dreams of surgical experiments, my (cruelly aborted) attempt to correct the misalignment of the Brush infant's skull, & other projects never realized, wafted before me like mirages as I sank into an exhausted sleep each night; & it seemed to me, this destiny awaited in Trenton, New Jersey.

A second time called to Trenton, in December 1851, with such satisfactory results that the Director wished to see me, to thank me personally; & to offer me a more permanent position on the Asylum staff, as a physician-surgeon, there being a sudden vacancy.

At first, I hesitated to accept this most welcome offer, as, during the course of our conversation, out of shyness I had not corrected the Director's assumption that my medical degree was from the University of Pennsylvania Medical School; & then, out of embarrassment, that a correction after the fact would call undo attention to the lapse; but when the Director reiterated his offer, in a kindly tone, I was thrilled to accept.

This position would pay a more steady wage than I could expect from the Rosencrantz family, who had fallen into the habit of taking me for granted, as I could usually be relied upon to be fetched at short notice. Scarcely did I need to consult my wife, who had long been unhappy with the situation in Ho-Ho-Kus, in which, as she charged, I was treated rather more like one of the Rosencrantzes' indentured servants than a respected doctor with a certificate of medicine.

Yet more wonderfully, my position at the Asylum brought with it a residence for my family on the Asylum grounds, in which we could live for a minimal payment; this boon, entirely unforeseen, made me weep with gratitude, like one who has struggled to swim across a turbulent river, & is staggering now on the shore, able to breathe at last.

"Dr. Weir, thank you!—you have saved my life."

Shaking my kinsman's hand so vigorously, tears streaming down my cheeks, I am afraid that I somewhat embarrassed the elder man, who quickly assured me that the position was "all that you deserve, Silas—for you come very highly recommended, & of course you are 'of good family'"—with a wink for me, that I might share in the joke.

Soon then, Pell was summoned into the Director's office, to discuss my contract, & arrangements for moving my family to Trenton; in the interim, I was to begin work the very next morning, for there were "urgent cases" that had gone untreated for too long.

Vaguely I had heard that the New Jersey State Asylum for Female Lunatics at Trenton, much heralded at its founding in 1837 by the reformer Dorothea Dix, as a center for the humane treatment of mental illness, was under attack by political enemies of the Director in the New Jersey legislature; much resentment had been stirred by the costly construction of the Asylum by the architect Kirkbride, whose vision was to build hospitals with windows exposed to the light as much as possible, instead of fortress-like buildings resembling prisons, with few windows. In those newspaper accounts which I had read, with a kind of morbid fascination, Medrick Weir was reported to be harshly criticized by ignorant legislators for wasting money on "hopeless lunatics"—"females who can never be cured"—rather than simply locking them away as in the past, & hoping that they will expire soon.

Of course, I was honored to be invited to join the staff at such a forward-looking hospital, for it was clear that Medrick Weir would be receptive to surgical experimentation of the kind I hoped to pursue. It had not escaped my notice that Dr. Weir somewhat resembled my father in bearing & appearance, as in age: both men in their early sixties, not tall, but carrying themselves with the authority of tallness; inclined to geniality, indeed to joviality, while masking a steely will which (I knew) it would be fatal to thwart.

Initially it was planned that I would have dinner with Medrick Weir in his private residence on the Asylum grounds, where we could discuss the terms of my employment in more detail, & become acquainted with each other; unfortunately, an emergency of some kind intervened, & these plans were postponed.

"I ask only that you be loyal to me," Medrick Weir said warmly, shaking my hand when we parted that evening, "—for I am surrounded by individuals whom I cannot trust. *You* will be my eyes & ears, I hope—my young kinsman, Silas."

The Vow

FROM *THE CHRONICLE OF A PHYSICIAN'S LIFE*
BY SILAS ALOYSIUS WEIR, M.D.

IT SOON BECAME EVIDENT, that there was a medical crisis at the Asylum, whether as a cause of *mental illness,* or a result, was not clear.

Not generally spoken of, in the Director's presence, as it was a source of keen embarrassment for him, was the fact that, over a course of twelve months, eleven lunatics at the Asylum had taken their own lives, in divers ways ranging from slashing of wrists, hanging with bedsheets, & drowning (in the Delaware River). Indeed, this was shocking to me! For *taking one's own life* is a most grievous sin, said to be the sole sin that God cannot forgive.

Benjamin Franklin, Benjamin Rush, Dorothea Dix, more recently Medrick Weir, & other reformers in the new science of psychology were of the conviction that "madness" was in fact "illness"—that is, *mental illness.* Not some sort of curse, or punishment, or affliction like Original Sin. To treat *illness,* as one might treat any *illness,* though the malady seemed to originate in the brain, one must not rely upon superstition but rather upon scientific observation; whenever possible, experimentation.

This was a most revolutionary idea! For in medicine, as in religion, authority has long resided with tradition, not exploration by questing young minds.

Experimental research at the Asylum at Trenton was headed by the Director & a small, trusted circle of younger doctors, which (I had reason to believe) I would soon be invited to join. Their goal was the "cure" of mental illness—which Dr. Weir believed to be a most reasonable goal, within his lifetime.

"Mental illness is caused by 'infection'—we must seek out the cause of infection." So Medrick Weir, M.D., had declared in the leading publications of the day, stirring a good deal of controversy.

It was exciting to me to hear such ideas articulated. The life of a rural physician is empty of "ideas"—treating patients is a practical goal, with the hope of returning the patient to his normal life of labor; there is no thought of discovering scientific truths, or "cures" for disease. In the Asylum at Trenton, caretaking of the mentally ill was the responsibility of the staff; seeking higher truths, the pursuit of the Director & his young researchers.

So far as mental illness was concerned, its primary manifestations seemed to be agitation, excitation, rapid & incoherent speech, "babbling"; or, mental & physical paralysis, refusal to speak or to listen, or to make eye contact. A wilder & more "colorful" sort of madness involved seeing & hearing things that did not exist, imagining communications with the divine, & being roused to violence with no provocation. In the female in particular, a disheveled appearance, untidy hair & broken fingernails, a strong body odor, above all a failure to dress suitably, including corsetry, were certain symptoms of madness, which the least trained of physicians could identify.

In medical school we were taught, & experience has largely confirmed, that females are more prone to madness than males, the seat of *hysteria* being the uterus. Tears come more readily to the female, at any age; as Aristotle noted, the tears of the female are of a "softer & less substantial texture" than the tears of the male. Emotions in the female arise from the specifically female organs, while emotions in the male rise from the cerebral. As it was firmly believed that immoral & criminal behavior was the consequence of degeneracy in certain races & in family lineages, sterilization of females so afflicted, mandated by the state, would be a necessary part of the surgical career of some physicians, entrusted with public health responsibilities.

Already as an eager young apprentice it had seemed to me a likely procedure for the treatment of *hysteria,* to remove the offending organ by surgery, & so it was my hope that I might pursue this avenue of exploration, once I was established at the Asylum at Trenton with its abundance of female lunatics, as it was my hope that I might pursue more successfully the "correction" of misshapen infant skulls begun at Chestnut Hill. As it might be requested, of course sterilization of certain elements of society would be another, more routine responsibility.

Medrick Weir listened to me with gratifying attentiveness as I spoke of my first, unfortunate experiment in Chestnut Hill; I confess, I somewhat glided over the fact that the Brush infant had expired beneath my hands, & focused on the fact that the skull of the infant had been misshapen at birth, & the infant no doubt doomed to an early death.

"I am sure, Dr. Weir, that I could perfect this procedure once I am in a position to operate on another infant, or two, who suffers from a similar condition. In fact, an older child—two, or three—might be an interesting challenge, for the skull hardens with age, as you know; the skull of an infant is still malleable, to a degree. Are there infants, or children, afflicted with misshapen skulls, available at the Asylum, for physicians on the staff to examine?"

In my enthusiasm I may have been speaking rapidly, & excitedly; it seemed to me that Medrick Weir directed a startled gaze at me through his glittering eyeglasses.

Surprising me, then, with the equanimity of his response, that seemed to both chide & forgive a young physician's overabundance of zeal: "Well, Silas! Your research is doubtless worthwhile & should be pursued, in time; it is true that, infrequently, there are illicit, bastard births at the Asylum, & of these, most are removed from the lunatic mother immediately, to be placed in adoption. But, if circumstances warrant, & a young experimenter has proven himself worthy, it is possible that an experimental subject might be provided for him, dependent upon a review of the Asylum board, of which I am Director."

At this, I was so deeply moved, I could barely speak. For it seemed to me that in this remote kinsman of mine, who had never set eyes upon me until very recently, I was discovering the benevolent, nurturing, *fatherly* father whom I had never had in my earlier life.

"But in the meantime, Silas, we are confronted with a dire crisis at the Asylum, a proclivity for suicide among the weaker-minded of the lunatics, as you have doubtless heard—for it is very hard to suppress such a growing scandal! My enemies in the state legislature—fed the most vicious rumors & falsehoods by certain of my adversaries in the field of psychology, who would like nothing more than to overthrow my Directorship here—are agitating for a 'public accounting' of conditions in my hospital; & so we must immediately put a stop to the suicides. Of course, we have locked up the most severely ill—we have restrained them, in the usual way. But it would look very bad, to *lock up all the lunatics as prisoners.* For then we would be signaling to our adversaries that we have given up trying to 'cure' them—which is our mandate." Medrick Weir paused, to fix his eyes upon mine, a most piercing gaze even through the polished lenses of his glasses. "*You,* my dear nephew, have been selected to head a team of young staff doctors, to deal with the physical maladies that may be precipitating these rash acts."

Among these many astonishing words, what most leapt to my ear were *You, my dear nephew* . . . for this was the first time that Medrick Weir had acknowledged me in so specific a way: as if he were not a very distant relative bearing merely my family name, & that a not-uncommon name in the New England states, but an actual close relative, who had known me intimately, as a *nephew.*

"Dr. Weir, I will not disappoint you. I vow, sir—*I am yours to command.*"

Brushing a hand over my eyes, that my kinsman Medrick Weir would not see how my eyes misted, with tears of gratitude.

Fistula

From *The Chronicle of a Physician's Life*
by Silas Aloysius Weir, M.D.

*F*ISTULA—indeed, Eve's curse, suffered by a goodly number of women after childbirth, but suffered for the most part in silence.

It should not have surprised me that *fistula* was the particular affliction of those female lunatics who committed the gravest of sins, taking their own lives; for *fistula*, repugnant in itself, could not fail to cast the afflicted one into despair, thus clouding her judgment even further. I had long known of this affliction, though not in detail, for physicians understood it to be a hopeless condition, like leprosy, or syphilis, in no way remediable. Among Dr. Strether's practice in Chestnut Hill there were said to be several women so afflicted, whom no one had glimpsed in years; women suffering from *fistula*, who were of the most distinguished families, were yet kept hidden away out of shame, or indeed willingly hid themselves away in their family homes, in a kind of quarantine, of which no one spoke. These unhappy women, though mothers & grandmothers, in many cases, could not mingle with others, & did not wish to mingle with others, knowing themselves repugnant; & preferring to be considered eccentric, or even mad, rather than be exposed as suffering from this affliction.

At the Hermitage, among those girls & women of lowly birth, common servants & laborers in the mills & on the farm, there were some afflicted with *fistula,* whom I had not been requested to examine; these luckless creatures were able to continue with their work, in isolation, by the charity of the Rosencrantz family, that they might avoid starving to death, at least.

At the Asylum, however, I was not to be spared these patients; in my zeal to uphold my uncle Medrick's high estimation of my skills, & his trust in me, I determined to do all that I could to pursue an actual *cure for fistula.* This, an entirely new field of experimentation for me, unforeseen until Trenton.

The particular misery of the *fistula*-sufferer is that she repels not only herself but others—all who come near her. No matter how she tries to keep herself clean, she cannot, for more than a few minutes; unless she forswears eating & drinking altogether, in which case she falls in a faint, & will soon die.

Such misery, it seemed to me, was possibly in excess of Eve's sin; though I hasten to say, I am not one to challenge the tenets of Christian faith as set forth by such esteemed leaders as John Calvin, of Protestant reformers the most admired by my father, for one.

In any case, the doctor's challenge is to *heal, & cure* the afflicted, not to pass judgment on them.

For those readers to whom *fistula* is a new medical term, it is in particular reference to perforations in the urinary tract of the female, leading to chronic & continuous incontinence.

Filthy, abominable, accursed—it was often said of the afflicted, who have no control over the inflamed nether regions of their bodies, thus should not be blamed.

Rarely was the affliction discussed in respectable company. A husband could not be expected to be aware of a wife's *fistula,* for the ignoble term would never be uttered in his presence. In medical school we learned of *ulcers*—not exactly a male equivalent of *fistula,* but bearing some relationship. The *ulcer* is a mysterious growth in the male intestine, a *fistula* is a tear in the female bladder, usually a consequence of a difficult childbirth.

Admittedly, it was something of a surprise, if not a shock, to me, to discover that my initial assignment at the Asylum at Trenton was to treat *fistula*-sufferers, surely the least attractive of all patients; & to realize, belatedly, that the terms of my employment, though generous & an improvement over my situation in Ho-Ho-Kus, was entirely dependent upon my serving in this way, under my uncle's direction.

Yes: It is tragic to report, Brigit Kinealy had become one of these despised females. Though not an Asylum patient Brigit was contracted to the Asylum, in some low-paying position; it was said of her that the Director himself had some concern for her as an orphan whose mother, an indentured servant from Limerick, Ireland, also contracted to the Asylum, had died a few years previously.

No sooner had I been relieved to hear that Brigit had not died of loss of blood, or infection, after the Cesarean birth, than I was informed, by Gretel, that the young mother was suffering from incontinence, like the others, & seemed to be deeply despondent.

"Shall I examine her? Where is she?"—eagerly I inquired, yet with some apprehension, for it would be dismaying to me, to see the angelic girl in such a state, & to smell the inevitable stench of urine & excrement that is a feature of *fistula*.

"Brigit keeps to herself, Doctor. She is usually assigned to the night shift, with other *indentured*. They have made little nests for themselves in a part of the cellar where no one ever ventures. They are kitchen & latrine workers, very poorly paid & readily fired."

This was painful to hear. That angelic face—a latrine worker!

"What has become of her baby? She does not nurse it, I suppose?"

"Certainly not, Doctor! They took it from her immediately. A 'white' baby is always valuable, even one of lowly birth. By now, it has been adopted by a 'worthy Christian couple' in Trenton, or Princeton. We will never know—we never do."

"What do you mean—'never'? Does this sort of thing happen often?"

But Gretel was easing away from me, frowning. Clearly she did not wish to be seen speaking with me in a main corridor of the Asylum, near the Infirmary.

No doubt, my face betrayed some incredulity, for I could not help myself, in feeling most astonished.

"But I hope, at least, that she is not 'suicidal'"—I would have called after Gretel, but dared not.

Soon, to my dismay, after examining a succession of wretched female lunatics, ranging in age from late adolescence to early senescence, more than two dozen at least, I became something of a reluctant expert on *fistula of the bladder,* hitherto an unexplored territory to me, as to any reputable physician.

Over all, the condition seemed to be caused by impregnation at a very young age, before the pelvis had time to grow sufficiently, to allow for a safe delivery of an infant of normal size (as in the case of sixteen-year-old Brigit). It was not uncommon for girls of a coarse background to become impregnated as young as twelve—I had been aware of this, to a degree, in rural New Jersey, & so it was hardly a great surprise.

Females in any situation of servitude—whether indentured servants, or Black slaves (for there were still slaves in New Jersey at this time, particularly in South Jersey), were likely to be impregnated at a very young age, being defenseless against their owners & overseers; lest one feel pity for these, it was pointed out to me that such girls were not above *seeking favors* in this way, & many were, at a young age, shockingly *mature.*

(I am somewhat reluctant to note that my wife's family in Vineland, New Jersey, owned a Black slave couple, & sold off their children as they were born; one of these had been intended to be Theresa's dowry, but I demurred, with the explanation that my family were staunch Abolitionists, & would disown me entirely if I brought a child slave into my household! From this awkward beginning, there was friction between my Cleff in-laws & me, that would not soon abate.)

As a result of torturous & protracted labor it often happened that a young mother suffered lacerations in the vaginal area, including perforations in the bladder; thus causing excretory fluid (urine) to flow directly into the vaginal canal, & out of the body in a near-continuous trickle. In this way the afflicted woman was rendered a pariah among her own family, who could not bear her "filth" & chronic stench. Even those who felt strong emotion for the afflicted, as close as a husband, a parent, a sibling, or one of her own children, could not abide the afflicted one for very long. The consequence being, women afflicted with *fistula* were not only banished from all semblance of normal life but were susceptible to open sores, festering infections, & raging fevers that soon brought their miserable lives to an end, often before their babies were weaned.

Indeed, in the most severe cases infants were victims as well—

abandoned by their wretched mothers, too frail or sickly to be placed with surrogate mothers.

Even in death, I discovered, the body of the afflicted woman gave off so pungent an odor, it was futile to attempt to wash it, following custom; a Christian burial was executed in haste, within hours, with little time to mourn. Over all, when a *fistula*-afflicted woman died, it was likely to be counted as a blessing, however sad to those who had known her in happier days.

Why, then, did young girls not strenuously resist impregnation?— one might inquire.

At such an age, & invariably out of wedlock, such sexual precocity is baffling to civilized society. A certain laxity in morals among the lower classes is the explanation, most likely; a failure to instruct their children in the Christian faith, as their parents had instructed them.

Often, I would ask in exasperation, to one of these afflicted creatures, "But why would you allow such a thing to happen? Surely you might have *resisted*?"—& was met with tear-filled eyes, & stony silence.

Once, overhearing me, Gretel intervened, laughing scornfully at my inquiry & telling me that it was not possible for any girl or woman to say "no" to any male—except if she was of a family with money; in which case, she could not say "no" to any marriage proposal approved by her father.

Though I much appreciated Gretel's assistance in the ward, I did not appreciate the woman's sharp tongue. I did not like her speaking so crudely of *males*—as if forgetting that I was a *male,* not to mention her superiors at the Asylum.

"That is not true, Gretel. There are decent, upright, God-fearing *males*—perhaps not of your acquaintance, but they exist, indeed."

I may have blushed at our speaking of such matters, so openly; for nothing like such an exchange could ever occur in my household, or that of my in-laws, or my family in Concord.

Gretel took note of my discomfort, adding, in her droll way: "Of course, Dr. Weir. It could only be *males* from elsewhere, not New Jersey, who behave so badly. They say that the Southern slave-owners are particularly uncouth, in their relations with their Black female slaves, though they are Christian gentlemen, too. But no doubt, that is but *rumor.*"

Others in the vicinity laughed, but I did not laugh. Indignantly I turned & walked away, leaving Gretel to stare after me with something like regret, I am sure.

For it is often, wisely said: If you do not insist that your subordinates *keep their place,* they will push out of their place, & take advantage of your kindness, mistaking it for a softness of conviction.

I vow, sir—I am yours to command.

Had I not made this vow to the Director of the New Jersey State Asylum for Female Lunatics, with an impassioned shake of my uncle Medrick's hand, I might have lost heart, & fled, faced with the seemingly insurmountable challenge of *fistula.*

Added to which, another female lunatic committed suicide very early on a Sunday morning in February, throwing herself from a window on the highest, third floor of the Asylum onto a snowy walkway, which broke both her legs, & badly cracked her skull; with but a scrawled note left behind—*Damn'd of God & man.*

(Though I felt sympathy for Medrick Weir, crudely targeted by enemies in the New Jersey legislature over this latest death, I did feel some relief, that the suicide had not been afflicted with *fistula* but with a more ordinary sort of malady, a chronic psoriasis over much of the suicide's body, & a chronic bronchial cough, in addition to the despair & despondency common to the Asylum; thus in no possible way my responsibility.)

It was all that I could do, & at times more than I could do, to examine the afflicted females, with Gretel, or another nurse-attendant, assisting; often, I had to cease abruptly, to hurry to a window, to lean out & breathe in fresh air, that I might not gag & vomit, for the smell was so very repellent. This, even when Gretel had seen to it that the patient's pelvic area had been thoroughly washed with borax-soap very recently.

Though I am reluctant to acknowledge it, my repugnance in those early days for my clinical work was such, I was required to sip small quantities of Scotch whiskey kept for that purpose, in my private office in the Infirmary; as well as, from time to time, cocaine drops & laudanum, out of the Infirmary supplies.

It was a startling discovery that not all of the afflicted females had been victims of forcible intercourse as young girls; indeed, most of the afflicted were older, married women, injured while giving birth, at any age. Gretel was likely to learn from them that they had had numerous babies—some as many as eight, or nine, or ten. That their bodies were ravaged, & their faces suggested despair, was not so very surprising. It was not always clear that these women were *lunatics,* when one spoke sympathetically with them as Gretel did; though, if I questioned them, they were likely to become silent, shifty-eyed, & anxious.

This was a diagnostic symptom of the *female mentally ill,* according to Medrick Weir: an inability to answer simple questions put to them by a physician, as if their brains had ceased to function, in thrall to infections from the uterus.

What I wished to determine was whether *mental illness* in these patients had followed as a consequence of *fistula,* or whether the two were only incidentally related; or whether, the experience of child-bearing in itself might have precipitated *mental illness,* & *fistula* exacerbated the pathological condition.

"Giving birth is a woman's fulfillment," I remarked to Gretel, "—so it does not seem to make sense that the more children a woman has, the more likely she is to become mentally ill. One would wonder why Providence had decreed so many women to be afflicted with *fistula,* if they are also 'blessed,' by becoming mothers."

"Not all women are so happy becoming mothers, Doctor. For some, it is a rude surprise."

"But for normal women, in stable Christian households, with loving & caring spouses, it is certainly a happy experience."

"For such women, yes—perhaps. But for women unprotected by a husband, contracted in servitude to a Master, it is another kind of experience."

This was the first time that I had heard Gretel speak of a Master, in somewhat the same rueful terms in which Betje had spoken.

"But who is your Master, Gretel?"—I could not help but inquire, in some surprise.

"The Director of the Asylum is my Master, Doctor," Gretel said, guardedly, "—but only as I am employed by the Asylum, under the governance of the State of New Jersey. I was sent here from a village outside Düsseldorf, at the age of fourteen—there were too many of us in the family. So long ago, I scarcely recall."

"I had not realized, Gretel. You are an indentured servant, too?"

"We are all 'indentured.' The only difference between us is that some have given up hope, & others have not—yet."

"You say you are from—Düsseldorf? Is that Germany? Are you not in communication with your family, over the years?"—this too surprising to me, as hitherto Gretel had not seemed to be an embittered person, like so many at the Asylum.

Gretel laughed harshly, showing small, badly stained teeth, which it was no pleasure to glimpse.

"A 'family' is a luxury, Doctor. Not for *us*."

Frowning, Gretel turned my attention back to one of the lunatic-patients waiting to be examined, with a look of chagrin, beside a part-opened window, that her bodily odor might be diffused; in this case one of the skeletal-thin females, with fraying frizzed hair like spun cobwebs about her head.

"Come here, Mrs. Brunner"—so Gretel spoke, in a kindly but firm voice.

What was particularly pathetic, women afflicted with *fistula* soon came to accept that they were as repugnant as others thought them; as women suffering from certain cancers, of the breast & pelvic area, were stricken as well with shame, & in some cases preferred to hide away & die, without seeking treatment. Since a *fistula* was something like an open, raw boil, a rent in the flesh, it was the more exacerbated by the continuous flow of urine from the torn bladder, in acid-like rivulets through the vaginal tract, down the inner thighs, & onto the legs, & staining the ground wherever the afflicted woman stood for long, which caused others to shun her, or shoo her, away irritably, like flies.

It was a particular pathos when young, attractive girls like Brigit Kinealy were so stricken, for inevitably their lives were over. They could never wed, they could never live in a normal household. The lowest, more despised sort of work was all they could do, for they could not work even in a clattering mill, among others. It was difficult not to assume that, so condemned by humankind, they were condemned by God as well, as the great John Calvin has taught.

How cruel!—I could not comprehend why God would create so winsome a creature, only to defile it.

.   .   .

At a distance one day in midwinter I had a glimpse of Brigit Kinealy, as I was approaching a rear entrance of the Asylum Infirmary; it appeared that Brigit had been headed for the same door, but seeing me shrank back, in great embarrassment.

I had been forgetting that Brigit Kinealy was, to the eye, a *freak of nature*: an albino, with unnaturally pale skin & ashy-white hair; & eyes so pale they appeared transparent like glass. Her face was of a startling beauty, yet such delicacy, I feared it might break, like the thinnest Wedgwood china.

On this blustery winter day Brigit was wearing a cloak of some coarse dark material that fit her slight body loosely, & was not very clean; on her feet, ill-fitting boots, that might have been a boy's. Though I waved my arms emphatically, to gain her attention—could not resist calling to her in a friendly manner, shaping my mouth to signal a warm greeting, and my identity—"Dr. Weir"—"he who delivered your baby"—clearly she did not wish to face me, & scurried away like a frightened cat.

Wafting to my nostrils, despite the fresh clear air of winter, a faint odor of urine—most pathetic, & repugnant.

"Poor girl! I wish that I could *vow*—to save *you*."

Later that day, I approached Gretel, to say that I had glimpsed Brigit, by chance; & wondered if Gretel would bring her to me in the Infirmary, that I might examine her, & see if there was anything that I could do, to help her; for I had a sudden fear, that Brigit might, like so many others, fall into a despondency, & take her own life.

Indeed, Gretel shook her head gravely, & said that Brigit shrank even from *her*, & was clearly most unhappy, following a recent death of a friend of hers similarly afflicted with *fistula*, who had been found dead in the Asylum cellar, starved as a skeleton by a refusal to continue to eat & drink, in her defiled state.

I expressed surprise that I had not heard of this death, but Gretel explained that since the girl was not a patient in the Asylum, a state institution, but merely one of the indentured staff, her death did not count in the public record; no one outside the Asylum would know of it.

"Are there many of these? Who do not 'count' in the public record?"—I was thinking of the likelihood of there being, in some capacity in the Asylum, undocumented individuals who might be available as experimental subjects; but Gretel had no idea.

"It would be a terrible sin, for Brigit to harm herself," I said sternly, in the hope that Gretel might pass my concern on to Brigit, "—an affront to God, even if she is suffering terribly."

To this, Gretel murmured a barely audible assent, whether in avid agreement, or with some covert mockery typical of her kind—*Yes, Doctor.*

"So I must insist, Gretel: You will bring Brigit Kinealy to me."

"But, Doctor—"

"*You will bring her.* Very soon, please."

"But I am not sure that she will come with me, Doctor. For, you see—"

"*You will bring her.* That is all, Gretel."

Quickly then, that Gretel should not see the expression on my face, I turned aside, & hurried away. My heart was beating rapidly, I knew not why. The firmness of my resolve was surprising to me, as to Gretel, for ordinarily I found it difficult to keep track of patients, particularly at the Asylum, where the female lunatics came to resemble one another, in two unappealing types: inclining toward soft-shaped, boneless obesity, or the gnarly boniness of a skeleton; piteously bald, or with hair frizzed & snarled as a rat's nest; sickly pale, or disagreeably swarthy, as with a fine scrim of grime too deeply imprinted to be washed away.

"But *she*—Brigit—is not one of them. *She* has been singled out, as you have been singled out, by Providence"—so this revelation swept upon me, with the power of a lightning-stroke.

Miracle

MARCH 11, 1852

―――――

FROM *THE CHRONICLE OF A PHYSICIAN'S LIFE*
BY SILAS ALOYSIUS WEIR, M.D.

YET ANOTHER TIME, Providence would guide me: & another time, unexpectedly.

My prayer of years, at last answered—at least, to begin.

"Dr. Weir—I have brought her: Brigit."

Some weeks had passed. I had given up hope. Yet now, on an unusually bright-dazzling March day, following a snowfall of the previous night, there appeared in the doorway of the Infirmary, led forward by Gretel, her face part-hidden by a hooded cloak, the albino-orphan Brigit Kinealy.

"Ah!—I see. Come *in*."

What a thud in my chest! The blow of a hammer.

Very strange to me, & unsettling, to find myself at last in close quarters with the albino-orphan, with whom I had been so intimately close, months ago. This time, Brigit was fully, acutely conscious, & I rose to my feet in a position of authority, not crouching between the straining mother's thighs so ignobly, as before.

Those staring eyes! The faintest blue, uncanny.

"Brigit, hello! How are you?"

Impassive, staring at me. Silent.

Requesting that Gretel prepare the patient for examination, I slipped from the room into my adjacent office, that I might take a quick sip of Scotch whiskey, out of the near-depleted bottle. For it seemed only sensible that the opened bottle, a gift from my benefactor, should not be wasted.

Rarely did such a precaution fail to release in me a vaulting sort of energy, & optimism.

For otherwise, my hope sometimes *ebbed.* My faith in my *destiny.*

"Ah, now! No one will hurt you, you know."

It was my way to speak lightly to (female) patients, to put them at their ease, if possible.

A tone of bantering, playfulness, appropriate with young children, who are particularly frightened of being touched by a stranger.

Never in my practice had I examined a *deaf-mute* patient, still less one lacking all skin pigmentation, with eyes so transparent, miniature capillaries were visible inside the eyeballs; producing in me a sensation of vertigo, if I peered too closely. *It is a trap, she will suck you deep inside. Beware!*

As Dr. Strether would have done, half in play, & half to test the "deafness" of the patient, I snapped my fingers behind Brigit's head; but Brigit did not flinch, either out of genuine deafness or in a stubborn refusal to react to me. For this Irish orphan was most stubborn, I could see.

"Hello? Hel-*lo*?"—though I raised my voice, Brigit did not seem to hear; yet must have felt vibrations in the air, & the heat of my breath, for she squirmed most uncomfortably.

"Let us see what the problem is . . ."

Frowning in concentration, I peered into her ears—as delicately whorled as a flower's petals, of a waxen-white hue; but could see nothing out of the ordinary in that shadowy interior. In medical school, we had studied virtually nothing to do with *ears.*

A very light down at the nape of the girl's neck, beneath the ashy-white hair that fell in limp curling tendrils to her shoulders . . .

Next, I tested the girl's vision by moving my hands about animatedly, in front of her face, to see if the pale gaze followed; when my fingers drew too close to her eyes Brigit flinched, blinking rapidly as a normal person would do.

When I held up three fingers, & asked her how many she saw, Brigit lifted three fingers in return, which seemed to me a witty rejoinder.

"Can you not say, Brigit—'three'?"

Brigit frowned, as a slight flush came into her cheeks. I felt that she was annoyed with me yet could not resist touching her throat, seeking the vocal cord.

"Can you not try to speak, Brigit?"

Stubborn silence. Her gaze was evasive now, she would not meet my eyes. When I touched her throat more forcibly, seeking the small "Adam's apple," which surely had to exist inside her throat, Brigit shrank away with a sharp intake of breath.

Yet, she would not speak. She would not placate me, even by making some sort of guttural sound deep in her throat.

"You know, Brigit, you must *try*"—I did not speak irritably but rather with an air of parental bemusement, as if I saw through her childish stratagem, & did not blame her; yet, might soon become impatient.

Gretel objected: "Doctor, I think you want to examine another part of Brigit—where she is sick & in pain. You will just upset her if you urge her to speak. Foolish people are always scolding her, saying that she can speak 'if she tries . . .'"

I did not like Gretel chiding *me,* with a reference to *foolish people.*

"Thank you, Gretel. But you are uninformed. In fact, it is commonly believed that the 'deaf-mute' may be a hysteric, & may be jolted into speech by the proper treatment"—so I spoke definitively; though, so far as I knew, this was not an entirely common belief in the medical profession, but one which seemed to me likely as the *uterus* is the seat of many pathologies.

However, I did have a suspicion that the albino patient was not totally deaf but might hear a loud voice, or a voice she wished to hear; she was staring most intensely at my lips, as if "reading" my lips.

I had heard that some deaf persons acquired a capacity to "read" the lips of others as they spoke; so it seemed, the albino girl was doing, as if by instinct.

"Has she always been 'deaf'?"—my question was put to Gretel, in such a way that Brigit could see my lips forming the question.

"People say that, as a little girl of three or four, Brigit went 'deaf & dumb' overnight after her mother died," Gretel said, "—for the death was sudden, an accident in the boiling-hot cauldrons of the laundry here at the Asylum, & the mother's face & body were much mutilated. This was such a shock to the child, she lost both the power of speech & the power of hearing. I cannot say: I was not yet contracted at the Asylum. But people say many things that aren't true, especially in the Asylum."

"Is it true, Brigit? You went 'deaf & dumb' with the shock of your mother's death?"—inquiring of Brigit in a gentle voice, shaping my lips with care, as I did not wish to upset her further.

Brigit did not reply. She would not acknowledge that she had heard my question, or even that she had "read" it on my lips.

A spasm of dislike ran through me. Indeed, anger.

But you are just an orphan-girl, who has given birth to a bastard child. And you are disfigured—deformed. Leaking excrement, even as we speak. Whence this pose of hauteur?

Managing a neutral voice I explained to Brigit that her condition might be remedied. If she had not been born deaf & dumb, she *was not naturally* deaf & dumb. But I had no wish to upset her further.

"In any case, whatever happened to you, or was done to you, was not your fault, for you were only a child. Indeed, you are hardly more than a child, even now."

These were placating words, that would have melted the heart of many patients. Still, Brigit refused to lift her pale eyes to mine. For possibly she felt some guilt, at having drawn another, presumably an older man, to carnal sin; & having given birth to a bastard child.

"Jesus forgives us, you know. Especially, Jesus forgave Mary Magdalene—a sinner from whom he had cast seven demons."

It seemed to me that this kindly reminder softened Brigit's stiffness, just slightly. As the Word of God suffused my being, like a rush of cleansing flame, so I felt the wonder of it, that I could uplift the heart of the Irish orphan, surely a sinner, yet an innocent.

I was feeling elated. The Scotch whiskey had warmed my throat, chest, even my hands, that were inclined toward cold-bloodedness.

Taking a cue from me, Gretel instructed Brigit to lie back onto the table—"You will let Dr. Weir examine you, Brigit. For you may die, otherwise."

In her stubborn-mute way, Brigit complied. A single tear ran down the ivory-pale cheek, shimmering like a pearl.

My beauty!—though in opposition to me, as to any man who dared put a hand on her, against her wishes.

Yet, Brigit Kinealy did cooperate. Thus, the first of countless pelvic examinations of mine, of the deaf-mute Irish orphan Brigit Kinealy, destined to play a prominent role in American medical history.

It should be stated that, though I had examined numerous females suffering from *fistula*, as well as performed divers surgical excisions in the region of the female genitals, at the bequest of guardians, like most physicians of my time I had proceeded in a "hit-or-miss" manner; I had not been able to examine the afflicted women thoroughly, lacking proper instruments. In the matter of *fistula*, for which no cure was known to medical science, I was further hampered by my conviction that the effort was futile.

As the usual procedure was *excision,* or *removal* of the diseased (female) organ, no great surgical precision was required; but in the matter of *fistula,* the bladder could not be removed, no more than the kidneys or liver, so another, more precise procedure was required.

With Gretel's assistance & calming manner, Brigit consented to be partly disrobed; lying on her back, on the examination table, her white-skinned thighs parted. At once I was forced to recall the hellish childbirth of months before, in this very room.

A wave of dizziness swept over me. For a ghastly moment I feared that I would fall to the floor in a faint.

"Doctor! Take care"—Gretel dared to steady me, as my knees had become weak.

As the examination was not proceeding well, but haltingly—(for I fumbled with part-shut eyes that flooded with moisture)—Gretel suggested another stratagem: Brigit on the table on hands & knees, that, from the rear, Gretel might "open" the girl's vagina, as best she could, for the doctor to examine.

This seemed to me preferable, as I would not have to face the patient; though in its way more repugnant, & likely as futile.

Yet, I sighed in agreement with the midwife—for I had no choice in the matter.

Little knowing that Providence was guiding me, even now, if circuitously, through the coarse figure of the midwife.

So, too, Medrick Weir had made it clear to me, I must investigate *fistula,* & try to find a cure, to prevent yet more suicides at the Asylum, & more scandal; & of all patients suffering from this affliction, the young albino-orphan seemed, to me, the most tragically afflicted.

Thus, Gretel positioned the girl another time, on her hands & knees on the examination table, & spread the lips of the vagina, which was covered in a fine, pale fuzz like the fuzz of a newborn lamb, at which I stared as if mesmerized. For here was a badly inflamed area, likely the mouth of the birth canal, ravaged by the delivery of several months ago, that must have been very painful. How was it possible, the poor girl had not perished in the interim!

I could see clearly now, how the small, slit-like opening in the vagina had been stretched & torn in childbirth, & was now flaccid & inflamed; but I could not see *inside,* where the *fistula* was hidden.

Unable to open the vagina further with just her fingers, Gretel hurried away, & returned not only with a needle & thread for stitching but with an object so commonplace, I stared in puzzlement.

"Doctor?—will you try *this*?"

"Good God, Gretel! What is it?"

A tablespoon! Of some cheap tarnished metal, a very ordinary tablespoon, presumably from the Asylum kitchen.

A bizarre notion, to use a tablespoon to open up the female body for examination, which I would have rejected indignantly, except, in these circumstances, I had little choice.

With much skepticism, I managed to insert the spoon into the inflamed vagina, as Gretel indicated I should do, & gave it a slight twist, in this way provoking an unforeseen result: an infusion of air rushed into the uterus, that must have been shrunken, & atrophied, causing the walls of the organ to expand instantaneously, with a soft *hiss*—revealing, to my astonished eye, the luridly infected interior.

"My God! What am I seeing . . ."

Gretel, too, stooped & stared, agape at the sight before us.

The *interior of the female* exposed to daylight, its labyrinthine secrets revealed!

Indeed, by stooping further, & craning my neck, & holding my breath, & with Gretel's assistance, I could at last see clearly the tear at the base of the bladder, that could not have measured more than half an inch: the *fistula.*

Until now, a hypothetical; now, a *medical fact.*

Excitedly, Gretel threaded the needle for me, with unusually fine thread, which my fingers could never have managed, & assisted me in the next, most delicate step.

"You must remain still, Brigit"—I attempted to speak firmly.

All this while, Brigit behaved with admirable stoicism, though her body was trembling as if with extreme cold; I could hear her panting, like a beast, but determined not to cry out, as I assayed to mend the tear deep inside her tremulous body: The first time, in medical history in all of the world, I believe, that a *fistula* had been so mended by any surgeon.

There was not even (yet) a medical term for the malady—*vesicovaginal fistula,* it would be called.

As, one day, the crude tablespoon I used to examine the patient's vagina would evolve into the *speculum,* to be adopted by all physicians to women, & indispensable to gynecologists & obstetricians.

(Unfortunately, it did not occur to me to patent the instrument with the U.S. Patent Office, in which case, today, the instrument would be known as the *Weir-speculum;* for in the exigency of the moment, wishing to treat a young woman in acute physical distress, I was thinking not in crass terms of commercial success but of *Providential destiny.*)

That night, late into the night, in a mood of exaltation & hope, I scribbled into my physician's journal these triumphant words:

March 11, 1852.

When air rushed into the collapsed uterus, forcing it into its former, proper position—that was the MIRACLE. In that instant, my eyes were opened. I could see now, as no mortal man had ever seen before, what had been shrouded in darkness & mystery, the *female vagina in all its complexity.*

As Columbus had gazed upon the *New World* in wonderment, as Copernicus & Galileo had gazed upon the *Heavens,* so Silas Aloysius Weir, M.D., gazed into the dark enigma of the female on this date, in the fortieth year of his life.

Miracle

———————

FROM *THE CHRONICLE OF A PHYSICIAN'S LIFE*
BY SILAS ALOYSIUS WEIR, M.D.

D R. WEIR!—*she is still 'mended.'"*
Following the procedure, each morning Gretel greeted me at the doorway of the Infirmary with these thrilling words, which were indeed heartening: for, it seemed, Brigit Kinealy no longer exhibited symptoms of incontinence, & gave every evidence of being *cured of her malady.*

Four days, five, six— "She is still mended."

Though I would have liked to re-examine Brigit, in the privacy of the examination room, deploying my newfound instrument, Gretel insisted upon reporting to me; for Brigit did not like to venture into this part of the Asylum.

"But why is that, Gretel?"—I could not imagine.

"I have no idea, Doctor. Brigit does not 'explain'—as you know. She has not the words."

"But why would she not want to see *me*? After I have cured her of that loathsome condition . . ."

"She may be reluctant to see someone else, Doctor. Someone on the medical staff, who did not treat her as kindly as you did."

These insinuating words of Gretel's, I did not dignify by acknowledging; for it is always a mistake to encourage subordinates to speak too openly to us.

Still, my suspicions were aroused: Could it be that the father of Brigit Kinealy's bastard baby was someone whom I saw routinely, on the staff of the Asylum?

It was my impassioned prayer, that the stitching in Brigit's bladder would prevail; for I had scarcely dared to expect such a success, following from the suggestion of a midwife, & not a fellow physician.

"Doctor Weir!—for you."

A most charming, childlike drawing of what appeared to be waves folding upon one another, or crevices, or folds in earth or rock, on stiff white paper, executed with a soft pencil; this was a gift to me, it was revealed, from Brigit Kinealy, who had not the capacity to thank me in person.

"But what is this, Gretel? Can you see?"

"A rose, held close to the eye. Those are rose petals, folded in upon themselves."

"Ah, a rose! Yes."

I believed I could see it: a multifoliate rose, with deep shadows & creases.

The particular pleasure of the childish gift was somewhat mitigated, as I learned that Brigit had given Gretel a similar drawing, as if her gratitude to me, her physician, was not greater than her gratitude to the midwife.

"Still, I will want to see Brigit soon, Gretel. I will want to check those stitches."

After eight days, I was feeling very hopeful, indeed; & had begun a draft of an article to be titled "A Successful 'Repair' of Vesicovaginal Fistula in a Young Mother," which I intended to send to the leading research journals in the field of surgery. Nor could I resist seeking out the Director of the Asylum, to boast of my (evident) success, for of all persons my great-uncle Medrick Weir would wish to be informed of this good news, which would reflect well upon him & the Asylum.

"After more than a week, the patient is still 'mended.' The stitching has held, the bladder is as good as new. May I show you the article, when it is finished, Uncle? I will not send it out without your approval, of course."

"Hmm! Very good, Silas."

Naturally, I was hoping that Medrick would invite me to join his elite *inner circle,* which had embarked upon experimentation of a quasi-secret nature, conducted in an upper floor of North Hall, to which I had yet to be invited; but he made no further comment, & seemed only just distractedly listening to me. Even as I described the most original employment of the tablespoon, & all that it revealed of the interior female genitals, the elder Dr. Weir was scribbling something in a little notebook; my description of the *mending of the fistula* with a needle & thread, for the first time (I was sure) in medical history, was rudely interrupted by Medrick's assistant Pell entering his office, with scarcely a knock at the door, bearing an "urgent" message that required an immediate response.

This was frustrating, & disappointing: for I had imagined that there was a particular *rapport* between my uncle & me that excluded Pell. I had every reason to believe that Medrick Weir favored me, among the younger doctors he had hired for his staff; the scene in his office reminded me of the distractions of my own household, of so many children, whom Theresa failed to discipline adequately, which often drove me out of my cramped residence on the Asylum grounds, to work in my office at the Asylum, well into the night.

Unfortunately, it seemed that my uncle's adversaries in the New Jersey state legislature were agitating for some sort of public tribunal, to question his methods at the Asylum; there being a number of complaints to authorities, by families of patients who had died by their own hand, or in ways considered suspicious.

To this, I tried not to listen; for I knew that my uncle would share his news with me, if he wished.

Indeed, I was admiring my uncle's office, which was a large, handsomely furnished room in a new wing of the Asylum, that overlooked a snowy garden above the Delaware River. At a comforting distance from the most noisome, locked wards of the Asylum, the Director's office was a gentleman's retreat, with elegant oil paintings on the walls, of American landscapes; bookcases of leather-bound classics, including Aristotle, Thucydides, Galen, & Gibbon. On a polished oak table was a brass telescope, aimed in the direction of the river; on a swivel, the telescope could easily be turned toward other wings of the Asylum, or toward a block of residences across a little park, where the more favored of the medical staff lived with their families.

I supposed that I should excuse myself, & leave my uncle to confer with his assistant; but there had been, several times since my arrival at Trenton, a suggestion of dinner with him, in his residence, some weekday evening; & it seemed quite plausible that we might dine this very evening, to celebrate my good news. But for the intrusive Pell, this might have come to pass. (I had taken a strong dislike to Pell, as much for his sneering, superior manner toward me as for his bullying behavior toward subordinates; it was said that Pell took advantage of females at the Asylum, both medical workers & patients.)

That evening, Medrick Weir was particularly preoccupied with politics, not only locally but elsewhere, as agitation between the Northern & the Southern, slave-holding states was increasing daily. As I wished to concentrate on my medical work, & the advancement of my career, I tried to avoid such discussions; I had learned never to discuss anything remotely political with my in-laws from South Jersey, who were anti-Abolitionist & sympathetic with the South. (As I had learned to avoid politics with my own family, who were staunchly Abolitionist, yet differed radically from one another, in how Abolitionism should be imposed upon the South, & at what cost slaves should be freed.)

"Of course, slavery is heinous, & must be abolished, by law, as England has done. It is like a gangrenous limb that must be amputated. Yet *insurrection* is also a terrible thing, & against nature—the rising up of the colored against the white, a subservient race against a superior race."

So vehemently Medrick Weir spoke, I had nothing to do but listen, respectfully. I gathered that while the immediate subject was a recent slave uprising in South Carolina, which involved the throat-slashing of half a dozen white persons, including the Master of the plantation himself, & all of his family, the more personal reference was to the New Jersey legislature, where Medrick Weir had "unscrupulous"—"venomous"—enemies bent upon destroying him, out of sheer jealousy of his position as Director of the well-funded Asylum at Trenton.

In 1852, issues of rebellion, revolt, & the need to *put down* such insurrections were much in the air. The terror of the South was the terror of the plantation: Black slaves turning against white Masters; great houses put to the torch. Lurid tales were told in the newspapers of slave-owners whose throats were cut by the very Blacks they had most favored, indeed by their own (unacknowledged) offspring, sired in shame, in the night. Christian white women cruelly raped by escaped slaves, left to die on the ground or, worse yet, to live out the remainder of their lives in disgrace.

I did not like to think of *race-mixing,* which seemed to me against nature; & not very probable, as the races naturally preferred one another, & shrank from such *mixing.* As I was an Abolitionist on principle, I did not need to be preached at, to be told that slavery is morally wrong; yet, I did not see any reason to believe that all races are *equal,* no more than both sexes are *equal.*

At last, once Pell was gone, my distracted uncle took notice of me, as I had been peering through the brass telescope, at icy rivulets in the Delaware River; & making myself as unobtrusive as possible, not to annoy or offend. Medrick asked me to repeat what I had told him, which I did; this time, he evinced more enthusiasm, & said that indeed, he would like very much to read my article on the treatment of *fistula,* when it was written.

He then inquired the name of the patient upon whom I had operated so successfully, & I told him that I had not operated on one of the Asylum patients, but upon one of the staff, a young Irish girl contracted to the Asylum who had given birth the previous September, & whose baby had been taken from her; in fact, the young woman for whom I had been originally summoned from Ho-Ho-Kus.

"Ah!—I see."

As Medrick did not speak further, & did not evince much enthusiasm, I feared that I had blundered: treating a *fistula* in an indentured servant, & not in one of the certified lunatics in our care, whose lives & deaths were a matter of public record.

Apologetically, I explained that the girl whose *fistula* I had mended was a most unusual specimen—*albino, deaf-mute, orphan, Irish descent*—whose mother, I had been told, an indentured servant from Ireland, had died in the Asylum, in a laundry-room accident.

In the exigency of the moment, I seemed to understand I should not utter the name *Brigit Kinealy* aloud, & so I did not.

Abruptly then, with a sigh, Medrick heaved himself to his feet behind the massive desk, like a man who has made a resolution. In a grave voice explaining to me that he was very sorry he could not invite me to dine with him that night as his wife, Agatha, was away in Providence, visiting relatives; & he did not "entertain" as a bachelor, unfortunately.

"But, if you would like to have a drink with me, Silas, to celebrate your good news, before you go home to your wife & children across the park—that would be a pleasure."

As already Medrick was pouring Scotch whiskey into two glasses, with a grimace of a smile cast in my direction, it would have been rude of me to have murmured anything other than most eagerly, *Yes! Thank you, sir.*

Misfortune

FROM *THE CHRONICLE OF A PHYSICIAN'S LIFE*
BY SILAS ALOYSIUS WEIR, M.D.

DOCTOR, I'm afraid I have bad news this morning."
At the entrance of the Infirmary the midwife awaited me. Even before the woman could speak, in her grating Düsseldorf accent, I saw the disappointment in her doughy face, & something like shared shame. Never had I felt such a blow to my pride.

"After twelve days, Dr. Weir! We have all been so hopeful. Poor Brigit has been so hopeful . . . This is a terrible disappointment to her."

To her! To *me*.

I must have stood staring vacantly, stunned by this news, as I had been basking in the glowing warmth of memory, of my meeting with Medrick Weir the previous night; & had been anticipating, with the fantastical imaginings of a child at Christmas, what my prospects might be at the Asylum—a promotion, to a higher rank; a much-needed raise in salary; the freedom of *experimentation* . . .

As Gretel hurriedly explained: After a succession of days of blessed continence in the patient, during which time Brigit gave every sign of being *restored to normality*, & had become almost lighthearted in the interim, early that very morning the old affliction returned suddenly, at first thinly, then as before—"What I think happened, Dr. Weir, is that the thread was not strong enough, but snapped."

Brigit had been so upset, Brigit had come to *her*—in tears of misery, & renewed shame.

So it was, Brigit Kinealy would become a loathsome pariah again, like her sister-sufferers. After all my effort! After all that abject *stooping*, & *peering* into a most wretched part of the female body.

After my boastfulness, to the Director of the Asylum.

All but impossible, following this dismal revelation, for me to concentrate on my work in the Infirmary. Nothing is more devastating to the soul than a succession of female lunatics to operate upon, about whom no one cares (to be utterly frank) if they live or die. When I had come so close to a medical discovery!

So extreme was my disappointment, I told Gretel that I did not want to see Brigit Kinealy, to re-examine her after all.

Yes, she is hopeless. Like the others. Death would be a mercy.

Yet, so fickle is the human heart, a day or two afterward, in my morose state I chanced to see the unearthly white-skinned, ethereal creature on the walkway behind the building, as before; as it was a balmy March day, Brigit was bare-headed, & her hair very pale, like spun silver.

In that instant, her wan beauty pierced my heart. I stopped dead where I stood, for my legs had gone weak.

Sighting me at that very instant, Brigit shrank away in shame, the pale ghost-eyes widening in her face. Quickly turning, & fleeing from me as I called after her: "Brigit! Wait . . ."

But it was not for me to pursue her, in so quasi-public a place, where anyone might have seen us; including, if he were seated at the brass telescope in his study, the Director of the Asylum.

This reversal of fortune, Gretel reported, left her concerned that Brigit might take her own life, as Brigit's young friend had done; for, in the brief interim of wellness, Brigit had begun to imagine a new life for herself, somewhere other than in the Asylum, which held such unhappy memories for her.

Seeing my expression of despondency, & wary of my petulance at being so thwarted, Gretel encouraged me not to *despair*.

Pointing out to me, with the shrewdness of her kind, that, considered objectively, the procedure had produced surprising results, for twelve days; during that time, Brigit had been more or less "normal"— what had failed was most likely the thread, not the skill of the surgeon.

"A stronger thread than cotton might hold fast, Doctor. Silk."

Irritably I said, "Oh! *Silk*. I think not. I don't have time for *silk*."

"Shall I acquire some for you, Doctor? A spool of silk thread—"

"No. No thank you. Gretel, you may leave me."

Veins in my temples throbbed, with impatience! I had to doubt that any self-respecting physician tolerated such impertinence from the nursing staff at the Asylum, as I did, in my effort to maintain cordial relations with them.

Yet, a scant week later, during which time Gretel & I resolutely did not discuss the sensitive subject of Brigit Kinealy, I surprised Gretel by producing, in the Infirmary, an actual spool of *silk thread*—purloined from my wife's sewing kit.

"Why, Doctor! You have the silk thread! Oh, this is very— unexpected! Shall I bring Brigit to you? When?"—like sunshine raying across a dun-colored landscape, the plain honest face of the midwife was alight, in enthusiasm & admiration for me.

So it was, the afflicted patient was summoned another time; & another time, reluctantly allowed herself to be partly disrobed, & examined; with the aid of the tablespoon, deftly applied, I was able to examine her interior organs, which were again shockingly inflamed, as the cotton thread had indeed snapped in the interim, as Gretel had surmised. Even as my countenance must have reflected my dismay Gretel reminded me, to recall that I had succeeded already, in repairing the *fistula*: "What you have accomplished once, Doctor, you will accomplish again—with better results."

This proved true: Wielding the needle that Gretel had threaded for me with silk thread, I managed again to repair the delicate tear in the bladder—*silk*, I had discovered, is indeed the strongest thread, beyond even catgut.

Following the arduous procedure, Brigit was visibly strained, & exhausted; her pale, thin skin seemed more transparent & fragile than ever. The pain she had endured at my hands had been, alas, considerable, even with an ingestion of Saint-John's-wort & laudanum; for I feared giving the girl too great a quantity of narcotics, that she might expire beneath my hands.

Yet, the pain the albino girl endured for my sake, as well as for hers, made me feel, for her, a certain *tenderness,* as well as a tremor of *excitation*—decidedly not a sensation I felt for other females upon whom I had operated at the Asylum.

My Ophelia!—out of nowhere the curious appellation came to me, quite unparalleled in my life; for I had never had such a whimsical thought when first encountering the pious young woman who would be my wife; nor, long ago, in what seemed to me now another, remote lifetime, my youthful infatuation with Tabitha Tyndale.

Post-surgery, I felt the need to retire to my cubbyhole of an office, to swallow a mouthful or two of what whiskey remained in the bottle.

Merciful God, I beg of you—do not allow me to fail her, again.

So it happened that, a day or two later, as if in response to my desperate prayer, Gretel came to me to report that Brigit had made a *miraculous recovery,* & was up on her feet, & walking about with but mild pain. Being able to relieve herself as normal persons do, at intervals consciously determined, & not as infants do, helplessly, she returned to her latrine & kitchen work, as productively as ever.

"Good news, Doctor!"—so Gretel informed me; yet, I was cautious about rejoicing, for Providence had chastised me, for my vanity & boastfulness, previously. As a surgeon must keep in mind—*Pride goeth before a fall.*

All too often, those Asylum patients whom I was obliged to treat in the Infirmary, like my patients at the Hermitage, did not recover from their maladies, though neither did they, usually, expire: their lunatic-lives persevering with the dull blind stubbornness of life itself, that plods onward, though the roadway is broken & leads nowhere; beyond the loss of intelligence, of speech & hearing & the mere ability to register the presence of another. Yet, we were forbidden to describe these patients as *hopeless.* The conviction of the reform-minded at the Asylum in Trenton was always *hopeful.* For the old way of treating mental patients was superseded with the new way, of experimental treatments, of the kind I could not pursue, just yet; for such projects were restricted to Medrick Weir & his "inner circle"—to which I was not (yet) privy.

Admittedly, if I could not experiment with them, there was very little interest in the female lunatics, for me. For lunacy is most monotonous, & dull; at least, in most female lunatics whom I encountered. (Of course, there were exceptions, in younger, attractive women, in whom lunacy had not yet set its talons, to render them shrill & repellent; but these prize specimens, it was rumored, the "inner circle" treated, exclusively; & some of us had no occasion to glimpse.)

So it was, in the Infirmary, as at the Hermitage previously, I was greatly restricted in my freedom to experiment; & began to chafe at restrictions beyond grinding mediocrity & conformity.

Thus my delight when Brigit Kinealy sought me out one day, to thank me as a deaf-mute might, with a smiling countenance, & an expression of gratitude; even as I insisted that it not been *I*, but God acting through my agency, that had "cured" her.

Fortunately, Gretel was present to act as an interpreter for the deaf-mute girl, as Brigit gesticulated, with a beaming face, of youthful beauty & radiance, that she had another gift for me, in gratitude for *saving her life*: a delicate little carving she had made, in some soft malleable wood, of a *mourning dove*.

Such emotion in the albino girl, which I had not seen before, was startling to me, & touching; & of course, I was admiring of the little carving, of a size to weigh lightly in the palm of the hand.

"Can you tell her, Gretel—'Thank you! & God bless *you*.'"

•

"But what is this, Silas," my dear wife, Theresa, inquired, with some surprise, having discovered the little wooden mourning dove in a bureau drawer in which were stored divers intimate items of my own, "—some kind of child's toy?"

"Yes! I believe it is," quickly I replied as Theresa examined the carving with a perplexed expression, "—a gift from a child-patient of mine, years ago in Ho-Ho-Kus."

"But why is it hidden away in this drawer, Silas?"

"Because the child died afterward, & I did not like to be reminded."

Taking the little carving from my wife now, & placing it back in the drawer, & shutting the drawer firmly; with the intention of removing the little dove on the morrow, & securing it a safer place.

Reversal of Fortune

FROM *THE CHRONICLE OF A PHYSICIAN'S LIFE*
BY SILAS ALOYSIUS WEIR, M.D.

D OCTOR, I—I am afraid that I have bad news this morning..."
    Ah, not again! God would not be so cruel to me: Would he?
    There stood the stout figure of the midwife before me, as in an all-too-familiar nightmare: not at the entrance of the Infirmary but on the walkway in front of my private residence, in a chill, lightly falling rain; with an expression on her face of utter vacuity, as in the contemplation of a shock too profound to be comprehended.

It was something of a shock to me that Gretel knew where I lived, with my family; & that she dared to confront me here, where my wife or children might observe her from a window.

Has it happened again?—failure? Dear God, I am accursed...

But the news that Gretel had to impart was of a magnitude unimaginable: not a new development in the medical history of a patient but a catastrophe befalling my esteemed benefactor & kinsman *Medrick Weir*—the very individual who had taken the place, in my heart, of my father, Percival.

I vow, sir—I am yours to command.

These words echoed in my mind, in the tumult of days following the shocking announcement, that Medrick Weir had passed away, at the age of sixty-three, of natural causes but under mysterious circumstances never to be satisfactorily explained.

Certainly it had been a *premature death,* as my kinsman was acknowledged, by detractors as well as supporters, to be unusually fit for a gentleman of his age, robust, hale & hearty & "ripe for combat"— "the very paragon of *controversy"*—one who "never backed down from a fight."

Indeed, Medrick Weir had become, over the years, something of a favorite Trenton personality, caricatured in the *Trenton Times-Herald* for his "radical notions" of reform in the treatment of mental illness & his spirited, ongoing feud with the state legislature, which had recently acquired a new bloc of votes condemning him, following an increase in suicides at the Asylum in the past year.

Hearing this, I wanted to protest: There had actually been a *diminution* of suicides among Asylum patients in the early months of 1852; at least, of reported suicides.

Yet, to make matters even worse: On the day following Medrick's death, his longtime assistant Pell was reported to have disappeared— "vanished"—(it would later be revealed that Pell had embezzled funds from the Asylum budget, allegedly as much as $20,000); soon then, several members of the Director's inner circle resigned their positions, leaving the Infirmary even more understaffed than usual, with much extra work falling upon my shoulders.

My wife was distraught, & my children apprehensive, that the Asylum might be shut down, & my job would vanish; we would lose our living quarters, & be forced to return to Ho-Ho-Kus, where I would be in the hire of the Rosencrantz clan, if I were fortunate.

Even as the Asylum board of overseers met in emergency sessions to appoint an interim Director, rumors spread through Trenton like wildfire: Medrick Weir had died not of *natural* but of *unnatural* causes, it was claimed; he had been stabbed to death, or had his throat slashed; he had been eviscerated; he had been castrated; he had died of a broken skull, as a consequence of being struck on the head with a brass telescope, a prized possession of the Director, a gift from a wealthy benefactor. There was said to be evidence of a scuffle in his office; there appeared to be documents missing from files, which had been opened & ransacked.

In the most lurid of accounts, a member of the custodial staff had discovered Medrick's lifeless corpse on the floor of his office very early in the morning, naked & partly burnt; or, naked, & his genitalia defiled in a most obscene way; or, reduced to an untidy heap of ashes, bone fragments, teeth in the fireplace, all that remained of the great man.

Hastily, a private funeral was arranged; shockingly few of Medrick's colleagues attended, but the word was, there had been no viewing beforehand & the casket had been *closed.*

Yes, I did feel terribly excluded; for I was sure that my uncle would have wished me to attend his funeral, & to mourn his loss.

Official obituaries noted that Medrick Weir had died of natural causes, presumably heart attack, or a stroke, for there had been no autopsy, at the request of the widow. Yet, it was widely speculated that the true cause of death had been *murder,* by one of the female lunatics whom the Director had personally treated, in his private quarters; or, by one of the male staffers, a rival for the affections of a woman, very likely a patient; or, by the mysteriously vanished assistant Pell. (It was certainly my conviction that Pell had murdered my uncle.)

Most scandalously, it was claimed that Medrick had been murdered by the deranged mother of one of his illegitimate offspring, grieving that her infant had been taken from her at birth, to be placed, for profit, with well-to-do parents.

At last, as these outlandish rumors faded in interest, it began to be speculated that Medrick Weir had ingeniously staged his own death, to make it appear to have been caused by another; thus protecting his reputation posthumously, & assuring that his (estranged) wife & (legitimate) children would collect insurance, as well as the consider-able sum of money, in cash, discovered in his private safe.

"It would be like the wily old fox, to flummox his enemies from beyond the grave," one of the staff physicians remarked, with an admiring chuckle. "In Hell, Medrick is gloating at us."

"In Hell, Medrick is lifting a glass of his favorite whiskey in a toast, to us; & invites us to laugh, with him"—so another colleague added.

How crude, how disrespectful, to say such things about a man who has passed away, & to laugh!

I did not like to hear such remarks. As often when I heard crude remarks among the staff doctors, of a kind not to be repeated in mixed company, I turned on my heel to walk away, my face burning.

As Medrick Weir's nephew, I allowed that I had been favored by him, to a degree; but not unfairly, as I had worked twice as hard as my colleagues, for a lesser salary, without complaint. Naturally, this had stirred resentment, in petty minds; now that Medrick had passed away, I felt as his kinsman that I must protect his good name.

In the meantime, I had been appointed head of the Infirmary, which responsibility I had already taken on as a matter of course, uncomplainingly; there being no one else available to deal with the chaos of a slovenly run wing of the Asylum, of some eighty beds, at full capacity.

These heroic words echoing in my brain: *I vow, sir—I am yours to command.*

In early April, as I made my way to the Infirmary, by chance I caught sight of Brigit Kinealy, walking with two other young girls, in work clothes; though the deaf-mute could not speak with the others, it seemed that she was in congenial relations with them, & that they accepted her, as one of them.

How fascinating it was, to see how Brigit communicated with other girls of her rank & age, using her hands to gesticulate, & staring most intently at their lips as they spoke.

My heart clenched in my chest with the wish to call to her. Yet, I remained at a distance, for fear that my presence might embarrass her.

How *normal* Brigit Kinealy appeared, despite her albino skin & unnaturally pale hair! I felt a thrill of pride, that at least I had accomplished *that;* before the supervision of the Infirmary had become my life, & all thought of surgical experimentation, with the repair of *vesicovaginal fistula,* or other corrections of nature, had to be set aside.

Yet it was a bitter sort of satisfaction, that Medrick Weir would not know of the extent of my first surgical success, with the silk thread; my article, titled "A Successful 'Repair' of Vesicovaginal Fistula in a Young Mother," would not appear in the *New Jersey Journal of Medical Research* until several months after his death. What fantasies I had harbored, that Medrick would read this with such admiration, he would write to his cousin, Percival Weir, in Concord, to congratulate Percival on such a son!

Yet, soon after this encounter, as if indeed Providence were preparing me for another astonishing reversal of fortune, the public announcement was made: that the board of overseers at the Asylum had voted unanimously to commission a twenty-foot copper statue of *Medrick Weir, Founding Director of the New Jersey State Asylum for Female Lunatics,* to be placed on the Asylum grounds near the front entrance; & that the new interim Director of the Asylum was to be— *Silas Weir, M.D.*

III

The Pioneer Reformer

Sacred Monomania

FROM *THE CHRONICLE OF A PHYSICIAN'S LIFE*
BY SILAS ALOYSIUS WEIR, M.D.

FOLLOWING my appointment as *interim,* & within twelve months *permanent,* Director of the Asylum at Trenton, in September 1853, I do confess that a kind of sacred monomania overcame me, to pursue my life's-work, in surgical experimentation upon the afflicted, who comprised virtually a hundred percent of the female patients entrusted to my care.

These, the "flotsam & jetsam" of any public hospital, or any publicly funded institution—anonymous persons, for the most part. At Trenton, numbering into the hundreds, a shifting population of as many as a thousand patients at the height of any "season of madness"—midsummer, or the Christmas holiday season.

In this, I made every effort not to slight my administrative duties, which were considerable, as it appeared my predecessor, Medrick Weir, seemed to have done in his concentration upon *his* particular experiments.

(As this is neither the place nor the time to further expose the former Director of the Asylum to yet more calumny, considering that the elder Dr. Weir is powerless to explain or defend his research methods, you will not find in my *Chronicle of a Physician's Life* any lurid listing of my predecessor's experiments, of a kind that thrilled & scandalized readers of the *Trenton Journal* in the early months of 1853; excepting those which, by happenstance, coincided with my own interests, namely the *Chair of Tranquility,* the *Bed of Tranquility,* the *Tranquility Jacket,* & some aspects of *hydrotherapy,* to be discussed in good time.)

As I was not, & am not, anything like so openly a rebel as my predecessor, I was determined to be more amenable than Medrick Weir to the expectations of the Asylum board of overseers, & the New Jersey state legislature; for I saw that where unfettered freedom to pursue my own research was the goal, it would be most pragmatic to *conform in every outward way,* to assure that the Asylum operated in such a manner that appeased the demands of individuals not themselves men of medicine, still less theorists.

To this end, I met with the board of overseers, & several of the more powerful state legislators, to ask their advice about hiring my administrative staff, & indeed to hire individuals whom they recommended, whether associates of their own who had proven reliable, or trusted relatives of theirs, who could be depended upon. It was quite natural, to my way of thinking, to offer contracts to a select group of local businessmen, who were connected with the board of overseers, or the legislature; for the maintenance of such a large institution as the Asylum, covering some two hundred acres of land, as well as new construction projects, was a large part of the Asylum's yearly budget. Unlike Medrick Weir, who proclaimed himself a *radical reformer,* & seemed too often to be granting interviews with newspapers & magazines, I vowed to keep out of the headlines, & concentrate on establishing a reputation as a serious research scientist, publishing my findings in professional journals exclusively. I understood how crucial it was not to antagonize influential local persons but to *enlist them in my cause.*

Instead of the supercilious, unreliable, & dishonest Pell, I took care to appoint an unfailingly reliable & honest assistant, a young relative of the chairman of the board of overseers with a background in finance & business administration; this person, Amos Heller, I could safely entrust with the routine & mundane operation of the Asylum, thus leaving me free for my experimental surgery. (Most of the routine surgeries in an institution like the Asylum at Trenton, of the type to be found across the United States, in all sizable cities, were *sterilizations* of the unfit & degenerate of both sexes, as mandated by state legislatures. These procedures being of no scientific interest to me, I was happy to delegate their administration to younger medical staffers who could be relied upon to meet the monthly quota.)

Another major appointment, a son-in-law of the New Jersey governor Horace Mackey, would prove most helpful, as an expert in legal matters. For it was no secret, there had been much litigation aimed against the Asylum, over the years, as against any institution providing health care to the masses; & the presence of the governor's son-in-law would be a deterrent to such frivolous litigation.

It seemed most practical for me to establish my private experimental Laboratory in the identical North Hall of the Asylum in which Medrick Weir's experiments had been located, though there was no need for most of Medrick's equipment (tubs in which hysterical females were subjected to near-scalding *hydrotherapy*, divers shackles & restraints, "sand bag blankets," etcetera), which was placed in storage. As all of Medrick's *inner circle* of research assistants had vanished from the Asylum, I took advantage of such vacancies, & did not hire curious & ambitious young M.D.s to take their place, reasoning that a reliance upon female staff, at their head the indispensable Gretel, would assure me far more privacy, & indeed loyalty—it being known that the female of the species is far more *loyal* than the male, because she is not in competition with any male, but takes her place naturally as his *subordinate & helpmeet.*

My dear wife, Theresa, lamented that I was at the Asylum such long hours, not only weekdays but weekends, from dawn until near-midnight, our (nine) children scarcely knew their father, especially the youngest; the older children, while flattered that their father was now locally revered as Director of the Asylum, & that they were now more comfortably housed in an eight-bedroom sandstone house overlooking the Delaware River, & not so crowded together as they had been in smaller quarters, complained of being subjected to taunting at their school in Trenton, that their father was a *lunatic-doctor.*

Such deprecations were hurtful to me, & roused my ire, as a net cast over the wide-muscled wings of an eagle whose destiny is to rise into the sky, cruelly & stupidly dragged down, by the small-minded!

So careless in their accusations were the ignorant, & the envious, it began to be reported to me, by my own children, notably my eldest son, Jonathan, who felt the insult most keenly, that our kinsman Medrick Weir had been "in league with Satan"—had "caused the suicides of hundreds of female lunatics" within a few years.

The children were tutored to reply to such ignorant remarks as calmly as they could: saying that *their* father was Silas Weir, who had nothing to do with his predecessor; & was a *personal friend of Governor Horace Mackey.*

In addition, the older children were tutored to explain that *lunacy* is but an *illness,* & that their father, Silas Weir, was a "pioneer" in the reform of the treatment of *brain illness,* as they would one day learn.

As to Theresa's charge that I was at the Asylum virtually every waking hour, I pointed out that she dared not complain, nor her family speak snidely of me, as they had been doing for fifteen years, since my income had greatly improved with my promotion to the Directorship; & my position of rising prominence in Trenton, as in the medical world generally, bespoke even more good fortune to come. I had set my sights, I informed Theresa, on the highest of goals: to take my place in the Parthenon of American pioneers of science, beside such paragons as Benjamin Rush, Benjamin Franklin, Samuel Thompson, & David Rittenhouse; indeed, her family would one day be proud of me, as my own father would be.

"You forget, my dear wife, that it is far better for a doctor to be too busy than to be idle, the lot of many young doctors; it is far better for a doctor to be overworked than underworked."

"But, Silas—do you not *miss us*?"—almost plaintively Theresa regarded me, as I prepared to leave the house for a very busy day.

To which I so patiently responded, Theresa could scarcely disagree: "What Providence has ordained for me, Providence has also ordained for you, & the children. We must all make sacrifices, my dear!"

Though it is true, as I often quipped, to the amusement of listeners, that I fled our lively domestic scene very early in the morning for the "relative quiet of the madhouse"—a joke that never failed to provoke hearty laughter among gentlemen, who, being family men, wholly understood what I meant.

Esther C____

NOVEMBER 1852

FROM *THE CHRONICLE OF A PHYSICIAN'S LIFE*
BY SILAS ALOYSIUS WEIR, M.D.

FOLLOWING my success treating Brigit Kinealy for *fistula*, there came into my care another, yet more grievous sufferer of *fistula*, soon after the establishment of my private research Laboratory on the third, topmost floor of North Hall.

Amid the mass of flotsam & jetsam in my Asylum, Esther C____ is a distinct, if unfortunate memory: a much ravaged, anemic, & sickly specimen estimated to be in her mid-thirties, who had been committed by her family to the Asylum, with the claim that she was "unclean"—"uncontrollable"—"possessed by demons." Following a failed exorcism, by a parish priest, when the subject was just twelve years old, Esther was said to have lapsed into a state of lethargy & had to be force-fed; eventually, committed to the Asylum in late adolescence, she was assigned to one of the locked wards, & had had no visitors for years.

How it happened that this unhappy woman, in appearance not unattractive, but with a sickly-pale, mottled skin, became impregnated, in what could only have been a most hellish & deplorable liaison, was not known; or at any rate, could not be explained satisfactorily to me, when I made stern inquiries of nurses & attendants responsible for the ward.

Giving birth in a birthing room in the ward, Esther underwent a most arduous labor, of eighteen hours, ending in a stillbirth; that left her lower body ravaged as if clawed by wild beasts. According to Gretel, who had assisted at the delivery, Esther would have bled to death, except that Gretel & another nurse managed to staunch the bleeding; yet, Esther remained in a perilous state, as infection had set in.

Piteous as the stillbirth was, yet it was generally conceded to be *merciful;* as the twins had been very small, & misshapen; the mother could not possibly have wished to keep them, & to nurse them.

As a result of the difficult labor, Esther suffered from a *fistula* more pronounced than Brigit's had been; a greater quantity of bloody urine leaked from her lower body, in a near-continuous stream. As there was little hope for the patient's recovery, I felt a stir of exaltation, reasoning that, as a medical practitioner, I might experiment imaginatively, with a miscellany of treatments; & if the patient expired, no one would dare fault *me.*

(For I often berated myself, for my blundering, in Chestnut Hill, when I had undertaken to repair the skull of the disfigured infant, damaged at birth & doomed to expire beneath my hands; a foolish decision, though the fault had *not been mine.* Yet, cruel rumors had buzzed through the town, & threatened to follow me to New Jersey; I vowed, nothing like this should happen again, to tarnish my reputation.)

Also, it should be noted that Esther herself, in a raving fever state, had abandoned all hope & prayed in a loud wailing voice for God to take her, & ease her suffering. That a kindly physician would examine her with care; that he should cause her to be bathed & soothed, & given medications to ease her mind; that he should cause her to be carried from the noisome ward to a quiet, sequestered place in another part of the Asylum, staffed by more experienced attendants; that she should be treated not as a contemptible "loose" female who had given birth out of wedlock, but as a *serious case,* was astonishing to her, & must have seemed a miracle.

Not counting Brigit Kinealy, who would remain a unique case, Esther C__ was to be my first experimental subject, at the Asylum in Trenton; the first of a *historic* number, as I could not have envisioned at the time. For that is the way of Providence, to totally surprise us, like grace.

Grace being that which we do not deserve, & cannot request, which falls from Heaven upon us, if, as John Calvin teaches, we are blessed by God.

"I will care for you, Esther. With God's help, I will *try*."

Wracked with shame, for the leakage from the (invisible) *fistula* was such, Esther had always to swathe herself in absorbent cloths, like a baby's diapers, she could do no more than murmur to me in a cracked voice—"Thank you, Doctor." Her shadowed eyes were fixed upon me with a desperate sort of hope, as the eyes of a trapped animal are fixed upon its captor, in a plea for mercy.

My pulse quickened in anticipation, for this *experimental subject* was so much more entirely my own than the pitiful Brush baby had been; & truly trusting in me, as no baby could.

Having requested of my assistant Amos Heller that Esther C__'s medical history be brought to me, I was stunned to see but a single wrinkled & torn sheet of paper, listing the patient's name & address in Trenton, the name of the person who had committed her to the Asylum, presumably her father, & very few notations as to *mental illness,* & treatments, with dates; the most recent date being several years ago.

"Why, this is useless! Embarrassing! We must update all our records, beginning with this patient."

"Yes, Dr. Weir."

"*You* will be in charge, Amos. Select a team to assist you, & begin immediately."

"Yes, Dr. Weir."

"There are—how many patients in the Asylum?—is the current number eight or nine hundred? You may need a sizable team."

"'Eight or nine hundred' is an estimate, Dr. Weir. What the exact figures are at this time, I am not sure."

"Well, see to it! 'Slovenly record-keeping' was one of the charges the legislature leveled against my predecessor. We will reform our record-keeping from top to bottom."

"Yes, Dr. Weir."

"Beginning with this specimen, 'Esther C__.'"

"*Yes,* Dr. Weir."

Poor Esther C__ was ailing in so many ways, it was difficult to know how I should proceed. That the patient was suffering from a *mental affliction* seemed less urgent, than her physical afflictions, like the loathsome leakage of excrement from her injured parts. Indeed, the afflicted woman scarcely seemed mentally ill at all, but stoic & resigned, with pleading eyes fixed upon my face that might have belonged to anyone.

At first it seemed to me that I should examine Esther internally, to ascertain if it was in fact a *fistula* that was at fault; but I did not like to use the clumsy tablespoon if I could avoid it, even with Gretel's assistance.

I would far rather have begun with the patient's fever, & attempt to cure that; but as fever is caused by infection, the *fistula* might be to blame. At the same time, the patient's acute weakness should be treated, which might have been the consequence of fever, but also of anemia, or some other imbalance of the blood. Except: Esther's weakness was probably caused by malnutrition, as she could scarcely keep food down, and (perhaps) I should begin with *that*; as we know that a lack of appetite is caused by fever, & a fever by an infection, so I was led back to the original—the dread *fistula*.

Fellow physicians may wonder: Why did I not bleed my patient, following the hallowed tradition of *phlebotomy*?—for indeed Esther was feverish, & it was known that "heated" blood caused fever, as Benjamin Rush had prescribed; & so relieving the pressure of the blood would bring about a "cooling" effect, helping to calm the excitable patient.

Ah, but—Silas Weir was to be a *renegade* in the Pantheon of Science! Going my own way, hacking my own path through the underbrush.

It would be said of Silas Weir that I weighed each patient's case individually, including even females as well as (rare in my practice, but not unknown) males, & treating the two sexes as (near)-equals; often, I came to unexpected conclusions.

As Esther was weak, white-skinned, & quite feeble, I felt instinctively that bleeding the poor creature would have a deleterious effect upon her; as, all too often, we had witnessed in Dr. Strether's office when treatment meant to restore health resulted in the patient's death.

At which time it would be muttered by Dr. Strether with flickering sorrow—*It was his time to die. God knows, we did all we could.*

At the time of the yellow fever in Philadelphia, in 1793, the revered Benjamin Rush prescribed bloodletting as many as seven times a day, as well as purging (of the bowels), of afflicted patients; this, a tradition of "heroic medicine," which I fully intended to pursue, seemed more feasible in male patients, with their heartier & "redder" blood, than in female patients with their "paler" blood.

Thus, I did not *bleed* Esther C__. Instead, experimentation with Esther was of divers sorts, very carefully chosen. Seeing the need to revitalize the patient's appetite, I administered a succession of medications (compounded by my own hand, as I took pride in my apothecary skills): Saint-John's-wort, belladonna, echinacea, quinine drops, cocaine drops, arsenic, black cohosh, & one or two others, to gauge their effects upon the patient, each in turn & simultaneously.

Such experimentation demands precision, since a patient is likely to vomit up certain medications, so that the attending physician cannot know whether the vomiting is caused exclusively by the medication or by the underlying illness or condition.

Also, it is ideal to have at least two experimental subjects: one who is given the medication, & one who is not. Both subjects would have to be in reasonably good health, a rarity among Asylum inmates. In such circumstances as the Asylum, with subjects so infirm, & uncooperative, results could not be absolute. (Though, when I wrote up my results to submit to the *New Jersey Journal of Physicians & Surgeons,* I did not emphasize this qualification, with the reasoning that the editors would be less likely to accept the article for publication if I did; & the general suspicion that other researchers, less scrupulous than I, would certainly not be forthright about their data.)

With the assistance of nurses' aides who held cold-wetted cloths against Esther's fevered forehead, & spent hours fanning the patient, at last I succeeded (I thought) in breaking the fever; which allowed the malnourished patient to swallow liquids, with only mild vomiting. This also reduced the patient's heart arrhythmia, which had (possibly) been accelerated by the Saint-John's-wort, unless it was a small dose of black cohosh, or the cocaine drops that had caused the arrhythmia, or, indeed, had diminished it. (Sometimes belladonna had a sedative effect, & sometimes the reverse! I have had contrary reactions in patients to these medicines, sometimes in the very same patient, for much depends upon the dosage, of course; & much depends upon the patient's condition, which may fluctuate within a single day.)

"Esther, are you feeling better? Stronger?"—so I inquired of the afflicted woman, in the kindliest tone; & Esther assured me, *yes,* with a weak nod of her head.

Considering the patient stabilized to a degree, the following day I decided to undertake, with Gretel's assistance, a treatment of those infected areas of Esther's body which were visible, reasoning that any of these infections could become lethal, sending their reddened poison-arrows to the heart; for, following the example of Medrick Weir, it seemed to me most convincing that most, or all, diseases are caused by infections.

In the case of Esther C___, however, I may have confused infections with boils, cysts, & goiters, which I undertook to drain of pus by lancing with a scalpel, hoping to "pop" the infection, & so drain it of impurities, as (I thought) I recalled from my apprenticeship with Strether; an effort that caused the patient to writhe in agony as these were on parts of her body (breasts, belly, pubic lips) that were particularly sensitive; & my scalpel was not, unfortunately, as razor-sharp as it might have been, if Gretel had remembered to sharpen it. Still, blood ran aplenty, mixed with a feculent-smelling pus.

Draining off pus was *good;* yet, an excess of blood, *not-good.*

When the patient showed no sign of recovering, nor even of maintaining consciousness for very many minutes, after several days I saw no other option than to undertake the distasteful pelvic exam, even as the patient lay panting & sweating like an exhausted beast, steeling herself against a further violation of her being, yet determined to impress the Director of the Asylum with her stoicism.

Always it was touching, among the flotsam & jetsam of the Asylum populace, how many of the female lunatics were eager to please their physicians, even while enduring pain; in this, in mimicry of females generally, who are raised to please men, & in that way improve their lot in life.

Yet, despite Gretel's hands firmly steadying the patient's hips, the mere insertion of the spoon-speculum into the mouth of the vagina provoked fresh pain, causing Esther to flinch away as if scalded, with a guttural cry.

"Woman! Do you *not want* to be healed? Do you *want to end your days mired in filth*?"—in disgust I cried, violating the professional reticence which I much preferred; but I felt provoked beyond endurance.

With Gretel's aid, Esther C__ rose again onto her hands & knees, panting hard, & resolving to hold herself still, that I might examine her properly.

"Esther!—*steady.*"

My heart would have been moved to Christian mercy except I understood that *my actions were mercy,* & the patient herself was the impediment, for resistance continued, despite my gentlest admonitions.

Wracking my brains how to proceed, for I did not want to *admit defeat* despite the length of the day's ordeal, for both the patient & the physician.

"Shall we wait, Doctor?—& examine Esther tomorrow morning? She will be stronger, then; & we will be more patient"—so Gretel suggested, practicably; which was a very sensible idea, yet annoying to me, as it was impertinent.

"Procrastination is the Devil's temptation, Gretel," I said, "—we solve nothing by failing in the present moment."

Surely, these were words of John Calvin, learnt by me as a boy.

"We will persevere, Gretel. But—we will put the fretful patient *to sleep.*"

In a flash of inspiration this came to me, for it was the very stratagem I had used with the Rosencrantz daughter, Bettina.

This solution was perhaps misguided—(as the alert reader may realize)—for I had already given Esther a considerable quantity of medications, which had not worn off entirely, so far as I knew; at mid-century the usage of sedation was not so commonplace as it is now, particularly the consequences of an admixture of belladonna, Saint-John's-wort, tincture of arsenic, etcetera, in combination with a sizable dosage of morphine. All too often, the patient so anesthetized would not wake up again—this being one of the arguments for not attempting anesthesia, a branch of medical science then in its infancy.

Still, I reasoned that I would use but a prudent amount of morphine, to allow the subject to relax into a deep sleep.

And so, morphine was ingested by the patient, in liquid form; & after Esther ceased struggling, & lay back unresisting on the table,

Gretel knelt between her legs & managed to gain entry to the ulcerated organ: a hellish sight, festering with infection, the sight & smell of which left me faint, & nauseated. Yet in this way, by stooping & leaning in, I succeeded in determining where the tear in the patient's bladder was; noting that it was at least twice the size of the tear in Brigit's bladder, & would require quite a feat of mending, with silk thread.

"Gretel?—please hand me the needle."

"The—needle, Doctor? I—I do not have a needle—"

"You *do not have the needle*? After all this effort?"

"I—I had not known . . ."

In disgust, I rose to my full height, & tossed down the befouled tablespoon.

In exhaustion then, staggering away from the reeking table, & with a dismissive gesture to Gretel, who stared after me most piteously, gave up my exertions for the day.

"Good night, Gretel! We will continue in the morning, when *you will remember to bring the threaded needle.*"

Retiring then to the spacious Director's office, in a farther building on the Asylum grounds, to throw myself into the late Director's leather chair, & pour a small portion of Scotch whiskey for myself, from a cabinet generously stocked with the late Director's whiskeys, bourbons, & wines, of which I had little need, as I do not ordinarily drink spirits.

Finally, when my nerves were somewhat steadied, returning to the Director's residence a short walk away, where I politely declined my wife's entreaties to eat some of the roast beef dinner kept warm for me, as I had no appetite; too demoralized even to wash myself properly, & insisting upon sleeping in a solitary bed in a quiet wing of the house.

So it was that, rising early before dawn, when I returned to the examination room where Esther C__ remained, it was to discover that the patient was lying very still on the table, beneath a sheet that Gretel had covered over her: shadowed eyes starkly open, pale-mottled skin grown ashy, the ghastly stiff smile on her face a cruel rebuke to *hope.*

"Esther! What has happened to you!"

Most frustratingly, the patient did not move, & did not appear to be breathing.

"Esther! I command you to *wake up*."

Appalled, I touched the woman's neck, seeking a pulsing artery: there was none.

Heartbeat: none.

Her skin not clammy-cold but dry, as mineral is cold; & a most melancholy odor wafting from the skin, like that of a sepulchre.

Christian Burial

1852

ABRAHAM LANGHORNE, OFFICIAL GRAVEDIGGER,
NEW JERSEY STATE ASYLUM FOR FEMALE LUNATICS AT TRENTON

IT WAS A SURPRISE TO ME, as the official gravedigger of the New Jersey Asylum for Female Lunatics at Trenton, a position inherited from my father, Moses Langhorne, who passed away in 1838, that, with the Directorship of Silas Aloysius Weir, there was a considerable alteration in the protocol regarding *deaths of patients at the Asylum.*

Prior to Silas Weir's administration, deaths of patients at the Asylum were duly reported to the health officials of the city of Trenton, & bodies of the deceased were buried in the Asylum cemetery, a portion of the grounds beyond East Hall, except if, in rare instances, families of the deceased wish to bury them in family plots, at their own expense.

Under the administration of Silas Weir, & seemingly by his direction, there came into being a category of patient re-evaluated as *null*—as a marriage, or a contract, might be *nullified.* In this, a female lunatic, deceased, might cease to *exist* in Asylum records; she would be buried in the Asylum cemetery as before, but no name was attached to the individual. Thus, no record of her death would be sent to the city of Trenton.

This category of patients, rendered *null,* would remain a relatively small quantity compared to the annual *deaths* at the Asylum, which continued to be reported, as before. But with a diminution in the numbers of deaths, including all of those considered *unnatural/suspicious,* or probable *suicide,* the air of hysteria among officials at the state capital quickly subsided. Perhaps surprisingly, no one made inquiries as to the cause of such a change.

In short, the younger Dr. Weir was spared the hostile scrutiny directed at the elder Dr. Weir through much of his turbulent tenure at the Asylum.

This alteration of protocol was carefully explained to me, by Dr. Weir's assistant Amos Heller, that there were "unique circumstances" involving some deaths, which would precipitate "legal complications" if made public; resulting in a "probable shrinkage" of the Asylum budget. That is, if Trenton officials resumed their close scrutiny of the Asylum, & their questioning of the nature of certain deaths, my position as gravedigger would be imperiled, with a likely sharp loss in revenue.

In addition, it was explained to me, Silas Aloysius Weir was initiating a new protocol altogether, of *moral therapy,* applied to the mentally ill; originally an idea of Benjamin Rush, who had not pursued it satisfactorily, being held back by traditionalists of his day. Following the strictures of *moral therapy,* mental patients would no longer be designated as *lunatics* but, simply, as *Asylum patients;* they were *ill,* & there was treatment for *illness,* a primary treatment being *active participation* in the operations of the Asylum, for all those not confined to locked wards.

Under this new agenda, patients would not spend idle hours in their rooms, or in group settings, perusing the Bible, or praying, or muttering to themselves, or quarreling with others, or staring into space; where Medrick Weir had subjected them to various sorts of *hydrotherapy,* involving a good deal of participation from Asylum staff, able-bodied patients would now be involved in *moral therapy:* in the Asylum kitchen helping to prepare & serve meals; in the Asylum laundry washing & ironing; scrubbing & cleaning floors; toiling on the Asylum grounds, shoveling snow in the winter, etcetera. Several acres of Asylum grounds were to be cleared, that a small farm might be established, with patients helping to plant, weed, & harvest, under the direction of Amos Heller. The fruit of these labors, no matter how deficient, or worm-ridden, would be served in the Asylum dining hall, to help defray costs for food, one of the highest expenditures at the

Asylum; so, too, patients of proven stamina & steady nerves would assist with the *deceased*, washing & preparing the bodies for burial, & in some cases, where appropriate, assisting in burials themselves, for modest rewards.

"You will have a staff to assist you, Mr. Langhorne! A team of *female lunatics* to follow your instructions, which will assure that you will have less work to do, with no loss in revenue."

To my shame, I quickly acquiesced to this proposition; for I saw that, if I did not, the shrewd Mr. Heller would cast about for another gravedigger in the area, to cooperate with him.

From that point onward, summonses came to me less frequently, for a good number of deaths were designated *null*, & dealt with summarily, at the Asylum, with clandestine burials in ambiguously marked graves, executed by staff; those deaths that were allotted to me were likely to be of *natural causes* like cardiac arrest, tuberculosis, stroke, & dementia. Almost overnight, *suicides* ceased to exist.

If there was a particularly sensitive *null* case, for my eyes only, a summons would come to me at my home, by messenger.

Mr. Langhorne—
   Please come quickly & do not tell anyone.
   There is an emergency need for a Christian burial here at the Asylum, within twenty-four hours.
   Your payment will be generous, it is assured.

                                                      A.H.

As I recollect, the first of these summonses came early one morning in November 1852, regarding the burial of a badly emaciated Caucasian female corpse whose face, in death, was frozen in a ghastly rictus of a grin; a most pathetic specimen, who appeared to have expired on a badly stained operating table, naked beneath a filthy sheet, in a Laboratory in North Hall.

Null meant an anonymous passing, to be recorded nowhere.

In years to come there would be a number of such requests, all issuing from the hand of Amos Heller, assistant to Silas Aloysius Weir.

A.H. was the name provided on the summons. But soon, *Butcher Weir* was the name whispered through Trenton.

The *Chair of Tranquility*

FROM THE DIARY OF MRS. THOMAS PEELE (1853)
TRENTON, NEW JERSEY

S O TENDERLY *he wrapt me in warm-wetted sheets, the firmness of his grasp was not immediately evident.*

A hood was placed over my head, of some light fabric, like muslin, through which I could see just light & not shapes, a suffusion of light such as one might "see" through closed eyes while facing the sun.

A thicker cloth was bound about my head & covered my mouth in a band. Not tightly—but with a hint that tightness would ensue, if I took advantage of this courtesy, & cried out for childish attention, as I had been chastised.

This, like the warm-wetted sheets binding my arms against my sides, & securing my legs as I was seated in the Chair of Tranquility, *was to pacify my more violent emotions, & my propensity for useless tears; that had led to such impatience, hurt, fury, & despair in my husband, he saw no recourse but to bring me to the Asylum at Trenton, where (it was believed) an illness such as mine might be cured.*

An illness such as mine, in olden days, could not ever be cured. For it was believed to be "demonic"—possession by Satan. But there is a new era now, of moral therapy for female lunacy.

By moral therapy *is meant an assault against illness, not "demons." A campaign waged by the guiding physician, to overcome the illness through the methods of common sense.*

The Chair of Tranquility *is a very solid chair, of a size somewhat larger than the ordinary, & a height well above the height of most men.*

The Chair of Tranquility *is well-cushioned, the soft downy fabric seems to clutch at you, & surround you. Taking your breath away.*

The Chair of Tranquility *is designed for deep rest, "dozing."*

It is true, I did harm to myself. Tearing at my hair & clawing at my face, & rending my garments.

It is true, I did harm to my "beauty." That my "beauty" was not mine to destroy but the possession of my husband was a lesson to be learned.

"Hysteria" is caused by a wandering womb, or broken-off parts of the womb circulating through the arteries, most virulent in the brain. So the revered ancient physicians have instructed us, beginning with Aristotle; even in our enlightened time, no man of science had persevered beyond this wisdom.

We were not impoverished like most of the patients at the Asylum. We were of comfortable parentage on both sides of our families & lived in a most prestigious neighborhood south of Trenton. My husband was himself a physician, of general medicine, & had heard of the "revolutionary" ideas of the new Director of the New Jersey Asylum for Female Lunatics at Trenton, Dr. Silas Weir, in the cure of women's madness.

For we were of a (joint) wish, to have children. Heirs.

This vow I had made in all but actual words, in marrying my husband at the altar of the First Presbyterian Church of Trenton.

Love, honor, & obey. In sickness as in health. Till death, part.

Yet, the crazed laughter bubbled up in me. There was released a frenzied kicking of my legs. If Mr. Peele should approach me in his nightgown on hands & knees like a panting beast. Kicked, kicked, & kicked, biting my lower lip until it bled onto the white linen of the marital bed.

Arrangements were made. Arrangements between men. There are none other except arrangements between men.

My father, too. Badly he wished a grandson. Grandchildren. Heirs.

There is little point to life, without heirs.

There is little point in accumulating wealth, except to leave to heirs.

God ordains. God commands—Increase & multiply!

My father, & Mr. Peele, & Dr. Weir. Arrangements were made, there was no need for my presence.

Private care, at private rates. In the state Asylum at Trenton, there would be a private wing, on the third floor of North Hall, for patients requiring special care under the auspices of Silas Weir.

None of us in private care would be required to brave the swarm of female lunatics in the dining hall, & none of us would be pressed into moral therapy in the laundry, or the kitchen, or the latrines, or with mop & pail scrubbing the floors.

We never saw. We never heard their shrieks. We never smelled their stench. We entered the facility, & exited the facility, by a special entrance reserved for private patients.

Our fates were decided by our husbands & fathers. Our fates were decided by handshakes.

Handshakes between the men behind the closed door. But you are free to imagine. Your hand is too soft & the bones are sparrow-bones. Crushed & broken in the man's handshake. You dare not risk.

Mrs. Peele!—you must lie still.

In his soft nasal voice instructing me. Through the muslin hood I could not see his face.

You must not resist, it is a woman's duty to submit.

You must meditate as a flower meditates. Each of the petals, in perfect stillness.

The face of a clock whose hands have stopt. For in the Chair of Tranquility, time ceases to exist.

Do not think, do not recall. Do not summon back printed pages—books. Your schoolbooks, these were in error. A girl-child does not need books. A girl-child of good family, of golden-haired beauty.

Rhyming verse, this is (sometimes) allowed. Verse carefully chosen for women, which will not excite or agitate them.

Do not allow (unrhyming) words to penetrate your consciousness. No more than tossing stones into a woodland pond. No more than tossing coals onto a pristine covering of snow. No more than shouting rudely in church.

Do not think, thinking is not natural in women. Do not think, thinking is harmful in women.

Thinking too freely led unhappy Eve to pick the fatal apple from the tree, to press upon Adam, her husband, to incriminate him in her sin of disobedience.

It has been prescribed that for eight to ten weeks, depending upon your progress, you will be seated very still in the Chair of Tranquility *through the day. You will lie very still in the* Bed of Tranquility *through the night.*

At all times, warm-wetted sheets will bind you. Your eyes will be closed, your mouth will be stilled. Your frenzied limbs cannot break free & will soon surrender.

Your heart cannot race wild & crazed & will soon surrender.

If still the nervous womb becomes dislodged & sends its particles of disease to all parts of the female body, most perniciously in the brain, a more drastic treatment will be added: The Waters of Tranquility.

Very gently, lowered into warm-lapping waves, while bound in the Chair of Tranquility. *Five-foot copper tubs, kept at a temperature soothing to the skin. An attendant at all times, to prevent an accidental submergence.*

Hydrotherapy, so-called, is a riskier measure than Tranquility, though it is an extension of Tranquility. It is not a punishment, though it may be necessary to quell the mutinous womb.

No, you will not drown! It is foolish, silly, childish, futile to fret over such a fate!—that will not happen, not under the watchful eye of Silas Aloysius Weir.

If you were a common lunatic, plucked out of anonymity, there might be reason to fret—but you are not common, your husband is paying a hefty fee (privately) to Dr. Weir.

Thus, you are protected. As the common lunatics are not protected.

You will be protected by the spirit of Tranquility, as the male of the species is protected by the spirit of Activity.

The soul of the female, which is passivity & placidity; the soul of the male, which is activity & restive.

The soul of the female, best realized in rest; the soul of the male, best expressed in motion.

The flesh of the female, soft, yielding, ample, boneless; the flesh of the male, hard-muscled, strong-boned, & quick in reflex.

As it is unnatural for the male to exult in stillness, so it is unnatural for the female to express herself in motion.

In bed, abed, bedded, embedded; marching, hiking, riding (horses), & hunting.

In the Chair of Tranquility, *you will consume eight meals a day.*

In calmness, in no hurry you will chew your food following the Weir method, which necessitates chewing solid foods no less than thirty-two times until they are liquified.

Never will you swallow any "solid" particles of food: You will only swallow liquid.

Rich broths & cream soups will be brought to you. You will consume butter, milk, specially prepared eggs, & rich breads & pastries. The hood will be removed, the cloth about your mouth will be removed, you will be fed by an attendant, you need not use your own hands.

As you are grievously underweight, & of a risk for childbirth, it is prescribed for you to gain somewhere beyond forty pounds.

You will become (again) an infant in the womb, to be nourished, to exult in absolute stillness as your (female) soul swells about you.

You will be given medications, prescribed particularly for you, & prepared by the hand of Dr. Weir, out of his own herbal medications.

In the treatment of hysteria, it is recommended that calomel be ingested several times a day.

Calomel (mercury) will be in granule form, sprinkled on bread & covered with a thin coating of butter or honey.

In the treatment of female frigidity & barrenness, it is recommended that Saint-John's-wort, black cohosh, castor oil, & milk thistle be administered in carefully regulated doses.

In the treatment of a spasmodic agitation of the limbs, to no purpose save agitation, a daily dosage of laudanum, to be increased if muscular agitation persists.

Never need you fear that the medications you receive will be bitter-tasting. All of the medications you receive will have a tincture of sweetness.

You are privileged. You are blessed. Providence has brought you to Silas Aloysius Weir.

Repeat: I will not read for a period of six to eight weeks. I will not write for a period of six to eight weeks. I will not imagine writing letters to my cousins, my friends, my mother begging for me to be released from this horror of swaddling & suffocation.

I will not speak for a period of six to eight weeks. I will not plead, scream, beg for mercy or release.

I will not agitate my brain for a period of six to eight weeks.

I will not need to "relieve" myself—a nurse-maid will see to it, that my bedpan is emptied whenever necessary & scoured clean.

Yes I am very, very sorry that I clawed at my face. For my face was not mine to claw.

Yes I am very, very sorry that I screamed & laughed & thrashed & kicked in spasms of madness in the sanctity of the marital bed.

In Tranquility I will drift to a place beyond words. In Tranquility I will exult.

In Tranquility I will gain thirty-two pounds of dense white flesh packed beneath my chin, swelling my belly, hanging from my thighs & from my bosom like great udders.

I will have a caregiver at all times. I will have a nurse-maid to answer all my needs.

At all times repeat to yourself: I am unique, I am in the care of Silas Aloysius Weir, a unique practitioner & pioneer, of Gyno-Psychiatry.

When I am cured of my illness I will be returned home to my husband. Only then will I be returned home to my husband to conceive our first son & heir.

In the interim, I have faith in Providence, & in Silas Aloysius Weir, M.D.

•

This, from a diary discovered amongst the personal possessions of Mrs. Thomas Peele, of 228 Lakeview Drive, Trenton, in April 1853, following her sudden death after her release from the Asylum at Trenton the previous week.

It did not seem to be known if the patient had died as a result of having gained forty-nine pounds during her hospitalization, thus swelling her belly, torso, upper arms, & the flesh beneath her chin, which came to resemble a monstrous goiter, & placing a great strain on organs already weakened from weeks of inactivity; or whether, by some devious female method, in defiance of all that is Christian, decent & wholesome, the unhappy woman had contrived to *take her own life.*

Halcyon Years

1853–1860

FROM *THE CHRONICLE OF A PHYSICIAN'S LIFE*
BY SILAS ALOYSIUS WEIR, M.D.

I N T H E S E Y E A R S, without parallel in the history of American medical science, what visions flooded upon me! A Burning Bush of revelations, & I, like Moses, gazing in rapture upon flames so brilliant, they blinded mere mortal eyes.

It was a frequent public statement of mine, made at official gatherings, for instance at the New Jersey state legislature, that it seemed to me only fitting that an American should be the first person to discover a *cure for madness:* indeed, a resident of Trenton, New Jersey.

Local newspapers, & some papers not local (including even *The New York Times* and the *Philadelphia Sentinel*), heralded such "optimistic" & "future-looking" statements as very welcome examples of "American How-To," in contrast to the "dismal pessimism" of "older, less vigorous nations" like those of Europe; it would be immodest of me to imply that, seeing my wife, my relatives, & even my older children perusing such headlines with smiles of pride, I did not feel a thrill of gratification.

For all that I have done, & all that I will do, flows to me from God; in himself, Silas Weir is but a frail vessel.

It was widely noted through the medical community, & much admired, that Silas Aloysius Weir, Director of the New Jersey State

Asylum for Female Lunatics at Trenton, was introducing a new & vigorous application of *moral therapy,* to the patients under his care; selecting the most practical forms of treatment explored by his predecessor, & eliminating the rest, that had proved unsuccessful.

Foremost, the *Chair of Tranquility,* & its auxiliary, the *Bed of Tranquility,* developed in my Laboratory in North Hall, proved enormously successful from the start, immediately reducing the degree of agitation in the female lunatics, as well as their likelihood of self-injury, always a high risk at a mental institution.

Related to these, a more expedient device was developed in the Laboratory, known as the *Weir-jacket:* a jacket of coarse fabric with arms that crossed over the patient's chest, in restraints held in place by straps; sometimes in conjunction with *hydrotherapy,* if required. If a lunatic began to throw herself about, rave & convulse, & attack the staff, she was at once restrained in the *Weir-jacket,* & if agitation continued, a *Weir-helmet* was fitted to her head, with a thick band of cotton over the mouth, to muffle cries. In the interests of sanitation, this band of cotton was so fitted into place, it could be easily removed & replaced with a clean band, if oversaturated with saliva.

(The reader may well recognize that the device rightfully designated the *Weir-jacket* has been wrongfully manufactured & sold to hospitals & asylums as the *straitjacket:* an unacknowledged appropriation from me, as a result of my failure to register the *Weir-jacket* with the U.S. Patent Office promptly in February 1853, when I first perfected it. At the time, I was so busy with my duties as a physician, surgeon, & Director of the Asylum, I had little thought for personal gain; & thus, someone on my medical staff, who shall remain nameless, stole the idea, in all its details, & replicated it at the Boston Lunatic Asylum, whose staff he had joined. Thus it seems to me unconscionable that my fellow physicians & hospital directors, who know well whose invention their "straitjacket" is, should fail to rightfully identify the *Weir-jacket,* so frequently used by their staffs.)

Also related to the *Tranquility* regime, a carefully calibrated use of *hydrotherapy:* not as Medrick Weir prescribed, in scalding-hot baths, into which lunatics were submerged by force, screaming & convulsing, but in waters of mild temperature, intended to soothe, not to inflame or punish. Far more rarely than detractors would one day charge, this modified form of *hydrotherapy* brought with it a risk of drowning, if the patient, arms & legs restrained by tight-bound sheets, was left unattended; but such a risk has been minuscule, set beside the ameliorative possibilities of the therapy.

Widely known are my pioneering experiments with the uses of medications in the treatment of mental illness, duly reported in such journals as the *Journal of the American Association of Medical Research* & the *Atlantic Journal of Medical Science*. For the interested reader, or medical practitioner, I will attach an appendix to the *Chronicle*, listing my bibliography.

In due course, I will discuss my innovations in the *surgical correction of madness*—which venture beyond Medrick Weir's insight that the cause of madness is not hereditary, circumstantial, "possession by demons," but *infection*.

The Humbling

1853

FROM *THE CHRONICLE OF A PHYSICIAN'S LIFE*
BY SILAS ALOYSIUS WEIR, M.D.

D R. WEIR! I'm afraid that I have bad news."
Accursèd words! I fear they will follow me into the next world.

In an abashed voice Gretel addressed me, another time; very early one morning at the threshold of the Laboratory on the third floor of North Hall; for alone of my staff, Gretel had a key to the Laboratory, that she might check the patients in their beds in the night, if necessary; & prepare them for my arrival.

Thinking that this "bad news" had to be related to one or another of my *experimental surgeries* of the previous week, which involved the removal of a particularly diseased & debauched uterus, in a female lunatic well into her forties, & the removal of a particularly deformed clitoris, in a female lunatic of late adolescence—(both Asylum patients recently committed by their families)—I steeled myself for the worst news that a surgeon can encounter: the unexpected death of a patient.

Yet: The surprise was even greater in its way, & more devastating, for Gretel's news had nothing to do with the Laboratory subjects, but with Brigit Kinealy, whom I had assumed I had cured of *fistula*.

"She has relapsed, Doctor. The silk thread must have broken."

Silk thread! Broken! For a stunned moment, I could not comprehend.

My progress in the Laboratory had been such, for months I had had few setbacks; with the exception of the loss of Esther C__, a moribund subject who had not been expected to live in any case; & one or two others, self-victims of extreme malnutrition due to *anorexia,* which not even the forced feedings of *Tranquility therapy* had saved. Indeed, my article titled "A Successful 'Repair' of Vesicovaginal Fistula in a Young Mother" had recently appeared in the *Atlantic Journal of Medical Science,* acclaimed by physicians with a particular interest in the field of gynecology.

I had refrained from following too closely the progress of Brigit Kinealy, who, having recovered from the stigma of *fistula,* had been given permission to train as a nurse's aide, a modest position on the medical staff, though a considerable advance from work in the latrines; for I had not wanted to intrude in the girl's life, & hoped to content myself with glimpsing her at a distance, as if by chance.

"*Broken?* And so her incontinence has resumed?"

"Yes, Doctor. I am afraid so."

Seeing the expression on my face, Gretel shrank back, to allow me to enter the Laboratory; & to make my way, without a glance at the half-dozen female lunatics in their beds, to my private office with its high windows; to shut the door, & sit heavily at my mahogany desk, with a sigh. There, with the solace of a small dose of laudanum from a beaker kept in a desk drawer, & a splash of Scotch whiskey in a glass, I would prepare myself for the fuller news that Gretel would recite to me; & to anticipate, with a heart both morose & hopeful, my meeting with the albino deaf-mute another time, not in triumph but in shared disappointment.

"Dear God! In Your mighty hands, I am as Job—humbled, humiliated, yet not broken."

As I have vowed to full disclosure of my life & career in this *Chronicle,* I must now speak frankly of my domestic life, where I experienced another sort of *humbling.*

For fortune did not always smile upon Silas Aloysius Weir, even in the afterglow of my promotion to Director of the Asylum at Trenton; still less in the stately rooms of the Director's house, which had seemed so spacious to my family when we had first moved in.

There was awkwardness between my wife & me, concerning the nature of my responsibilities at the Asylum, for Theresa seemed vexed that I was away much of the time, yet, when I was home, & sought to engage her in conversation about the Asylum, her gaze soon grew blurred & opaque; for it was very distasteful to her, as a genteel wife, to imagine her physician-husband in close proximity to female patients, still more, to gaze upon their partially clothed, or unclothed bodies; indeed, to imagine such was to shudder, in reproach & dismay. (In our marital life together, Theresa & I comported ourselves with unfailing dignity: in all our years of marriage, neither of us had ever had the occasion to gaze upon the other unclothed; & our expanded space in the sandstone house allowed for an even greater respect for mutual privacy.) If I spoke of conflicts with my staff, which arose almost daily, & which is natural in the maintenance of so large an institution as the Asylum, Theresa would say, with a crinkle of her pert nose, "Why, you are the 'Director,' Silas—just tell your underlings what to do."

In fairness to her, Theresa was never altogether happy with the housekeeper assigned to the Director's household, nor most of the staff of four servants, who lived in the house, in modest quarters at the rear; still there remained resentment on her side, that my Abolitionist principles had cost her the gift of a slave child belonging to her family in Vineland, New Jersey, intended as her dowry, who would have grown now into maturity.

Thus, Theresa & the Cleff family had a penchant of referring to me, even within my earshot, as *Holier Than Thou Silas*. Which, overhearing, I had no choice but to interpret as an affectionate sort of teasing, & not outright contempt.

"You have your 'indentured servants' at the Asylum, Silas: How do they differ from slaves? I'm of the impression that you work them to death, just as slaveholders work *their* slaves to death." Maddeningly, Theresa would laugh at this exaggeration; for much of her formerly girlish charm had lain in airily exaggerating when she spoke, to entertain & to tease.

When I protested, that all of the work-staff at the Asylum were treated equally, Theresa interrupted to say, "But are they *paid equally*? You don't pay your indentured staff, just as slaves are not paid. You work them as hard, & you cast them out when you are finished with them."

"Theresa, that is not true! No one on the staff is ever whipped, or cruelly treated. When an indentured servant comes to the end of his contract, he is given his 'freedom dues'—& walks away, free. Now I think we have had enough of this subject."

In fact, the matter of *indentured servants* on the Asylum staff, who had been engaged by the previous Director, as their contracted Master, had become a sensitive matter of late, which I had no intention of discussing with Theresa.

Nor did I feel comfortable in confiding in her of my hopes for a career beyond New Jersey, once I had secured a *national reputation,* as a pioneer in the reform of the treatment of mental illness. My model was Dr. Francis Brickman, formerly Dean of the Harvard Medical School, who had been named the President's Chief Medical Adviser, with an office in the White House in Washington, D.C.; it was said that Medrick Weir had frequently been discussed as a successor to Dr. Brickman. But if I were to speak too carelessly of my hope that one day my achievements might come to the attention of the White House, Theresa could not have been trusted not to speak boastfully to her sisters, & they to their family; which would prove mortifying to me, if the summons from the President never came.

Intensely feminine by nature, & of a class & background in which femininity was identical with modesty, Theresa could not abide any frank discussion of *physical matters;* that is, anything pertaining to the *physical being.* Even after nine pregnancies, during the course of which she had grown to ample matronly proportions, weighing down her side of the marital bed, Theresa blushed if certain subjects were broached, to which polite society objects. So delicate were Theresa's nerves, like her mother's, & grandmother's, I had not learned that we were expecting our first baby, until informed circuitously by my father-in-law, Myron Cleff, in a gruff & joshing sort of way, to my surprise & discomfort, as a young husband at the time.

"Why, sir, I am not sure if I understand what you are saying . . ."—so I floundered, my face going very red; while Mr. Cleff bared his teeth at me in a pitying sort of grin, laughing, & saying that there was no need to *understand,* Nature would make her way nonetheless, in nine months' time.

Nine months' time. Ah! Belatedly, foolishly, I understood.

Mr. Cleff laughed at me, in a companionable sort of way. But I could not help but feel that, in his heart, as in his (begrudging) bank account, he did not think so highly of his daughter's husband as one might have wished.

In other circumstances I would have been curious to know if, among Theresa's family of many female siblings & cousins, there were cases of *fistula;* but of this I dared not speak, for my inquiries would have been met with stunned silence. Very likely, Theresa would not have known, for the condition would have been kept secret; the disagreeable word *fistula* unknown.

Once, when my father-in-law inquired of me, what kind of *surgery* was I performing at the Asylum, that kept me away from home until late hours, I replied as decorously as I could, alluding to *female maladies;* whereupon Mr. Cleff shuddered, & said, with averted eyes, "Enough, Silas. Thank you."

Yet more humbling, my eldest son, Jonathan, was proving a disappointment, indeed. With the hope of enticing his interest in clinical medicine, that Jonathan might one day join me at the Asylum, & take over the Directorship upon my retirement (far in the future!), I brought him to the Asylum upon several occasions, & one memorable time to my Laboratory in North Hall. But here, to my surprise & dismay, Jonathan reacted most childishly, stammering an excuse as he fled from the Laboratory with a look of horror, white-faced & sickly; giving the explanation afterward that the smells alone had made him ill; & the sights of the slatternly female lunatics in the beds, some of them shackled to iron bedposts, had been upsetting to him.

Nor had Jonathan felt comfortable with barred windows in all of the wards, & locks & bolts on many doors, & tall husky attendants brandishing truncheons, though it was explained to him that the Asylum was a *mental hospital, not a picnic ground.*

"How would *you* treat a raving lunatic, son? Do *you* have any alternative remedy?"—so I inquired of the boy, in a voice of heavy sarcasm; but Jonathan did not put up any defense, merely shaking his head vehemently—*No, no! No.*

"I am following the dictates of science," I told Jonathan, "—determining, by rigorous experimentation, how best to excise 'madness' from the soul of the lunatic, by attacking *infection.* It had been my hope that you, my eldest son, would take some interest in the work to which your father is dedicating his life . . ."

Still, Jonathan would not engage with me; avoided speaking of the subject at all, as if the mere contemplation of it made him physically ill.

Following this debacle, which took place when the spoiled boy was in his eighteenth year, I could not bring up the subject of medical school without Jonathan becoming agitated; he declared that he had not the stomach for *experimental surgery,* or dealing in any way with *lunatics.*

Indeed, to my acute disappointment, Jonathan had decided that he would not pursue studies in science at all.

"How can I do the most good for society?—humankind? I think—by studying the law. Putting an end to slavery: *That* is the great challenge, which your generation has not solved."

Earnestly the boy spoke, as if echoing the pompous, self-righteous sermonizing of my New England Abolitionist relatives, whom he had never met; with the fingers of both hands brushing unruly strands of hair from his forehead, in a frettish gesture I found most annoying, as disrespectful to me.

Yet, Jonathan was willing to accept, from me, tuition for the Lawrenceville School, with the expectation that I would pay further tuition at the nearby College of New Jersey to follow—(this attractive institution, formerly a theological seminary, would one day soon be known as Princeton University); though both schools were favored by the sons of the wealthiest Southern slaveholders, and were places of entitlement & privilege, not at all sympathetic with the Abolitionist movement. (Indeed, it was a tradition at the college to become Princeton that its undergraduates brought their personal slaves to campus with them, to reside in slaves' quarters near the student residences.)

The hypocrisy of youth!—particularly, *liberal-minded youth.* Yet, Jonathan seemed to gaze upon his distinguished father with particular scorn, & a kind of pity as well.

At my request, Gretel brought Brigit to me in the early evening of a weekday, when most of the medical staff was gone from the Asylum, & no one was likely to approach the Laboratory.

Indeed, Gretel had not been able to bring Brigit to me for several days, as the *relapsed patient* was despondent, & reluctant to return.

Ah, how sickly Brigit looked! Scarcely did the white skin appear radiant, rather its light was dimmed, as the light in the pale blue eyes had dimmed, since our last encounter when she had presented me with the carved wooden dove, & gazed at me with eyes of *reverence*.

Now, Brigit could not bring herself to raise her eyes to me, at all. Though, with Gretel's assistance, she had washed the offensive regions of her body thoroughly, yet there clung to her, as a miasma about a swamp, a feculent, piteous odor.

"Help her to disrobe, Gretel."

"Yes, Dr. Weir."

"Up on the table. On hands & knees. As before."

"Yes, Dr. Weir."

Gretel's manner of late had been subdued. Her eyes seemed less focused, her cheeks thinner & less ruddy. A handsome woman, with a fleshy round face, she had lost, like Brigit, a certain inner *glow*.

Dread came into my heart, that something would happen to Gretel!—the only female on the staff whom I could trust, which included the supervisor of nurses at the Asylum & others with proper nursing degrees, as Gretel did not have; indeed, it appeared that the midwife had been trained by older midwives, with no formal nursing classes at all.

From Amos Heller, I knew that there had been problems with our numerous indentured servants at the Asylum. For it appeared that under some duress or coercion, of an unclear nature, the previous Asylum administration had extended the terms of contracts for some of these workers, inveigling them into signing sub-contracts, which they had not fully understood at the time. (Most of the indentured servants were not literate; if they spoke English, it was with heavy accents.) Gretel was one of these, & it appeared that Brigit was, as well; very likely, her own mother had sold her into servitude, for cash with which to buy gin. (Gin-drinking was one of the plagues of the Asylum staff, & said to be commonplace in Trenton among the lower classes.) It seemed to me a practical matter that these female employees of the Asylum were contracted to me, as Director of the Asylum; for I would protect their legal interests as no one else would. If Gretel, with her poor background, were to attempt to leave the Asylum, to work else-where, she would soon be starving; there was no thought of Brigit sur-viving outside the Asylum, for it was all she knew, since birth. Who, beside Silas Aloysius Weir, would care for *her*!—an albino deaf-mute orphan, hideously afflicted with *fistula*.

With a gloved hand, & Gretel's assistance, I succeeded in peering into the patient's inflamed vagina, with the spoon-speculum, wielded now with more expertise, if not complete ease.

What a shock!—indeed, as Gretel had surmised, the silk thread had rotted, & snapped; part of it seemed to have become embedded in the bladder itself, which appeared to be swollen & discolored. The tear was now appreciably larger, as a consequence.

That morning, a radical new idea had come to me, that I would repair the injury in Brigit's bladder not with more silk thread but by compressing the tear with a heated forceps. Gretel expressed some surprise at this development but knew better than to object or raise an inquiry, somewhat reluctantly, yet dutifully heating the copper instrument on an open flame, & bringing it to me, that I might insert the heated end into the patient, tremulously poised on hands & knees on the table.

"You must remain still, Brigit. This may be a bit *warm*."

Unfortunately, as I tried to push the heated forceps into place, Brigit could not suppress a scream, & a cry of what sounded like *Oh God!* issued from her throat, the first words I had heard uttered by the deaf-mute; which did not surprise me, as I believed that Brigit was neither deaf nor dumb but afflicted with a type of hysteria.

"Brigit! You are not a child. Resume your posture here, & stop being foolish. I have told you—the interior of the vagina is known to be insensitive to sensation, like the birth canal. There are no nerve endings in these organs. Gretel, hold her still."

After waiting several seconds for the heated forceps to cool slightly, I resumed the procedure, with some difficulty; for despite her effort to be stoical & brave, the subject was trembling badly now, & had to be soothed by Gretel.

Nonetheless, after persevering, I succeeded in suturing the wound with the heated forceps; taking care then to insert, at the base of the bladder, a minute piece of sponge to soak up blood & urine. This, a temporary measure, to be removed after forty-eight hours.

Even so, I worried that the oversensitive patient may have sabotaged the procedure, by flinching when the heated forceps was first inserted. Had it been *fully heated,* as I had intended, the procedure might have had a better chance of success.

By the time the operation was completed, a full hour must have passed. My neck & back were very strained, & my eyesight clouded with tears of concentration.

"Well, Brigit! We have both earned a respite, I think!"

Gretel helped Brigit from the table. With surprise I saw that Brigit's face was ashen with strain, & her eyes shimmering with tears.

After Gretel helped Brigit wash her lower body, & put on fresh attire, I thanked Gretel for her assistance, & bade good night to her; insisting then that Brigit swallow a small quantity of laudanum, that, after her ordeal, she might sleep peacefully through the night. In a festive if muted gesture, I joined Brigit in pouring a very small quantity of laudanum into a glass of Scotch whiskey, for myself.

"You have been very brave, Brigit! I am hoping that, this time, Providence will smile upon us."

So exhausted was poor Brigit, she had not the strength to respond to this, even mutely. Her eyelids were drooping, the flesh of her face had grown slack.

It seemed a kindly gesture to offer Brigit a pallet for the night, not in the foul-smelling hospital ward but in a corner of my private office, where I spread blankets on the floor behind a mahogany bookcase; that she might make a little nest for herself there, instead of in the airless cellar of the Asylum, where she was reputed to dwell.

This offer Brigit accepted, out of sheer exhaustion, perhaps; too fatigued to protest, or to hesitate, but sinking to the floor, with what sounded like a murmur deep in the throat which only I could hear— *Yes thank you, Dr. Weir.*

"Silas? Where have you been so late?"—so Theresa inquired of me, with concern; for it was near midnight, & most of the house was darkened, as I ascended the stairs to the second floor, holding a lighted candle aloft.

"'Where have I been so late?' Why, in Heaven—where would you expect? Hell?"

Despite this jaunty reply, I was very tired. The ordeal of the suturing, the ingestion of both laudanum & whiskey, had so suffused my being, I could barely move past my frowning wife as she stood in the doorway of our bedchamber, in voluminous nighttime attire. With a murmur of vague apology, I retired to my corner of the room, to fumblingly disrobe; & from there to our four-poster bed, with a sigh drifting off into sleep like one borne aloft on the most tumultuous of Atlantic waves.

Slander

FROM *THE CHRONICLE OF A PHYSICIAN'S LIFE*
BY SILAS ALOYSIUS WEIR, M.D.

IT WOULD BE CLAIMED by the low-minded, knowing nothing of our circumstances, that Brigit Kinealy, an indentured servant contracted to the New Jersey State Asylum for Female Lunatics, was abused by me, the Director of the Asylum; that this underage girl, not only orphaned but an albino of uncertain health, a deaf-mute, with no family to protect her, was exploited most shamelessly, as an *experimental subject;* that I forced her to undergo as many as a dozen surgeries, through the 1850s, in order to advance my career as a pioneer in Gyno-Psychiatry, while caring little for her sufferings.

Still worse, it would be (crudely, unconscionably) claimed by some that I drugged Brigit Kinealy, held her captive in a sequestered area of the Asylum reserved for the hopelessly insane, bound her to her bed, starved her, or overfed her, that I might pursue an *illicit, clandestine, unnatural* relationship with her—an abominable accusation, & totally erroneous.

An orphan-indentured servant, young enough to be my daughter!

In fact, as Brigit Kinealy many times attested, she owed her life to me, as her Savior; & was grateful for my attentiveness to her, alone of all doctors to care for her particular, most loathsome affliction, which would have condemned her to die in misery otherwise.

It is true that, from time to time, to calm the patient's fears, & my own, I prescribed for us both, at the conclusion of an arduous day in the Laboratory, a very small dose of laudanum—*sweet balm of Lethe*, as I called it; a very modest quantity, indeed, less than physicians prescribe for their genteel women patients.

True, too, that I may have directed the supervisor of the kitchen facilities, to provide nourishing meals for Brigit, or to allow her to prepare meals for herself, with privileges not provided for others on the work-staff of the Asylum; for the girl was of a very slight build, & underweight, thus in danger of becoming tubercular, like many of the accursèd patients in the Asylum.

Beyond this, to answer such slanderous charges is to dignify them, which I refuse to do.

Indeed, such obscenities were (& are) circulated by my rivals, as similar obscenities were circulated by the sworn enemies of my predecessor & kinsman, Medrick Weir, driving this pioneering martyr of Gyno-Psychiatry into an early grave.

Another accusation, commonly circulated amidst my detractors, was that I maintained a locked Laboratory at the Asylum, where *hellish experiments* took place, perpetrated upon lunatic subjects against their will, & without anesthesia; that this Laboratory was in a remote, desolate place on the Asylum grounds, forbidden of entry to all but a few carefully chosen nurses & attendants, who were sworn to secrecy, in thrall to Silas Aloysius Weir, as their Master; & that, here patients were shackled to their beds, bound in wetted sheets, & caged like beasts; the corpses of those who did not survive were hurriedly taken away, under cover of darkness, & their bodies buried on the Asylum grounds, with no grave markers.

Shameless slander! *Lunacy.*

That such absurdities have been uttered, & have found their way into newsprint, is outrageous, & actionable; but, as a devout Christian, I am not a litigious person, & have no wish to call further attention to the libelous remarks, by attempting to sue for defamation in a court of law. Nor would I wish to expose myself to the whims of a Mercer County judge who might be prejudiced in my disfavor, corrupted by local gossip.

It is true, most of my surgeries were performed without *anesthesia,* for the practical reason that, in the early years of my Directorship, *anesthesia* was scarcely known. Also, it is a scientific fact, as I had explained to Brigit, that female organs have fewer nerve endings than other parts of the body, no doubt to make the rigors of childbirth less painful.

In fact, I did experiment with chloroform & tincture of opium, from time to time, in my Asylum patients, who were not likely to register alarm, nor even awareness of such a procedure. As "putting a patient to sleep" was an uncertain procedure, I was hesitant to employ it for my private patients, for fear that they might never awaken again.

The average layman has no idea how frequently even the most skillful & experienced experimental researchers *fail,* & how rare it is for them to *succeed;* that an experimental surgeon might be required to operate upon a subject as many as one dozen times, or more, before any progress is made; how devoted, how persistent, how *stubborn* the researcher must be, in the light of such odds! That one hundred experimental subjects might die, in order that a single subject might live, to advance medical science: Why is that so difficult to grasp? We scientists do not *prey upon* the expendable, but *make use of* what Providence has provided for us, in the way of individuals of questionable worth, like lunatics, convicts, & other inhabitants of institutions, housed at the public's expense.

None of this should be the material for *slander,* rather more for praise, in a just world!

Therefore, let the heathens rage: My experimental surgeries upon Brigit Kinealy resulted in a *complete cure* for the patient, of her gruesome malady; & not least, a *total success* for me, as her physician, assuring for me the honor to be conferred upon me at the zenith of my career—*Father of Modern Gyno-Psychiatry.*

Nurse-Assistant

FROM *THE CHRONICLE OF A PHYSICIAN'S LIFE*
BY SILAS ALOYSIUS WEIR, M.D.

How do you feel this morning, Brigit?"—calmly I inquired, in defiance of my rapidly beating heart, shaping my words carefully with my lips, as I had fondly learned to do in this circumstance.

Casting her eyes downward, Brigit allowed me to know, by a movement of her small perfect lips—*I think—I am well . . .*

"Did you say, Brigit, you are feeling—*well*?"

How strange it was, how like a caress, the transparent-blue eyes of the albino fixed upon my mouth, as if *reading* my words, that could not be heard by her.

Yes—Brigit nodded.

How rarely the orphan-girl smiled, & how radiant this smile!

"It may be, then, that God has smiled upon us, Brigit. We will pray, & we will hope."

Following the *heated suture* procedure, the first of its kind (I was sure) in any treatment of *fistula,* I requested of the patient that she report to me each day, that I might examine her in private, to see how she was recovering.

Having failed in the past, in my efforts to "repair" *fistula,* I must confess, I had great hope for this new treatment; & each day that Brigit reported good health, with no relapse, was a (tentative) victory for me, for which I gave thanks to God, with a hearty sigh.

Soon, I planned to transcribe my copious notes into an article to be titled "A Successful 'Repair' of Fistula by Heat Compression"; I would include clinical notes (pencil sketches of the *fistula,* injured bladder, etcetera), for possibly, the details of my experiment would one day be of great value to other men of science, as the anatomical drawings of Leonardo da Vinci are today.

(It seemed to me, too, that it was within my power to treat Brigit Kinealy's alleged *muteness & deafness.* Another pioneering effort!)

Traditionally, in clinical studies, the identity of the subject is irrelevant; for the patient is but the material upon which the physician-surgeon labors, to bring forth a medical advancement. It is appropriate that only the physician-surgeon is granted an identity in professional publications, as the author of the article, & the experimenter behind the experiment.

However, between this experimenter & his subject, there was a strange & inexpressible intimacy, which could not be described in scientific or medical terms. For I was convinced that I had come to know Brigit Kinealy as I knew no one else in the world—certainly including Theresa & my children.

(Ah, it seemed that I knew Theresa less with each passing year! Each childbirth, of nine, she had been attended by a midwife, & certain of her female relatives; while the father-to-be had kept at a discreet distance, steeling his nerves against muffled screams from another part of the house. When at last the newborn was presented to the father, time had elapsed, & the father brought into the intimate scene belatedly, as an observer.)

Doctor you have saved my life. Doctor—I owe my life to YOU.

So Brigit Kinealy allowed me to know, without words; with little smiles, & a nodding of her head; a flash of adoring eyes, & charming gestures of her delicate hands, that made me wish to reach out to seize them, & lift them to my mouth, to kiss . . . As never in my life I had done, nor even wished to do.

But—*I did not touch her! Not in that way.*

It was at this time that I appointed Brigit Kinealy to the rank of nurse-assistant in the Laboratory, to report directly to *me.* Though indentured servants were paid no wages by the Asylum, & were provided only with food & board, I suggested to Brigit that, if she distinguished herself as my assistant, I might pay her a modest wage each week, out of the Director's private budget.

At this generosity of mine, Brigit's pale eyelids fluttered, in an effort not to weep.

Doctor—thank you!

"But you must earn it, you know, Brigit. 'The laborer is worthy of his hire.' "

Brigit's living quarters, too, were radically improved, from a squalid place belowground, to a private room with a hospital cot, at the rear of the Laboratory; for the first time in her life, the orphan was granted a measure of privacy, & the privilege of a door she might close. (Though she could not lock it, from within.)

Most prized of all, to an easily impressionable young girl, Brigit was given a very attractive nurse's uniform, with a long pale gray skirt, a white cotton smock, a white cotton apron, & a pert little white starched cap; white cotton stockings, & more practical dark shoes, of a quality quite unlike anything the Irish orphan had ever owned in the past.

All this, as I recognized that Brigit Kinealy was a young person of high intelligence & unusual sensitivity, possessed of a most beautiful *soul*; hardly to be found in any medical worker at the Asylum, of any age.

When she learned of the promotion of a mere indentured servant at the Asylum, the supervisor of nurses, whose surname was Furst, vehemently protested that Brigit Kinealy had no medical degree, nor even minimal training as a nurse; that my elevation of her could not be justified, & would not be justified, by Furst; the entire maneuver, in Furst's words, a "shameless ruse," more egregious even than a similar undeserved promotion had been, earlier in the year, of my assistant Gretel.

Furst complained, too, that "reputable nurses" assigned to the Director's Laboratory had been summarily dismissed; & among these, nurses personally known to Furst, & highly valued.

"Dr. Weir, I am warning you: I feel that I must, in defense of my administrative position at the Asylum, & in support of the integrity of the nursing profession, render a formal complaint to the board of overseers, of the Asylum; & possibly, too, if that complaint falls on deaf ears, a petition to the New Jersey state legislature as well."

This threat took me by surprise. For I had considered that, by elevating Furst to the position of supervisor, after the resignation of Medrick Weir's appointee, I had enlisted a powerful loyalist; now, I realized that the devious woman might well have been an enemy of Medrick Weir, with a hand in destroying that great man.

Coolly I replied, "As I am Director of the Asylum, & you are but the supervisor of nurses, Miss Furst, your judgment is not a match for mine."

One would have expected the foolish woman to keep silent at such a rebuttal; but the harridan could not resist:

"Dr. Weir, as I am the supervisor of nurses, with credentials from the Nursing School of the University of Pennsylvania, I would argue that my judgment is more sound than yours, in the assessment of nurses & our standards of excellence over all."

To which my reply was: "Furst, you are dismissed from your office. You may apply to Amos Heller for your severance pay. Then, you may clear out your office & depart the Asylum grounds at once. That is *my* assessment."

So eager was Brigit Kinealy to distinguish herself as more than a common laborer, she began assisting me in the Laboratory, before she had fully recovered her physical strength. I did not encourage this, for I remained in dread of the *fistula* reopening.

Yet, quickly I discerned that my judgment had been correct: Few nurses were so capable as Brigit, & none would be so loyal to *me*. And there was pleasure in Brigit's silence, in contrast to the oft-ignorant remarks of the nursing staff.

It was a relief to me when each morning Brigit allowed me to know, by a small shy smile lifting to my face, that she remained *well;* that is, *normal.* Though I continued to fear a relapse of the *fistula*, & prayed each day for the suturing to prevail.

Did I imagine, the ethereally beautiful pale-blond nurse with luminous eyes whispering to me—*Thank you Doctor! I love you, Doctor.*

Though muted, these words pierced my heart with a most potent power.

So it was, Brigit gave every appearance of being healed; yet still, each evening I provided her with a small quantity of laudanum, *our sweet balm of Lethe,* that she might sleep peacefully in her private quarters in the Laboratory, on her own narrow cot, after a day of heroic effort at my side.

The Laboratory: The Experiment

(1853)

FROM *THE CHRONICLE OF A PHYSICIAN'S LIFE*
BY SILAS ALOYSIUS WEIR, M.D.

IN ALL, more than seventy *experimental subjects* were housed in the Laboratory in North Hall, over a period of years; at its fullest, there were eleven bed-patients in the main ward, & half a dozen in adjacent rooms, as these were likely patients who required special restraints & protections (like the *Weir-cell*, my invention, whose walls were ingeniously padded, to prevent violent patients from self-injury).

Initially, the Laboratory was very well-kempt, with daily cleanings & scrubbings by the custodial staff of the Asylum, & a rigorous scouring of bedpans; in time, as there was more need for privacy, to protect me from hostile scrutiny, the custodial staff was dismissed, & housecleaning fell to my personal assistants & those patients well enough to participate in *moral therapy,* by helping to keep their living quarters tidy.

A small, select team of young researchers from the Asylum medical staff were invited to conduct their own experiments in the Laboratory, under my supervision; until such time, when their use of the facilities became distracting to me, & required too much of my oversight, to make such collegial use practical.

Of the numerous surgeries performed in the Laboratory by me, records show that eighty-three percent were fully successful, while twelve percent were successful to a degree; the remaining small percentage were *inconclusive,* or *null.*

Of necessity, there were often several surgeries performed upon a single patient of which only one—(inevitably, the last)—might prove *fatal;* which should not reflect upon the degree of success, of the earlier surgeries.

Thus, contrary to rumors, *virtually all of my patients recovered;* of these, a high number were returned to full sanity, & discharged from the hospital to return to their families. (There is some disagreement over these figures, unfortunately lost to public scrutiny after a conflagration in the Laboratory which destroyed all such records.)

Over all, matching the records of the Asylum at Trenton with other, similar facilities, including the New Jersey State Lunatic Asylum for Men at Newark, it appears that the Asylum at Trenton could boast the most cures, & the most discharges; all the more remarkable in that *lunacy* is far more prevalent in women than in men; & notoriously much harder to cure.

From my earliest days as a young apprentice in Chestnut Hill, attached to an older, hidebound clinician, it had always been my conviction that *mental illness* is *illness*—caused by, & exacerbated by, *physical illness*. Within a scant decade of effort on my part, in the Laboratory at the Asylum, great advances were made (by us) in expanding knowledge of such pathologies of the female as "tilted" uterus, lactation inadequacy, vaginismus/"hysterical" vagina, neurasthenia, infertility, ovary atrophy, irregular monthly periods, overly heavy monthly periods, premature cessation of monthly periods, menopausal fevers, prolonged melancholia & depression, mania, frigidity, nymphomania, pelvic & breast tumors of every size & variety, etcetera— maladies loathed by the great majority of physicians, yet scrupulously examined, & treated, by Silas Aloysius Weir, as all bore upon *female lunacy.*

It was crucial, however, that ignorant, uninformed persons not intrude into my Laboratory, bearing with them outmoded notions of *moral rectitude* that cannot apply to the experimental realm. I have noted the childish reaction of my son Jonathan, in his response to our little ward of "restrained" subjects; a failure of imagination deeply disappointing to me. As well, my *prize patient* Brigit Kinealy reacted in a weak semblance of my son, when first viewing the female lunatics confined *in restraint,* shackled to their cots, or tight-secured in wetted sheets, or, the most dangerous, in hutch-like wooden enclosures with bars, for their own safety.

As I had escorted Brigit into this area of the Laboratory, she was amazed to see half a dozen wretches, & to smell the most repellent smells; even as those wretches who were not comatose began pleading, & moaning, & cursing at us, as if they would have liked to tear us limb from limb.

By this time I was alert to Brigit's *mute speech,* as I thought of it; & could hear her soft voice clearly, in my mind.

Asking of me—*Dr. Weir*—*why are they in* cages?

So, calmly I replied to her: "These are not *cages,* Brigit; they are 'restraints.'"

But—*why?*

"Because these patients have proven themselves dangerous to others, as to themselves."

What—*what are their names?*

"Their *names*—?"

At this query, I had to laugh: The notion that these wretches had *names* was so pitiful a sentiment.

The nearest to us, in one of the hutch-cages, a bestial creature, diagnosed as syphilitic, leered at Brigit & at me in a most threatening way; not once had this creature expressed a modicum of gratitude, for my having attempted to repair her *fistula,* & for having extracted from her inflamed gums two rows of rotted teeth. Except that I pushed Brigit away from the cage, the lunatic would have spat vile poisonous saliva on the naïve young girl.

I explained to Brigit that the patients secured in this annex of the Laboratory were distraught & confused, & had no idea how to behave in a civilized hospital setting; of the more acutely infected lunatics, they were consumed by a compulsion to *run away.*

"If they break free of the Asylum, they will surely come to harm. So many of them are determined to throw themselves into the Delaware River, for instance."

Very still, with widened eyes, Brigit stared about the (windowless) room, in a cringing sort of way that reminded me of my son Jonathan.

"The penalty for trying to run away from the Asylum has to be forcible restraint, Brigit," I said, choosing my words with care, so that the orphan-girl would not misunderstand, "—otherwise too many of you would run away, & come to a grave end."

·

Herewith, one of my earliest experiments in the Laboratory, presented in a vocabulary that should give the layman no difficulty.

TREATMENT FOR (SUSPECTED) BILIOUS REMITTENT FEVER IN TWO FEMALE MENTAL PATIENTS (FALL 1853)

Subject #1—"Beulah": age 37; high fever; chills; nausea; very thin; chronic cough; listless, intermittent delirium & aggression.
Subject #2—"Mary": age 51; high fever; chills; nausea; weight loss but still "obese"; moods of calm/resignation alternating with excitation/delirium.

Given this rare opportunity (i.e., an identical illness in near-identical patients) the research scientist is in a most practical position to experiment with medications.

Medications tested: blue-mass (mercury) pills; black cohosh; echinacea; ginkgo leaf; quinine drops; mustard plaster; oil of fennel; belladonna.

As it was beginning to be considered in medical circles that "quinine" in a diluted form helped to reduce bilious fever, my methodology was to administer some combination of these medications to Subject #1, including quinine drops, but, to Subject #2, all of these medications, excluding quinine drops.

Noting how, within a relatively short period of time, Subject #1 began to recover from the more evident symptoms of bilious fever while Subject #2 gradually worsened.

After two days, Subject #1 was able to swallow liquids (water, chicken broth), being clear-eyed & not in a fever-delirium; Subject #2 remained severely ill, with high fever, nausea, delirium.

At this time Brigit Kinealy had just begun to assist me in the Laboratory, & was of particular value when Gretel could not be present. (For there had begun to be episodes when Gretel was not so capable & trustworthy as she had been, indicating, by her manner, a combination of impudence & docility, a failure to engage, with enthusiasm, in my experimental ventures.)

Initially, in awe of her altered circumstances, & intimidated by her responsibilities in helping to oversee a small ward of patients, Brigit followed my instructions unquestioningly—indeed, *gratefully.* In the albino girl's pale eyes there shone a clear adoration for me, her Savior, as one might see in a companion dog, that never distrusts her Master.

But then, as days passed, the albino's pale eyes began to widen, & to *see*—withal, the nurse-assistant began to hesitate, in following my instructions; particularly as my instructions indicated a *radical disparity* in medical treatment of the two subjects. A totally naïve comprehension, or lack of comprehension, of the *very foundation of Experiment.*

As Brigit could not speak to me, as a normal person might, even a subordinate like herself, she turned to other means, to communicate: indicating one or another medication on a shelf of the armamentarium, & (gently, timidly) tapping my arm, to indicate that the patient should be given *this medication*—so brash an act on the part of a subordinate of such a lowly rank, I was too astonished at first, to respond.

Growing more frustrated, Brigit sought a piece of paper & a pencil, to write laboriously on it, as a small child might:

Giv Ky nine to Mary tow

What was this gibberish! I tossed the piece of paper down to the floor, with a sigh of exasperation. My own children had soon learned better, to not attempt to capture their father's attention by such ploys; as if I had not better/higher things to puzzle over than childish riddles!

Had Gretel been present, she would have prevented the rash young assistant from persevering; but blindly, Brigit insisted upon presenting the paper to me again, lifting it to my face in an audacious gesture, scarcely an inch or two from my eyeglasses.

Giv Ky nine to Mary tow

As I stared at her with undisguised hostility Brigit dared to shape with her lips the command *Give quinine to Mary, too.*

" 'Give quinine to Mary, too'—what, you are daring to order *me*?"

This impertinence on the part of a wholly untrained "nurse" in the first week of her new employment might have been amusing to me, but was not; had the offender been one of my children, severe discipline would have been immediate.

Yes, it was a time of *discipline*: "Spare the rod, spoil the child" being a tenet of Jesus Christ Himself, in His wisdom, as John Calvin has declared.

"Let me remind you, Brigit, a doctor depends upon a loyal nurse, to do his bidding; not to suggest to him, in utter naïveté & ignorance, what his bidding might be."

Brigit's eyes widened. What, had the naïve young girl imagined that there was some *rapport* between us, that she might address me, her superior in every way, the very Savior to whom she owed her life, with such brash intimacy?

At last enlightened, Brigit shrank away; slunk away, as a kicked dog; & busied herself in mopping the Laboratory floor, which had become unconscionably filthy in recent days, about the beds of the loathsome *fistula* patients.

Indeed, it had been my plan to administer quinine to Subject #2, shortly; this, I intended to synchronize with the withdrawal of all medications from Subject #1, & the introduction of Saint-John's-wort, a medication to which I had become attached, & about which I had written several articles. (I often took small doses of Saint-John's-wort myself, with my nightly *balm of Lethe,* as these seemed to aid in digestion, clarity of thought, male virility, & general well-being.)

Beyond that, the experiment was to alternate medications, giving to one subject, & ceasing to give to the other, in a complicated stratagem by which I might isolate the effects of individual medications on the sick women; for it is one thing to "cure" a patient, but quite another to know precisely *why* the patient has been cured.

All science is based upon facts, not fancies. A medical treatment that cannot be replicated is useless.

Of course, the risk in the Laboratory was: Would patients live long enough, that I might do a thorough job of testing medications? All too often in the Asylum, a patient who had seemed but moderately ill took an abrupt turn for the worse, without any self-evident reason; for our patients were ailing in such complex ways, over long periods of time, the treatment for one malady might exacerbate another.

In this case, *would the bilious fever endure long enough, that it might be clear what had cured it, if indeed it was cured?*

On principle, however, to emphasize my disinclination to take the advice of my nurse-assistant over my own better judgment, I decided to withhold all medications from Subject #2, even as I interspersed doses of Saint-John's-wort with quinine drops to Subject #1.

Consequently Subject #2 continued to worsen, & was now rarely conscious, with an ashy-"burning" skin, while Subject #1 remained stable. It was my plan to introduce several provisional medications (arsenic drops, powdered aloe, calomel) when I returned from a lengthy day of administrative meetings; & after re-examining both subjects, initiating a new regimen of doses.

During my absence Brigit was allowed to press cold-wetted cloths against the face of "Mary" (an older female with a hairless, dented head & sunken eyes), & to fan her, to cool her heated skin; of course, Brigit was expressly forbidden to *administer any medication.*

Yet, somehow it happened that, when I returned at the end of the day, it appeared that Subject #1—"Beulah"—had suffered a sudden relapse, even as Subject #2—"Mary"—seemed to have stabilized, to a degree.

This was not what I would have expected, & so I quickly revised my stratagem: I would revert to the original regimen, quinine drops for "Beulah" & no medications at all for "Mary," with the result that "Mary" gradually began to weaken with a renewed fever, even as "Beulah," with a lessened fever, nonetheless weakened as well.

Indeed, as if to spite me, "Beulah" began to convulse, her eyes rolling back into her head.

How unexpected this all was! (Was the illness bilious fever at all? Or something else? *Yellow fever?*) Truly, a bafflement to me.

"This does not seem possible, Brigit. This is not *likely.*"

Very still Brigit stood, though her face was yet more pale than usual, with exhaustion & strain. Clearly, my new young nurse-assistant was exuding girlish "innocence" to hide guilt beneath, like a child who has misbehaved in a parent's absence & is hoping not to be found out.

Whereupon the thought struck me: *Why, Brigit has been "dosing" my patients on her own! The "nurse" has been playing doctor in my Laboratory.*

This charge, Brigit naturally refuted; & seemed to have had no difficulty hearing, from my lips.

Calmly I examined the supply of medications seeking to determine if any had been pilfered.

"Brigit, I see what you have done. Of course, I see: I am no fool."

In truth, I was but bluffing; I had not the faintest idea which medications Brigit might have pilfered, & administered to the experimental subjects; or indeed, if she'd touched any at all.

In the Laboratory, there was a considerable armamentarium of useful medications, with which I intended to experiment, as part of a long-term project; a dazzling array, to the untrained eye, like Brigit's.

Meekly, with quivering eyelids, Brigit stood before me, neither denying nor confirming my accusation; though, seeing the girl so contrite, I relented somewhat, supposing that she was innocent.

"Well. I will overlook your insolence for the time being," I said, sternly, "—but you know, you must know your place."

Hesitantly, Brigit lifted her pale eyes to mine, as if pleading. *Quin-nine. Will you give Mary—?*

How bizarre, such a word as *quinine,* in the subliterate brain of an indentured servant, of Irish extraction!

The stubbornness of the girl was impressive to me, if disagreeable. All this, very surprising.

I could see that, since moving into the Laboratory, with a cot, & a room, of her own, Brigit Kinealy would seem to be *aping* the behavior of the medical staff, where once she had been quite at home with the lowly Asylum workers. The previous day, I had noticed her leafing through a medical journal I had brought into my office, frowning like a schoolgirl—*Was she capable of reading such material?*

I could not imagine that anyone had taught the illiterate Irish orphan how to read, still less how to write, nor could she have attended public school; it must have been, the sharp-witted girl was picking up such knowledge on her own, as a desperate creature will sniff into all the crevices of its surroundings, to learn what it can.

" 'Will I give Mary *quin-nine*?' No, I will not."

As far as I could recall, I *had* resumed the quinine drops for Beulah, but not (yet) for Mary. Yet, as the meetings with my administrative staff which I had attended that afternoon had left me vexed & distracted, I could not be certain of my memory; & there seemed to be no record of this in my notes for the experiment, which were copious, & much annotated.

As it would not do to appear befuddled or forgetful in Brigit's presence I maintained a stern countenance, & would not give in. Though it was beginning to be suspected in medical circles that quinine was helpful in curing fevers involving "heated blood," still I did not like to be ordered about by a girl of the size of my eldest daughter, Florence Nightingale. (So named, in a frolic of exuberance, with the hope, waning now, that this daughter might have wished to study nursing, with the intention of assisting her father one day.)

With astonishing boldness & tenacity, Brigit offered to administer the quinine drops herself to the patients!—but firmly I told her *No.*

"My experimentation follows a definite *plan*. You can see that plan—I have written it down. I am not going to be deflected from that *plan* by impulsive suggestions."

For a moment, Brigit seemed about to protest—then, pursed her lips tightly, & mimed not a word.

"As you are new to the Laboratory, you will soon learn: The Director of the Asylum *will not* be deflected from his master plan."

Next morning, when I arrived at the Laboratory, Subjects #1 & #2 were now near-identical in their condition, a feverish delirium, approaching coma; & there had come into my head, during the night, a brilliant, radical experimental idea: to treat bilious fever, I would *extract infected teeth.*

For had not Medrick Weir confided in me, that *mental illness* was caused by *infection*!

So clearly, this seemed the solution. Already I had treated several excitable female lunatics by extracting their abscessed teeth, which should have been extracted long before, with results that had seemed, on the whole, promising. It was beginning to be believed that ailments as various as gout, hysteria, & many varieties of fever were caused by infections of the jaw & gums; since such infections were near the brain, & blood loss following extraction was a practical sort of phlebotomy.

Thus it occurred to me that Subjects #1 & #2 being now near-identical in their conditions, I might extract teeth from one, but not the other, to make a useful comparison.

Pull teeth, Doctor? Now?—Brigit seemed to be pleading with me, in mute frustration.

"Yes. Fetch the pliers."

Brigit complied, but in a dazed sort of way; assisting me, not nearly so capably as Gretel would have done, but not resisting me, at least.

With some effort, I extracted several badly rotting, yellowed teeth from the gums of Subject #2, "Mary," & dropped them into a tray; it was amusing to see how Brigit stared at these savage-looking teeth, bloody-rooted, giving off a pungent odor.

"Eh, you see, Brigit—these are the teeth of jungle beasts. If they could, they would sink these teeth into *you*."

These extractions resulted in considerable bleeding of the patient's gums, & a general weakening of the patient; while, in the next bed, Subject #1, "Beulah," was observing us, with eyes dilated in horror.

"Brigit, what in God's name have you done now!"—in an instant I was furious, for Brigit had so distracted me, with her wincing, & pursed lips, & facial mannerisms, that exerted a fascination upon me, I had made a stupid blunder: meaning to extract teeth from Beulah, to alleviate convulsions, I had extracted teeth instead from Mary, who was not (yet) convulsing.

"On purpose to humiliate me!"

Brigit gazed at me with such repentant eyes, I had not the heart to further chastise her.

Also, I had no intention of explaining to my assistant that I had confused the patients, who so resembled each other, like most female lunatics of a certain age beyond the attractions of youth, I could scarcely distinguish between them.

By this time there was much bright glistening blood on the patient & in the patient's bed, & on the surrounding floor, which would require considerable cleaning up, before Brigit could feed the other patients in the ward, before stopping to rest for the night; her immediate task was to staunch Mary's bleeding gums, with gauze & bandages, as best she could, & to see that Beulah was comfortable for the night. To both experimental subjects, dosages of belladonna, mercury, & extract of nicotine were recommended, which, I believed, I could entrust Brigit to administer. (But no more quinine! Not for the time being.)

"*You* will deal with them, Brigit. Since *you* have insisted upon having a hand in this, usurping the role of the *M.D.* Good night!"

For truly I was very tired suddenly, & hungry for dinner; our cook would have prepared a roast for the family, with every sort of trimming, which I felt, after the vicissitudes of this long day, I richly deserved.

Later that evening, in my home study, while perusing a recent issue of the *Journal of American Medical Research,* I discovered that extraction of teeth in female patients was recommended for *hysteria,* but not for *convulsions.*

What a blunder! For some minutes I pondered this revelation, stricken with doubt; to calm my nerves, pouring a minute quantity of Scotch whiskey into a glass, to down in a single swallow.

Soon then, Providence consoled me, in a kindly voice: *Do not despair, Silas. Hysteria is indeed a kind of convulsion specific to females.*

·

Unfortunately, very early the next morning Subject #1—"Beulah"—suffered a massive convulsion & ceased breathing; Subject #2—"Mary"—seemed to be stabilized but then, as her badly swollen gums developed infected cysts, preventing her from ingesting even the thinnest liquids, she lapsed gradually into a coma, & expired after several days.

Nonetheless, in drawing up my conclusions, to be published in *The New England Journal of Medicine* the following year, it seemed clear that quinine drops had *significantly reduced fever* in a female mental patient suffering from bilious remittent fever; even as tooth extraction in a similarly ill female suspected of infected gums, without quinine treatment, had had a lesser yet not negligible effect upon reducing fever. In both cases, Saint-John's-wort was recommended as well as quinine, in moderation.

This seminal article, titled "Two Cases of Bilious Remittent Fever in Female Mental Patients: Two Treatments & Their Outcome," would prove to be one of my most popular publications, many times reprinted in American medical journals.

Fever

From *The Chronicle of a Physician's Life*
by Silas Aloysius Weir, M.D.

WHAT! Is the little deaf-mute *malingering* on us, already?"—so I joked to Gretel, for such was my manner, in dealing with female subordinates, to put them at their ease; though, indeed, my blood had *run cold* at this new development, & my teeth fairly chattered with alarm.

For, it seemed, Brigit Kinealy had been stricken overnight with a sudden malaise & a high temperature. Fortunately, Gretel was attending to her, in Brigit's very small but private quarters, when I arrived.

It was heartrending to me, to see my *prize patient,* whose cure had been a point of pride for me, lying so very still on a narrow cot, beneath a thin sheet; shivering, even as her skin burned with fever, though ghastly pale. Nervously I joked to Gretel, I had seen *corpses in the morgue with a healthier skin color than this.* But Gretel seemed scarcely to hear my well-intentioned banter, in her concern for the stricken patient.

Like any good nurse, Gretel had been placing wetted cloths on Brigit's face & chest, to arrest the progress of the fever; also, to keep away flies & mosquitoes, which were a plague in the Laboratory, as through the Asylum generally, along with roaches & rodents.

Very gingerly, I touched the back of my hand against Brigit Kinealy's brow. It was a measure of the patient's illness, she made no reaction, & her bluish, shut eyelids scarcely quivered.

Fever! My first thought was *bilious fever*. (Contracted from my most recent experimental subjects, whose lifeless bodies had been carried out of the Laboratory, by the back stairway, only a few hours before in the still of the previous night.)

In fact, whatever was meant by *bilious fever* in the 1850s was never clear. No doubt, several fevers were conjoined, including *malaria, yellow fever,* & *dengue*. All that "bilious" meant was "bile." Not all of these fevers were contagious, & not all were predictable. Some were lethal, & some were harmless; yet, their initial symptoms were near-identical.

Since I had (evidently) healed the *fistula* in Brigit's bladder, I saw no reason for re-examining that surgery, to spare my fevered patient the ordeal of a pelvic examination, & myself the ordeal of the examiner. I ordered quinine drops to be administered to Brigit, which seemed most sensible; as for *bloodletting*, which most of my physician-colleagues would have prescribed for fever, I hesitated to proceed. Brigit was already in such a weakened state, & the albino tincture of her skin so suggested anemia, I could not think that the fever was caused by an excess of *heated blood*.

"You will be well soon now, Brigit! *Quinine* is the cure—as we have learned from our experiment."

Yet, hours passed, a day & a night, & Brigit's fever did not lessen.

To quinine, I added a dollop of Saint-John's-wort, & powdered belladonna, to quicken the patient's (listless) heartbeat. These medications, Gretel duly administered to the patient.

Still, Brigit did not seem to be improving.

Lying motionless beneath the sheet, scarcely breathing; her eyes shut in so tremulous a way, I imagined that I could see through the thin eyelids, fixing my gaze upon hers.

My Ophelia! I vow, you will not die.

It was touching that, as Gretel was needed elsewhere, other patients in the Laboratory, who were well enough, volunteered to care for Brigit. (Indeed, it should be noted here, how, if they were well enough, the Laboratory patients cared for one another; a feature of female patients in general, that, in dire situations, in which they themselves might well be afflicted, they will set aside their own discomfort, to care for others more in need. Thus it has long been recognized by the medical profession, that females are *natural-born nurses, midwives, & caretakers;* & much of this labor is out of pure charitable instinct, with no need for financial remuneration.)

One of these was a new arrival in the Laboratory whom I had not yet examined, named Nestra, who, despite being in some pain herself, remained with Brigit through much of the day & night, pressing cold-wetted cloths against Brigit's face, when Gretel was not available.

So distracted was I by Brigit's illness, I found it difficult to concentrate on my work elsewhere in the Asylum; for, as Director, I had myriad responsibilities, & could not linger in the Laboratory as I would have wished to, as the attending physician. I did not—yet—wish to call in one of my more experienced staff physicians, with a greater knowledge of fever than I, to examine her; for I did not want more gossip to circulate, regarding my connection with the *indentured-servant deaf-mute* about whom, I had reason to suspect, associates at the Asylum were already whispering.

Vicious tongues! Determined to bring down the new Director, as they had murderously brought down Medrick Weir!

In the wake of the scandalous end of my predecessor, I had vowed to oversee my staff far more assiduously than Medrick had done. Clearly, my kinsman had put his trust in persons who did not warrant it, like the repellent Pell (who had never been discovered by local law enforcement, but was believed to have fled to a western state with ill-gained spoils from Medrick Weir's private safe) & others. My reputation for exacting high standards from my subordinates was such, I made unannounced visits to the more problematic locked wards, where mental patients were particularly vulnerable to mistreatment by staff, & indifferent care from physicians. It had been my statement publicly, when first appointed to the Directorship, that I intended to devote myself wholly to the Asylum, to provide *individual care* for patients, none of whom would be deemed "hopeless"; & to seek & find a *cure for madness,* that would eradicate it utterly, for future generations.

Distracted now by my concern for Brigit, I was not able to concentrate on the chatter of my medical staff; I stared at patients gloomily, with the thought—*Let the lot of them die, if she lives!*

Nor had I patience for my family, particularly Theresa, who seemed less content with her life now, in the Director's spacious house, than she had been in smaller, cramped quarters in Ho-Ho-Kus in bygone years; for she fretted that, in the highest echelon of Trenton society, the wife of a *lunatic-doctor* was not held in high regard, despite the fact of my elevated status. My sons & daughters, too, seemed distant to me, as the children of strangers; as they regarded me uneasily, at a little distance, for I knew that they, too, resented their father's association with *female lunatics.* (No matter that my profession paid for their costly private schooling & other benefits of their pampered lives!) Particularly, since his childish flight from the Laboratory, I had not felt comfortable with my eldest son, Jonathan, nor he with me.

We understand that Death is commonplace; cemeteries are crammed with grave markers, & ever expanding. Yet, a singular death is devastating: so the death of Brigit Kinealy would have been, to me.

"She is still very ill, Doctor," Gretel said quickly, seeing the expression in my face, "—but she is not worse. Her eyes . . ."

Seeing me, her vision not entirely in focus, Brigit tried pitifully to lift her head, to shape words with her pale lips; but was too weak. The cast of her eyes was no longer blue-tinted but somewhat yellow— could this be *jaundice*?

How less attractive the radiant-skinned albino would be, sicklied over with a *urine-hued yellowish cast to her skin.*

With the back of my hand, cautiously I touched Brigit's forehead. Burning-hot, yet strangely clammy.

(Yes, it was most unusual for a physician, to *touch the forehead of a patient,* as a nurse might do; especially, if the patient were an attractive young female.)

With no other option to pursue, I continued the regime of quinine, belladonna, & Saint-John's-wort, to which I added a small dosage of extract of nicotine, to quicken the patient's pulse; though not able to recall whether, in previous experience, such a *quickening* had proved fatal in a fever patient.

"Swallow this, Brigit. You will be well soon—I predict."

But it was with difficulty that Brigit swallowed anything—gagging liquid back up, as she choked & gasped.

Standing in such a way that no one else could see, especially the sharp-eyed Nestra, I removed partway from my coat pocket the little carved dove that Brigit had given me months before; wanting the feverish patient to glimpse it, to lift her heart just a little, that she might recall a time before this illness, & anticipate a time when she would be well again.

"D'you see, Brigit? What I have here?"

But no, Brigit's pale eyes seemed not to see.

It vexed me that Nestra, a commonplace sort of lunatic-slattern, indistinguishable from hundreds of others like herself (long-term residents in the Asylum, abandoned by their families), had attached herself to Brigit, & was tolerated by Gretel; though I encouraged the Laboratory patients to tend to one another, as well as keep their quarters tidy, & provide assistance to me, whenever required. This was but a logical extension of *moral therapy,* which involves the mentally ill in the practical circumstances of their lives, & does not detach them from the normal routine, as, elsewhere in the Asylum, under my supervision, those patients who were capable were doing a good deal of the housekeeping, kitchen & latrine duty, etcetera, thus reducing the Asylum budget.

Not only Nestra, but one or two other Laboratory patients had formed some sort of friendly attachment with Brigit, as with Gretel; it is often the case in such circumstances that the nursing staff may forge attachments with patients, & vice versa, in a way that physicians can scarcely comprehend. It is a matter of some unease, as well as perplexity, among men that women form such attachments, to so little evident purpose, as they do with children not their own.

As Gretel could not always be at Brigit's bedside, it was only practical that Nestra watch over Brigit, volunteering to sleep on the floor beside Brigit's cot, on a blanket removed from her own cot; soon joined by another, huskier & more aggressive female lunatic, improbably named Bathsheba. These two took turns feeding Brigit, or trying to feed her, & moistening her lips with a sponge.

What unattractive creatures, these female lunatics!—both afflicted with *fistula,* unkempt in their (filthy) hospital attire, & hair like rats' nests, unwashed & unbrushed for years.

Nestra was eerily disfigured, with a blind left eye & a deformed spine; a female of about forty, with an unnerving habit of muttering & laughing to herself, as if vastly amused. Yet, Bathsheba was arguably more unattractive, missing her right leg to the knee, & in a habit of lurching & careening about, with a perverse sort of lunatic energy, using a cudgel for a cane. Both women were slated for experimental surgery under my hand within the month, a plan I did not intend to alter.

I wondered if the tender solicitude of these females for Brigit Kinealy was maternal; for, it was noted in their records, both women had had babies in the Asylum that had been taken from them & given up for adoption, with *therapeutic sterilization* following.

Such adoptions, in the days of Medrick Weir, seemed to me of dubious morality; but my board of overseers argued most convincingly that, for the protection of the infant, a newborn must be taken from a lunatic mother. A lunatic asylum is, after all, *not a nursery.*

If, then, adoption into a good Christian family was the practical solution, it was also practical to allow adoptive parents to pay a small fee for the much-desired infant. To that, no one could reasonably object.

That some resentment accrued in the lunatic mother, from whom an infant was forcibly taken, could not be avoided, unfortunately. Especially, the Asylum staff made every effort to keep those female lunatics who had been so deprived from one another's company, to prevent an atmosphere of grievance & mutiny.

On principle, I did not approve of *alliances* between patients, that seemed to divide them from me, their physician.

In the Laboratory, there could be but one Master: a truth so obvious, it scarcely needed to be uttered.

Yet it seemed to me that neither Nestra nor Bathsheba granted me the respect owed one in my position. This, not in any overt way, but subtly, & slyly, as if these brain-damaged individuals believed that I, with my vastly superior intelligence, was not aware of their attitude!

Of the two, it was Bathsheba who seemed the more insolent. A mean little smile played about the savage woman's lips, which were curiously thin & tight against her large discolored front teeth, the only teeth remaining in her jaws following an extraction that had helped to reduce the patient's hysteria, but had clearly not tamed her. Whenever I appeared in the Laboratory, Bathsheba managed to hobble herself into such a position that the shiny stump of her half leg was exposed beneath the ragged hem of her garment, an obscenity which I tried not to notice.

As if *I* had been responsible for the creature losing half her leg! The troublesome female had been delivered to the Asylum many years before, already disfigured, as she was already raving mad. The crude amputation, which looked as if it had been made with an ax, had nothing to do with *me.*

Indeed, it was rare, now that I had shifted my area of specialization to mental diseases, that I amputated any limbs, or digits; specializing in *surgery of the (female) interior*—hysterectomies, ovariectomies, & the like.

Yet how curious it was, & worrisome, that sometimes I seemed to hear in my wake, as I strode through the ward of the sick & impaired awaiting my ministrations, the murmur *Butcher! Red-Handed Butcher!*—but if I turned to stare, not a one of the lunatic females seemed to be gazing in my direction.

Before Brigit's illness I had been intending to enlist Bathsheba in one of my nutrition experiments, in which the subject would subsist on a severely limited diet of greens, grains, & a single cup of water each day, for several months, while undergoing frequent bloodlettings, to see if her "fiery" blood might be controlled in this manner; in addition, seeing that one-legged Bathsheba had learned to hobble deftly about with a cudgel, it whetted my curiosity as a scientist how the subject might adjust if her other leg were also removed to the knee.

(It was not uncommon, to see one-legged individuals; but fairly uncommon, to see individuals missing both legs, who might learn to swing their torsos forward, with the use of crutches. I recalled several amputations of the lower leg, in Dr. Strether's surgery, that required more exertion than surgical skill, in combination with adequate sedation; all of these had been performed on male patients, but I had no doubt, the female femur would be less difficult to detach from the knee than the male. In this experiment, I would be exploring the *adjustment of the physical being* to its altered condition; my theory being that the adjustment would be mental, before it could be physical. For the mysteries of *neurology,* or *brain science,* intrigued me greatly, as a corollary of seeking a cure for madness.)

But for the time being, to my frustration, such revolutionary experiments were in suspension; my only hope was that ambitious rivals would not forge ahead of me!

Annoying, too, that my usually loyal Gretel was behaving strangely of late: wincing with pain as if her joints ached, & often short of breath; evincing anxiety for Brigit, yet somewhat slow-moving, & clumsy, in caring for Brigit; surprisingly negligent of the other patients in the Laboratory & in the adjacent rooms, who were helpless to care for themselves, being shackled to their beds or held fast in the *Bed of Tranquility*, or comatose.

It vexed me that Gretel had begun inquiring of me as to her *legal status in the United States:* for she was but an indentured servant, whose German father had sold her into servitude many years ago, & not a *citizen*.

"But Dr. Weir, do you have a contract for me?—does it have my name on it?"

"Of course, Gretel! Your contract is with us, in safekeeping."

"But—how would they know the name on the contract is *me*?"

"Why, what do you mean, Gretel? Anyone can see, you are *you*." In a joshing manner I spoke to the nervous woman, though I did not like her leaning so close to me, as she exuded a yeasty odor, as of unwashed female flesh.

"My contract—was it for seven years? How many more years remain? Before I am 'free'?"—almost shyly Gretel asked this impudent question, not for the first time.

(*Impudent* because it suggested that my nurse-assistant was not altogether happy with the state of things as they were, but wished that things might be otherwise.)

"Why, Gretel, you are 'free' at the present time. Unlike Bathsheba, you have two legs, & can leave the Asylum whenever you wish—to sleep & starve in the gutters of Trenton, if your throat is not cut by runaway Black slaves beforehand."

Confusedly, Gretel smiled as if not sure whether my remark was meant to be mere banter, or a warning.

"But if I left, Dr. Weir, *I* would be a 'runaway.' They would hunt me down, like a dog."

Such bitterness was surprising to me, & distasteful, in one whom I had long trusted; I had to wonder if it might be a symptom of imminent mental illness in Gretel.

It was a newly forming theory of mine: Since madness is caused by infections, & infections are contagious, *madness might be contagious in the Asylum.*

"Why, I would not let anyone hunt you down, Gretel—'like a dog.' So long as you are *my dog*, I will protect you."

This, with a joshing sort of laughter, to put the woman at ease; & to encourage her to return to her responsibilities in the Laboratory, where she was greatly needed.

Following this exchange, Gretel did seem to come to her senses, & ceased asking impudent questions. With renewed diligence, she returned to the sick & infirm in the Laboratory; tending to Brigit as to a beloved daughter, preparing herbal teas for her, & wiping down her clammy body with sponges. It was gratifying to me, that Gretel as a caretaker temporarily banished Nestra & Bathsheba.

Herbal teas? It was necessary that the fever-patient drink nutritious liquids, or she would waste away & die; yet, I had to wonder if Gretel's herbal teas constituted a kind of medication, unauthorized by me, the attending physician; for, without my knowledge, the canny midwife had cultivated an herbal garden at the rear of North Hall, an area of the Asylum grounds neglected by groundskeepers & allowed to flourish in tall grasses, thistles, & wild rose. Among Gretel's herbs were sage, chamomile, peppermint, & rose hip—a veritable witches' brew!

At times, as I approached the closet-sized room where Brigit lay on her cot, I could hear Gretel singing softly to her, as a mother might sing a lullaby to a sick child; the words were not audible, or intelligible, yet evoked a strange sort of beauty, ceasing as I drew near; as the shadow of a cloud might fall across a bright landscape.

> *Wollst endlich sonder Grämen*
> *Aus dieser Welt uns nehmen*
> *Durch einen sanften Tod!*
> *Und, wenn du uns genommen,*
> *Laß uns in Himmel kommen,*
> *Du unser Herr und unser Gott!*

I wondered if this might be a heathenish sort of music. Sweetly seductive, but of the Devil. The more intensely I listened, the less I could *hear*.

At times, I seemed to hear the midwife's voice, wafting, in the stillness of night, into my study, on the first floor of the Director's residence; though it was some distance between my private residence & North Hall, across the overgrown stretch of Asylum grounds. For often of late I spent the entire night in this room, working by lamplight, taking notes on my experiments & planning a succession of experiments for the future, as a General sits up through the night sleepless, plotting a military campaign, while his soldiers sleep unheeding outside his tent, the heavy sleep of animal innocence & oblivion. When at last I did succumb to sleep, it was on the massive leather couch that my kinsman Medrick Weir had purchased, in happier days before his martyrdom at the hands of his enemies destroyed him.

This, a soothing sleep, preferable to climbing the stairs to the master bedroom to slip into the high four-poster bed beside my dear wife, whose slumber I did not wish to disturb.

"Dr. Weir?"—Gretel called to me, in an abashed voice, as I stood at the threshold of the door to Brigit's room, "—you are with us early today . . ."

"Yes, of course—I am *here*. Where else would I be?"

I was irritated by the woman's bovine stare, & spoke coldly.

With a stoic demeanor I approached Brigit's cot. A physician becomes frightened of his patient, at such times; but a physician dare never show weakness.

You cannot fail me, dear Brigit, by dying! God would not allow this.

If God allows this, there is no God . . .

I feared that Brigit's pale eyes would close & never again open; never again would I see Brigit's soul shining in them; never again, the deaf-mute's adoration of *me*.

Gretel had been sponge-bathing Brigit in a soothing, languorous manner, but now, seeing me, made a quick move to cover the girl's slender shoulders & breasts. Though I had looked immediately away, yet the after-image of the pale breasts with dark, berrylike nipples, shimmered against my eyelids, & made me feel faint. For the nakedness of any female apart from his wife is naturally repugnant, to the decent, Christian husband.

Also, the sight of the sponge in Gretel's fingers was disturbing to my eye, as it had been a new, clean sponge brought into the Laboratory by my own hand, for Gretel's use with Brigit, but it was now as badly stained as one of the older sponges.

Why this sight was so *disturbing* to me, I could not have said.

"Dr. Weir?—I have been giving Brigit the medications you prescribed, as well as the fluids. But—you can see—there has been little change in the patient . . ."

Little change! This was not the news I wished for; but it was not so upsetting as it might have been.

Then, to my consternation Gretel added, with a brash sort of timidity: "Did *you* do something to Brigit, Dr. Weir? With the heated forceps—"

"Gretel! What on earth do you mean, 'Did I *do* something to Brigit'—of course, as a surgeon, I *did something* to my patient. It would be very strange if I had not."

I must confess, I was somewhat stunned at this latest impertinence from Gretel. For a mere midwife, & not even a trained nurse, to question a physician in so blunt a way, that might be overheard by others—this was quite unheard-of.

Nor did I like the way Gretel regarded me as if she knew how I had been listening to her singing to Brigit, here in the Laboratory; & also in the night: a pagan sort of music, as wild thoughts rushed through my brain like great bruised clouds on a windy night.

With scarcely disguised sarcasm, I explained to the dolt of a female, as I had previously explained, that Brigit had *recovered completely from the recent surgery.* "But now, this damned bilious fever has complicated her recovery . . ."

Suddenly, the realization came to me: *The sponge! I had forgotten to remove the sponge from Brigit's bladder.*

A tiny fragment of a sponge, which I had left at the base of the sutured bladder . . . intended to be removed within forty-eight hours; yet, somehow I had totally forgotten it, for fourteen days.

So shocked was I by this realization, so mortified, I did not pause to consider how I might preserve my pride, but blurted out to Gretel what I had done: what I had forgotten to do; & how, very likely, it was the foreign matter inside Brigit that was causing the infection, not bilious fever!

In Gretel's face, a flush of something like indignation, dismay.

Yet, (to my shame, I record this) not altogether surprise.

"A sponge! Yes! We must act quickly, Doctor! Before it is too late."

Immediately then, with tremulous hands, & with Gretel's help, I examined the near-comatose patient with the spoon-speculum, awkwardly positioning her on hands & knees, in bright sunshine, so that I could see, with appalled eyes, that indeed, the minuscule sponge was still lodged inside the patient, at the base of the bladder, brackish-dark with urine, filthy & festering . . .

God, forgive me! I had come close to murdering my most prized patient!

This filth-saturated bit of sponge, I removed with tweezers, but in so doing must have nicked a small vein in the lining of the bladder, as blood began to flow out of Brigit, at first in a trickle, then more copiously.

It was unlike her—unlike any professional medical worker—to give a small stifled shriek like a wounded parrot, as Gretel did; commanding me to sew up the wound, quickly staunch the blood, if I could.

Commanding me! Yet, in the exigency of the moment, I did not hesitate but follow Gretel's instructions; only when my clumsy hands fumbled did Gretel snatch the needle from me, & mend the little wound herself.

If only a woman could be a *surgeon,* how much more merciful for the patient!

Indeed, if a woman like Gretel could be allowed to execute such tasks, with her practiced eye & deft hands!—but that could never be, any woman wielding a scalpel, let alone an illiterate immigrant female.

At last Brigit lay in repose breathing more evenly as Gretel fanned her face, & soothed her with one of her lullabies, unintelligible to my ears—*Wollst endlich sonder Grämen, Aus dieser Welt* . . .

The filthy bit of sponge, the very emblem of my shame, I quickly disposed of in a container of pestiferous waste, & washed my hands ferociously afterward.

Day of Triumph

APRIL 28, 1854

FROM *THE CHRONICLE OF A PHYSICIAN'S LIFE*
BY SILAS ALOYSIUS WEIR, M.D.

QUIETLY I explained to Gretel that I would have discovered the sponge myself shortly—"Since I was planning to examine Brigit's suture."

To this, Gretel mutely conceded: *Yes, Dr. Weir.*

So grateful were we that our most prized patient was beginning at last to recover, my nurse-assistant & I did not pursue petty disagreements.

It would require some time for Brigit to recover from the near-fatal infection, & regain the weight she had lost; nor did she sleep easily, being prone to disturbing dreams. To her chagrin, her old *fistula*-ailment had begun again, with a slow leakage from her bowels, causing pain as well as mortification.

So it was, Brigit avoided the Laboratory, where she had so enjoyed her promotion to nurse-assistant to the Director of the Asylum; & returned to her old work-place, in the cellar of the Asylum. For one so incapacitated, no matter how frequently & how desperately she washed herself, it was not possible to be a medical worker.

Avoiding me, as by chance I encountered her outside North Hall. Out of her old shame, fleeing, as a pariah.

"Brigit?"—I called pleadingly after her; but she paid me no heed, shrinking away like a wraith into the twilight.

"Dr. Weir! I had a most amazing dream last night, that Jesus appeared before me in spotless white robes & in His hand was a 'thread' that could not break or rot—*wire*."

At the Laboratory entrance Gretel awaited me, ruddy-cheeked, smiling a wide gap-toothed smile. For a moment I could not think how to reply—an indentured servant at the Asylum, daring to dream of *me*!

Seeing my astounded expression Gretel more discreetly repeated her words, in a less exuberant tone.

Wire? What was the woman saying? Threading with—*wire*?

"If you mean repairing a *fistula* with wire, Gretel—it would be too thick, for such a small tear. There would be no way a surgeon could 'thread' wire through a needle, then through a patient's bladder, without destroying the organ."

"Some kind of very thin metal, Doctor," Gretel persisted, "—like silver. I have heard, watchmakers have *silver wire*."

"I am sure that there is not *silver wire*, Gretel. You have been dreaming."

"But, Dr. Weir—"

"No. *Ridiculous*."

Yet the notion lodged deep in my imagination, that there might indeed be a very thin, but strong, wire, to take the place of thread, that might be used surgically. I inquired among persons of my acquaintance, who seemed not to think that *silver wire* was an impossibility, as I had thought it; indeed, it was Theresa who suggested that I visit a prominent Trenton watchmaker, who might be of assistance.

Ah, a watchmaker! Of course: Watches are so very finely constructed.

So it was, I visited one Erasmus Tunney—said to be the preeminent watchmaker in New Jersey—inquiring of him if he could fashion for me a length of very thin silver wire: which was not so difficult after all.

Returning then, next morning, to the Laboratory, with a length of the finest silver wire, of an astonishing thinness—with which I shortly sutured the tiny wound at the base of my patient's bladder!—in this, the *dozenth surgery* undergone by Brigit, at my hand: the one that would prove historic.

The reader will understand how ignorant, & how cruel it is, for detractors to focus upon the number of surgeries Brigit Kinealy underwent at my hand: for each of the surgeries was a sincere attempt to cure the afflicted girl, & only after these numerous failures could a successful surgery be performed.

By this time it was not surprising that Brigit herself had become resigned to never being cured of the *fistula*. Despite Gretel's encouragement, & mine, it was piteous to see how melancholy the poor girl was, like a creature that has turned its face to the wall.

"Brigit! You must have faith. *This* treatment will be the last."

Always I would recall how Gretel managed to thread a needle with silver wire, not without difficulty; how with prayers uttered by both Gretel & me, Providence guided my hand. Once again, with the spoon-speculum I gained entry to the infected area; once again, with Gretel's assistance, I mended the minuscule tear in the bladder—this time, the suture would be *permanent*.

Of course, we could not know this at the time—that silver wire would prove to be *the* cure, after so many failures; & Silas Aloysius Weir would be guaranteed a place in the pantheon of American medical pioneers.

So it happened that days would pass, without leakage from the bladder, not even a trace of bloody urine.

A week passed, with no (event) infection.

The suture appeared to be holding! Each day was fraught with anxiety, yet—each day proved a triumph.

I took copious notes in my journal. I prayed to God, to have mercy on us & reward us for our zeal at last. Meekly I vowed, I would dedicate myself to the salvation of all females so afflicted, as well as female lunatics. *I would be a medical Savior, should Providence continue to guide my hand.*

After four weeks it appeared that the patient might be permanently healed, as the natural process of excretion had resumed; & the subject was strong enough to return to the Laboratory, as my nurse-assistant.

Thus, a miracle: a cure for *fistula,* at last!

Which results would be published in the article to become the most acclaimed of my career, "On the Repair of Vesicovaginal Fistula in a Young Irish Mother," in the *Journal of American Medical Science,* November 1854.

The Gift

FROM *LOST GIRL, FOUND: AN ORPHAN'S TRUE STORY
TOLD BY HERSELF* BY BRIGIT AGNES KINEALY

*I*T IS TRUE, *I owe my life to Silas Aloysius Weir.*
It is also true, Silas Aloysius Weir was a butcher of girls & women.
This contradiction, it is not possible to explain.
*This contradiction, I must accept, as I must accept my life, in grati-
tude for the life itself, the divine gift that eludes comprehension.*

IV

Red-Handed Butcher

God's Chosen

1854–1861

FROM *The Chronicle of a Physician's Life*
BY SILAS ALOYSIUS WEIR, M.D.

NOW INDEED, the *sacred monomania* consumed me.

In the years following this initial triumph & well into the spring of the fateful year 1861, when Providence smote me a blow from which I would never fully recover, it would have seemed to me, as to all who knew me, that God had blessed me with His very hand guiding mine, unerring.

Silas, surely you are one of My sons, in whom I am well pleased.

It seemed only natural, that Providence was granting me the freedom that must be granted to genius, to experiment where I would, with the goal of advancing human knowledge, & benefiting humankind.

Admittedly, it is a relatively small world—*gynecology*. I could not even recall why fate had led me thus! Yet, a man's fate is *his*.

It is a generally loathed & avoided specialty—*gynecology*. Unlike the more elevated medical care which my brother Franklin chose to pursue in his Beacon Street bastion, amid wealthy Bostonians; the result being, my brother Franklin would perish in obscurity, as a rich clinician, who had contributed naught to medical science as his younger brother Silas would contribute.

Very soon then, in 1854, it was known that Silas Aloysius Weir, Director of the New Jersey State Asylum for Female Lunatics at Trenton, had discovered an *unfailing technique* for the repair of *fistulas* in afflicted females; or, more generally, for repairing minuscule tears in inner organs of patients of either sex.

In articles for the most prominent medical journals, I would report on the phenomenon of *reducing mental illness,* through such repairs to afflicted females; in addressing medical gatherings, to which I began to be invited, I would speculate that *mental illness* in American females would be reduced by as much as eighty percent, as the practice of this procedure spread through the country—"As no physician-surgeon can patent his discovery, as inventors of the most trivial gadgets can patent theirs, I bequeath, to all of you, the boon of *silver wire,* to save the lives of the afflicted among us."

(So I was likely to conclude my talks, to boisterous applause.)

For some months at the Laboratory, in the wake of my success with "the young Irish mother," as Brigit Kinealy was to be identified in medical history, I continued to experiment with *silver wire,* repairing *fistulas* in several female lunatics under my care; as it had become a procedure which I could perform with a certain degree of skill, provided Gretel assisted me in positioning the patient, & assuaging her fears. Thus, *fistula* repair soon began to lose its appeal for me, as it was now a mechanical procedure any capable surgeon could perform.

Even then, there was some resistance to my procedure, for it is the way of physicians & surgeons to be skeptical at first, & conservative in their attitudes toward revolutionary developments; so, too, with subsequent experiments of mine, no matter how self-evident, there would be sporadic pockets of resistance, & these often among the more "elite" of my colleagues in places like Boston, Philadelphia, & New York City, in their disdain for the plebians of *Trenton, New Jersey.*

Here follows, for the layman versed in the fundamentals of science, & with an interest in the advancement of science-knowledge, a selected miscellany of my major experiments in the Laboratory at Trenton, on the basis of which Silas Aloysius Weir, M.D., was elected to the National Academy of Medicine, & the American Association of Medical Practitioners, as well as the National Institute of Science, in addition to being a perennial candidate for Director of the United States Department of Health & Chief Medical Adviser to the President of the United States.

Including, in the final years of my father's life, the admiration &

blessing of Percival Weir, who had so long withheld his acknowledgment of my achievements, as he had withheld his love. *My dear son, I am proud of you at last. Even if the President has yet to choose you as Chief Medical Adviser.*

CASE STUDY: HARELIP REPAIR IN A THIRTY-SEVEN-YEAR-OLD FEMALE LUNATIC (1854)

It had always intrigued me whether such deformities as harelips, club-feet, cleft-palates, crossed eyes, & the like, believed to be caused at birth by careless midwives, were a mere sign of mental illness, or a consequence; or had no relationship at all.

And so, if repaired, would the mental illness be alleviated, or cured, or neither?

If the patient were not only mentally ill but of a reduced intelligence, would the repair allow for the emergence of a higher intelligence? As the patient's brain could not help but be affected by deformities of the skull, so if the skull-bones were realigned, would the brain expand more normally? Questions which no one asked—except Silas Aloysius Weir.

God Himself seemed to promise me: *If you have repaired fistula, My son, you can certainly repair mere harelips!*

In this type of surgery, which might be called *cosmetic,* as it is *superficial,* it seemed likely that a successful procedure for correction could not fail to be financially rewarding; as many disappointed parents of the deformed would eagerly pay a high price to have their offspring rendered *normal,* & not go through life as *freaks of nature,* embarrassing to all of the family.

"Zenobia D__" seemed a most promising specimen, a female lunatic of thirty-seven years of age, exhibiting a (minor) birth defect of the upper lip accounting for garbled, incoherent speech. Though Zenobia could not speak to be understood by most persons, yet she appeared to be of average intelligence, although markedly willful, & "difficult."

It was reported that since the age of nine, Zenobia had toiled in a Trenton granary, to help support her large family; with the result that Zenobia's lungs had been affected by airborne grains of wheat, causing her breathing to become hoarse & labored. She was susceptible to respiratory infections, & an inflamed pelvic region seemed to indicate forcible assaults of divers kinds, as well as numerous pregnancies; with a diagnosed syphilitic infection, sporadically treated with tincture of mercury.

Through most of her life a reliable worker in the granary, Zenobia had suffered some sort of collapse in her early thirties, following an accident in which her right hand had become mangled, & her overall health diminished; given to fits of weeping, laughing, & raving, Zenobia was dismissed from the granary, & committed to the Asylum at Trenton by her relatives, out of impatience & exasperation with her.

As I had long been eager to develop a surgical procedure to correct harelip—(as well as crossed eyes, cleft-palates, club-feet, & deformities of the skull)—the arrival of Zenobia in the Laboratory was most fortuitous. I had recently acquired at auction several surgical instruments formerly owned by a Philadelphia surgeon, for facial use, with which I was keen to experiment.

Zenobia D__ was, like others in the Laboratory, in so weakened a state of health, & generally demoralized when she arrived, as, Gretel reported to me, all of her five or six children had either died or had been taken from her; subsequently, Zenobia was too weary to offer any resistance to surgery, & may even have consented, in her wish to be *cured* of whatever it was, that had imprisoned her in the Asylum.

Like many of the female lunatics in my care, Zenobia was not predictable in her moods: She might appear to be near-lucid, but soon flare up in bursts of rage or despair, requiring restraint; then again she might weep, & plead with the staff in her garbled way, that *one of the doctors* should help her, for otherwise she had no hope, & did not wish to live. Naturally, the unhappy woman was chided for expressing such a blasphemous thought; & it was promised to her that Silas Weir, the Director of the Asylum himself, would *do what he could* to restore her to some modicum of health, that she might return to the Trenton granary to earn her own keep & not persist on the charity of taxpayers.

Hearing this, Zenobia laughed, sadly & wistfully, as if such a hope were beyond reason, provoking a twitch of the disfigured upper lip.

Not surprisingly, my younger nurse-assistant Brigit showed signs of sympathy with the harelip Zenobia, as the woman's garbled speech made her a sister, of sorts, to the albino deaf-mute; often in the ward

I would see Brigit lingering by Zenobia's cot, head inclined as she listened to the patient's gibberish, with a flattering sort of comprehension. When I inquired of Gretel whether Brigit really understood Zenobia, or only wished to give that impression to assure the harelip-female that she was *not alone*, Gretel replied, "You will have to ask Brigit, Dr. Weir. Only she can reveal what is in her heart."

As we prepared for the harelip surgery, positioning the frightened patient on a table, to which she would be strapped for her own protection, I could see that Brigit appeared uneasy, as if she had something to ask of me; & waited for her to appeal to me, without my intercession.

Finally turning to me, lifting her pale eyes to mine, hesitantly. *Doctor, I think . . .*

No one else could hear Brigit, as Brigit's silent speech was addressed only to me. So it may have surprised Gretel, or any onlooker, when I replied to Brigit: "Brigit, *no*. You *do not think*. That is not your task."

In a lighthearted tone I addressed Brigit, for I found it amusing, rather more than offensive, that this slip of a girl, of the size of my youngest daughter, so often dared to *proffer medical advice to me,* beyond what Gretel might have dared.

"It is *my task* to think, Brigit. It is *your task* to 'assist.' "

No doubt it was an inevitable consequence of the propinquity of physician & nurse-assistant in such close quarters, as well as a passage of time, now several months, that allowed Brigit to imagine that she might address me as she was daring to do now; miming Zenobia's respiratory condition by tapping at her own chest, & coughing; then, with certain gestures of both hands, miming the inflammation in Zenobia's lower body, that (possibly) meant an (undiagnosed) *fistula;* communicating to me, in such a way, her notion that, of Zenobia's various ailments, the harelip was not so crucial to treat first.

At this, I was doubly annoyed: for the correction of harelip seemed to me more crucial, as it was *visible* to the naked eye; & indeed the prospect of examining, with the spoon-speculum, another female likely afflicted with a raw *fistula*, did not appeal to me. (I might have appealed to God Himself, to spare me any more female *posteriors* for the time being; I had toiled in that particular vineyard for too many years, it seemed to me. Nor was Zenobia at all attractive, as a female into whose *nether region* one might wish to peer.)

Nonetheless, Brigit persisted, pointing to her own mouth, & shaping words in an exaggerated way, as if addressing a deaf person; what I gleaned of this was that Zenobia had lived all her life with a harelip, & could continue that way, as the harelip did not endanger her life, like the condition of her lungs & lower body, which might prove fatal.

"You seem not to realize, Brigit, because you are 'deaf', or claim to be 'deaf', that Zenobia's speech is garbled, & causes her great distress, as well as annoying the people around her, who have to listen to her babbling like a baboon."

Almost, I could hear Brigit laugh in derision: *Baboon! Have you ever heard a baboon, Dr. Weir?*

"Yes! I have heard many human baboons, my dear girl. Chittering & chattering."

We can understand Zenobia, Doctor. You just have to listen.

"Ridiculous! Only another freak could begin to understand what this woman is saying."

If Zenobia can understand what is said to her, what difference does it matter, that she can't speak to them? She has little to say, that they would want to hear. But if her lungs are weak, & her blood is poisoned—

"If her blood is 'poisoned', Brigit, it has been 'poisoned' for a long time. A little while longer will not matter."

But, Dr. Weir—

"No more, Brigit! Either you will be still, like Gretel, or you will be banished to—you know where."

At this, Brigit was suddenly contrite. The threat of *you know where* had the immediate effect of dampening the girl's impertinence.

(When Brigit was behaving childishly, challenging my judgment, neglecting to help Gretel as I wished her to, forgetting *her place,* she was banished to confinement in one of the storage rooms at the rear of the Laboratory, called by the staff the *cadaver room,* where pestiferous waste materials were stored, including even, occasionally, for expediency's sake, the bodies of patients who had expired, & were awaiting the arrival of the Asylum gravedigger to quietly cart them away for burial. This seemed to me sufficient punishment, for an indentured servant with a dread of corpses; rather than manual punishment, blows with fist or cudgel, or whipping, that were deemed more appropriate for male servants at the Asylum & which, as a reformer, I was attempting to banish from the facility.)

With Brigit's nonsensical mimings silenced, I was able to examine Zenobia's upper lip soberly. The surgery would have to be as delicate as a *fistula* repair, but, fortunately, it could be much more easily executed, & free of the repulsiveness of those surgeries; though there was another sort of discomfort in working at such close quarters with the patient, having to inhale her breath, that smelled of the ashy taint of panic, & having to withstand the female lunatic's very *nearness*, that roused me to extreme unease.

Though I had, in the course of my career of many years now, stitched together numerous lacerations on various parts of the human body, including deep wounds flush with blood, in which bone was exposed, I had had little experience with what might be called *facial surgery*, with its more precise requirements.

As no one on my staff was trained in such a specialty, & I did not like to consult with another surgeon, I was beginning to acknowledge that this might be a new & challenging area of surgery for me. I could see clearly what was required: cutting into the cleft running from the patient's upper lip to the base of her nose with my (newly acquired, razor-sharp) scalpel, which I was eager to use; a forcible (manual) realignment of tissues; stitching up the wound with a thread (silk) sturdy enough to keep it closed, but not so coarse as to cause scarring.

Indeed, the cleft was very narrow, resembling the interior of a third nostril; I was sure that, when it was stitched together & healed, it would "grow together," leaving scarcely a scar.

Already I could envision a pictorial representation of the harelip, which I would undertake to draw myself, or enlist Brigit in drawing for me, to accompany my article for the popular *Harper's Weekly:* "Before Harelip Surgery/After Harelip Surgery."

With the assistance of both Gretel & Brigit, the patient was secured to the table; yet had begun to shudder & quiver, in anticipation of the scalpel. Sternly I reprimanded Zenobia, reminding her that she had, indeed, requested this surgery, to correct her disfigured face; & that I was doing a favor for her, a selfless act bringing with it no reward for me. In her garbled speech Zenobia muttered that she would *lie very still.*

"You had better, Zenobia! If you do not, the scalpel may slip, & you will not have one harelip, but *two.*"

This warning had the effect upon all three females, of silencing them, most gratifyingly.

However, it was disconcerting that, as I peered more closely at the disfigured upper lip, I could see that the lurid fissure was more than just a superficial cleft, but seemed to continue grotesquely *inside the mouth.* I had not examined the patient thoroughly until now & was dismayed to discover an *actual hole* in the roof of the mouth, of the size of a grape!

Where the exterior cleft was disfiguring, yet a familiar sight, this *interior hole* was terrifying to behold. A fainting sensation rose in me, & my legs grew weak, for there was something in this hellish vision to suggest the *nether regions* of the female, which I had avoided examining.

In dread that either of my assistants would guess at my surprise & alarm at this new development, I gripped the edge of the table to steady myself, & said not a word. The thought came to me, as it had often when I had been a young doctor—*God help me! I have no idea what to do. Yet, I must do it.*

It would be unseemly for a physician to reveal such ignorance in the company of female subordinates; I could only imagine how they would whisper of me, behind my back in the Asylum, & elsewhere.

Of all things a physician most resents, & is infuriated by, it is baseless slander & libel pertaining to his integrity as a physician.

Seeing from the expressions on both Brigit's & Gretel's faces a sort of appalled impassivity, I realized that both assistants would have liked to ask of me to administer some sort of painkiller to the patient; but as I had expressly forbidden advice, they dared not.

A game of bluff—was it? I had not considered the harelip surgery to be serious enough to require sedation, calculating that it would take only about ten or fifteen minutes; now, I wondered if morphine drops might be a reasonable idea, since I did not trust the leather straps, nor the promise of the patient to lie still, & not thrash & scream like a maniac.

As my scalpel hovered above Zenobia's stiffened face, tremulous in my right hand, the patient whimpered, & shivered; which vexed me mightily, for *I could not bear to be distracted.*

"I have warned you, Zenobia: Do not move!"

Zenobia shut her eyes, & steeled herself for the scalpel; even as, by her side, Brigit stood in a most strained posture, regarding me fixedly as if she had something urgent to say, yet was not saying it.

"Yes, Brigit: What is it?"—in exasperation turning to the white-skinned girl & seeing in her hand a beaker of—was it morphine drops?

"*You*, Brigit: What are you suggesting?"

Meekly, mutely, Brigit lifted the beaker, as if not precisely offering it to me, only just identifying it.

"So, now, *you* are prescribing 'anesthesia'—is that it? *You?*" Laughing irritably, I turned to Gretel: "And *you?*"

But canny Gretel remained impassive, neutral. Her acquiescence was so impartial, I could not determine its meaning. (Yet, when I reconsidered this scene, later that evening, I would realize that *of course, Gretel had surreptitiously handed the beaker to Brigit,* with the supposition that Brigit, rather than herself, would be more persuasive with me.)

"Very well, then! It can do no harm, I suppose."

Sighing loudly, to indicate how I was but humoring female foolishness, I took the beaker roughly from Brigit, forcibly opened the patient's mouth & shook out a small quantity of liquid morphine into it; which caused Zenobia to cough & choke, as she was hesitant to swallow at first. For it was believed among the superstitious Asylum patients that such medications put the subject into so deep a sleep, there was no return from it.

"There! Ridiculous. As if this were not *very minor* surgery."

Awaiting the morphine drops to take effect on Zenobia, I left the operating table, with no explanation to my assistants staring after me, to retreat to my office, where, though it was somewhat early in the day, I took several therapeutic swallows of Scotch whiskey, to fortify my nerves; & to proffer a murmured prayer to God the Father, my Benefactor; in a vexed mood, having allowed my nurse-assistants to coerce me into behavior of a kind I could not countenance, as *coddling.*

When I returned, it was to find both my nurse-assistants looking abashed, if not contrite. The patient had lapsed into a gross sort of unconsciousness, a disconcerting sight, for this female lunatic was most unattractive, her eyelids but thinly shut, her mouth drooping open, so that, by stooping to peer inside, I could see the grape-sized hole in the roof of her mouth. How on earth had the poor woman lived, from childhood, with such a deformity! If such a birth had been Theresa's, & the baby puny & undersized, I should not have made any great effort to keep it alive, God help me!

In medical school we had stared at such freaks of nature illustrated in our textbooks, shuddering in revulsion, & a wild sort of hilarity, at something called a *cleft-palate;* such aberrations had to be marks of lower-class debauchery, & would rarely be found in families of reputable background. It would not have occurred to me that, one day, I would be obliged to attempt to "repair" such a horror, in a slatternly female lunatic of all persons, with but slatternly females as witnesses.

With Brigit & Gretel looking on, with rapt expressions, I proceeded with the surgery: The first incision, in the patient's upper lip, was hesitant; the second, more forceful.

At once, blood began to flow, running down the side of the patient's mouth, like glistening-red tusks, which should not have been a surprise to me, yet was; for there is something about bleeding from the mouth which is particularly disconcerting to observe. Something of my old queasiness at the sight of blood stirred in me even as my nurse-assistants deftly wiped away blood with rags, allowing me to proceed.

Ah, my hand did tremble!—just slightly.

For a panicked moment, it looked as if Zenobia were about to wake suddenly, screaming in pain & indignation; but instead she only quivered, & shuddered, panting loudly, like a beast; but not otherwise resisting.

A third incision, & a fourth. My hand grew steadier. A consoling voice came to me—*You are one of My sons, in whom I am well pleased. All that you do, Silas, is ordained.*

Opening the exterior cleft more deeply, cutting now into the patient's upper gum, I calculated how the two (clefted) parts might be brought together; it had often seemed to me, as a surgeon, that indeed Providence guided my hand, so that my deployment of the scalpel was *intuitive, inspired.* So now, with the (bloody, slippery) fingers of both hands, I struggled to bring the flaps of skin together, wondering if I had cut too deeply; deftly Brigit came to my assistance, securing the site of the wound while I worked with the needle as best as I could, holding my breath against the foul breath of the patient, in the hope of completing the operation before she awakened.

No, I did not touch the hole in the roof of the patient's mouth. My reasoning was that this freakish feature had little to do with the exterior cleft, as it could not be seen; presumably no one except Zenobia knew about it.

If Zenobia had lived with this disfigurement her entire life, why meddle with it now?

There was no need for haste: Zenobia did not awaken until hours later, sometime in the night, it seemed, while Brigit kept watch by the patient's bedside, changing gauze bandages as they became saturated with blood.

The following day, it seemed to my critical eye that my stitches were very expertly executed, in the patient's face; & so it was curious how neither Brigit nor Gretel praised me for the procedure, but moved about somber-faced, & eyes avoiding mine.

Had I forbidden my nurse-assistants to speak, the previous day? Had I hurt their feelings, by *scolding*? How childish their behavior, now.

As the *harelip repair* had seemed, to me, very skillfully rendered, with a minimum of bleeding & bruising, it was something of a surprise when, after twelve days, the stitches were removed by Gretel, & it was revealed that the harelip had not exactly healed but had been replaced by a curious cleft of flesh: not a modest fissure as before but a growth, with a serrated edge, of about an inch in height, so that Zenobia now resembled, not a hare, but some species of wild boar with a single miniature tusk on one side of her face!

Brigit, who for twelve days had been dutifully tending to Zenobia's surgical wound, keeping it moist with ointment of aloe, & pressing cold cloths against Zenobia's face to reduce swelling, & all the while brushing away noisome flies, mosquitoes, & gnats, now frowned at me, with the slyest hint of adolescent sarcasm as if to say—*Dr. Weir!— well done.*

Irritably, I said, as if the brattish girl had spoken aloud, "Yes, it is *well done.* The surgeon has *done something,* not nothing. It is very easy to criticize, on the part of the ignorant & uninformed."

In her way of impertinent silent speech the deaf-mute communicated to me—*At least, Zenobia does not look like a hare any longer.*

This rude remark, I did not indicate I had heard; for an insolent deaf-mute is silenced, if her listener declines to hear.

The patient, who had been, for twelve days, compulsively feeling the stitching in the wound with inquisitive fingers, was not so surprised, perhaps, at the outcome; as if indeed, with the air of melancholy resignation that is the predominant emotion of the Asylum inmate, rather than outright mania, she had expected nothing better, ending up finally with a tusk-like growth in her face more disfiguring than the original harelip.

As I stood at Zenobia's bedside, uncertain what to say, but inclined to speak in a jolly manner, as one does with patients to put them at ease, I saw that Zenobia's eyes were sunken & bruised & yet intelligent, & alert; though she did not lift them to me with anything like gratitude.

This, I resolved to ignore, speaking cheerfully, asking the patient how she felt; & stooping to hear her muttered, garbled speech—no different from what it had been before the surgery.

"Is that so, Zenobia! Ah, I am happy to hear that."

Undaunted, I spoke in a loud voice, that others in the ward, as well as my nurse-assistants, might overhear.

"As to your other medical problems, Zenobia, do not fret. We will cure them in time—I, or another doctor on our staff. This, I promise!"

This pioneering surgery I would describe in great detail in my major article "Surgical Correction of 'Harelip' in a Mature Female," published in the *Journal of the Association of American Physicians and Surgeons,* Winter 1855, & many times reprinted.

CASE STUDY: MANIA, EPILEPSY, & "HEARING VOICES" IN A MATURE FEMALE LUNATIC: TREATMENT & CURE
(1855)

Let us call her "Mahala H__": of a particular swarthy coarseness, as in the crude physiology of certain races of southern Europe, as distinct from the lighter-skinned Protestant north; in age somewhere beyond thirty; stout-bodied, with short muscled legs & swollen ankles; prognathic jaw, recessed pig-eyes; "jittery" nerves; shivering, shaking, (occasional) convulsing; painful pelvic region/suspected (undiagnosed) *fistula;* interludes of mania, hysteria alternating with muteness, catatonia; refusal to speak save in menacing mutters & growls; badly scarred back & thighs, incompletely healed & partly infected, possible evidence of having been *whipped.*

By a rare coincidence, Mahala was an indentured servant previously contracted to the Hermitage, in Ho-Ho-Kus; where, I suspect, she had been whipped, very likely by one of the brute foremen whom I had known there; following her banishment from that community, she was employed as a mill-worker in Trenton, also with disastrous results, for, in response to a reprimand, or a blow, from a mill foreman, Mahala had allegedly gone "berserk" & bitten off a part of the man's ear; in retribution, beaten & whipped & dismissed from her job; declared "worthless"—"useless"—taken into custody by law enforcement & dispatched to the State Asylum for Female Lunatics, as a last stop before the boneyard.

So sordid a history, & the woman not yet forty years old!

As my newly appointed Supervisor of Nurses routinely shunted to me likely specimens for use in the Laboratory, I did not question Mahala being transferred to my domain, but set out to examine the remarkable female, combining so much of *psychiatric interest,* in a single person! For indeed, as Supervisor Fussell well knew that my plans for the upcoming year were unusually ambitious.

"One of the wretches of the earth, eh, Gretel?"—so I inquired of my doughy-faced assistant, to spur her to smile; that her lot, as an indentured servant contracted to me, as her Master, in very civil settings, was not so unfortunate after all, compared to Mahala's lot; whereupon Gretel with downcast eyes replied, "Yes, Dr. Weir. We are all so fortunate to be here, with you."

I was not so happy, however, in discovering that Brigit had befriended this new resident in the Laboratory, no doubt out of pity, & some naïve sort of presupposition of kinship, between the "tongueless" deaf-mute, & the swarthy-skinned woman incapable of speech beyond muttering & growling.

Yet, it was characteristic of Brigit to take on more responsibility in the ward, as if to demonstrate to me, her Master, that my promotion of her was not ill-advised; & so Brigit labored to sponge-bathe Mahala's stout, gnarled, scarified body, with particular concern for the ulcerated wounds, from whippings, on the patient's back & massive thighs, which had not healed, & were a breeding ground for disgusting maggots.

Yet, the following day, mistaking Brigit for someone else, or in an expression of crude jealousy or envy of the attractive young girl—(for Brigit had become luminous with beauty, since the repair to her bladder, & her return to youthful health & vigor)—Mahala cursed Brigit as an "English devil," & sank her rotted teeth into Brigit's hand, causing Brigit to scream in terror, & nearly collapse in a faint.

Fortunately, I did not witness this savage assault, being elsewhere at the time, in a luncheon meeting with the Mayor of Trenton & his aides; but it was reported to me in lurid detail, by Gretel, & by others in the ward, with a lascivious sort of zest. (The lunatics thought it particularly amusing that Brigit should be mistaken for English by the brute Mahala.)

"Brigit, you have been very foolish. A bite from a human is far more dangerous than a bite from an animal!"—so I chided my nurse-assistant; for it was true, as every physician knows, that human bites carry more risk than animal bites, & here was my *prize patient* an innocent victim.

It was not generally known what accounted for infection or tetanus—"blood poisoning"—but the prescribed procedure was for bloodletting at the site of the wound, followed by oral ingestion of garlic, belladonna, calomel, & tincture of arsenic.

"You see, Brigit, you must take more caution with these lunatics. They are not *of your kind.* Indeed, I think they have no souls at all, like the flies buzzing about, & these filthy sponges."

Following her attack on Brigit, the patient lapsed into furious raving. Like a wild animal, she could not abide being shackled to the iron posts of her bed—yet, there was no alternative, short of calling our husky male attendants & throwing her into the padded & windowless *Weir-room.*

I doubted that Mahala would live long, & anticipated an autopsy & dissection of her brain, to determine if *epilepsy* could be detected, in any notable way; or whether the cause of her mania might not be syphilis, which was common in the Asylum.

I could not hope to examine such a creature, even at a distance; the very sight of me roused Mahala to yet more rage: her fierce pig-eyes raked over me, & her savage teeth flashed.

No doubt, judging from her chronic incontinence, Mahala suffered from the malady common to most of the women in the ward—a *fistula* of the bladder; but I did not see the point of repairing this loathsome patient, for her usefulness lay in her other symptoms, fits of madness that seemed to precipitate epileptic seizures.

Following such outbursts, Mahala was likely to be calmer, & even remorseful. Though she could not recall clearly what she had done, only that it was "something bad" for which she hoped to be "forgiven," she apologized to Brigit in her broken speech.

When she made the effort, it seemed that Mahala could speak almost normally, & be understood. She blamed "devil-voices in her head," clamoring loudly for her to "tear off white-devil-doctor faces" with her teeth.

In medical school we had learned that *hysteria* is a distinctly female malady & that it has one primary cause: a "tilted" or diseased uterus. I believe that this discovery originated with the great Greek philosopher Aristotle, & has been borne out by clinical research through the centuries. It seemed to me that in Mahala's case such *hysteria* was likely the cause of *epilepsy;* unless her *epilepsy* was the cause of the *hysteria.*

Disorder of the uterus & the brain both, possibly caused by a misalignment of the plates of the skull; with additional pathology supplied by "heated blood." Most evident, the rotted & debased condition of the patient's mouth: Many of her teeth were missing, & those remaining in her gums were a sickish yellow in hue, raggedy-looking, & the gums inflamed.

It seemed clear to me that the patient required severe *bloodletting,* to cool her heated blood; this routine procedure I entrusted to Gretel, who had become a skilled phlebotomist under my tutelage. So, too, the patient's teeth would have to be extracted, to reduce infection & poisoned blood, as well as, more practicably, prevent the savage lunatic from *tearing off* anyone's face with her teeth.

To execute such procedures, since the awkwardness of the harelip surgery, I had lately designed an ingenious wooden device, to be known as the *Weir-wheel,* which a staff carpenter had constructed for me: an actual wheel into which the patient's head was inserted, which was then tightened, like a vise, to secure the patient firmly, that she might not injure herself flailing about in panic. (For additional security, leather straps were often used as well, to restrain the patient's limbs.)

And so, with Mahala's head secured in the *Weir-wheel*, & a sizable dosage of laudanum, with the help of my nurse-assistants I managed to extract the few rotted teeth remaining in Mahala's jaws, using a common pliers.

Deftly then, I lanced the patient's inflamed gums to the bone, that pus would be drained from them, & cleansed by the free rush of blood.

Tossing the hideously yellow teeth into a blood-splattered pan, I remarked to Brigit, who was looking faint by this time, "How fortunate you are, Brigit, that your new friend didn't sink these fangs deeper into your hand! She might have bitten off your delicate little paw entirely."

As if to protect it, Brigit held her bandaged hand by her side. In response to my lighthearted banter, her lips twitched in a faint smile.

Following this treatment, Mahala was much improved. To the relief of all in the Laboratory, the bouts of mania faded, & the patient lacked the strength to "convulse." I was strongly of the conviction that her epilepsy was cured as well, removed with the rotted teeth.

Indeed, Mahala confided in me that the devil-voices in her head were still instructing her to hurt the *white-devil-doctor*—but she *would not*. These same voices had instructed her to hurt her little sisters, long ago; & to "strangle with bare hands" a man who claimed to be her husband; as well as to "bite off the ears" of her overseers at the Hermitage & the Trenton mill.

I inquired of Mahala if the "voices" were in her head at the present time.

Cocking her head, Mahala appeared to be listening intently; saying then *Yes*, for the voices never went away, day or night.

The voices were quieter at some times than others, it seemed; but always there, inside her head.

As if to extract the noisome voices, Mahala poked her forefingers into both her ears, as a child might do. The thought came to me— *Could these voices be lice? Fleas? Ticks? Inside her head?*

Was this a new idea?—had any clinician ever thought before, that the sounds heard by the mad might be *real*?

Voices in the head was hardly a new malady, usually attributed to "madness"—"insanity"; yet, if there was an actual cause to explain "voices," there might be an actual cure.

Having gained the lunatic's trust, as one sometimes gains the trust of a large, unpredictable beast, I proceeded to examine Mahala's ears, positioning her in the brightest sunshine, & opening the (badly caked, discolored) ear tunnel with a teaspoon-speculum. In this awkward effort I enlisted Gretel; each of us with the identical result, that, no matter how we peered inside both ears of the patient, we failed to find anything out of the ordinary. True, filthy clumps of gnarled wax had accumulated in both ear canals, but I had seen accumulated wax as extreme as this in even my private, well-to-do patients, both female & male.

(As I am not an ear specialist, I did not feel obliged to attempt to remove this wax; but suggested to Gretel that she might make the attempt, or enlist another young nurse in the effort, at a later time.)

Next, I listened at the patient's ears with my stethoscope, to see if I could detect a rustling or murmuring suggestive of vermin, or, indeed, voices. At first I seemed to hear nothing except perhaps a pulse-beat of blood in the patient's brain; then, as I pushed the stethoscope harder against the ear, it began to seem that I did hear something unusual, a kind of murmuring or muttering, resembling voices at a distance.

How curious this was! Expecting a scuttling sound of vermin, I seemed to be hearing actual human voices, albeit muffled & indecipherable.

As Brigit was in the ward, changing bedclothes & cleaning the floor beneath the patients' beds, I summoned her hither, to press my stethoscope against her ears, but detected nothing unusual.

"I am listening for *voices*, Brigit!"

At this, Brigit affected surprise; but did not question me, for she was learning the etiquette of a nurse-assistant, which is to say little, & betray no surprise at all.

Several times, I tried again: listening with my stethoscope at Mahala's ears, at Brigit's ears, at Gretel's ears, even at Nestra's ears—(for Nestra was often on the prowl in the Laboratory, too restless to remain in her bed, but not frantic enough to justify being shackled). In each case I could hear nothing save a faint pumping of blood, that may have been the pulsing of the eardrum.

Next, I next listened to Mahala's heartbeat—a hard defiant *thud! thud! thud!*—not at all resembling the softer liquidy beating of Brigit's heartbeat. Out of curiosity I pressed the stethoscope against Mahala's back, which was covered in ugly welts & scabs; & was astonished to hear what sounded like voices again, muffled & indecipherable, with an undercurrent of anger or argument commingled with the *thud* of the heart.

When I peered inside Mahala's ears again, as into a filthy burrow, it seemed to me that her eardrums were inflamed; this might have been related, I realized, to the inflammation of the patient's female organs; as Aristotle observed, an infected uterus disintegrates & wanders through the female body wreaking havoc.

What was required was *cauterization of the diseased eardrums,* that they might be purified of vile voices, or the devil-voices; not to discount a possibility of actual vermin in the ear canal, like lice.

When I made this announcement, Brigit stared at me in disbelief. Almost, I could hear her impudent question—*Dr. Weir—I wonder if you are joking?*

"I am not 'joking,' Brigit! I will use heated copper knitting needles to treat the diseased eardrums."

At this, Brigit glanced about, to see if she could catch Gretel's eye. But Gretel had backed away & would not engage with her.

Timidly, Brigit shook her head, as if to indicate that she did not think my idea was a good one; provoking me to ask, in a voice heavy with sarcasm, whether the proposal was not a feasible idea for us, with our limited surgical instruments, or whether it was not a *good idea,* over all.

Brigit was wincing, pressing the palms of both hands against her ears. Now I could quite clearly "hear" her, though her lips were pressed together tight.

Not a needle, Doctor! Not in her ear!

Bluntly I interrupted such nonsense: "See here, Brigit: This is a matter of curing disease. It is not a frivolous undertaking. The patient *hears the Devil's voice*—instructing her to do evil things. We can, & we will, cure her."

But, if the needle pierces the brain, Mahala will die . . .

To this (unvoiced) objection, I said, to deflect the subject, which I was finding distinctly annoying, as it cast an unflattering light upon my expertise as a physician, "I suppose you will suggest morphine drops, Brigit, to precede the needle," & to this somewhat satirical suggestion Brigit responded, with a look of hope: *Yes! Thank you, Doctor.*

Yet, when I sent Brigit scurrying to the armamentarium, it seemed that the supply of morphine drops was all but depleted; & there was not enough laudanum currently on hand to squander for such a cause.

As I had to allow that thrusting heated knitting needles into a patient's ears might be *cruel & unusual punishment*, even for a female lunatic, it occurred to me that I might use this occasion to experiment with the new anesthesia discussed in medical journals: *chloroform.* This was a sharp-smelling liquid whose mere fumes were sufficient to have a calming, numbing, soporific effect upon the human brain, female more readily than male. From the Philadelphia physician whose surgical instruments I had purchased, I had acquired a pint jar of chloroform; or, at least, the liquid had been so identified to me, *chloroform.*

Forcing a patient to inhale an anesthetic, rather than to swallow it in pill form, was a distinct novelty; though it was generally warned that chloroform was dangerous, & should not (yet) be used on most patients, until more was known of its properties. (Indeed, this was the precipitating factor in the Philadelphia physician's retirement, that he had caused the deaths of several patients through an excessive use of chloroform.)

I recalled the unfortunate example of Esther C__, who had expired prematurely, as a result of a defective supply of morphine which I had, all trustingly, administered to her; but that was some time ago, & was not chloroform of course, but morphine, ingested orally.

"Chloroform it is, Brigit! *You* will assist."

As I would report in my article for the *Journal of American Medical Research,* I instructed the Irish nurse-assistant to soak cloths in liquid chloroform, which were very strong-smelling, & caused our eyes to water; these cloths I then pressed firmly over the terrified patient's nose & mouth, that she might inhale the fumes & cease her fretting. Though resisting initially, the patient was safely restrained in the *Weir-wheel* & could not do injury to herself or others, & soon relaxed, sinking into sleep as a great beast might, with a great sigh of submission; at which point the cloths were removed, & my assistant heated one end of a twelve-inch copper knitting needle over an open flame, which, with infinite care, I inserted into the patient's (right) ear canal; having calibrated how deep I might penetrate before touching the actual eardrum, & with what degree of pressure, to pierce the eardrum. (For I was well aware, without one of my subordinates informing me, that the brain is immediately beyond the eardrum!)

Though knowing that the patient was *sedated,* I prepared myself for howls of anguish, & a physical altercation—except, with a little cry, it was Brigit who panicked, & dared to push away my hand, which was gripping the heated needle.

"What! What on earth are you doing, Brigit?"—so I shouted at her, that all within earshot might hear, for I was disgusted with the nursing staff in the Laboratory; no matter that the nurses were all hand-picked by me, & should have been loyal to me to the death.

Miming her distress, Brigit indicated, by gesticulating & cringing, that she did not think it was a good idea for me to insert the heated needle into the patient's ear; whereupon I told her that she was free to leave the Laboratory at once, & take herself into *that place,* where she deserved to be whipped. (For it was an old custom at the Asylum, that indentured servants on the staff could be whipped or cudgeled if they failed to follow orders; this was not illegal, as such servants were not American citizens, & were not protected by American law.)

Even now, the Irish deaf-mute protested, mutely—as I interrupted: "I have spoken. Stop these foolish gesticulations & 'miming.' I am your Master. You are in breach of contract. *You are banished to the cadaver room.*"

At once, like a kicked cat, Brigit shrank away, & crept out of the Laboratory. If the disobedient girl was not in the *cadaver room* when I checked later that day, if Brigit had disappeared from the Asylum, I would have considered it *good riddance.*

For I was tired of indulging the albino deaf-mute, & should have initiated corporeal punishment long before this.

In a state of fury, with shaking hands, I summoned Gretel to me, to take Brigit's place. This experienced midwife would not dare disobey a physician, though by the expression on her bovine face Gretel was appalled at the procedure—whether at the heated knitting needle or the chloroform, or both.

Irritably I shook out more liquid chloroform onto a rag, & placed this over the patient's impassive face; for I did not want Mahala to awake suddenly, & push away the knitting needle from her ear for the second time. *Damned to Hell, if I would be laughed at by the females.*

This time Mahala fell into a deeper sleep, her wide toothless mouth gaping open. The gnarled body went limp, covered in a chill sweat; even as her head was held fast in the *Weir-wheel.* Calmly I inserted the red-hot copper needle into the (right) ear, another time; meeting slight resistance as the needle encountered the eardrum, & pushing forward, with much precision. Repeating then, with the left ear, this time detecting burnt & sizzling flesh, which I hoped that Gretel did not notice.

Nothing is so delicate as the human eardrum, I had read in a text-book that very morning. It is positioned at a strategic point inside the ear canal, to function, I believed, as a sort of tiny *drum,* amplifying sounds to register in the brain. Unfortunately, there were pages missing from the textbook, that presumably dealt with the ear, including the "inner ear"—only vaguely could I recall perusing these pages, for an examination in medical school.

While assessing the procedure afterward, it was not clear to me that I had inserted the needle to the same degree in both ears. I *had* penetrated the eardrum each time, I was sure; but had no clear idea how thin or thick an eardrum was, & if the needle had extended beyond this.

By this time I had an uneasy feeling that Mahala was not breathing properly. Granted the peculiar, shallow panting of the breath under sedation, her breathing was erratic & ragged, & seemed to cease altogether for long seconds.

I wondered if the "voices" in the patient's head had ceased—whether the scrambling of vermin, or otherwise. With the stethoscope, I tried to listen at both the patient's ears but heard only the rapid beating of my own heart.

"Mahala! You may wake now."

As if in defiance of me there was no response from the slatternly body, slumped on the operating table.

"Mahala! You may wake. Now."

Seeing my distress, Gretel came quickly to my side. As I stood transfixed, unable to move, a smell of burnt flesh wafted to my nostrils; I wondered if in my zeal to cure the patient of her maladies, I had penetrated her brain after all.

"Doctor, let us try this"—Gretel struggled to release Mahala's head from the viselike grip of the *Weir-wheel,* & grasped Mahala by her shoulders, & shook her roughly—commanding her *Wake up!*—even as blood leaked thinly from Mahala's ears.

Awkwardly I tried to steady the patient, that she might not fall to the floor; but the woman was very heavy, & inert, slipping from our grasp & falling to the floor like a bag of cement.

"Mahala! Mahala!"—Gretel squatted beside the unconscious woman, urging her to wake, & slapping her cheeks; which had some effect upon the patient, causing her eyelids to flutter.

It was Gretel's idea to grip Mahala's stout legs, & lift her partway from the ground, that blood might run into her head, & in that way revive her; seeing the logic of this, & driven by desperation, I joined Gretel in lifting the heavy body; gripping the ankles & legs, & shaking her roughly.

Recalling now an episode in Dr. Strether's office: A heavy-set middle-aged man had become dizzy, & seemed about to faint; Strether had advised him to sit down, & lower his head to his knees, that blood might rush into his brain, to revive him—which was very good advice.

Ah!—after ten anxious minutes it appeared that Mahala was breathing again, weakly, yet regularly; but when we attempted to lift her from the floor, into a seated position, she lapsed into her previous state, & ceased breathing.

"Damn you! You are determined to *die*"—in my distress these words sprang from my lips.

Gretel lay Mahala down again on the floor, in such a way that her head was lower than her body; we tugged at her ankles, grunting & straining as before, & managed to lift her somewhat; again, after several anxious minutes, Mahala began breathing again, & her eyes fluttered open, unseeing.

"Mahala! *Breathe*"—Gretel commanded; repeating several times that "Jesus loves you"—"Jesus wants you to live, Mahala"; until at last Mahala seemed to revive as blood returned to her face, & a certain animation. In perplexity, Mahala glanced about the room, as if she had no idea where she was.

Relief swept through me. The creature would survive. In my hour of need, Providence had not betrayed me.

Soon then, with Gretel's ministrations, the patient appeared to have *stabilized*, though still confused & uncertain, & leaking blood from both ears. By this time I felt confident that I might leave Gretel in charge; I had become drained of energy in the effort to save the life of the patient, a most disagreeable ordeal that had prevailed for more than an hour.

That evening there was a private dinner at the home of the chairman of the board of overseers, attended by both myself & Mrs. Weir; it was an honor for me to be seated to the immediate right of the hostess, as my wife was seated to the immediate right of the host.

When it was inquired of me what might be happening at the Asylum that would be of interest to the gathering, I replied, with quiet pride, "We are experimenting with a cure for epilepsy, & that kind of madness in which 'voices' are heard—it is the first such work in medical history, I believe; & it is being done here in Trenton, New Jersey."

.

"Mania, Epilepsy, & 'Hearing Voices' in a Mature Female Lunatic: Treatment & Cure" would appear in the *Journal of American Medical Research*, Fall 1855, & would be many times reprinted.

Following this treatment, the patient was never again troubled by "voices" in her head. She no longer succumbed to fits of rage, & was altogether placid & affable; the savage pig-eyes were replaced by softer, bovine eyes; a general stiffness impeded her movements, as arthritis gripped her joints. Perhaps most therapeutic, her hearing was greatly diminished, which added to her placidity, along with a newfound propensity for Christianity; her only aberration was a fixed idea, that not Dr. Weir but Jesus had saved her life—*raising her from the dead, like Lazarus.*

So docile had Mahala become, when she recovered some of her strength she was attached to the Laboratory, as one of our trusted staff; her duties were emptying bedpans, scrubbing & scouring, & hauling away medical waste, with the eager compliance of a trained beast.

Wilhelmina S___: The Twins

FROM *THE CHRONICLE OF A PHYSICIAN'S LIFE*
BY SILAS ALOYSIUS WEIR, M.D.

I vow, *with God as my witness, I will make amends for my weakness!—
from this time onward.*

Coolly planning how, the next time Brigit publicly disobeyed her
Master, & gave me ample reason to discipline her, I would not hesitate
to act upon my better judgment.

The whip! You must not be weak, but rise to the challenge.

This steely resolve in me, Brigit seemed to sense, as did others with
whom I interacted at the Asylum among the large staff of subordinates. It was recalled to me, by Supervisor of Nurses Fussell, that Medrick Weir, in the zenith of his career in the Asylum, had not hesitated
to exact discipline when merited; including, at times, wrenching a
truncheon from a hesitating attendant, to wallop an unruly patient
with his own hand; for it was Medrick Weir's credo: "They respect you
more when you are Master to them. They will emulate you then, what
is *masterly* in you, & not what is *madness* in them."

Indeed, it is true, as proponents of the new field of *psychology* have
discovered: Control, discretion, & resolve are characteristics of *sanity*;
while a lack of control, emotional excess, & a general chaos of resolve
are characteristics of *madness*.

The former, distinctly *masculine traits*; the latter, distinctly *female*.

Following her banishment to the *cadaver room,* where she was made to spend the night, Brigit behaved much more prudently than in the recent past. She did not question my judgment, by a crinkling of her nose, or a rolling of her pale eyes; & often went for days in succession without expressing any rebellious thought that I could detect.

More frequently, with a nod of her head indicating—*Yes, Doctor.*

Or, it might have been, had I peered more closely—*Yes, Master.*

I am assuming that, among readers of this *Chronicle of a Physician's Life,* there are those who, like its chronicler, have never been comfortable with the principle of corporeal punishment; yet, we have grown up amid a society, indeed a religion—(Protestant, sternly moral)—that recognizes the logic of discipline. *Spare the rod, spoil the child*—this truism is as deeply embedded in the heterogenous States of America as the principle of democracy itself.

Particularly, I have been uncomfortable with discipline of a corporeal kind, since my father, Percival Weir, had not stinted in doling out such, to his children; though in truth there was little active mischief I had perpetrated in our household, as a boy; my sins, in Father's eyes, were those of omission, inadequacies. My brothers participated in *roughhouse* activities, but our father took pride in them, even as he chastised them with the rod—"Boys will be boys," was Father's adage.

Poor Silas! Mother pitied me, that I was, if not the youngest of the Weir brothers, in manner & behavior the youngest, & the most cautious, if not callow, in Father's critical eyes.

For such reasons I hesitated to order the corporeal punishment of anyone at the Asylum; though I did not exactly forbid it, but chose, with the seasoned wisdom of the administrator, to "look the other way" if the issue came up.

My kinsman Medrick Weir had advised me—*Do not interfere with your staff, Silas: You must have them on your side. You do not want your staff to be your adversaries.*

What had been most distressing was that Brigit, of all persons, should question my judgment in the presence of others; when, previously, she had made it clear that she considered me her Savior, who had (literally) saved her life on several occasions. This contradiction, I found very hard to comprehend, & to forgive.

To my consternation, it seemed to be bruited about that Silas Weir was an uncertain Director, & favored some of his (female) staff over others. *He will punish some of us—but not others, his favorites.*

Almost, I could hear these whispers. Even as spiteful eyes drifted onto Brigit, & onto me, with salacious intent.

Most distressing, Mrs. Weir began to make veiled remarks in our household, as if she had been hearing gossip from other Asylum wives, who gathered in one another's homes all too frequently, having much idle time on their hands. Worse, I began to sense a general disapproval & disdain among my Cleff in-laws, whom we never failed to see each Sunday at our residence, or theirs.

The Cleffs allowed me to know that I would soon be held in contempt, & my reputation in Trenton seriously diminished, if it was suspected that I could not control the indentured servants among my staff; my father-in-law, Myron, took me aside, to warn that if I could not control those persons, soon I would be unable to control my wife & daughters as well—"That is how it begins, Silas. Once they perceive weakness in a man, they will burrow into you like the boll weevil into cotton."

When we were alone together, I inquired of Theresa who had been saying such things of me, & Theresa replied tartly, that no one had to tell her, it was becoming well-known in Trenton, that the new Director of the Asylum was a *weak disciplinarian* when it came to his female staff.

"If you did not expose yourself to such rumors, Silas," Theresa said, tears of hurt & indignation flooding her eyes, "—such rumors would not circulate."

•

Shunted into the Laboratory by my esteemed colleague Supervisor Fussell, who knew of my interest in a particular field of *experimental psychology*, was a recent arrival at the Asylum, "Wilhelmina S__", in whom indeed I did take a considerable interest, in the winter of 1856.

Wilhelmina S__ was a lanky-limbed, rough-hewn female in her early thirties, cast off by a farm family in Basking Ridge, New Jersey, who despaired of "controlling" her; a "brawler"—"easily prone to violence"—"unpredictable in her behavior"; believed to be of a defective intelligence, & lacking in morals; so grotesquely pregnant when she was committed, by force, to the Asylum, it was believed that she would soon give birth to twins, if not triplets—her aggressive manner being such, it was feared she would harm the newborns.

Surprising to see, then, that Wilhelmina was an attractive young woman, with striking hazel eyes, & a clear brow; snarled hair of a lustrous burnt umber, & a manner of speech that did not, initially, appear to be raving or lunatic. Admittedly, I had but glanced at the new patient in the Laboratory, as I was distracted by other experimental subjects (who were not thriving as expected) at the time; but my nurse-assistants reported to me that Wilhelmina S__ was suffering from myriad ailments, including gastric distress of a type common in advanced pregnancy, swollen ankles, shortness of breath & vertigo, & a prevailing *malaise*—a proneness to fits of weeping, & deep sadness, alternating with outbursts of anger, against relatives who had had her committed, having driven her to Trenton from Basking Ridge, in the rear of a horse-drawn wagon, with wrists & ankles bound, & a rag stuffed into her mouth, to prevent her *spewing obscenities*.

Symptoms of a "brawler" nature soon emerged as Wilhelmina defied the Asylum staff, insisting that she was *not crazy;* refused to cooperate while being examined, & bathed; & struggled with attendants, who had no choice but to put her in shackles, to prevent her injuring herself & others. In the midst of such agitation, the patient went into a difficult labor, lasting well beyond a day & a night; with both Gretel & Brigit attending, & a considerable loss of blood, Wilhelmina gave birth to female identical twins, somewhat undersized & wizened, but seemingly normal, with fair hair like corn silk, & hazel eyes like their mother's; which infants Wilhelmina demanded to be allowed to nurse, but which were kept from her, in another part of the Laboratory.

My colleague Supervisor Fussell had correctly predicted, this serendipitous birth was, for me, an ideal opportunity for an experiment I had long planned, involving identical twins with a parent suffering from *mental illness.*

In this experiment, the twins would be separated at once, from each other; one to be nursed & nurtured in the usual way, by its mother & other females in the hospital, who were sure to enjoy fussing over it;

while the other infant would be kept in its crib in a pitch-dark space, in a windowless storeroom in the Laboratory, for twelve months, not held by its mother, or anyone; not allowed to hear any human voice, & "nursed" only with a bottle containing skim milk, by an attendant with a masked face.

While Infant #1 would be allowed to nurse at its mother's breast, & fed the usual soft-mushy foods which infants are given, Infant #2 would be fed the *Weir-diet* of mashed grasses, mint, & Saint-John's-wort; in this way, I would be able to determine how the ingestion of food promotes the growth of bones, teeth, & the skull in infants, as well as other organs. Infant #1 would be allowed to "play"—Infant #2 would lie in its crib, inert. In this way I could provide data of inestimable value to science, as to the effects of *sensory deprivation* in an infant: Would such an infant be able to see, when finally brought into the light? Or would such an infant be blind? Would it be capable of acquiring normal speech, when finally allowed to hear speech? Would such an infant have a full-sized brain, or a wizened brain? Would such an infant "recognize" its twin, when finally allowed to see the twin? *Would such an infant be "human" or—more resembling an "animal" unable to walk upright but snarling & groveling on hands & knees?*

Of paramount importance, would Infant #1, nursed by a mentally ill mother, begin to exhibit symptoms of mental illness, despite all other conditions being "normal"?

When I outlined this experiment to my board of overseers, with a reiteration that such pioneering advancements in Gyno-Psychiatry would be credited to the Asylum at Trenton, under their oversight, it was greeted with much respect & enthusiasm, if not total comprehension; for comprehension of scientific research is limited, in the imagination of the layman.

When I gave the first directives to Brigit, to have Infant #2 removed from its mother, to be placed in the (darkened) storeroom in a crib, Brigit responded with a look of utter perplexity: seeming not to have heard my instructions, & requiring me to repeat them.

After which Brigit stared at me, communicating to me her alarm in all but words—*Dr. Weir! You are not serious—are you?*

"Indeed yes, Brigit. *I am most serious.*"

Brigit simply stared at me, from her diminutive height of less than five feet; the albino eyes glowered in mute incredulity.

An infant separated from its mother will cry & cry—it will just cry. *If its mother cannot nurse it, or hold it, it will waste away & die—there can be no surprise in that!*

"Well, Brigit. That is what the experiment will determine for us."

It can be no surprise, Doctor. The baby will die.

"Not if the baby is kept alive, which will be your task, Brigit. After twelve months—when it's brought out into the daylight—we will compare it with the other infant, weighing & measuring it, & seeing how the skull has grown, & we will learn much. This will be an experiment of historic proportions, originating here in Trenton: You will see."

But most stubbornly, Brigit did not see. Miming to me, with pursed lips, & crinkled nose, & glaring-pale eyes, how she resisted seeing.

You would not be so cruel, Doctor—would you? Taking the baby away from her mother, for such a purpose?

"Enough, Brigit. Do not provoke me."

It is very wrong to take a baby from its mother . . .

Seeing the stricken look in Brigit's face, I recollected how Brigit's baby had been taken from *her;* a recollection that was painful to me, & repugnant.

. . . the worst cruelty, which God will repay.

"I said, Brigit: *enough.* You are being emotional—a nurse should know better. Go into the ward, you are wanted there. Immediately."

But, Doctor—

"*Away.* I am losing patience with this 'deaf-mute' idiocy."

Lifting my fist at Brigit, & shaking it, in righteous indignation; if the canny girl had not shrunk back instinctively, at this show of force, it is likely that I would have struck her, not a hard blow, but a forcible enough blow, to knock her back onto her heels, & wipe from her face that smirk of Irish insolence.

This impulsively *manly gesture* quite took me by surprise; & certainly, Brigit.

Enough for the time being, Brigit crept away in mortification. And how much more shameful to her, that others in the ward overheard our exchange.

It is a measure of the curious blind pride of the Irish, that certain individuals of their species, though immigrants of the servant class exclusively, because of an attractive face or figure imagine themselves elevated above the rest, & so naïvely forget their station in life; as if, if they can speak at all, they do not speak a most bastardized form of English, ridiculous & unintelligible to the ear, & at other times, exude an air of obstinacy, by not speaking at all. And when they are reminded of their status, it is like the pricking of a child's balloon, immediately they shrink to their proper size.

In confidence that Brigit would soon overcome her insipid moral objections, & agree to care for Infant #2, I proceeded with my plans; for I knew that Brigit would wish to keep the infant alive as long as possible, this softness being her nature. Without her presence, the baby would soon die, & the experiment founder.

It is true, I might have enlisted Gretel in this experiment, or another of the younger female staff smilingly eager to assist me, but, alas!—the Irish albino orphan remained my preferred assistant.

(Indeed, I was contemplating sending Brigit Kinealy to the nursing school at New Brunswick; following which, she would return to Trenton, to assist me.)

(Except that, in my wilder musings, I could not risk the girl getting into mischief, away from my scrutiny; recalling that my first sight of her, a most hellish one, was of bloody spread legs, & the enormous strain to her frail body, of *giving birth to a bastard child.*)

Gretel, too, expressed some doubt as to the feasibility of the experiment, since Wilhelmina was in failing health, following the arduous pregnancy; some part of her female organs had been badly strained, & blood leaked from her, days later. And still the distraught mother wept for her babies, convinced that she would save her soul from the Devil, if she could but nurse them as God has intended.

It was Gretel's argument, that Wilhelmina be allowed to nurse her babies, as this would be a solace both to her, & to them; whereupon I retorted: "You know, Gretel—this is a laboratory, not a *nursery.*"

Like many females of her age, Gretel was becoming a *tedious presence.* Her thick Germanic tongue, doughy glum face, & inquisitiveness where it was not desired reminded me of my own dear wife, & other female relatives who, as they outgrew the attractive clothing of their youth, outgrew their charm.

Yet, this revolutionary experiment, which would have assured the position of Silas Aloysius Weir in the pantheon of modern medicine, quite apart from the discovery of a cure for *fistula,* was sabotaged before it began: To my astonishment, Theresa somehow learned of it, & declared to me that she *would not hear of any "experiments" perpetrated upon white Christian infants.*

When I inquired of my wife where had she heard such gossip, she replied to me that neighbors & friends living on the Asylum grounds were speaking of nothing else: that light-skinned "angelic" baby girls had been born of a "mixed-race" lunatic mother, a drastic situation that had to be remedied, at once.

Soon then, such gossip spread to the wives of my board of overseers, who provoked a great commotion, & enlisted the aid of the Anglican archbishop, as well as the Mayor of Trenton; with the result that the infants were removed from the Laboratory, & placed with an older childless Christian couple living in the prestigious Riverside community of Trenton, who professed their gratitude by donating a sizable sum of money to the Asylum, with particular thanks to Silas Aloysius Weir.

"Spare the rod, spoil the child . . ."

FROM *THE CHRONICLE OF A PHYSICIAN'S LIFE*
BY SILAS ALOYSIUS WEIR, M.D.

I AM NOT PROUD to record the following. Yet, I am not ashamed, for I did what was required to be done; not realizing how Fate would cruelly reward me, with the eventual betrayal of my own eldest son & heir.

For at last it came to a climax in the Laboratory: the insubordination of the Irish albino deaf-mute, & the discipline required to confront her.

Increasingly it began to happen, as news spread of *miraculous cures* at the Asylum at Trenton, not solely of mental illness but of other maladies, that private persons brought their infirm family members to me, most of them females; as in Ho-Ho-Kus, soon in the Trenton area & beyond, Silas Weir acquired a particular reputation as a physician-surgeon with *gynecological skills.*

For it was clear, *mental illness* in females is a consequence of infection, particularly of the female genitals; accounting for a vast array of moods, fugues, eccentricities, "whims," & the like, as well as the more serious eruptions of what is deemed *lunacy.*

Indeed, I was likely the sole surgeon in New Jersey trained to treat *vaginismus,* at the request of frustrated husbands, who brought to me their hysterically "frigid" wives, to undergo a delicate surgery widening the mouth of the vagina, while at the same time severing nerves in the surrounding flesh, to kill all sensation; this, often combined with a clitorectomy of which the wife was unaware, & where indicated, an ovariectomy. (See my "Clinical Notes on Corrective Vaginal Surgery," originally published in *The American Journal of Medical Sciences*.)

Occasionally, an unhappy husband might bring his (unsuspecting) wife, likely to have given birth more than once, for the reverse sort of surgery, in which a slack & flaccid vagina was tightened to the specifications of the husband. (See "Further Clinical Notes on Corrective Vaginal Surgery.")

In these surgeries, anesthesia was cautiously employed; for a genteel female patient could not tolerate one-tenth of the pain the Asylum patients tolerated, & I would not have subjected them, or their families, to such ordeals.

So popular did I become, I thought it prudent to open a second bank account, in which to deposit my earnings from private sources, as distinct from my salary as Director of the Asylum; for this account, using a pseudonymous name, *Dr. Adam Percival.*

That I might hone my surgical skills, it was necessary for me to experiment with Laboratory subjects; in this, I was aiding these subjects as well in reducing the degree of their infections, thus the degree of their mental illness, by the removal of infected organs.

Still, in the most infected, nodules of mental illness would remain, like traces of dirt beneath a laborer's nails, even when (it appeared) there was no *visible infection;* one could infer *imminent infection.*

If an organ is not diseased, Dr. Weir, why would you remove it?—so I understood Brigit Kinealy to be inquiring, with a crinkling of her pert Irish nose, & a frown of disapproval.

"To prevent it being diseased, of course! What an ignorant question."

Seeing that Wilhelmina was in constant pain in her lower body, as well as distraught with grief at the loss of her infants, it seemed necessary to remove her female organs entirely in a single marathon surgery; with the beneficial consequence, Wilhelmina became less troublesome immediately, & inclined to Christian piety & cooperative behavior.

So, too, others in the Laboratory, offered the possibility of release from the Asylum when their mental illnesses were cured, were eager to consent to my experiments; which included also testings with chloroform & ether. Springing from this, soon I became skilled in the removal of cancerous & precancerous breasts, uteruses, ovaries, & the like, which resulted in a yet further increase in my private patients. (Such services were kept confidential, as there was shame involved in the mere hint that women might be in need of such surgery; indeed, the word *cancer* could not be uttered aloud in mixed company.)

It is true, few of the cancer patients survived; yet, without the removal of the cancerous organs, none at all would have survived.

Perhaps I was not altogether gratified that my patients were now exclusively *female;* it was not choice but Providence that set the course of my career. This I could not explain to my father, or others in the family, including also my in-laws, who seemed invariably to slight my achievements—*But Silas is a women's doctor! A female-lunatic doctor.*

Nonetheless, as a result of my rising reputation, & the services I provided for certain prominent fellow physicians, in the late winter of 1856 I received an invitation to join the exclusive New England Association of Physicians & Surgeons, to which my elder brother, Franklin, though less deserving, already belonged.

Among the treasures of those years was a telegram sent to me that, though somewhat terse in its phrasing, was very welcome to me after years of paternal penury:

Dear Son,
     Congratulations on this honor. I am proud of you both.
                                        Your loving Father,
                                        Percival

·

Following their surgeries, two of my Laboratory subjects developed a particularly virulent sort of *bloody diarrhea,* & lay in bed with dazed dilated eyes, incapable of speech; it could not have been mere happenstance, it seemed to me, that the patients' cots were close beside each other, & the befouled breath of Lucy commingled with the befouled breath of Juel.

An opportunity for an (unscheduled) experiment!—so Providence seemed to suggest.

Quickly I drew up a plan: Each subject was to be treated with a distinctly different regime, & daily results recorded by my nurse-assistant Brigit.

One subject was given a particular medication, the other an alternate medication. One subject was bled each day, the other bled not at all. Teeth were extracted from one subject, & not from the other. (In each case, infected teeth had already been extracted during previous surgeries, as well as infected vulvas.) One subject was moved to a cot near an open window, & the other removed to a cot in a windowless room, with no light. One subject was severely restricted in diet, ingesting virtually no liquids or solids, & the other provided with routine Asylum food from the kitchen.

What a basic idea it was, to treat diarrhea by simply restricting liquids!—immediately, diarrhea lessened in the subject so deprived; even as it continued in the other subject.

After some days, *bloody diarrhea* ceased entirely in Subject #1 (Lucy), even as the condition prevailed in Subject #2 (Juel), though oscillating from day to day, unpredictably. So varied were the contingencies, it was very difficult to know if, for instance, Saint-John's-wort was helpful in the treatment of diarrhea, or harmful; or, if it had no effect at all. Of the arsenal of medications, laudanum appeared to be the most beneficial to curtailing diarrhea; but it was known that a protracted use of this medication resulted in severe constipation, dementia, & death. Similarly with exposure to bright sunshine, by an open window, resulting in a spike in temperature in the subject, & a cessation of diarrhea, for the time being; but some possibility of heat stroke, bringing delirium, & death. Extraction of teeth, too, could not be linked to specific alterations in the subjects, though it was not possible to prove that extraction *did not* have any effect.

All this, Brigit observed in silence, & did not interfere; but it was clear to me, from the orphan-girl's stiff facial expression, that she did not approve of my methods, & followed my instructions only because she had no choice.

Indeed, it seemed to me that *Brigit was praying, in silence*—not daring to even move her lips, lest I understand what she was doing. (The more annoying, that it would surely be the Catholic God to whom she was praying, & not the Protestant!)

Though finally, as Lucy seemed to be growing weaker, & Juel stronger, Brigit protested, with a pained facial expression, & a fussy gesture of her hands, that Lucy would *perish of thirst* unless she was given water; & that Brigit was begging me, to be allowed to do this.

Ah, I was awaiting this! I knew that Brigit would object to my plans, in her habitual way; placing sentiment over science, like a headstrong child. Sternly I rebuked her: "This is a pioneering medical laboratory & the eyes of the world are upon us. We are committed to the advancement of medical knowledge, not the coddling of childish patients."

Brigit winced; yet could not resist suggesting, with a miming of her hands, gripping a sponge, that she be allowed to lift the sponge to Lucy's lips, to suck moisture from it; to which I retorted, that would sabotage the experiment, which was an exploration into the effect upon subjects of liquids, ingestion & deprivation.

Tears welled in the pale-blue eyes. Ridiculous!

But, Dr. Weir—

"There is no 'but,' Brigit. 'But' is but the ticket to the *cadaver room.*"

—it is not humane, Dr. Weir. Lucy will die of thirst—

"Do you not hear me, Brigit? Are you truly *deaf,* as well as *dumb*?"

As if I had raised my fist to her—(indeed, I had not)—Brigit shrank away like a frightened cur, & did not trouble me again for several days.

Though I had to smile to myself, as a father might smile, bemused & proud that his young child had learned to pronounce a fancy word, that the little Irish orphan had picked up from somewhere the word *humane*—(which I believe to be French in origin).

After six days of this rigorously imposed regimen, Subject #2 (Juel) was still suffering from diarrhea, though it was no longer bloody; while Subject #1 (Lucy) was entirely cured of diarrhea, having had no further attacks in days.

Thus, one of my major experiments, to be published in *The American Journal of Medical Sciences* (1857) titled "A Cure for Chronic Diarrhea: Clinical Notes."

Following this, Brigit sulked about the Laboratory, & would not lift her eyes to mine when I greeted her in the morning.

When I inquired of Gretel, in Brigit's earshot, what was wrong, Gretel informed me in a neutral voice: "Brigit is very upset, Doctor, that you allowed Lucy to die."

"What! I did not 'allow Lucy to die.' The experiment was to determine how diarrhea can be cured, & I am quite satisfied, the experiment demonstrated how."

To this, Gretel made no reply; but Brigit, seemingly having read my lips, mimed to me, insolently, *Yes, you did. YOU ALLOWED LUCY TO DIE.*

Now, this was indeed shocking, & offensive. That Brigit would dare confront me like this, in full view of others in the ward; even if the deaf-mute did not speak aloud, her meaning was painfully clear.

Sternly I rebuked Brigit, but she refused to apologize. That Lucy may have expired, as patients frequently do, of one ailment or another, does not exclude the fact that *Lucy was cured of diarrhea.*

Now Brigit was pretending, in the most insulting way, like one of my most willful daughters, to be unable to hear, or understand me; even as patients in the ward looked avidly on, troublemakers Nestra & Bathsheba most of all.

"You have gone too far this time, Brigit. You will be whipped."

Astonishingly, Brigit laughed! Clearly miming—*Whipped! I am not afraid.*

No one had ever opposed me in such a way in my adult life. For a dazed moment, I could not absorb the insult.

Stunned, I staggered out of the Laboratory & into the corridor, & summoned one of the Asylum attendants, commanding that Brigit Kinealy be taken at once, & confined in the *cadaver room,* which was at the rear of North Hall, near the entrance.

"Do you want me to whip her, sir?"

"No! I do not want you to whip her."

"Do you want me to beat her with my truncheon, sir?"

"No! I do not. Just—confine her."

"Do you want her restrained in the *Weir-jacket*?"

"No! I do not want her restrained in the *Weir-jacket.* Just—do as I have said."

My voice rose in exasperation. How I am tormented, surrounded by dull-witted staff!

Only a few hours previously, the corpse of the deceased Lucy had been laid in this space, neatly wrapped in a tarpaulin, in preparation for being hauled away to the cemetery. This alone, I believed, would be sufficient to bring the rebellious Irish orphan to her senses; but when I confronted Brigit, in the *cadaver room*, later that afternoon, she remained defiant, a mutinous figure in her nurse's white uniform, which had become splattered with blood & grime.

"You will apologize & repent, Brigit! You have insulted me, grievously." These words I mimed with cold fury, gesticulating with hands and arms.

In reply, scarcely troubling to move her lips, that I might understand her muted words: *Doctor, I will not. I have done nothing wrong.*

"Do you want to be whipped, then? Is that what you are saying?"

I am saying—I have done nothing wrong.

I am saying—Lucy SHOULD NOT HAVE DIED.

Astonishing to me, such opposition! Even as the girl betrayed evidence of having wept, for her stark-white face was stained with tears.

I went away again, shutting the door firmly behind me, & locking it; seeking out a whip in the Asylum, from one of the husky young attendants, who stared at me in amazement, for he had never spoken to the Director of the Asylum, before this hour.

"A—whip, sir? You are asking for a—whip?"

"A whip! Yes."

Returning then, brandishing the whip, to the *cadaver room*, which had a very bad smell, & was nauseating to enter, somewhat unsteady on my feet. It was surprising to me that the whip was smaller than I had expected, not a *bullwhip* evidently, such as might be used to whip a Black slave on a plantation, but measuring about four feet in length.

By this time I was quite light-headed, with my collar tugged from my neck, to allow me to breathe.

"Brigit, do you apologize? Do you *repent*?"

I—I do not, Doctor.

"Do you see what I have in my hand, Brigit? This is a whip."

I see, sir. A whip.

Boldly I gripped the stubborn girl by the upper arm, & gave her a shake, as one might shake an obstreperous child; & was somewhat taken aback, by how petite the girl was, how small-boned her arm, inside the starched sleeve of the uniform. This, despite the strength Brigit often demonstrated, in helping to lift, or to lift, heavy patients in the ward.

"Brigit, you will disrobe. Now."

I will not.

"You *will*. For you are going to be whipped, across your back."

I will not.

"You *will*."

Almost, I could not speak; my voice was hoarse & cracked, for this was so shameful an episode for me, a gentleman, I could not wish anyone else to hear.

"You are an 'indentured servant.' I am your Master."

You are not my—Master . . .

The pale blue eyes flashed, with what seemed to me a frantic fervor, of rebelliousness. This was the *Irish,* in defiance of their *English* Masters.

Was Brigit daring me to remove her prim nurse's uniform? To tear her clothing from her? At the Hermitage, I had been an unwilling witness to more than one whipping, by the brute foreman; invariably the victim was part-naked, his torso bared, that the whiplash would cut deeply into his flesh. All of the whipped had been indentured servants but none had been females, that I had observed.

As a physician, I had been repelled by the spectacle; for I was a pacifist, at heart. Yet, as I was a man, I was somewhat excited & thrilled; for such rebelliousness should be punished, & a manly man would know how to wield a whip, to assure that subordinates know their place.

With Brigit, the situation was different, in ways difficult to elucidate. Almost, my nurse-assistant was taunting me, & daring me to strike her, as (I recalled) my eldest son sometimes did, not so much in words as in a certain insolence of the eyes & mouth; for Jonathan was the most willful of all of the children, badly spoiled, evincing not the slightest interest in following his father's noble career, & forever hinting of *joining the Abolitionist movement.*

It occurred to me that, as a physician, I had vowed to uphold the Hippocratic oath, to *do no harm;* yet reasoned, such ethical restraints surely did not apply to subordinates but only to persons like myself, of the ruling class.

As Brigit cowered before me, I raised the whip, with a shaking hand: "You have brought me to this! *You*—who pretend to be a child of Jesus—*you are a pagan romanish devil.*"

A kind of raving came over me, as I had never before experienced in my life. The nurse-assistant cringed, & sank to her knees as in a pose of prayer, yet clearly unrepentant, maddening to see. In blind frustration I raised the whip higher—yet—could not make myself bring it down on the girl's back, which was clothed, & not bare as required . . .

My knees were weak, barely could I see for moisture in my eyes, & a most disagreeable sensation in my groin, that was ordinarily numb, like a limb that has gone to sleep, now hellish in indignation & rectitude, throbbing, & swelling . . . So distressful to me, the whip fell from my fingers clattering to the floor.

Next I knew, I was staggering from the rear of North Hall, blinking & gasping in the open air, at dusk; through a patch of wild grasses & brambles, toward the Director's residence, which was only just in view. Badly wanting to find a private place, to splash cold water onto my face, & calm myself. For my heart was beating hard in my breast, & my blood pressure was so high, I knew that my face had gone beet-red, & my glasses opaque with steam.

Seeing then, as if he were an apparition out of Hell, my eldest son, appearing before me on the walkway with a look of utter astonishment, as if he had no idea who I was.

"You!—what are you looking at?"—my voice croaked, in fury; & my fingers twitched, that I had not still the whip in hand, to wipe that expression from the youth's callow face.

"Father? Is that you? What is wrong?"

"What is *wrong*! Much is *wrong*!"

Jonathan's gaze dropped to my feet, & lifted, taking in my disheveled appearance & heated skin, as tears of mortification ran down my cheeks. Having failed utterly in my own eyes, I must now contend with failing in the eyes of my eldest son, whose respect I so urgently desired.

I had wished my children—my eldest boys, in particular—to be evidence, to my father, Percival, that I was *a man among men; indeed, as I had sired sons, a Weir among Weirs.* As I was an heir of our distinguished family, albeit one of the less prized of my father's heirs, so, too, my sons would be heirs of the Weirs, & contribute to their reputation.

It was painful to me to recall how, as a naïve young father, I had gazed into the face of my infant son, as if seeking some echo of myself in him; without ever satisfying myself that I found it. Now, seeing

Jonathan at a little distance, I could not resist feeling a twinge of pride, that my son was tall, taller than I, with a strong-boned profile & hair that was fawn-colored, thick & wavy; his eyes were a startling deep cobalt-blue, the irises appearing black in certain gradations of light, which gave him a look of wariness, even duplicity.

So Jonathan looked upon me now, as in a quavering voice I commanded him to go immediately to the rear of North Hall—to enter the first room he encountered, where the door was ajar—this room, known as the *cadaver room,* but also a place for discipline, where insubordinate Asylum staff were sent to be punished.

"Go there, son—you cannot miss it!—& take up the whip I have dropped—& administer *not less than twelve lashes* to the cowering Irish girl inside; not overly hard, but hard enough to impart some pain. You will recognize this person at once: She is wearing a nurse's uniform, which she has defiled. She is one of our indentured servants, & she is in breach of contract. We may whip them, or we may dismiss them; but we cannot send them back to their home countries, for that is the contract. If she begins to whimper, or sob, or beg for mercy— you have permission to cease whipping; but if she remains, as I am sure she will, defiant & rebellious, you must whip her until she comes to her senses."

"Father? *What?*"

Jonathan stared at me, for indeed he had never heard such a torrent of words rushing from his father, whose demeanor, in the household, tended toward the reticence, if not the withdrawn.

In a calmer voice I repeated what I had said. Still, Jonathan stared at me in disbelief.

Stammering that he *did not want to whip anyone*—certainly not a girl . . .

Whereupon I told him, in no uncertain terms, *he dared not disobey me.*

"But, Father—"

"You will *do as I tell you.*"

With almost a look of fear, Jonathan took a step back from me. I had to wonder what wildness shone in my face.

No doubt, the callow youth was debating whether to turn & flee from me; I would not have put it past him if he had run home to appeal to his mother, for Theresa had spoiled all of the children, & turned them against their father.

Just two or three years before, I had hoped to imbue Jonathan with the idealism of the physician & scientist; he had rebuffed my overtures, which I found it very difficult to forgive.

"Jonathan: I have commanded you. Go to North Hall—you see the door, I am pointing at it. Do not look at me, look at the door. Inside, the girl is waiting. She is to be *whipped.* The whip is on the floor. She has defied me—my authority. She has defied *the entire race to which we belong.*"

"The—'entire race'—?"

"Yes! *You* are of that race, I believe, are you not? Don't stare at me like a lout! You are of revered English stock, your ancestors came to this country long before it was the United States! *They* are like vermin, they come to our shore to breed, & to undermine our authority. They are in league with Black slaves! Give her no less than twelve lashes."

"*T-twelve—?*"

"Are you a parrot, Jonathan? Just—go! *Go!* Before it is too late, & I disown you."

From whence came this wild threat, I had no idea; my attire was disheveled, & my starched collar loosened from my neck; certainly, my face burnt red, & oozed sweat; & it may have frightened my son, that his father was near to having a stroke, as he had never seen, nor heard, me in such a state.

The argument seemed to persuade the youth who swallowed hard & said, "Very well, Father. If you insist."

"Yes! You have been hearing me—*I do insist.*"

At this I plunged past Jonathan, in such a heightened state of nerves, I could not bear to be in his presence for a moment longer.

At the house, I entered at the rear breathless & agitated, yet failed to avoid encountering my wife, Theresa, who was in the kitchen conferring with our cook, & turned to me now to stare at me as at a madman.

"Silas! What on earth? Your collar—what has happened to you?"

"Nothing! Nothing has happened to *me.*"

"Silas, what is it? Are you ill?"

"Just—*do not touch me,* Theresa! I warn you—*do not.*"

Making my way to my study, & shutting the door behind me; sitting down heavily at my desk, with hands pressed over my ears; scarcely aware of my surroundings, like one who has wakened from a nightmare, only to find himself in yet another nightmare.

Fumbling to open a desk drawer in which, beneath medical journals, was a pint of whiskey, from which I drank hurriedly.

For some minutes, I simply sat—my brain in a whirl, like dried leaves blown in a windstorm.

Not wanting to hear a sound of hushed voices outside my door, belonging to my wife & one or another of the children. How annoying they were! Theresa was telling them to *shush,* in such a way that I could not fail to hear.

"God help me. God help *him*—to whip the girl soundly."

This prayer I uttered softly, so that no one might hear, who might be listening outside the door.

The carved wooden dove Brigit had given to me in a happier time, I had placed at eye-level, on a recessed shelf of the rolltop desk; & gazed at it now, with a hard-beating heart.

"And God help *her*—to repent."

To the whiskey I added a tablespoon of laudanum. Some minutes later, by which time I had swallowed several mouthfuls of the warm, soothing, auburn-colored whiskey, which kindled a small glowing flame in my chilled breast, I was feeling more expansive, & less despairing: A generous thought came to me, that I would pay tuition & board for Brigit Kinealy to train as a nurse at New Brunswick, following which she would return to the Laboratory, to work closely with me.

There came then, as I had been both anticipating & dreading, a cautious knock at the door.

"Sir?"—it was Jonathan.

Hurriedly I put away the whiskey, in one of the desk drawers. The carved dove I pushed back on the shelf, so that it was hidden from sight.

In another part of my desk I kept, hidden amid old account books, an accumulation of U.S. currency, paid to me by my private patients; amid the distractions of my life, I had neglected to deposit this in the account of *Dr. Adam Percival,* about whom Theresa knew nothing.

This drawer was always kept shut & would have been locked, except it had no lock, unfortunately.

As Jonathan knocked again, I bade him enter. How pale he had become, with a strained look, moist eyes, & a grim mouth! In his hand, the whip I had left for him on the floor of the *cadaver room,* quivering still with the dark energy of a snake, which he dropped onto my desk in a brusque gesture, without explanation.

"Well, son—did you? Whip her?"

It was remarkable, this husky, fit youth was out of breath, as if he had been running. That he could not meet his father's eyes with his own suggested how the experience had tested him; for never had any pampered son of mine lifted a whip to anyone.

"Yes, Father. I whipped her."

The Penitent

FROM *THE CHRONICLE OF A PHYSICIAN'S LIFE*
BY SILAS ALOYSIUS WEIR, M.D.

D<small>R. *WEIR*</small>—*forgive me! I beg of you.*
These repentant words, mimed in Brigit Kinealy's muted voice, haunted my (troubled, broken) sleep in the hours following the debacle, & through much of the following day, as a wraith may haunt the living; yet, in truth, when I next set eyes upon the insolent Irish girl, on the morning of the next day, in her usual station at the Laboratory, she did not communicate with me at all, but stood at a little distance, in her nurse's uniform—(that had been, at least, freshly laundered & was properly starched)—awaiting orders from me, or from Gretel: neither disobedient, nor entirely obedient, but poised to act as a subordinate must be, with an impassive expression on her face, that seemed somewhat stiff & drawn, as if with pain.

(Covertly I watched Brigit Kinealy: She *did* move as if she were feeling pain, as one might move with an injured knee, or back; but I refused to look fully at her, & could form only a vague notion of what her *naked, whipt back* must look like, covered in reddened welts; the mere vision of which left me weak-kneed & faint.)

Yet, smarting with indignation, I refused to speak to Brigit, or even acknowledge her; addressing my instructions to Gretel, who appeared, in her manner, entirely as usual, not seeming to know of what had transpired between Brigit & me the previous day.

(But was the entire Asylum gossiping of it? For I had made a blunder, I was sure, in summoning an attendant to confine Brigit in the *cadaver room,* & to bring me a whip; & this, without warning him not to speak of it, to a living soul.)

So it was, Brigit occupied herself with her duties in the ward, & I turned away, for I had commitments elsewhere. I had hardened my heart not to forgive her, even if she begged.

Much of that week, I was obliged to be away from the Laboratory, tending to administrative matters; & when I returned, to check on my experimental subjects in their beds, & confer with Gretel, I took care to avoid Brigit, as Brigit took care to creep about quietly in my presence, without calling attention to herself.

(And now yes, it did appear that Brigit moved about wincingly; no doubt, her soft-skinned back was covered in welts.)

(I felt an impulse, to examine Brigit's whipt back—yet, I dared not. For doing so would acknowledge that I felt that I had caused her injury, while I should only have felt that I was exacting justice; the insolent girl had caused injury to herself.)

(I *had* examined the whip, which Jonathan had dropped on my desk; which seemed to me darkened with a rank-smelling liquid that might have been blood, & which I hid away from my sight, for I could not bear seeing it.)

(I wondered if Gretel had cleaned & bandaged Brigit's wounds; but I could not inquire.)

(I did not think so: for if she had, Gretel would not be behaving so matter-of-factly with me, but would be regarding me with astonished & disapproving eyes, as if I were not her Master, but a monster.)

(Which might mean, then, that someone else had nursed Brigit's wounds, as patients in the Laboratory often cared for one another. But I had no way of knowing this, nor any wish of knowing.)

(For how inappropriate it would be, for the Director of the Asylum to be making inquiries after his lowest nurse-assistants!)

After five days, it seemed to me that Brigit Kinealy had fully recovered from her punishment & had regained her usual zeal for work, tending to our patients in a way that could only be described as *tender & efficient.* Indeed, there appeared to be a new hesitancy in her step, which could only indicate a new maturity; as there may have been the faintest of lines in her brow. Here was a maidenly *penance,* in all but words.

As my stature was in every way superior to hers, I saw that the wisest course for Silas Aloysius Weir, Director of the Asylum at Trenton, was to behave as if nurse-assistant Brigit Kinealy had begged for his forgiveness, & he had magnanimously granted forgiveness: for such is the Christian way.

Ah!—if Providence had but directed me, to be less trusting, & to examine the Irish girl's unclothed back, things would have turned out very differently, & the singular catastrophe of my life averted.

God's Blessing. God's Wrath.

FROM *THE CHRONICLE OF A PHYSICIAN'S LIFE*
BY SILAS ALOYSIUS WEIR, M.D.

NEVER GUESSING that in my triumph would be my destruction. In the establishment of my experimental Laboratory, unique in North America, & staffing it with persons deemed to be loyal to *me*, above all else, I had unwittingly assured my own betrayal, as one who nurses a viper in his bosom.

What greater irony, which the historian of American medicine will note: how a pioneering research scientist might ascend the highest echelon of scientific discovery, yet be made to suffer the most abject humiliation & physical distress, within the same small sphere of time!

God's blessing & *God's wrath*: tragically conjoined.

First, triumph! For my reputation grew steadily, as a major figure in medical research of our era, bringing with it such honors as my election to the New England Association of Physicians & Surgeons, of which I have spoken; & the yet more prestigious honor of an award from the National Institute of Science, for my pioneering work in the treatment of *fistula*, as a prevention of mental illness, with a most flattering citation in which it was claimed that *Silas Aloysius Weir, M.D., is the Magellan of female genitalia.*

More fiercely than ever in those heady years I threw myself into my work! My dear wife, Theresa, who had often complained of rarely seeing me, became at last placated by our steady rise in income, for my salary at the Asylum, a generous one, was supplemented ever more by my private income. As my children were growing in maturity, they were more able to measure the significance of their father's work in the larger world; complaints of being shamed among their well-to-do peers, that their father was a *female-lunatic doctor,* faded gradually, & were no more. Even my Cleff in-laws had to concede, my fortunes were on the rise—their beloved Theresa had not made an egregious mistake, after all!

Older physicians & surgeons who had once doubted my methods, & had looked with disdain upon the little-known field of Gyno-Psychiatry, were obliged now to pay respectful attention to me; & even to inquire if they might observe me performing, as if they were but apprentice doctors in the presence of a master.

With each surgical procedure repairing *fistula,* I grew more experienced, & more skillful. Where initially I had struggled simply to perform the pelvic examination of a patient, now, with the use of a *Weir-speculum,* the shadowy interior of the vagina could be exposed to view; with the use of silver wire, sutures were possible in the interior of the body that had not been possible before. Add to which, my experimental surgeries in the treatment of lunacy, or, as it was coming more commonly to be called, mental illness, involving the removal of infected parts of the female body, began to be emulated by leading practitioners of the day, at the most distinguished hospitals.

By invitation, I performed surgeries in Boston, New York City, Baltimore, & Cleveland; in Chicago, Philadelphia, Buffalo, & Cambridge; in a tour of the South, I performed surgeries in Montgomery, Atlanta, Charleston, Richmond, & New Orleans, traveling everywhere in the most luxurious train suites, & staying in the most luxurious hotels. Owners of the largest cotton plantations in the South sought my services, for their Black female slaves were almost universally stricken with *fistula*—a condition that usually condemned many to an early death by starvation, as slave-owners saw no purpose to keeping a useless laborer alive.

Thus, in the Southern states, plantation doctors were eager to learn the technique of mending *fistula* with silver wire, clamoring to be allowed to observe my surgical methods when I demonstrated the technique at medical schools.

Ah, I did miss Gretel at my side, at such times! But had to do with nurses & aides at the site, who proved on the whole quite satisfactory.

Following a successful surgery in an esteemed hospital, it was not uncommon that a grateful patient kissed my hands, & spoke of me in the most elevated terms as her *Savior*—when other physicians, among them prominent names, had rebuffed their pleas & declared their conditions hopeless.

Here was a most delicious irony: My usually aloof father-in-law, Myron Cleff, was obliged to bring his ailing wife to me, for a uterine prolapse repair with silver wire at Trenton General Hospital, which surgery I performed with a carefully calibrated dose of chloroform, with great success.

Nothing more gratifying than a father-in-law humbling himself, with a muttered *Thank you, Silas!*

To my wife's relief our eldest daughter, Florence, became engaged, at the perilously mature age of twenty-one, to a respectable cotton broker with an office in Baltimore. Our second-eldest son, Solomon, was studying business at the University of Delaware. Our eldest son, Jonathan, had managed to graduate from the College of New Jersey with a useless degree in philosophy & history, but with ambitious plans to study law at Yale in another year or two; in the interim, Jonathan was working in Philadelphia as a junior associate in a law firm, but modestly paid.

Between us, there was an awkwardness as palpable as the mist that settles over the city of Trenton, when wind from the east bears smoke from factories on the Delaware River—indeed, I was given to suspect that Jonathan sought to avoid me, when he could.

Seeking some measure of independence, Jonathan lived alone in a rooming house within walking distance of the Philadelphia law firm; yet, as I eventually discovered, Jonathan frequently returned to visit home, by happenstance when I was away.

Why Jonathan frequently returned to Trenton was not quite understood, at the time, by either of his parents.

"Jonathan misses us," Theresa remarked with a wistful air, "—he's still so *young*. I wish that you would not be so harsh on him, Silas."

"'Harsh'! I am not harsh on Jonathan," I said, astonished, "—it's Jonathan who is harsh on me."

Recalling how Jonathan had dropped the whip on my desk, that had seemed to smell of the Irish girl's smote flesh; with an expression that seemed to me, in retrospect, both regretful & contemptuous.

It was a measure of my naïveté regarding our eldest son; I had no idea that he maintained a surreptitious relationship with Brigit Kinealy, & that while visiting home, he arranged to meet with her, without Theresa's knowledge; all this, to be revealed most scandalously, in time.

Also unsuspected by me: As a rank dim-lit atmosphere promotes the growth of toxic fungi, my frequent absences from the Asylum were allowing for an atmosphere of increasing misrule & discontent in the Laboratory; my faith in nurse-assistants Gretel & Brigit, to oversee the hospital while I was away, would turn out to be cruelly misplaced.

So it happened that, on a mild March day in 1861, out of nowhere the *wrath of God* struck like a whirlwind.

Riding upon the heels of the *fistula*-success, I was next planning to embark upon a campaign of popularizing the removal of infected female organs, in the treatment of mental illness, in which I had been doing research for years in the Laboratory. Ever more in the United States, *hysteria* was becoming an epidemic among white women of the genteel classes, very possibly linked to rising tensions between North & South, which were dominating headlines, to the exclusion of other issues. My knowledge of the female genital region was without parallel; as my knowledge of female anatomy & physiology over all, revealing the crucial connection, in the female, between genital & reproductive organs & the brain. As recent studies have shown, the pursuit of so-called "higher" education among white women endangers the rate of flow of blood from the uterus to the brain, increasing it tenfold, with the consequence that such an activity is likely to shrivel a woman's ovaries & prevent her from discharging her motherly duties; this being the case, rigorously controlled experiments in this area of physiology were gravely needed.

My intention was to follow a methodical plan, to surgically remove female organs—ovaries, uterus, clitoris, vulva, & other residual parts of the vagina—one by one, in a series of subjects, in my Laboratory; to see which, if any, might be responsible for hysteria; or whether hysteria was generalized throughout the genital area in the female; or whether, as Aristotle & Galen had theorized, the loosened womb might shift within the female body, & travel into the torso, for instance, with grave results if making contact with the lungs or the heart.

That is, in Subject #1, I would remove the ovaries; in Subject #2, I would remove the uterus; in Subject #3, the clitoris; & so on. (In the case of a pregnant subject, injections into the birth canal & uterus of belladonna, ammonia, mercury: to see if it is possible to precipitate what is called *stillbirth.*) In one or two subjects, depending upon the degree of garrulity, I might remove the tongues, for it has been long suspected that mental illness is primarily expressed through speech: If a subject were deprived of her tongue, & could not rant & rave, would her illness be diminished?—possibly, *cured*?

It goes without saying that the surgeries would be carefully spaced, so that I could observe the patients closely afterward: to what degree *hysteria* had diminished, or grew worse, or seemed unchanged.

I intended also to combine some of the surgeries with practical experimentations with morphine, chloroform, & ether; even after years of administering *anesthesia,* I was not satisfied that I knew how best to use these powerful chemicals, whose results, in my experience, often seemed random & unpredictable.

As the female subjects in my Laboratory were, for the most part, sturdy specimens, insensitive to pain that would immobilize more genteel women, as their diminished intelligence rendered them less curious, the circumstances for such experimentation were ideal; for, in all things *gynecological,* if in no other significant way, it appears that the genitals of females of all classes are *identical.*

I intended to begin with Bathsheba, whose quick temper & devious ways were clear symptoms of hysteria, giving instructions to Gretel that, on the eve of the surgery, she was to slip into Bathsheba's food a strong dose of morphine, that Bathsheba would sleep deeply through the night & not wake in the morning, but remain unconscious & unresisting. Indeed, after Bathsheba sank into a deep sleep that night, Gretel & Brigit were to carry her quietly out of the hospital ward & into the operating room, without her knowledge; for I feared a fierce resistance if Bathsheba knew that she was scheduled for one of my surgeries.

By her concerned expression, which seemed to me both comical & annoying, Brigit wished to inquire of me: *What was wrong with Bathsheba?*

"Bathsheba is in dire need of emergency surgery, having shown symptoms of *uterine prolapse*"—so I replied, as earnestly as if I were speaking to a fellow M.D.

(This pathological condition, the collapse of the uterus into the birth canal, where it might sag out of the female's body, through the vagina, was the singularly repulsive affliction suffered by Dr. Cleff's wife, which I had successfully repaired.)

Indeed, the mere words—*uterine prolapse*—were grave enough, if the little deaf-mute could read my lips, she need not inquire further.

To Gretel & Brigit, I gave careful instructions: "As soon as you carry Bathsheba into the surgical room, secure her on the operating table with the leather straps. Make sure that they are *tight*. Though I don't expect her to wake up prematurely, we may as well take precautions."

At this, both my assistants were very quiet. Evidently there was no need for the little deaf-mute to inquire further. With grave bovine air Gretel murmured, *Yes, Doctor.*

Surely, I had no reason to suspect an imminent mutiny!

Nor did Providence prepare me, as the covenant between the Creator & me would seem to have promised.

Eve of March 13, 1861. Nearing nine p.m. Through a part-raised window in my home office, in the Director's residence as I was perusing a medical text by lamplight, I heard, or believed that I heard, a plaintive voice—*Dr. Weir! Oh, Dr. Weir! You are badly needed in the Laboratory* . . . At first, I was not sure that I was hearing correctly, & lifted my head to listen more acutely—*Dr. Weir! Please come, you are badly needed* . . .

Here was the (mute, melodic) voice of the Irish girl, wafting to my ears, borne by a breeze of early spring! This summons to my blood made my heart leap, for I was already in an aroused & anticipatory mood, preparing for surgery in the morning.

That evening, several of my in-laws had been guests at dinner, including Theresa's sisters & their children, so it happened that, following the heavy meal, as I retreated to my office with the excuse of needing to prepare for a very early morning, the rest of the company gathered in the parlor; talking & laughing gaily, in a way that would have distracted me ordinarily, & greatly vexed me; but tonight seemed to me serendipitous, for amid their clamor no one heard Brigit's siren-call for *Dr. Weir.*

At once, hearing, I leapt to my feet, for I did not want one of our house servants to intercede, & knock at my door. Hurriedly I prepared a lighted lantern to take outside, & snatched up my physician's valise, in a state of excitation.

Dr. Weir—come quickly!

Exiting the house from the rear, I discovered to my amazement both my nurse-assistants, Gretel & Brigit, awaiting me in the shadows, in their prim nursing uniforms, starched white caps on their heads; each holding a lighted candle that flickered somewhat coquettishly in the wind. Gretel's face was doughy-grim & Brigit's radiant with the reflected candlelight, her pale eyes shining like a cat's eyes.

With thick-tongued urgency, Gretel told me that one of the experimental subjects needed emergency help: "She is bleeding badly, Dr. Weir!"

"'She'—? Who is it, Gretel?"

"Juel."

Juel! What did I care for *Juel!* I had expected the subject to be Bathsheba, & the nuisance of a surgery postponed.

Juel was the most wretched of patients, a survivor of several surgeries, who clung stubbornly to her miserable life, as if to spite me; so ravaged, so malnourished, so wizened, & more resembling a large bat than a human, I had no more reasonable use for her, as a subject for further experiments; & always she defied me, for no removal of any infected organ of hers resulted in curing her lunacy, so far as I could determine. Yet, as a Christian physician, I could not betray indifference. Also, it was a law of my Laboratory that no physician should be summoned to it, except me, even in emergency situations, for I did not want anyone on the medical staff to step inside my restricted space, & pry into my private research.

I sighed heavily, to signal to Gretel & Brigit that their vigilance was vexatious to me; yet, as a responsible physician, I would humor them.

As they led me to the imposing structure of North Hall, along a walkway overgrown with tall grasses & thistles, it seemed that two voices addressed me, & not just Gretel's—

So suddenly it happened, Dr. Weir—

—so much blood—

—h-hem-or—

—hemorrhage—

Hurry, Dr. Weir! Only you can save her.

My heart was beating rapidly, in anticipation. Though the countenance I showed to my nurse-assistants was one of vexation at being interrupted in my own household, in truth I was thrilled to be routed like this, so unexpectedly, while a most irksome gaiety reigned in my household, from which I was exiled.

High gusts of wind blew strange, sculpted-looking clouds across the sky, great schooners & galleons, ships boasting many masts & sails, illuminated by a glowering moon, then cast into shadow, & then again illuminated. Rare that I stepped foot into North Hall after dusk, as I did now, lifting the lantern high before me, that I might not trip on the stairway, as the nurse-assistants hurried before me holding their candles aloft, & beckoning me to *Hurry!*

By night, the interior of the red-brick building exuded a funereal aura. The natural smells of the madhouse—camphor, rancid food, matted hair, desperation, & rage—were denser now than by day. The staircase seemed far steeper than usual, as we climbed to the third, topmost floor. Corridors led in several directions, for the architect had stipulated, as many windows as possible are desirable in a mental hospital, for the suffusion of light into the wounded soul.

But at night, windows emit no light, & rather reflect a shimmering interior, distorted by candlelight.

How altered by night, my own Laboratory—the hospital ward so familiar by day, quite unfamiliar by night! As I entered, almost hesitantly, I could scarcely make out the shadowy figures of the patients. Some were in their beds, too weak to rise; others were standing beside their beds, for some odd reason, ragged nightgowns falling to their ankles. All, it seemed, were holding lighted candles aloft, in preparation for my arrival, or celebration; positioned about the room & emitting a ghostly sort of illumination.

How quiet they were, where, by day, these female lunatics kept up a noisome din in the ward, forever chattering, to themselves or to others, ranting, braying, weeping, praying. And how curious that the dozen or more patients, familiar to me by day, were, by night, scarcely recognizable. There was—Mahala? Zenobia? Nestra? Others, whom I would have sworn I had never seen before. Silently they observed me, their eyes flatly reflecting a tawny light, like shards of glass, glaring out of their ravaged faces, blending with shadows like African masks.

—*through here, Dr. Weir*—

—*Juel is in here*—

Hurry!

Now I remembered, I had ordered fractious Juel to be removed from the ward after her surgery & placed *under restraint,* in an adjoining room, to prevent her harming herself, or others. I did recall, the bat-like creature had tried to bite me, with but a very few teeth remaining in her head.

—*here she is, Dr. Weir*—

—*Juel, here is Dr. Weir!*—

—*he will save you . . .*

Airless & stifling as the Laboratory ward was, with its double row of hospital cots, & the smells of numerous female bodies commingling, the anterior of the Laboratory, the corridor of *restraining rooms,* was more repugnant. Only wretches were housed here, hopeless cases of mental infirmity, homicidal madness, filthy habits. Here, not merely *minds* were diseased, but *brains.* Experimental subjects who had outlived their usefulness, yet continued to live, were housed here, out of necessity; for in their altered post-surgical state they could not be transferred back into their original wards in the Asylum without arousing questions among the nursing staff, for which there could not be answers.

Naturally, the mortality rate in this part of the Laboratory was high. No patient who entered it was likely to emerge from it alive.

These lunatics, categorized as *null.* That they would not undermine the statistics released annually by the Asylum.

At the present time there were three of these creatures in separate cells, of whom two were glaring out at us, with murderous eyes like owls' eyes; the third, wizened Juel, lay on the floor of her cell, on a bed of filthy straw, coiled upon herself like a snake so that her face was hidden from us.

Juel! Dr. Weir has arrived, he will help you.

Was this Brigit, speaking so clearly? In the darkness, I could not see her delicate lips move, but I was certain, this bell-like voice, so different from Gretel's voice, was that of the Irish girl.

"Juel? Is that you? Look here, what is wrong?"—putting the question to the patient, in as courteous a voice as I could summon.

All this while pressing my lantern against the bars of the cell, at shoulder-height; but unable to see well into the enclosure, nor would the patient cooperate by turning her wizened-bat face to me. Indeed, the straw beneath the coiled figure was dark-stained, with blood or other foul liquids, I could not discern.

As I had no choice but to unlock the cell door, with a key kept on a heavy ring of keys in my valise, my nurse-assistants stepped forward to assist me.

Dr. Weir?—allow me to take the lantern. So it seemed, Brigit spoke.

Dr. Weir?—allow me to take the key. So it seemed, Gretel spoke.

It was not unusual that an attendant would unlock the door of such an enclosure, as well as perform preliminary tasks, prior to a physician's arrival; I had time to wonder, here, that so little had been done of a preliminary nature, such as sweeping away old, befouled straw, & replacing it with fresh straw, before the attending physician stepped inside.

So, too, in that instant of wonderment, I heard a sharp intake of breath. Many breaths. A footfall behind me, heavier than I might have expected. Another footfall, heavy. And another.

"What? What is—"

In a haze of confusion, I turned to see leering mask-faces & tawny-glaring eyes, beyond the familiar faces of my nurse-assistants; & more, crowded in the doorway; even as something struck me on the side of the head, devastating as a mallet, felling me at once, stunned & uncomprehending as a steer destined for slaughter, onto the filthy floor.

As my soul shrank to a pinprick of consciousness, as fragile as a flame, from all sides came cries, murderous shrieks as of predator birds rushing at me—

Butcher! Butcher! Red-Handed Butcher!

V

The Insurrection

Lost Girl, Found: An Orphan's True Story Told by Herself

1868

BY BRIGIT AGNES KINEALY

I.

. . . we had not begun murdering the Red-Handed Butcher before it was over. He had fallen at once to the filthy floor like a dumb beast smote by the hand of God, slip-sliding piteously in his own blood. Weeping like a whipt child bereft of all hope & shamed & his clothing torn & yanked from him, in his nakedness mangled genitals bleeding between sallow old-man thighs we screamed with laughter to see. *Hallelujah!*—the cry of the wrathful Jehovah God of the Israelites pushing forward in the fury of joy like flood-waters overspilling the riverbank, the boldest of us were bent on murder, the joy of murder, our knives were hungry for the soft-fleshy chest of the Red-Handed Butcher who had kept us captive, the heart of the Red-Handed Butcher who had tortured us, the belly of the Red-Handed Butcher who had sodomized us even as the wisest of us cried—*No! No, we must not!*—*it will be our doom, if we murder the Butcher-doctor.*

Hid my eyes for I could not look upon it, what we had wrought.

. . . each night prepared specially for me a syrup like chalky molasses to drink, *sweet balm of Lethe* he called it, for himself the physician as for me *his* nurse, for the physician-hands trembled from the excitement of the scalpel slicing into female flesh, eruption of bright blood like a shrill cry, insertion of the scalpel into the obdurate female flesh of one whose name he had already forgotten, could not have recalled, for *names* of the *female lunatics* upon whom he operated did not register to one who wields the knife; yet, he knew my name, in his low thrilled voice murmuring, *Brigit!—you are so beautiful, look at you!—so beautiful, not like the others who are so ugly, abominations in the eyes of God.* And I would wish to resist yet could not. I would wish to draw a razor swift & unerring across the Butcher-throat yet could not. Instead the numbness was welcome to me, God forgive me. Memory of my mother forgive me. All whom I have helped to wrong, my sisters forgive me. In sorrow grateful for the numbness rising in me, *sweet balm of Lethe.*

Nothing so pleasurable as numbness to one so miserable in affliction as I, so shamed in the flesh as I, as the scalding-hot pain between my legs eased & there came merciful darkness into which I could sink, a thousand thousand cobwebs soft to the touch. So that all that was fearful & craven in me, & despairing, would be obliterated—how my mother was taken from me long ago, they said she had *died in a horrible accident, scalded to death through her own fault drunkenness God forgive her.* So long ago, her face is lost to me except in dreams of such sweetness tears streak my cheeks & though I am sleeping (I know) *I can feel the wet on my skin,* & in the dream I can speak, my throat is not shut up tight but open, I can breathe freely, I can speak, but only in the dream. For awake, now I cannot speak. Their terrible words, I cannot hear. I am shielded from them, for I am *deaf & dumb.* In their eyes, I am an imbecile. I am damaged in my brain. My ancestors, who are Irish, are trash to them, who are English-born, & some of them Scots-born. We are Catholic, they are Protestant. Their cruelty has followed us to the New World. Their cruelty, I have been told of, in broken-off tales. We are not slaves but servants, it is explained. We are not *chattel slaves,* we are *contracted servants.* We are not Black like the Africans kidnapped & brutalized into slavery, we are white, yet we are *white trash.*

Why I cannot speak, I am in terror of speech. I am in terror of screaming to the Red-Handed Butcher not to touch me. For he is my Master, he has the right to touch me. He has the right to whip me. He has the right to force me, to have domain over my body. There is no way for me to scream how my baby was taken from me, pulled from my riven body howling in pain, a knife slicing my belly to release the big-headed baby with his father's high broad brow, cried for my baby to be returned to me but they *would not,* saying I was *unfit to nurse.* For I was too young, & my breasts too small. For I was too white-skinned, & a freak & now *deaf & dumb.* And where I was torn, inside, there was a hole, a tear, a leak of excrement down my legs, melting flesh from my bones. And ever after, in a torment of shame that such things were done to me, & I could not say no; & more than one of them, the male staff, & the doctors, & the Director, to none of them could I say *No.* For I am a servant, I am the lowest of servants, indentured. Because my contract can be extended. Because if I am *in breach of contract,* it can be extended. Because if I am sick, if I am not able to work, it can be extended. Because I am Irish Catholic trash. Because my baby was of worth because it was its father's baby & so taken from me to be adopted by a rich couple, Protestant, English-speaking, known by the baby's father, of course he would lie to me he would tell me, *Your baby has died, Brigit. That is a blessing.* But if my baby had died it was of the shame of his father not-named. *Medrick Weir*—never would he see his own baby, he did not wish to look upon the Devil's spawn. Bitter memory of Medrick Weir praising me for my beauty when I was just a girl, cupping my face in his hands to peer into my eyes into my soul yearning to be loved, cherished, protected soon after my mother died, all of them praised me, petted me, women as well as men, how pitiful that the child is an orphan, how pitiful that her mother had no husband, how pitiful that her mother died in such a way, a laundress to the very end, her skin peeled off her bones in shimmering skeins of scalded flesh. Exclaiming at my white hair, my white skin, my eyes the palest blue like glass, exclaiming how like an angel I was, but then later, how like a devil, a heathenish little devil scorning me when my belly started to swell. Scorning me for the shame of the birth, & for the stink of my body after the birth. For the beauty of a face cannot compensate for the stink of a female body rent in two. Banning me even from the laundry, the rough heat of the cellar, in disgust of the stink of me, that I could not help. Banning me from aboveground, sending me belowground to work in the latrines.

For it was a curse of God, how my body leaked filth. For I could not deny, it was a curse. For I could not even speak, out of shame at such a curse.

Envy of my sisters who have plunged into the wide, rushing river— into the black muck of the shore, of the river—sunk to their deaths in the rich black muck of the swamp beside the river. If I had the courage. If I had the strength. Run from here, into the black muck of the swamp & breathe the rank rot-water into my lungs to extinguish my life which I *could not bring myself to do.* No more than I could have known to ask of my mother, *Who is my father?—is he one of the Masters?* For this was pride, to be raised above the others. If only to be cast down cruelly, at least for a time to be raised above the others, & suffused with a false hope.

The melting icicle, its beauty is not less real, that it is melting & will be gone.

Though it was known that the Director took a special interest in me, in the pretense of an interest in me, as an orphan. Cast-off orphan, no family, a mother who died of drink (it was claimed), & no father (no father who would declare himself). Not even was the woman a *good Catholic,* she was a *lapsed Catholic* & bound for Hell.

But an orphan cannot ask, *Who is my father?*—for the answer is a whipping. An orphan cannot ask, *Are you my father?*—for the answer is a whipping. An orphan cannot ask, *Why will Jesus not save me?*— for the answer is a whipping. As an orphan with no schooling, no one to care enough to send me to a school, the Irish girls are natural-born servants, they are laundresses, they toil in latrines, they are not allowed to be nurses, it is enough for them to aspire to be nurses' aides, & still they will be held in contempt. No need to waste schools on them! Teach yourself to read, if you care so much for reading—so they laughed at me. For few of them can read. Few of them know of the Gospels bringing good news of Jesus our Savior. The poor, the despised, the meek. Like dogs the orphan children were summoned to *him,* the Master. A snap of his fingers, the frightened orphan-girl is summoned to the Director's residence. There is a secret way, a rear entrance. All of the servants know, & some of these are Irish & practiced in holding their tongues. If they heard cries, screams. If they saw evidence, on the bedsheets in the morning. Hold their tongues, they are not citizens, they have not the rights of the ruling class.

Pull off the befouled bedsheets, scalding-hot the washtubs, still the faint stains remain, nothing can remove them.

Your baby has died, Brigit. It was ordained by God.

Your baby it was, & not his. Not ours. And this baby had not died, I knew well. But taken from me as I am trash, & unfit.

3.

Nowhere to run, nowhere to hide, in desperation running from the grounds of the Asylum into the bog beside the river. An orphan-girl of eleven, nearly twelve, grown to a dangerous age for the eyes of men have drifted upon her, *his* eye has fixed upon her, in a way that is new.

Panting for breath as her (bare, bleeding) feet sink into the black muck, as the black muck sucks at her feet, ankles, legs in a delirium swallowing her whole like a great fish might swallow her, in mercy. In excited flurries mosquitoes settle upon her eager to drain her dry of blood, in the marsh that has no end running until her girl's-heart bursts & she collapses in the marshland shimmering with irides-cent insects, dragonflies, bees, bright-feathered songbirds & black-feathered scavenger birds, nowhere to hide except deep in the marsh where her pale-blond hair grows into the roots of the swamp trees, her fingers & toes grow into the tangled roots of the swamp trees, where sleek glittering snakes as fat as a man's forearm swim lazily in the dank dark water in which her girl's-soul is a tough little nut, it will grow into a tough little tree, it will grow into a tough little invincible tree, it will not exude light but suck light into it, a soul more beautiful than any light, but nothing like this will happen for rough hands discover her within hours, within a mile of the Asylum attendants will track her down, seize her hair, brusque fingers closing about her rib cage with the power to crack her bones, lifting her with no more effort than if she were a very young child & not a girl of twelve.

Medrick Weir has sent us—find her, the little Irish slut.

Bring her back alive.

4.

Sweet balm of Lethe that makes the unbearable, bearable. But the price is, much is taken from us, those bearing the yoke of servitude have forgotten, in order that we might live.

5.

Then came the younger one, a relative—*Silas Weir.*

Gentler than Medrick Weir, his face pale in panic & disgust at the sight of me, in the delivery room.

Female gaping bloody riven body heaving to give birth, raw shrieking unbearable to the (male) ear, yet if he'd wished to flee, he had not; if he'd wished to allow the orphan-girl in agony of childbirth to die, he had not; remained with her, & with the midwife Gretel, grasping the handle of the bloody knife, to slash open my abdomen, to save the life of my baby, & of me; for otherwise, we would both have died.

And of his own choice afterward, seeking me out. For he remembered me, & saw now what distress I was in, a mother who has lost her baby, a female whose body has been rent & torn & has become repulsive, & felt pity for me. For then, he was not (yet) the Butcher, he was the Director's young kinsman, it was claimed: not (yet) the evil he would become.

Beginning then, the succession of examinations, surgeries. Opening my tight-clenched body with a tin spoon!—excruciating pain, I could not draw breath to scream.

No other doctor at the Asylum would have wished to touch me. To come near me. For I was not a patient, but an indentured servant-girl, of no worth in my condition. A burden to feed, offensive to see. Yet: *That girl—Brigit? I vow, I will find a way to help her. I have daughters her age. I will help her, & others afflicted like her, with fistula. This is my promise for Providence has decreed, such is my destiny.*

Shame I am feeling now, how grateful I was, to be so singled out, by Silas Weir.

How craven in my obsequiousness to him, who would become my Master. Out of gratitude, we will crawl like beasts. Not knowing if you will be allowed to *live* & then it is granted you, the most meager *life* you would cherish. No one in the world except Silas Weir would care for me, enough to cure me.

In this, Silas Weir did not deceive. He was true to his word, in time. A dozen surgeries—& finally, success.

For too long, I shut my eyes against the harm he was doing to the others. For you will shut your eyes, in a glaring light. You will *refuse to see,* that which is blinding in your face.

It was not long ago, yet I was very young then. I was a girl—a girl made to give birth, & made to lose her baby; an orphan-girl, an Irish albino deaf-mute girl, lowest of the low.

Then, I could barely read, & I could not write at all. I am not that person now, writing this memoir. But I wish to be honest, in recording what I remember of Silas Weir's Laboratory in North Hall, in the late years of the 1850s.

These are your private quarters, Brigit! This room, this cot.

No one has a key to this door, Brigit. Except me.

A storeroom in the Laboratory, close by the ward. Windowless. Close by the restraint rooms where female lunatics were held captive in barred cells & every night moaned, wailed, wept in despair.

Yet it was *my place,* private & secret. For I had had nothing like this before in my life.

As Gretel had advised me—*You are an orphan, an indentured servant, no family to protect you—take what you can from them, to save your life. As we all do.*

So it happened, the meals provided for me in the Asylum kitchen were not the meals provided for most of the population of the Asylum, but the very meals provided for private patients, under Silas Weir's care.

Not meager, tasteless, & frequently rancid food the others had no choice except to eat but rather nourishing food, freshly prepared—porridge, puddings, corn bread & rye bread, pork, beef, chicken—potatoes, greens & grits, even pies—blueberry, cherry, rhubarb!

It gave the Director pleasure, to so reward me. His *nurse-assistant.*

It gave the Director pleasure, as I was deaf & dumb, & could not speak to him, that he might speak to me, anything that came out of his mouth that was boastful, thrilling—*Our secret, Brigit. No one must know!*

A plan he liked to speak of, he would send me to nursing school in New Brunswick, where I would be trained in Gyno-Psychiatric nursing, & return then to Trenton, to work closely with him for the remainder of my life.

Secrets to be kept from everyone else. But of course, they knew.

In a stream like a turbulent river each week new *female lunatics* were committed to the Asylum & of these a select few were brought to Silas Weir's Laboratory in North Hall hopeful (at first) that Dr. Weir's *experimental surgeries* would cure their lunacy, & free them; & with time, gradually there were fewer patients remaining who knew of my origin—my mother's death, the pregnancy forced upon me, that I was the *Irish deaf & dumb orphan* to be pitied. Hearing tales that I had had a baby & the baby had been taken from me, the boldest of these patients inquired if Silas Weir had been the father; & if the Red-Handed Butcher (for so Dr. Weir was beginning to be known) had delivered his own baby, & seeing that it was disfigured or misshapen was sickened by it, & cast it away from him, in utter ruthlessness.

No!—no! It was not—not Silas Weir . . .

Miming such protests, with facial contortions, & gestures of my hands; yet there were those in the Laboratory who did not wish to believe otherwise, & who would not trust me, no matter how kind Brigit Kinealy was to them, no matter how tenderly she nursed them, for I was the Red-Handed Butcher's favored *nurse-assistant,* & so loathed.

6.

In my hiding-place in dead of night with but a stub of a candle & a flickering flame by which to *read.*

Shaping my lips to the printed words, that leapt to my eyes from the page. Such joy, a rush of joy, for printed material was forbidden to the indentured, any effort of *reading* forbidden, for the waking hours of the indentured are not their own but their Master's.

It was said, the piteous Black enslaved in the South might be whipt to death if they purloined printed material, to attempt to *read;* & even a white person would be grievously punished for teaching a slave to *read.*

For *reading* must be forbidden, to keep the despised helpless, & powerless.

Cruel as our lives were in the North, as indentured servants, yet for the Black enslaved Africans in the South, life was far worse.

As I was *white-skinned,* I knew myself not totally damned. For if I could escape my situation, I might pass for a free citizen. (Though, as Irish, I was as close to damned as might be possible, in the eyes of the English.)

He did not know, or did not seem to care, how I hoarded printed materials—old newspapers, magazines, a medical textbook he'd cast aside, & would never miss.

As a parent would not care, if his child played with *reading,* who was illiterate; for what harm could *reading* do, in mere mimicry?

Yet: thrilling, to hold a book in my hand.

Thrilling, to turn the pages of a book.

And very gradually, it seemed, words leapt to my eye, which I was capable of recognizing.

Fascinated by the battered old medical text, some of its pages badly stained.

Drawings of what are called *anatomies.* Insides of human bodies, so that the *organs* are exposed.

It was Dr. Weir's half-serious suggestion, I might study the anatomical drawings that I might better assist him in his surgeries.

This was joy to me. Amid so much that was pain & humiliation, this—happiness!

My mother was illiterate, it was believed that all of her family were illiterate, in Limerick, Ireland. Most of those toiling in the Asylum, illiterate.

Or their poor brains so blasted, *words* passed through them as through a sieve.

Dr. Weir did not notice, for Dr. Weir did not *see,* much of what surrounded him. Took little notice that his nurse-assistant was curious about pamphlets, books—retrieving from the trash what others had cast negligently aside.

Dr. Weir was like the others—men like himself—had to laugh at girls & women struggling to *read, think.* His own daughters did not require education beyond eighth grade, he believed—*It will only tax*

*their brains. It will drain blood from their brains. Womanly instincts
will guide them in being wives & mothers, not ideas in books!*

Fascinating to me, drawings in the medical text. Insides of the
human body: *heart, lungs, esophagus, liver, spleen, kidneys, pancreas,
gallbladder, stomach, small intestines, colon, bladder, uterus.*

With a pencil & paper, I copied these.

Thrilling!—to dare to copy what had been printed, in the possession of men like Dr. Weir.

Here was a drawing of the human (white, male) head sliced in
two so that you could see little rooms inside the skull where kinds of
behavior were located: *truth-telling, frugality, intuition, reasoning, fortitude, courage, charity, foresight, philanthropy, worship, respect, sympathy, justice, integrity, hope (future), hope (present), tenacity, mendacity.*

(How strange this was!—for I had many times seen the bashed-out
brains of animals, that were bloody suet, & flesh, mixed together, & I
was sure that human brains were like these, & not like the drawing in
The Science of Phrenology.)

Yet stranger were individual drawings of female organs: *uterus,
birth canal, vulva, vagina.* Here was a baby inside a womb, in a position to be born, shown with a forceps already gripping its skull—so
ugly! You were meant to believe that the baby could not be born,
unless the (male) hand was gripping the forceps, to pull out the baby.

Another very ugly drawing was something like a skinned baby
rabbit with a little extrusion like a fish's fin & a dark hole at its
center—*vagina.*

I thought I recognized this. I could not read the word—*vagina*—but
grasped the logic.

For only a man would draw something so ugly!—I could not help
laughing, for it was very funny.

Looking sharply at me, Dr. Weir took the book from me, & frowned
at what he saw, & a crude blush came into his face.

Saying, he hoped that I would tell no one, that I had been looking
through his medical books.

Quickly miming, *No Doctor.*

"For it isn't advised for indentured servants to take up book-
learning. That would set a very bad precedent, you know."

Yes Doctor.

"You can't really 'read,' Brigit, can you? You are just pretending—playing."

This was more a statement than an inquiry but I knew to murmur piously, *Yes Doctor*.

Hiding from his eyes behind the glittering eyeglasses all that I wished to keep from him, that was forbidden to me, & would save my life.

7.

... one night waking from the *balm of Lethe* to discover myself naked, hot-skinned, & sweating lying helpless on my back. For all volition had drained from my limbs, I was just barely awake. Airless inside the secret space, the room whose door I could not lock, the room whose door only *he* could lock & unlock. On my back helpless. Flickering shadows of candlelight & above me grunting & moaning the face that was both familiar & hideously altered. Rough fingers poking & prying inside me, where formerly the surgeon's fingers & the surgeon's instrument had pushed, pierced to excruciating pain. Now grunting, moaning. For it was not expected, that the *balm of Lethe* had released me. For it was not expected, that I would wake, & see that face as enormous as a moon. And inside the opened trousers a stubby flesh-knob sprouting like a small skinless creature so that I cried in astonishment, *Dr. Weir? What are you doing?*

But it was not me, Brigit. You know that.

Yes, Dr. Weir. I mean—no.

It was your dream, a laudanum-dream. For these are dreams all women have, for whom laudanum is prescribed. For in the weakness of the female, such lurid dreams arise.

Yes, Dr. Weir.

These persons you believe you see—they are not real. They are not known to us.

Yes, Dr. Weir. "Not known to us."

8.

Arms & legs spread, wrists & ankles bound tight. This was the *Bed of Tranquility*, which Dr. Weir was testing in the Laboratory.

Wetted sheets tight about me, that were allowed to dry, & to tighten. So close to suffocation, it is a risk to be taken, that the *perverse will of the female* will be broken by the physician.

Which day this was, I do not know. Time is broken, as a mirror is broken. Spooning *balm of Lethe* to my lips, that had gone numbed. Yet, it would not be enough to dull the piercing pain.

But this is day. Midday. Sun streaming through the window, so that the surgeon could see what his instruments were doing.

Those months, years. Determined to cure *fistula*.

Lie still, Brigit! It will not hurt if you lie still, it will be over before you know it, shut your eyes.

For I will make you whole, Brigit—that is my vow. I will cure you, I am sent by Providence to cure you, & to enter the pantheon of American medicine, that has been promised us both.

9.

When did *butchery* begin?

It is difficult to recall. For we did not see calendars, we had little awareness of time.

In the Asylum there were clocks, & clocks were to be rigorously obeyed. But not calendars. In the Asylum, we floated free of time as on a river without end.

When does *butchery* begin, when they mean well at the start. Meaning *to help, to save*.

He would cure *lunacy*, he was determined. He would rid the female body of *infection, disease*.

In this, he was doing the will of God, he believed. Jesus Christ Savior. John Calvin, His emissary.

Repairing *fistulas*, removing teeth. Organs. Bloodletting.

Scream until your throat is stripped raw, no one will hear who does not wish to hear.

The medical staff at the Asylum, in the hire of Silas Weir. They did not hear what they did not wish to hear, only a few nurses, perhaps, who refused to continue, who quit the Asylum & were never heard of again.

Yet it was true, he had saved some of us. Certainly, he had saved *me*.

Yet, the scalpel had always wielded terrible pain, anguish, terror to those whose flesh it cut into.

Because he did not *feel it*. He saw, he heard, he understood; yet, he did not *feel* another's pain.

Commanding me, *Stuff a rag into her mouth, to quiet her.*

Be sure she's strapped down—tight.

Ridiculous! She is not *feeling pain, I assure you.*

Writhing in agony, droplets of sweat oozing through the pores of her forehead, eyes rolling panic-white as a horse's eyeballs roll in their enormous sockets.

Washing away blood, urine, & feces afterward. Helping to carry the dazed patient back into the ward, securing her to her cot.

Gretel's grim face, eyes downlooking. For Gretel had cast her lot with *him,* as I had. To save our lives.

Through the night praying, that the patient would not die.

No laudanum for this one. Too costly to waste on the doomed.

Through the long day, through the long night, tending to the comatose patient in the aftermath of the *hysterectomy*. For the surgeon needs practice, his skills come only through practice. For the surgeon's private patients, he must be prepared.

Skillfully Gretel changed bandages that soaked quickly with blood. Not needing to speak to me, but impatiently gesturing to me to assist her, seeing that the coarse black stitching Dr. Weir had hastily executed had begun to loosen, & bloody flesh sagged out of the ravaged vagina. Pressing wetted cloths against the patient's face as she lay feverish, moaning in pain, & at last, in mercy, slipping into a coma, scarcely breathing.

Shooing away flies, that buzzed on all sides.

In the early morning, our task was to prepare the (stiffened) body for the gravedigger, who had been summoned; to carry away the corpse in his mule-cart, to that part of the cemetery where the gravestones were trim white wooden crosses.

10.

It is my task to think, Brigit. It is your task to assist.
In my destiny, you have a role to play.

11.

. . . in the airless heat of late summer in New Jersey. The first of the flying beetles appeared. Out of nowhere they came. And then everywhere, we could not escape them.

Tiny glittery eyes & transparent wings throwing themselves into our sweating faces, as we screamed, & slapped them away but still they pelted us, & some (of us) could hear their tiny cries that were the Devil's cries—*Kill! Bite! Tear off the Butcher-face!*

You were very frightened. Laughed jamming knuckles against your mouth.

Pressing his stethoscope hard against Mahala's ears Butcher-doctor did not hear the Devil's voices for they were not meant for *him*. Pressed his stethoscope against Brigit's waxy-white delicately whorled ears but did not hear the Devil's voices for they were not meant for *him*.

Commanding Brigit, whose will he had broken, whose spirit he had corrupted, to heat the copper knitting needles in a flame, that he might penetrate Mahala's ears to rid her of the Devil's voices which he had (yet) to hear even while allowing for the possibility that they were not in fact *voices* but lice, fleas, ticks, or other sorts of vermin nesting inside Mahala's head.

Securing Mahala's head in the wooden device, he would boast to call the *Weir-wheel.*

As Mahala stiffened & began to resist, eyes rolling in panic.

Chloroform? A wetted cloth, to press against the panicked mouth, nose.

Heating the copper needle in the open flame. Is it possible, Butcher-doctor really means to pierce Mahala's eardrums . . .

The (small) hand of the nurse-assistant daring to touch the (larger) hand of the Butcher-doctor!—as if God had urged her, despite the risk to her.

Butcher-doctor's surprise, fury. For *how dare she*, his nurse-assistant!
Banished then, *you know where* for the night.

Smells of the *cadaver room*, Brigit would never escape. Smells of
death, dying, & the decomposing of the bodies of her sister-captives,
she betrayed.

So many, over years. Could they forgive her!

In the Laboratory were countless surgeries, not recorded in the surgeon's journal. Not in the Asylum's records. Countless deaths, corpses
trundled by night to unnamed graves.

With each, the flying beetles with their tiny glittery eyes & transparent wings plagued us. *He* never saw, for *he* had no idea.

Tiny cries for only us to hear—*Kill! Bite! Tear off the Butcher-face!*

12.

Who is your Master, girl?

You, Dr. Weir. You are my Master.

You do not sound convincing, Brigit. Are you mocking me, Brigit?

Master, forgive me: I am not.

You are contradicting me, Brigit: declaring you are not?

Master, I—I am n-not . . .

*Not so insolent, are you, Brigit? In this place of disgrace, where you
belong.*

I am very sorry, Master . . .

Of course you are sorry, now that you are you know where. *In our
secret place where no one will hear & no one will see.*

. . . did not mean, Master—to be "insolent."

*D'you think you can behave, to me, like one of my own daughters?
Smirking & rolling your eyes. Daring to sass me?*

I do not mean to "sass" you, Master.

*Would you rather that I amputate one of your legs, or one of your
arms?*

I—I would n-not . . .

*Like what's-her-name—"Nester"—who gets along very well with just
one leg & a stump—& no teeth . . .*

That is not Nestra, Master. That is—

Ridiculous! These wretches have no names, except what has been given them.

Yes, Master . . .

You have not said, Brigit: a leg, or an arm?

I—I—I would . . . I would not want to lose an arm or a leg, Master.

But I am asking you, Brigit: Which would you prefer to lose?

An—an arm, Master.

Then you could not assist me! With one arm, you would be useless & lazy, of no worth in the Laboratory.

I—I would try . . .

I would have to return you to the latrines. An Irish deaf-mute, with but one arm! Ridiculous.

N-no, Master . . .

If I amputated your tongue, there would be no temptation for you to sass me, then.

I—I do not "sass" you—Master . . .

Ah but yes you do, Brigit! You "sass" me every day, if not in words—in thought.

N-No, Master . . .

At this very minute, while you are pretending to be mute. I see in your eyes, you are utterly transparent to me. Of course you dare to sass your Savior, but you are gravely deceived if you think that I am unaware.

Master, no.

You have dared to object, to my plans for amputating tongues?

It would be very cruel, Master. You are not cruel . . .

I have told you, Brigit!—in the matter of scientific experiment, there is no cruelty, as there is no kindness. The object will be to determine if a subject can learn to "speak" without a tongue—some sort of speech, even if gibberish. All that is required is the removal of several tongues in persons who utter mostly gibberish anyway.

Y-Yes, Master . . .

Yet this gibberish they utter, which I overhear, has "meaning" to them—to you; without tongues, it's my theory that you would invent your own gibberish-speech, & you would understand each other—the lot of you.

I—I do not know, Master. Please do not amputate my tongue . . .

But the tongues of the others, I may amputate?

Master, no—please.

"Please"—what?

I—I do not know, Master. I am so frightened . . .

But not of me, Brigit? For I am your kind Master, I am the Master who saved your life.

Yes, Master.

Who saved your life more than once, & is determined to heal you, by God.

Yes, Master.

You are not frightened of me, then?

N-No . . .

You must never be frightened of me, Brigit.

Y-yes, Master . . .

Because it is true. I am a good man—I am the Director of the Asylum who has reformed it, after the outrages of my predecessor.

Everyone knows, I am renowned in Trenton. I am renowned in all of New Jersey, & in Manhattan & Philadelphia. As I am elevated, so you, the lowest of the low, are elevated with me: my nurse-assistant.

Because God has sent me to you, alone of your race. Exalted above your insidious race.

Because it is ordained by Providence, I shall make you whole again— I shall heal you—that tiny little flaw, in you. I shall raise you above your station. I will raise us both. You will see.

One day, when Providence ordains. Not just now, for the time is not now.

Ending the long day now with the balm of Lethe, Brigit, which we both deserve. For we have worked very hard in the service of the Lord.

As my eyelids grew heavy, & a drowsy weakness suffused my body. Hidden from sight of the others, in the privacy of my quarters. It would be late in the day, nearing dusk.

In his merry mood which few saw, very few except me, Dr. Weir forced open my jaws to grip my tongue in his fingers. In play, such things Dr. Weir did in play, yet when I gagged, & tried to wrench away from him, he held me fast, my head caught in the crook of his arm.

Would you like me to apply the *Weir-wheel*, if you insist upon resisting?

Would you like me to soak a cloth in chloroform, to put you into the deepest & meekest of sleeps?

As the *balm of Lethe* spread, coursed through my body, I lacked all strength to resist.

How strange it was, & how terrifying, Dr. Weir would play with my tongue with his fingers. Strength drained from my limbs like water, & seemed to flow into the physician, to suffuse him with a virility not ordinarily his, & the quickened breathing of lewdness. I tried to shrink from him, yet without offending him, for we must never offend our oppressors, lest they punish us severely. In this way quick-breathing, the Butcher held me fast, my pale hair in a waterfall straight & flattened against his shoulder in a hellish embrace of mock-intimacy.

Soon then, I gave up all resistance. Eyelids so heavy, I could not keep them open.

What relief to sink into sleep, a hot sodden sleep, an unbroken sleep until the chatter of birds woke me hours later at dawn; what gratitude then to be alone on the lumpy cot amid stained sheets in the windowless storeroom with the taste of the Butcher's fingers in my mouth & the dreamlike memory of—I knew not what.

For I am your kind Master, I am the Master who saved your life, Brigit.

13.

Lucy did not have to die.

There! Boldly I declared to Dr. Weir, shaping my lips unmistakably, glaring at him, accusing him, that he could not help but hear.

Starved & denied water, Lucy died a most wretched death, in fever & convulsions over a period of twelve days. For the Butcher had denied her liquids, as a requirement of his experiment. Which I had told him, was *not a humane experiment.*

In astonishment gazing upon me, a mere nurse-assistant, as if a dog had stood on its hind legs to protest in human speech. *Humane! What are you saying! This is* science, *not* sentiment.

(In fact I had smuggled water to Lucy, & a sponge soaked in cool water, for her to suck when she was too weak to swallow; but Lucy had lost so much weight in the throes of diarrhea it was far too little, & too late for her.)

You have gone too far this time, Brigit. You will be whipped.

"Whipped!" I am not afraid.

For suddenly, I was not afraid; as Lucy was beyond fear, so I was.

Not even of the filthy & foul *cadaver room,* to which I was banished; & where Dr. Weir followed me panting & stuttering, grasping a whip in his hand.

A whip! From one of the attendants, the Director of the Asylum had acquired a *whip.*

I am commanding you, Brigit: disrobe.

I will not.

Are you disobeying me, Brigit?

Shaking my head, in certainty. The Butcher would have to remove my clothes himself, for I *would not.*

A flame seemed to rise in me, of pure Irish obstinance & mutiny.

Over the years at the Asylum, I had never once been whipt, for Medrick Weir had been partial to me, when he had been my Master; & others on the staff had favored me, too, or pitied me, for my disabilities, as for my white *angel-face;* & the transparency of my skin, in which delicate blue veins were visible, as in a porcelain doll of particular fragility.

But I had witnessed many frightful whippings, & beatings, & kickings, & pummelings, as the orderlies held dominion over the *lunatics,* with their whips & clubs, & every device with which they were supplied, to quell resistance.

It was my belief that Silas Weir was not prepared for such an act of discipline, as his orderlies were. His barbarism was of another sort, the barbarism of the scalpel & the curette, the *therapy;* he could not be brutal without such a mask, the pose of the gentleman, who must think highly of himself, that allowed him such cruelty.

Thus, with a shaky hand Dr. Weir raised the whip to me, not a bull-whip such as the worst of the orderlies used, but a smaller whip, that might be used for a horse or a mule; threatening to strike me, with the accusation that I was an *Irish devil;* even as I stood unflinching before him, determined not to cower.

For a moment it seemed as if, in very frustration, Dr. Weir might bring the whip down upon me, not on my back (for I stood resolute, facing him) but on my head & shoulders; to allow this, he even shut his eyes, & contorted his face.

But then, with a garbled cry, he threw down the whip, onto the floor of the *cadaver room,* & turned to stagger outside, like one desperate to breathe fresh air.

How laughable it was, the gentleman-physician had *flung down* his whip, as if the touch of it were scalding—a sight no Irish servant had ever seen before, I was certain.

Thank you, Jesus!—so the words came to me, in silence, as I sank to my knees on the filthy floor, badly trembling.

Hiding my face in my hands. In reaction to how close I had come, to being whipt, feeling very light-headed, giddy. Yet apprehensive: for I knew that the Butcher would not spare me, & that my punishment was yet to come.

Though truly I did not have much faith in Jesus, as so many others did, without question; for even if Jesus had helped *me,* in the moment, He had not helped my sisters. He had allowed Lucy to die most horribly, & had not protected the women upon whom Dr. Weir had experimented for years.

Jesus had done very little for the meek & helpless—we who, it was promised, were to inherit the earth, & be privileged in Heaven. Jesus had done nothing for the Black enslaved Africans—*that* was certain. Yet there remained the hope that, if you thanked Him most profusely, & God the Father, Creator of Heaven & Earth, & flattered both with their goodness & mercy, they would do some good for you eventually, if you did not give up & curse them, instead.

Butcher-doctor can go to Hell, Nestra laughed. *Jesus will set His foot on Butcher-doctor's neck & grind him to dust.*

When we could, we laughed. Even those of us locked in cells or shackled to our beds.

Howls of hilarity, spasms of coughing & wheezing.

"Are you—'the Irish girl'?"

Lowering my hands from my face to see, in astonishment, in the doorway of the *cadaver room,* a stranger, of about my age or a little older, not (evidently) an orderly, for he was not wearing an orderly's uniform—a very startled-looking young man whose face seemed to me familiar but whom I was sure I had never before glimpsed.

Declaring to me, with a flushed face, as I stared hard at his lips: *I am Jonathan Weir, his son. But—I am not—*his.

14.

In this way, entering my life.

In this way, altering my life, as the course of a river may be altered by a seemingly chance intervention, that may be indeed providential, determined from the beginning of Time.

Jonathan Weir!—Silas Weir's eldest son.

Though son & father did not resemble each other—much.

In a state of distress, I could not interpret much of what Jonathan said. Indicating to him, cupping my hand to my ear, & with expressions of childish mimicry, that I could not *hear* him.

In confusion Jonathan stared at me. Saying something, no doubt an apology, which I could not interpret.

Uncertain, Jonathan stood just inside the doorway of the *cadaver room*. His nostrils twitched with the smell, nervously he glanced about at the stained floor, walls. He had no idea what this room was, I knew. No idea, probably, what his father was.

Fair, fawn-colored hair that lifted from his forehead like a pale flame.

Eyes of such intelligence, sympathy, intensity—clutching at mine, in indecision.

As if considering—*Should he remain, or should he leave?*

Out of courtesy then, squatting on his heels. Since I was on the floor, my legs had so weakened. He did not wish to loom over me, to intimidate me.

Sighting the whip, that lay on the floor nearby. I understood, his father had sent him—to whip me?

The Butcher's son. What was the name—*Jonathan.*

He was a young man of about twenty-two. Lanky-limbed, & taller than his father. Lacking his father's morose manner, though his forehead was creased like dough by a fork's tines. In his eyes a piercing pain, I did not (yet) recognize as the pain of filial shame.

From a distance of several feet we regarded each other like furtive animals, each waiting for the other to make a move.

But *he* was the Director's son. *He* had been given instructions.

What to say? How to say? What speech? What words? In his hand the short, blunt whip.

Weighing in his hand like the weight of duty. *Shame, chagrin.*

Shaping with his lips, so that I could understand each word—*He sent me to whip you. He said you'd insulted the entire English race.*

Which made him laugh. Two of us laughing, breathless.

Declaring to me, he *would not whip anyone.* He did not believe that anyone *had the right to whip anyone else.*

But he *would whip someone,* he said, who *dared to whip* him. Or dared to whip *me.*

All this, with some difficulty, Jonathan Weir managed to communicate to me.

Yet it was not so very difficult, so strangely. For from the first, Jonathan Weir could understand me, as I could understand him, or nearly.

In slow enunciated words asking me if I was injured?—if his father had hurt me?—& I shook my head *No.*

Asking me if I was sick, if I was one of his father's patients, in the Laboratory, & I shook my head *No.*

I am one who cares for the sick. The women your father has injured.

Avidly he stared at my face. My lips. My gesturing hands.

He asked if I was hungry?—thirsty? I meant to indicate *No* but faltered.

For no one from his world had ever addressed me in such a way. Not condescendingly, not in pity. Rather, with tenderness. A brotherly solicitude. And so, I found it hard to respond, I did not want to betray myself, by weeping.

He went away, & returned with a glass & a pitcher of water, & a covered plate of food, I had to think had come from his home, for I knew that the Director's residence was not far away.

How readily this was accomplished, how forthright & assertive Jonathan Weir was, once he had made up his mind to act!

Yet again, maintaining an air of courtesy, or shyness. Squatting on his heels just inside the door, & keeping a distance between us.

I was very thirsty, & ravenously hungry. Tears welled in my eyes, I could not remember when I had eaten last. I could not remember that long day, that seemed to have begun with Lucy's death.

Like an animal, eating. Tears spilled down my cheeks. I thought—*He will pity me now. He will despise me.*

But Jonathan Weir was thinking of something that made him laugh.

Enunciating to me, with a smile—*You are a mighty small girl to have insulted the entire English race.*

I wondered if this was something Dr. Weir had told him. Yes, it was funny!

Suddenly together, laughing. *We,* against *him.*

That sensation of wildness that overcomes us, when something has been decided, of which nothing was known, until that very moment.

He went away, yet I knew—*I will see you again, Brigit.*

Taking up the ugly little whip, & striking it against the floor.

Bared teeth, an angry grin.

One day I will whip him—all of them.

15.

The lies we are told, as children we are told, we are not you & you are not us. That is the lie, Brigit. That those who are "blessèd by God" are deserving & those who are poor, who have no property or possessions, who are unwell or disabled deserve their fate & not our sympathy.

My father knows this is a lie because he is a doctor, he knows that all human beings are brothers & sisters beneath the skin.

In God, there are no Masters & servants. There are no Masters & slaves. The conqueror English are not superior to the Irish.

This I believe, & will not betray as my belief.

Know that I love you, Brigit, as my sister. And I vow, I will free you from the Asylum. I will free you from servitude. I will defy the fathers.

16.

Weeks & months like a rushing stream whose giddy froth hides rocks & boulders below the surface, how many times Jonathan Weir arranged to meet with me at the edge of the Asylum grounds overgrown with thistles & wild rose; often in silence, smiling, & staring, & touching—lightly, tentatively.

You are so beautiful, Brigit.

Your soul, shining in your eyes. Such beauty.

Framing my face with his hands. Strong hands, yet gentle.

As his father's hands were weak, & acquired strength only through dominion, & through the terror of the knife.

This delicate blue vein at your temple, Brigit! Such beauty.

What a gift to me, a revelation. The Butcher's son. In *his eyes*, I was not loathsome, I was not Irish trash & contemptible.

Touching my throat, as I tried to speak. Listening, as I tried to give *sound* to words—a matter of breathing, pushing with the breath.

. . . yes like that, Brigit. Yes!

He would teach me to speak (again). Already, I could hear (again)— *his words.*

Where there is trust, we can speak. We can hear.

Maybe I can buy out your contract. Set you free—from him.

And he would teach me to read, his eyes lighting in a promise of pleasure & rebellion, as if we were young children together, brother & sister.

In spring, wild growing wisteria whose odor left us dazed, giddy. Daring to touch, to caress.

Bringing me children's books, from his household. Of course, I could read these—most of these.

Sheets of paper & colored pencils with which I could copy A B C D E F G H I J K L M N O P Q R S T U V W X Y Z in inch-high letters in dreamlike succession, memorizing in my sleep & in the exhausted stupor of my (resumed) work in the Laboratory. (Where the Butcher was pleased to pretend that nothing had altered between us: & his Christian charity it was, to forgive *me*.)

Jonathan was astonished, Jonathan was amazed & laughing in admiration that I, who had never had a day's schooling, could spell out with a colored pencil such prodigies of language as

ESOPHAGUS, LIVER, SPLEEN, KIDNEYS, PANCREAS, GALLBLADDER, STOMACH, SMALL INTESTINES, COLON, BLADDER, UTERUS, VAGINA, SPINE, VERTEBRAE, BRAIN

—with little idea what most of these words meant nor how to pronounce them.

More commonplace words which I printed out in bright colors—

TREE, HAND, TABLE, CAT, FIRE, SKY, FOOT

—made us laugh very hard, we had no idea why.

Poetry my friend read to me by the soft light of the lantern. Each word enunciated like a pebble in a stream. Soft sibilant soothing words, words like caresses mingled with cries of nocturnal insects & birds, nighthawks, owls in the tallest trees & in the eaves of the Asylum outbuildings.

For by slow degrees *hearing* was restored to me. That I could feel, *hearing* would not be injurious to me, *hearing* would not be terrifying to me, I could accept *hearing* again.

Since my mother died, *hearing* had faded. On the morning following her death *hearing* had become muffled. And when I tried to speak, my throat shut up tight.

Speech is a riddle, that is its power. Most of all poetry. As elusive as moths drawn to lamplight softly striking their beautiful powdery wings against the glass lantern.

Poetry is the speech of the soul. Stirring hope in my heart. Flaring into flame in the hope that one day when I am healed I might take pencil to paper, to *write*. Not merely to spell words like a child but to *write*—as adults do.

In Jonathan's ardent voice:

> Calm and serene thy moments glide along,
> And may the muse inspire each future song!
> Still, with the sweets of contemplation bless'd,
> May peace with balmy wings your soul invest!

Rhyming words were fascinating to me. Even as I was unsure of their meaning.

This poet, Phillis Wheatley. Born in Africa, brought to America as a slave, in the previous century. She'd had the good fortune to have been purchased by an educated Bostonian & his wife, Jonathan said, not by a Southern plantation owner who would have forced her to breed & worked her to death; she'd had the good fortune to be valued for her intelligence & not punished for it. Her owners had not only taught her to read & write but had found a publisher for her poetry, & had emancipated her at the age of twenty.

Emancipated! A Black slave-girl, yet emancipated? I wondered at this, how it could be. There were many tales of the terrible things done to Africans in the South, whipt to death, thrown into swamps to be devoured by alligators. Torn to pieces by bloodhounds.

These rumors, to indentured servants. To placate us—*You are white, you are spared such punishments. Praise God, be content with your lot.*

Jonathan explained that Phillis Wheatley was a very famous poet, a gifted person. Her experience was very different from the experience of most African slaves.

Because she was brought to the North, & not the South. For the South was purely Hell, for the enslaved.

My heart near-stopped, to hear such things spoken of, so frankly.

In the Asylum, no one spoke of what lay outside the Asylum. Only vaguely did we know of North, South. Only a few of us had had glimpses of African faces, in Trenton.

All that Jonathan said, of the Black poet, I could not entirely follow. Though I stared at his lips & could "hear" most of his words, I did not always comprehend. For speech flows rapidly, & understanding lags behind.

Something in me balked, I did not want to hear. *Emancipation!* Frightening to me, to think that such a possibility might exist for me . . .

Except, Jonathan did not speak lightly about such matters. Anything to do with indentured servitude, slavery, bondage, "emancipation."

(Which was a word I knew—*emancipation*.)

My eyes filled with tears, I could not have said why. Except to think of a Black girl named Phillis Wheatley who had written poetry read now by white people like Jonathan who would read to me. And the courage given me, who had so much easier a life than she had had, by her example.

Jonathan took my hand—not to draw me to him (as for a moment I had feared) but to comfort.

One day soon, Brigit. Your day will dawn.

17.

. . . *Your day will dawn* like faint cries of birds at dawn, in the oak trees above North Hall, it was now a gift returned to me after years of silence, to hear.

18.

When you have nothing you greedily hoard what comes into your hands. No matter if it is the detritus of others, cast off & abandoned.

In all institutions like the Asylum, the lost possessions of those who die are eagerly found & cherished by the living.

Living as we did, the lowest of the workers. What came into our hands we did not let slip through our fingers.

Not stealing but cherishing. Our caches.

Butcher-doctor had promised me, he would begin paying me, if but a pittance he would pay me he had promised. For I was his favored *nurse-assistant*. For my labor for him had no end, I might be summoned at any time. Or any hour. For he was my Master, a fact of law.

For I had no key, to lock the door of my cubbyhole from within.

Weeks, months passed & he said nothing further. Regarding me coldly, or cruelly. Regarding me with damp eyes, & grim mouth. *Balm of Lethe,* I dared not resist.

Shameful to me, to confess, I did not dare speak of it to the Butcher-doctor, for fear of stoking his wrath; nor did I speak of it to Jonathan, for there were secrets between us, I could not reveal.

(That I had had a baby, & it was taken from me. That I had had *relations,* as it is called, with Medrick Weir, & with others who had forced themselves upon me over the years.)

(If he knew, he would be repelled by me. If he knew how young I had been at the start—not yet thirteen. That he was the gentleman-doctor's son, how could he bear it?—the knowledge of how my body had been ravaged & defiled past redemption.)

When we were together, it was Jonathan who spoke most of the time.

Jonathan Weir, who would be a lawyer one day, for whom words were as easy to maneuver as small smooth pebbles in his hands.

It was my place to listen, to strain to *hear*.

And his fingers against my throat, where my "voice" vibrated, it was joy to him to feel (he said) with his fingertips.

In this way teaching me to speak, as I had once been capable. Teaching me by example, & never coercing.

So hoarding what I could find amid the detritus of the Asylum. As silt sifts downward in a body of water, to accumulate in the muck at the bottom. Each of us in North Hall had her own piteous cache of possessions. Even those in cells & rabbit-hutches (so low, they could not stand upright but had to squat on their haunches like beasts in filthy straw) could make little burrows in the straw, in which to hide their treasures.

My most precious things were not articles of clothing, stockings, hair barrettes, & combs like the others but magazines, pamphlets, newspapers, & calendars. Such treasure came into my possession out of trash containers, blown along a walkway in the unkempt grounds beyond North Hall.

A battered old Bible that looked as if it had been in Noah's flood which was a prize possession of mine, Jonathan laughed sadly at the sight of it—*Oh Brigit!*—if he had known, he would have brought me a Bible of my own.

If I promised to tell no one, who had given it to me. And eagerly I said, *Yes. I promise.*

For it could not be known by anyone, Jonathan said, that he visited me, & that we were *friends.*

For his father would be very angry, & cause a rupture between us. And some harm might come to me that Jonathan could not prevent.

Could not prevent *yet*. But one day, soon.

His father's anger against him, Jonathan could accept, but not his father's anger against me.

"He will never hurt you again, Brigit. I vow."

Not the Holy Bible but the New Testament, in a black soft-cover binding, Jonathan brought for me, with illustrations meant for children, & from this gift Jonathan read to me of Jesus's miracles in so fervent a way, I had to wonder—*Does he believe? In Jesus? In miracles?*

I did not trust the Christian Jesus, but hoped that, if Jesus did exist, & Jesus was aware of me, that Jesus would take pity on *me*.

With loving patience Jonathan ran his forefinger beneath the line of printed words, that I could follow with my eyes. Repeating this, to allow me to learn.

Indeed, as if I were a child. Cleansed of all sin, in my soul a child again, grateful for all that Jonathan had brought into my life.

By slow degrees I was learning to speak again, as I was learning to read.

In my raw hoarse girl's voice, that could scarcely rise above a whisper, & only in the presence of my beloved friend.

For though, with Jonathan, I could *hear* & I could *speak,* however roughly, I was not prepared yet to do so in the presence of others.

Slowly enunciating these words as Jonathan moved his forefinger beneath them.

Blessed are the poor in spirit: for theirs is the kingdom of Heaven.
Blessed are they that mourn: for they shall be comforted.
Blessed are the meek: for they shall inherit the earth.
Blessed are they that hunger & thirst . . .

I faltered & fumbled. Jonathan provided the words, as required. Never was Jonathan impatient with me. Nor did Jonathan laugh at me when I became discouraged.

"Reading is practice, Brigit. We learn to read without knowing that we are learning."

This was not true—was it? Some days, I forgot all that I had learned. Words known to me dropped away from me, like fledgling birds too soon fallen out of the nest.

Yet, another time, when I returned to read what Jonathan had taught me, these words leapt to my lips at once, I could "say" them aloud with no hesitation!

With great patience, too, Jonathan taught me arithmetic. Much of this I knew, I did not have to be told, yet it was consoling, to be told. Copying out numbers carefully: 1 2 3 4 5 6 7 8 9 10 11 12.

Adding, subtracting. Don't question what numbers *are,* just think of numbers as things, like pennies, shoes, trees.

Confused by a problem, my instinct was to make a wild guess, like shutting my eyes & plunging into the dark, but Jonathan assured me—
No, no! Take time, Brigit.
There is always enough time.

Instructing me to use pencil & paper. Not to feel impatient with myself. There is no trick to math, just a single answer which is the correct answer.

Just one solution to each problem.

Just one solution to the injustice of the world, that makes so many the captives of so few. Servants, slaves.

In the Bible, there was *Heaven*. In our world below, there was *Freedom*.

Ever more excitedly Jonathan spoke of *our escape*. That he would come into a sum of money, he would *purchase my contract*.

If his father refused to cooperate, we would *run away together*.

To Jonathan, I did not reveal much in my heart. To others who had befriended me, like Gretel, I had never revealed much, lacking speech at the time, & the wish to confide in another.

While Jonathan spoke with much animation, I was very quiet. For it was urgent to me that the Butcher-doctor's son would be *my friend*, & never think of me as one who might think for herself, apart from him. I did not mind that Jonathan pitied me, for the circumstances of my life, for if *pity* might be a means of *escape*, then *pity* was a good thing.

That Jonathan would think of himself as *my friend* did not mean that I was Jonathan's *friend*. This, I understood instinctively.

To him, I was like a child, indeed I *was* a child. Though not so much younger than he, yet small in stature, & ignorant of so much that he knew well, of the way of the world outside the Asylum, & of wisdom, & knowledge, & schooling, & books, & the *normal lives of persons* as alien to me as another species of being. And so I was quiet in his presence, in awe & adoration of him, & in wariness.

What was softest in me, Jonathan felt a need to protect. His eyes were beautiful eyes moist with the tenderness of his own feelings. And his gripping of my (chilled) hand, in his (warm, strong) hand, to comfort & steady.

An obscure guilt pervaded him, that he was the son of the Director of the Asylum, who was our Master & oppressor. Jonathan had never known want, he had never crawled on his belly in despair, he had never dwelt in filth, & had been grateful even for filth, for the breath of life to persist in him, if but for a few hours.

Never so ravenous, he had devoured food containing grubs. Never so thirsty, he had drunk discolored water, tasting of sewage.

The guilt of his father's position pervaded the son, & had become an exquisite sort of wound, half pleasurable. Because *he* was not the wicked Master. Never would *he* be the wicked Master.

Yet, he was the son of the Master, & had benefited from the Master's position. He had never gone hungry, he had never gone without clothing, or schooling; his brain was sharp, & quick, for he had been well-nourished, he was one of those who had thrived, as others fell by the wayside, & perished.

All this, Jonathan knew. He was conscious of knowing, & to a degree, ironic in his knowledge. For it was thrilling to Jonathan, to speak critically of his father, & his relatives; to indicate to me, that he differed from them. Though he was not so different from them, to the casual eye, yet he was *not as they were, in his heart.*

Thrilling to Jonathan, that he might meet with me, the Irish orphan-girl, in secret. Even as his father, Silas Weir, was not so very far away, in actual distance. Even as (Jonathan told me) he & his father scarcely spoke, & never spoke of *Brigit Kinealy.*

Thrilling to Jonathan, that he might claim that, so often did he think of me, it was as if I had become his *soul-mate.*

Such a claim made me laugh, in surprise & disbelief. Heat rose in my cheeks, my hands lifted to hide my face in sudden shyness.

So, too, I was stricken in silence when Jonathan dared to inquire about his father's surgeries performed upon me, of which (he said) he had heard. Pained to allude to anything involving *female matters.* Between us, there opened an abyss.

Truly I did not wish to speak of such matters, with anyone. What had happened, what had been perpetrated upon me, was past now, & forgotten.

What my body had endured, it *had* endured. And was beyond such memories now.

Jonathan acknowledged, his father had brought him once into North Hall, to the Laboratory. Where he had seen such sights, he had near-collapsed, & had to quickly flee.

Saying to me, in a lowered voice, that he had heard his father had "experimented" on me, as on others in the Laboratory.

Quickly I shook my head, *No.* I did not wish to speak of this. *No.*

He had heard—*Terrible things are done, to the helpless.*

These words, I could not hear. A roaring in my ears, I turned aside. *No.*

Father has been honing his skills, with the indigent, to prepare for surgery with private, well-to-do patients.

Someday, he will be held to account! Somehow.

I did not hear, none of this.

It was true: Butcher-doctor had "experimented" on countless female lunatics, held captive in his Laboratory. In these experiments, he enlisted my help, for I was his favored *nurse-assistant*.

But Dr. Weir had never experimented with *me*. All that he had done with me had been to cure me of *fistula*.

For I was special to him, to Butcher-doctor. In this, I took a small, sick pride.

None of this I would tell Jonathan Weir, of course. My shame, I would not share with one who thought well of me.

Turning a deaf ear to him, when he spoke of such things. As in the past, *not-hearing* was my solace.

19.

He must not know. He will not know—ever.

Soon then, I had little thought of anyone or anything but Jonathan Weir.

It became a desperate need of mine, to keep secret all that had befallen me, before Jonathan had entered my life to transform it utterly.

He spoke of loving me, as a sister. Yet, I could not believe he would continue to feel for me, anything like this, should he *know* the despoiled person that I am.

He had completed his studies at the College of New Jersey—he had learned, from his professors there, all that they had for him to learn; now, he would enroll *in life*—he would work part-time at the Philadelphia Abolitionist Society, in Rittenhouse Square, & take courses in law at the university.

He had not informed his parents of this decision—just yet.

In his new, independent life, Jonathan hoped to earn a decent salary. He would have few expenses, & would save every penny he could, in the hope of one day purchasing the remainder of my contract from the Asylum.

So quietly Jonathan informed me of this decision, almost I could not believe what I was hearing.

For *hearing*, to me, was a most fragile state; where I could not trust the speaker, I could not *hear*.

Jonathan explained that he had made inquiries into the contract binding me to the Asylum, in the guise of a "disinterested" party concerned for the welfare of Irish immigrant offspring; but had not wanted to press the inquiry, for fear of attracting attention to himself, & alerting his father, who would be hostile to his efforts, he knew; & might act to make things worse for me.

According to the law, indentured servants were awarded "freedom fees" when their contracts ended—sometimes, an acre or two of land as well. Much depended upon the goodwill of the local magistrate, who could also rule in favor of the Master, to extend the contract "for cause."

He would insist upon my rights, Jonathan declared. He would not allow anyone to exploit me. His field of law would be *emancipation law.*

When I was free, we would travel together, he hoped—*As man & wife.*

Wife! The word hovered in the air between us like a most beautiful moth struck in mid-flight.

It had been deeply moving to me, that Jonathan had spoken of me as his *sister.* Though I could not believe him, truly.

But now—*wife*!

He had brought me a ring, as a pledge. A very delicate silver setting, with a small opal—so identified by Jonathan himself, as I had no idea what it was. This stone, but a *semi-precious stone,* he hoped I would keep close about me, perhaps on a chain around my neck; as, he knew, I could not openly wear it.

The little stone was not gaudy, its beauty was subtle—shifting hues of pale blue, iridescent green, very faint gold.

Of course, I would share this ring with no one. I would show no one, not even Gretel.

Most secretly I would hide this ring, in the most secure of all the caches, as a rat will do, in distrust of its own kind.

I could not properly thank Jonathan—the Butcher's son. There were no words. It was all I could do, to hide my face of raw hope from my dear friend's searching eyes.

A part of me wished to believe that *wife* might be possible, with Jonathan Weir; but another doubted that Jonathan had any clear idea of what he was saying.

It is his Butcher-father he is defying. It has little to do with you.

Such voices came to me, in the night. To rebuke my most foolish hopes, & yet to console.

20.

It is too late for Lucy, & for the others. We must save Bathsheba.

Tonight! For tomorrow will be too late.

Laughing, & her breath smelling of gin. Stumbling into my arms, Gretel panted hotly into my ear—"No one knows! No one ever knew."

Ever knew—what?

"Who murdered him—in his bed. The one before this one."

Murdered—who?

"Medrick Weir"—pronouncing the name, in her heavy Germanic accent, as if nothing could be more hilarious.

If a horse could laugh, such loud ribald laughter. Lips drawn back from big stained horse-teeth, half falling, half sitting onto the step.

I was staring at Gretel, in amazement. Seeing her lips carelessly shaping these words, she may have believed that I could *not hear.*

"Yes! I was the one. Because of *you*—what he'd done to *you.*"

Wiping her mouth, that glittered with saliva. Laughing & shivering.

I knew, Medrick Weir had forced himself upon others, as well. No doubt, when she'd been younger, Gretel.

"Slashed his throat, like the pig he was. In his filthy bed."

Cradling me in her arms, as our hearts' beat quickened together.

It was the eve of Bathsheba's surgery. We were to drug her with morphine in her food, & carry her into the operating room, & shackle her to the table, in preparation for whatever it was planned by the Butcher-doctor, the Red-Handed Butcher, for the morning.

Bathsheba is in dire need of emergency surgery, having shown signs of uterine prolapse—so the Butcher had proclaimed, with a look of repugnance.

Why it was, Gretel clutched at me, why I did not push her away in surprise, this is not known, never to be known. But know: *Brigit was not drunk on gin.*

Together we were laughing, as young girls laugh when they are tickled. Gretel's heavy breasts loose inside her nurse's tunic, the heat of her panting breath, wild-rolling eyes.

Laughing, trying to speak. Taking Gretel's hand coarsened from years of servitude & pressing the fingers against my throat so that she could feel the thrill of the vibration of words straining to be released.

We will refuse—to betray Bathsheba.

We will not drug Bathsheba. We will not carry Bathsheba into the surgery, & shackle her to the table.

We will not prepare Bathsheba for sacrifice by the Butcher.

Will not, we will not! We will not, ever.

Too late for Lucy, & all who had perished by his scalpel.

But time now, for the Red-Handed Butcher to die.

21. BEARING WITNESS

From now forward I am recording these words not as Brigit Kinealy but through the hand & pen of Brigit Kinealy.

Though she was an orphan of a despised race, yet, through her effort to save herself she acquired a privilege denied her sisters, who were trapped in the Asylum as lunatics. And of these, very few could read & write beyond the level of a very young child.

For she was favored by the Butcher-doctor, as I have revealed in this narrative. As she was befriended by the Butcher-doctor's son.

It is true, Brigit Kinealy was "saved" by the Butcher-doctor—that will not be denied.

For which, she is grateful. Yet—her bond is with her sisters, with whom she must cast her lot.

As Gretel declares. When the die is cast, we stand with our sisters to the death.

22. INSURRECTION. MARCH 13, 1861

Hallelujah!—female lunatics' triumphant cries as flames rose, out of the topmost floor of North Hall the lair of the Red-Handed Butcher.

Hallelujah!—flames quickly spreading through the Laboratory, & downward to lower floors, & to adjacent outbuildings exploding like tinder in a conflagration to illuminate the night sky above Trenton, New Jersey.

Wishing that *all of Trenton* might perish in these purging flames! *All of those who have held us captive as lunatics, & thrived amid our misery, to Hell.*

Among us there was spirited debate, whether to allow the Red-Handed Butcher to lie where he had fallen murdered in filth, or whether to drag the bloody body down from the topmost floor of North Hall, to display the mutilated Butcher-body to the world.

No time to linger! Before the first of the firefighters arrived we would flee in men's clothing along the banks of the Delaware, to a bridge to take us into Pennsylvania. Some of us to be apprehended within a day or two, in the wilds of Bucks County, others never seen again—*vanished!*

As if the Earth had opened up, to swallow us.

Freed forever of the prison of the Red-Handed Butcher. Though all of us marked for life by the Red-Handed Butcher.

Years captive in the Laboratory of the Red-Handed Butcher. No one would know of our sorrow & the horrors committed against us except that one of us, writing these words, will bear witness.

One of us, spared by a miracle. Of so few of us, granted life, & the privilege of *reading & writing,* to bear witness for all.

All of us, abandoned by our families. Insulted & injured & shackled to bedposts. Locked in cells, & some of us, the *most obstreperous* held captive in hutches scarcely large enough for rabbits, too small for us to sit up, still less stand. It may have been an *experiment* to see how bone yields to an enforced posture, how diet turns bones brittle, bent like bows. Filthy straw for us to sleep on, dream upon. Open sores on our bodies seething with maggots.

Jesus help me! Jesus help me!—in the night, our cries lifted mingling with the forlorn cries of night birds, blown away in the wind, unheard.

One by one we were summoned to him. Through glittering eye-glasses examined by him. A crude instrument, to *open us up* to the Red-Handed Butcher's eyes.

In prim dark gentlemen's clothing, starched white cotton shirt, starched white collar, & necktie, beneath a white a surgeon's apron soon smudged & splattered with our blood.

Strapped us to a table stained dark with the anguish of our sisters. Sank his scalpel into us, scraped us raw with his curette, cut away our lives with scissors, rarely dulling our pain with morphine, chloroform. For *anesthesia* was costly, reserved for private patients.

Amputations of toes, fingers, feet, legs—to prevent the spread of *gangrene,* which he had deliberately delayed treating until it was too late.

A plan to amputate tongues—to see if we could learn to speak without tongues.

Gibberish of *female lunatics,* who can comprehend it?—of no worth, none.

Boasting, the trick isn't to *amputate* but to *keep the patient alive, following.*

Tying off veins & arteries, stumps cauterized. Treatments for "shock." For the mortality rate is as high for "shock" as for loss of blood.

Post-operative. Patient-care. So little is known, the Red-Handed Butcher declared. An entire field of science, his to explore.

His to conquer, to raise him to the heights of fame.

Most cruelly, some (of us) were made to assist the Butcher in his surgeries. Knowing that soon we, too, would be strapped down, rags stuffed into our mouths to muffle our screams of agony.

Unless we wished to be whipt, or sent into *restraint.*

Chair of Tranquility, Bed of Tranquility. Weir-room, Weir-wheel. Weir-death.

Only to his favorites was the Red-Handed Butcher merciful. But then, not always.

Gretel, & later the younger, albino deaf-mute *Brigit.* The one stolid & ruddy-faced, reliable as a milk-cow; the other, with eerie-white albino skin, glassy pale-blue eyes, *Devil's soul* inside the *angel-face.*

Also, on this night in March 1861 we were *Nestra, Bathsheba, Wilhelmina, Zenobia, Mahala, Juel.*

God's wrath, & the jubilation of God's wrath illuminating the night sky above the accursèd city.

Never will the Red-Handed Butcher let you go, never release you of his own volition. You must rise up against him. You must seize your freedom.

Colleagues of the Red-Handed Butcher knew of his cruelty, & for years turned a blind eye, turned a deaf ear, that cruelties & perfidies of their own would pass unacknowledged.

Nurses, nurses' aides & orderlies, administrative staff, work-staff, board of overseers—all knew, or should have known.

Families of medical staff, who lived on the Asylum grounds, had reason to know. Surely heard our screams from the topmost floor of North Hall & smelled our terror. Dense hedges of wild rose & sweet-smelling wisteria were encouraged to grow, tangled English ivy over the brick façade of North Hall, masking the odors of the *cadaver room*.

We died young. For we were all younger in years than our strained faces showed.

Beneath the cloth carelessly wetted in chloroform pressed against our mouths & noses. Died hemorrhaging, as an *infected organ* was hacked from us, by the Red-Handed Butcher to drop into a slop pail, in triumph.

Though the Red-Handed Butcher boasted that he owned no slaves, he did not believe in slavery but in the Abolitionist creed. Though still his power in life was to command the lowliest of us to be worked to death & to be whipt & truncheoned, if we disobeyed.

Commanding the lowliest of us to be carried screaming into the surgery, shackled to the operating table & our heads secured in the *Weir-wheel*.

When we died, we were removed by night, & buried in the most remote corner of the Asylum grounds, with but small wooden crosses to mark the common grave, that no one would take note of us, & mourn for us.

It was said that, in the *cadaver room*, the gravedigger Langhorne dared not look closely upon our broken & mutilated bodies, which it was his duty to carry away & bury. That tears of pity might leak from his eyes. In a lifetime a gravedigger sees much to turn him against humankind & to question the mercy of God, yet Abraham Langhorne would marvel he had not seen such *deliberate butchery* as he was obliged to carry away from the rear entrance of North Hall.

Though the Red-Handed Butcher was a very clean & fastidious man, yet flies, roaches, & other vermin bred freely in the locked wards of the Asylum, where few visitors ventured; & on the topmost floor of North Hall, where no one visited.

It was known, the public spaces of the Asylum, in the main building, including a reception area, a visitors' lounge, private dining rooms, & even a small ballroom overlooking a garden, were handsomely furnished, & kept very clean; so, too, the wards & private suites housing the less *mentally ill* patients, for here visitors came frequently, & were always greeted with courtesy, & informed medical staff.

It was known the Red-Handed Butcher took much care that these public spaces were maintained as they were, that the remainder of the Asylum was not suspected of such neglect.

With the passage of years, it was said that the Red-Handed Butcher grew more dependent upon his nightly *balm of Lethe*—laudanum, whiskey, cocaine drops.

With the passage of years, more careless & savage in his appetites.

The Red-Handed Butcher's vanity was this weakness, as it had been the weakness of his kinsman Medrick Weir: that he wished to imagine that his patients admired him as a Savior, & looked upon him with awe & reverence as a physician-surgeon of great repute.

Medrick Weir: whose death was shrouded in mystery, like his life, for none should know that an individual of such stature had died in a pigsty of a bed, throat slashed as a hog's throat might be slashed, soaking an entire massive mattress in his blood, with myriad drippings to the floor of the Master's bedroom.

Thrilling to us, to know that one of us had slashed that throat & let the butcher knife fall in contempt from her fingers, on the pig's fatty naked torso.

Such vanity, they could not guess how we loathed them, & conspired to rise against them, as (we were told by Gretel, who knew of such things) a Black slave named Nat Turner had led a revolt against white oppressors in Virginia, killing more than fifty of them in a single night.

Our eyes widened, hearing such tales. For Gretel was one of us who could read, perusing newspapers discarded by the medical staff.

Thrill of slashed (white) throats, at the hands of (Black) slaves.

Most amazing, it was recounted how young Nat Turner, like an Angel of Wrath, had murdered even white women who'd been kind to him, had taught him to read. Even white children, who had done him no wrong except through the accident of their birth—as *white.*

But the insurrection had not turned out well, Gretel said. For Nat Turner could not convince other slaves to join him.

With justice on his side, & God surely urging him, Nat Turner's mistake had been to kill his oppressors savagely, instead of simply *fleeing with his life & leading his people to freedom.*

So Gretel cautioned us, *YOU MUST NOT KILL. NO SLASHED THROATS.*

Badly we wanted to slash throats. We had not realized until now how badly we wanted to kill not only the Red-Handed Butcher but those others who aided him, his fellow doctors, administrators, brute orderlies, & even certain of the nurses, who had had no sympathy for us. Badly we wanted to slash the throats of the entire Weir family, for we knew where the Director resided, which residence large & stately as a mansion was his. Some of us had had glimpses of the Weir children, no idea of their names nor of how many were still living at home, all of these we'd have liked to murder, even the young girls, even the innocent young girls bearing the Weir name like a curse, while the Red-Handed Butcher & his wife were made to look on in horror, & then we would slash their throats, we would gut them like pigs!—hang them upside down, drag their intestines out of their bellies with our bare clawing fingers.

Hearing the excitement in our voices Gretel grew alarmed—*No.*

Stolid Gretel with her warm brown cow's eyes, widening in alarm—*No!*

Chiding us that *escape* is the means, *emancipation* is the destination.

Just to free ourselves from the Laboratory, to flee into the State of Pennsylvania, seek asylum in the countryside. Declare ourselves no longer *lunatics* under the care of the State of New Jersey.

It would be a grave error to do as Nat Turner had done: to kill.

For killing will beget killing. All swords are double-edged.

This was the midwife's warning to us. For Gretel was one of the older nurses in North Hall, where few nurses remained on the staff beyond the age of forty.

Unknown to the Red-Handed Butcher in the blindness of his vanity, it was his longtime nurse-assistant Gretel, whom he trusted above all others, who had first begun to speak of *revolt, insurrection.*

Unknown to the Red-Handed Butcher, but not unknown to us, it was Gretel who had understood years before, Medrick Weir must be stopped, in his very bed.

For no one else will stop them, the rapacious physician-surgeons who prey upon us, suck the marrow from our bones, & cast us aside when they are finished with us.

So many of us, & only one of him—so Gretel whispered to us, in our captivity.

Until Gretel uttered those words, we had not realized. For most of us were ill, weak, beaten, & broken. Our bodies leaked blood, female filth. Our bodies were mere sacs of flesh, commandeered by others. Blood was drained from us, our organs removed as sites of *infection.* Unfit in the world of the *sane* & so cast off & left to die in the Red-Handed Butcher's hell-hospital.

Like a grimy barred window that has been broken, to let in gusts of fresh air, the very thought of *revolt, insurrection* was rousing to us. Wild-flapping flags of independence, our hearts leapt to salute.

Such visions as *slashing throats, setting fires* suffused us with bursts of strength.

Quickly it happened, like a contagion of yellow fever, this fever for revolt. Even those of us long kept caged, in restraint, even sickly moribund Juel, & Mahala, who had lost her mutinous spirit after several surgeries, began to feel the sharp thrill of revolt, wanting now badly to live, & to wreak vengeance upon our oppressor.

Tossing a lighted match onto grasses dried & desiccated following the drought of summer. Soon then, dreams of *revolt* stirred our sleep.

Even as Gretel cautioned—*We will take our time. We will not act in haste. We will have a plan.*

Gretel was in contact with persons in Morrisville, Pennsylvania, through her church, who would help us in our escape & could provide *safe houses* for us, such as African slaves were provided, in their efforts to emancipate themselves; but we must not act rashly, & do unnecessary harm to any person, however culpable, for if we do we will be badly punished.

It was Gretel who warned us, no other patients in the Asylum should know of our plans. Not even our sisters in the locked wards, living & dying in filth similar to ours. For if they knew, their excitement would overcome caution, & soon we would be found out, & terribly disciplined.

Nor could you trust nurses' aides, & orderlies—even the lowliest of the low. For they will not join with you, they will inform on you, to win favor with the Master.

Gretel did cunningly engage one of her oldest friends in the Asylum, who would keep our secret, out of a blood-hatred for the Masters dating back for decades, a sister midwife who had access to storerooms of civilian clothing & could provide for us men's clothing in particular.

We must disguise ourselves not just as *sane persons,* but as *male persons.* If we are identified as *female,* we will be apprehended at once.

Making our way into the State of Pennsylvania, & away from urban areas. If we are lucky, we will *vanish into thin air.*

Through all this, Gretel held firm & would not agree to slashing any throats: even the throat of the Red-Handed Butcher.

Gretel's plan was: The Butcher would be overcome, & his keys taken from him to unlock the caged captives, & free all of us from the Laboratory; but it was crucial that the Butcher not be injured, or not injured badly. For there was no practical purpose to this—severe injury, or death.

Most practical to shackle the Butcher as he had shackled us, & stuff rags into his mouth as he had stuffed rags into our mouths; giving us hours through the night to make our escape from the Asylum, each taking a (separate) route.

Not revenge but escape. Revolt, & escape. To freedom.

No need to set a fire. In fact—no fire!

No need to approach the Weir house. Gretel insisted.

But *no.* For there were those of us most aggrieved who spoke yearningly of entering the sandstone residence of the Director & *slashing the throats* of everyone surprised in their beds, & setting fire to the house—nothing less! For it seemed to us, we had been dreaming of such justice, all of our lives.

Even as Gretel spoke more sternly in rebuke, as if, being a midwife, & long an indentured servant at the Asylum, in fact one of the *nurse-assistants* most closely trusted by the Red-Handed Butcher, she was in some way superior to others of us, who were mere *female lunatics* in the Asylum; in this way offensive to us, for, having tossed the match, having given us the spark, Gretel had no right (we felt) to deny us all that we deserved of vengeance & blood lust, & we did not like the Butcher's *nurse-assistant* to instruct us, like one of the staff physicians, or a head nurse, in what we should or should not do.

Now, too, the little Irish albino deaf-mute began to protest, in her wincing way of mimicry, just barely able to speak, a whispery-throaty voice scarcely audible begging, *We should not injure anyone. Especially not the Weir family, they are not guilty of his crimes.*

There were daughters still living at home, it was believed. And of course, the wife.

Knowing nothing of us, & had never done us harm.

But they are *his children,* it was pointed out by Bathsheba. And that woman, *his* wife.

Juel, too, argued, we were obliged to slash the Butcher's throat, as the Israelites rose against their oppressors, to crush them utterly, & any of his family whom we could lay hands upon. North Hall should be put to the torch, & the Director's residence—burnt to the ground, & let whoever was unlucky enough to be trapped therein, die in the flames.

In fact, there was a directive from Providence: The captives must rise against their captors & burn down the hospital, where so many (of us) had suffered & died.

To this chorus of voices all (of us) vehemently agreed, except Gretel & Brigit, who urged calm & caution, like persons trying to beat out a wildfire with their bare hands—too late.

Gretel repeated to us, we must promise not to act rashly, & do unnecessary harm to any person, for if so, her church-friends across the river in Morrisville would not wish to associate with us, & we would be badly punished.

They will pursue us, they will drag us back in shackles. We will be interred anew, as female lunatics who are homicidal. The story of our insurrection will be turned against us, support for our plight will be sabotaged, we will end up worse than we are, & all "female lunatics" will be branded by our actions, as "homicidal."

However, if Gretel's plan succeeded, those of us who fled the Asy-

lum would be mere runaways from the hospital, & not criminals needing to be punished; there would be little sympathy for the Butcher
Weir, whose injustices would be revealed, perhaps in the Trenton
newspapers. Indeed, all who knew of the Butcher's reign of terror at
the Asylum would be relieved, to be rid of him.

He must be allowed to live, in shame & ignominy. His naked assailed body seen by all.

If so, he would retire from his position. He would be no threat to
any female patient at the Asylum, ever again.

Above all, *there should be no fire. For in any fire, innocents might
perish.*

To this logic we (reluctantly) agreed. We understood, Gretel was
correct. As mere runaways, we were not of significance, no one would
care greatly about capturing us, there would be no rewards.

Not revenge, sisters!—insurrection, freedom, & escape.

Dr. Weir! Dr. Weir! You are needed . . .

On the eve of Bathsheba's scheduled surgery, in the darkness following dusk of this March day, a pleading call of the little Irish deaf-
mute seemed to waft to the Red-Handed Butcher's ear some distance
away in his lavishly furnished study in the sandstone residence.

Did the Red-Handed Butcher hear, or did he imagine he heard, the
Irish girl's tremulous voice floating like a (dark, shimmering) feather
in the still air?

How could the Butcher resist such a siren call? Of course, *old fools
like Silas Aloysius Weir, M.D., could not.*

At the massive mahogany desk in his office, in half-light sipping
laudanum, whiskey. The Butcher-surgeon was meant to be taking
notes on the *hysterectomy* he would be performing in the morning on
the one-legged lunatic, what was her name, glaring-eyed, aggressively
ugly, with a shiny stump most obscene to see.

The *hysterectomy* would be performed without an anesthetic, not
even morphine drops, for it was not thought that the trifling surgery
would bring much pain, not to one so insensitive, a mere brute, with a
wicked tongue, in fact, *the surgeon might remove her (infected) tongue*
if circumstances warranted.

Thinking such thoughts, & his mind adrift, lewdly fondling the little carved dove that Brigit Kinealy had given him years before, in abject gratitude.

More dear to Silas Weir than his own daughters, whom he scarcely knew, this little Irish orphan. Or his own wife, whose girth oppressed him. The good Christian wife!—more than once, Silas Weir had prayed, he might have a few years to outlive Theresa, when his little Irish nurse-assistant might come to dwell in this very residence.

Pride could not bear that his yearning for the Irish orphan was so deep, it had pooled in his soul as a poison, as a stagnant swamp breeds poison. As a gentleman of stature, he could approach so lowly a person only as a Master for whom cruelty must precede tenderness.

As night came on, this yearning rose in the Red-Handed Butcher like a mist out of which was conjured the cry: *Dr. Weir! Dr. Weir!*

Cupping his hand to his ear, listening avidly.

With clumsy excited fingers lifting the lantern, to bear with him outdoors.

Taking up his valise, containing the precious key ring. Key to the Laboratory, & keys to other private rooms.

Calling in a gruff voice—*Yes? What is it you want from me now?*

In the dark outside, Silas Weir's two *nurse-assistants*. In their starched nurse's uniforms, white-starched caps pert on their heads. Ah, his trusted slave-girls! The midwife, & the little Irish girl, who has stolen his wizened heart.

One of your patients, Dr. Weir. Bleeding badly.

In flickering candlelight, a face of such beauty to take away a man's breath. And close beside her, somber-faced Gretel, with whom he had long associated common sense, practical wisdom, & a ceaseless concern for his well-being. And so without hesitation, the Red-Handed Butcher unwittingly followed his *nurse-assistants,* holding aloft his lantern in one hand & gripping his valise in the other.

In the sweetness of delusion unaware of how high overhead thin fleece-like clouds were blown across a glaring-white moon-face bemused at what was past, passing, & soon to come in Trenton, New Jersey.

Led by the two candle-bearers along the windswept walkway to the rear of North Hall, & into the familiar entry; up the narrow stairway, breathless; & into the Laboratory on the top, third floor of the building, where lunatic-patients stood beside their beds as if at attention, holding lighted candles as the Red-Handed Butcher passed; & at last to the *restraint* corridor, where the Director rarely set foot, for patients assigned to this part of the Laboratory were likely to be soon rendered *null.*

There, in cells too small to allow them to stand up, three wretches were confined. The Red-Handed Butcher had no memory of these lunatics except that one was named *Juel,* on whose behalf he had been summoned by his *nurse-assistants:* Juel had collapsed, Juel had begun to hemorrhage, please would he examine Juel?—for no one could save Juel, except Silas Weir!

To make his burden lighter the younger of his *nurse-assistants* offered to take the lantern from his fingers, to make his task lighter the elder *nurse-assistant* offered to take the ring of keys from his fingers, & so unlock the cage herself; & in that instant, like a stroke of lightning splitting the sky, the panting horde of us swarmed up behind the Red-Handed Butcher & leapt at him in a fever of vengeance we had promised we would resist, as Gretel had begged us; except our blood beat so hot & so hard in that instant, like ravenous predator-birds too long denied our prey, we were upon the Red-Handed Butcher before he could draw breath to protest, before he could draw breath to scream for help, clawing at him, pummeling him, striking blows with our fists like iron, felling him like a shrieking goat, onto the sacrificial altar. Thrilling to us so long deprived to see the first glisten of the Butcher's blood, that we had never before glimpsed, even as, a thousand times, he had glimpsed our blood; thrilling to us to inhale the first smell of the Butcher's blood, that roused lusts in us we had never known in life. Eagerly our fingers tore at his hair that was graying & scanty, of the hue of pewter; our nails tore at his thin scalp, & at the lobes of his over-sized ears; we seized the starched collar & tore, & with much glee tore at the prim dark trousers yanked to knobby white ankles, revealing the man's nakedness in its flabby pallor; in derision & mockery we clawed at the soft-shrinking genitals & wobbly white buttocks as the Butcher pleaded for his life like a beggar, whimpering stunned & bawling on hands & knees, trying to crawl to safety, as a broken-backed snake might try to crawl; how we roared with laughter at him, the fool imagining there could be *safety* in this hellish place he had devised for us.

Filthy rags we shoved into his mouth, fistfuls of filth-encrusted straw we shoved into his mouth, gleeful, giddy, as piteous in his nakedness the Butcher pleaded for mercy, shielding his bleeding face with fingers roughly pushed aside by ours in a delirium of joy as the Butcher begged, wept, prayed to Jesus his Savior, God the Father to spare him as each of us brandished an instrument from the Laboratory with which to "treat" the Butcher—scalpel, curette, spoon-speculum, forceps, catheter, hypodermic needles, pliers for teeth-extraction, knife for bloodletting, handsaw for amputations, *écraseur* with ingenious wire hoop encircling the terrified shrunken penis & testicles & by gradual tightening cruelly squeezing until the soft flesh became bloody liquid-gel in a puddle beneath gaunt white-man thighs, stupefied with pain & in an agony beyond measurement.

Hallelujah!—by this time those of us locked in cells & cages were freed & roused from lethargy to action, for the first time in months able to stand upright, with the strength of exhilaration able to lift our heads; there came Juel resembling a wizened bat, weighing no more than seventy pounds yet ferocious with nails grown as long & sharp as a rodent's nails sinking into the pale-fleshy chest of the Butcher clawing for his heart; there came Zenobia with mangled upper lip serrated as a hog's bristles snarling & snorting & clawing for his guts; there came Bathsheba lurching on her stump-leg bright & fierce with the handsaw to amputate the Butcher's (infected) toes, & Nestra gripping the spoon-speculum to pry open the Butcher's tight-clenched anus & inject by hypodermic needle into the anus a fiery suffusion of black cohosh, ammonia, red pepper, belladonna, & mercury; there came Wilhelmina from whose ravaged body the Butcher had once tugged twin girl-babies with the very forceps he had used now brandished by Wilhelmina gripping the Butcher's torn guts to tug hard, as a headless chicken is eviscerated; & there was vengeful Lucy returned to us with a sharp knife to sever veins & arteries & rolls of white gauze for tight, tight tourniquets, & astonishing in our midst a furious ginger-haired girl with a pale, freckled face whom we had never seen before slashing at the Butcher's groin with a straight razor—*Have you forgotten me, Doctor? I am Bettina, whom you butchered in Ho-Ho-Kus* & those of us whose teeth the Butcher had extracted from our jaws with no anesthetic taking turns now with the pliers, extracting his ugly stained teeth from gouged & bleeding gums with shouts of laughter as the

Butcher's mouth filled with blood, & the Butcher's throat filled with blood, drowning in his blood the Butcher had not the strength to further plead for mercy for by now even his trusted *nurse-assistants* had abandoned him, had given up the effort of trying to stay our savage hands, for in fact both Gretel & Brigit in their proper nurse's attire had joined us like hyenas exulting in the kill, lapping with our tongues the bloody remains of the Red-Handed Butcher as he lay lifeless on the filthiest of floors for there could be no mercy, there could be no forgiveness, no more than acid-hot lava erupting from a seizure of the Earth is forgiving as it rushes forward, ravishing everything in its path.

VI

Epilogue: Afterlife

The Promise

TESTIMONY OF JONATHAN WEIR

*T*HERE HAS BEEN A FIRE, *your father is gravely injured. Come home at once!*

This first telegram of my life came to me at my lodgings in Philadelphia on the morning of March 14, 1861, & so without question I returned to Trenton on the next train.

That there had been something like an *insurrection* among patients in the Asylum, as well as a "cataclysmic fire" in which a number of patients had perished, was stunning to me, as to all who were beginning to hear of this alarming news.

My great fear was that Father would die of his injuries. That by the time I arrived at our house, Father would have died. My fear was as much for what would become of the rebellious patients, as for Father himself.

For I was thinking of Brigit Kinealy: Had she, too, been injured in the fire? Had she been *killed*?

Stunning to me, to think that something might have happened to my beloved Brigit, whom I could not protect.

It was a thorn in my heart, that I had not seen Brigit for some time. When we were last together I had had to reveal to her that I was moving to Philadelphia, for I could no longer dwell beneath my father's roof, & accept my father's charity, as I had for all the years of my life until then; I promised that I would write to her, & return to visit when I could, & there came into Brigit's face a look of such surprise & hurt, to recall it is to weep . . .

I did write to Brigit as I had promised, having only the Asylum as an address, but did not hear from her; nor had I any assurance that my letter had been received by her.

Three times more I wrote to Brigit at the Asylum & to my dismay did not hear from her.

Still there persisted a plan of mine: that I would return to Trenton with sufficient funds & so purchase Brigit's freedom from her contract. I would speak frankly & without fear to Father. I would not allow him to threaten me or bully me with a prospect of *disinheritance*.

I would make it plain, *I did not care for any patrimony.* In life, I would make my own way. I would not compromise with my elders to advance my career.

I would ask Brigit Kinealy to be my life-companion—*sister,* or *wife.* Regardless of the howls of disapproval of my family.

If Brigit were to say *yes,* I would bring her to Philadelphia with me & see to it that her education was continued. I would enlist Brigit to be my helpmeet in the Abolitionist cause.

We might move to Boston, for I was attracted to the bold publications of William Lloyd Garrison's Anti-Slavery Society. I was attracted to the Anti-Slavery Society, where women worked beside men as equals, to promote the Abolitionist cause. The presence of a freed white Irish *indentured servant badly mistreated by her Master* would be welcome in such circles.

But now—this shocking news! My mother's elder brother sent the telegram, a terse message that conveyed little; like most messages sent to me by my mother's relatives, who did not approve of my political sentiments or my move to Philadelphia, a "hive" of Abolitionist activity.

En route to Trenton reading in *The Philadelphia Inquirer* of the fire at the New Jersey State Asylum for Female Lunatics: An unknown number of patients in locked wards had perished by flame or smoke inhalation. An uprising of patients was blamed for the fire, begun with rags set aflame in a "research laboratory."

The Director of the Asylum, Silas Aloysius Weir, had been discovered unconscious on the ground outside North Hall, the extent of his injuries "not known."

So much was in the air in the early spring of 1861—every kind of threat, or rumor, of *slave uprisings* in the South, & much fear, among the oppressors. Virtually every day, some lurid tale was told of a slave revolt *put down*. Yet still, tales erupted, like flames bursting out of smoldering matter.

It would have been little surprise to me if the wretched female patients held captive in the Asylum had been inspired by the insurrectionist spirit of the African slaves, to revolt against their oppressors.

So it seemed, Silas Weir's captive patients in North Hall had risen against him, & succeeded in injuring him; yet, I could not imagine that such a revolt would not end tragically, & dreaded hearing of Brigit's arrest, or worse.

"God, let them both be spared—Brigit, & Father!"—so I prayed silently.

For though I did not believe in the stern Calvinist God of my father, Silas Weir, I did believe in a more benign God—of justice, mercy, & forgiveness.

Initially it was not known if the renegade "female lunatics" (as they were called in the press) had actually managed to escape the fire set by their own hands; or whether a fire had started accidentally, & all had perished in the fire, which swept through North Hall, & one or two outbuildings close by.

It was a relief to me, to learn that the Director's residence had not caught fire, & that everyone in the house, including my mother & my (six) brothers & sisters still living at home, had managed to avoid any injury; & were staying temporarily with my mother's family in Vineland.

It was assumed by authorities that, since most of my father's patients were classified as severely ill, both mentally & physically, they were not likely prospects for survival in such a cataclysm, & so had probably perished in the blaze with the others.

Within a few days some portion of the mystery was resolved: Several disheveled, distraught females, one of them with but a stump for a leg, & all of them toothless, were apprehended some miles away in rural Bucks County, clad in men's ragged clothing, & wandering lost; the one-legged woman spoke wildly as in the voice of an Old Testament prophet that *God had smote a fire on the Butcher's head* & bade them flee for their lives; another, a wizened bat-like creature who could speak in only a hoarse whisper, claimed that *Butcher Weir had set the fire himself out of repentance for his sins.*

Others seemingly missing from the Asylum would be reported *vanished into thin air.*

With Father's (private) records lost in the fire, as Father would claim, & Father himself in no condition to speak with authorities, it was not known, & would never be known, exactly what the circumstances had been preceding the fire; or even exactly who had been involved, whether as perpetrators or hapless victims.

All that seemed to be clear was that *some persons were missing, alive or deceased.*

Again I tried to learn of the status of the indentured servant Brigit Kinealy, said to be contracted to the Asylum, but was similarly rebuffed by an officious administrative assistant; when I insisted upon speaking with the Supervisor of Nurses, I was told outright that no one with such a name was ever on the nursing staff of the Asylum.

"But that is not possible," I protested, "—Brigit Kinealy was assigned to Dr. Weir's Laboratory, I am sure."

"Well, I *am sure* that she was not."

So Supervisor Fussell rebuffed me, with such an incensed set to her jaw, she seemed to know how I was plotting to further injure her protector, Silas Weir.

Within the family, all attention was focused upon Father, who, though living, having survived the worst of his injuries, was said to be, by all who knew him, *gravely altered in spirit, as in body.*

Such relief I felt that Father had not died, allowed me to realize that I did—I *must*—love the man: as well as disapproving of him strongly.

Pondering whether I should beg forgiveness of Father, for my disrespectful behavior in the past; for the deceit of my relations with "the Irish girl" he had sent me to whip; & for the difficult son I had been for some time, while living beneath his roof.

Prudently deciding, for the time being, that it might be kinder to wait until Father was more recovered.

It had been my brother Solomon who, hurrying toward the fire, as firefighters were arriving, had discovered our father's body motionless on the ground between North Hall & our family residence.

At first, stooping over the naked & ravaged body, Solomon believed that Father must be dead: He could detect neither breathing nor a heartbeat. He called to Father, to awaken; pleaded with him; to no avail. One of Father's eyes was swollen & blackened & the other stared sightlessly into space. His nose had been broken, oozing blood. Much of his hair was missing, as if it had been yanked out in handfuls. Several teeth appeared to be missing from Father's bleeding lower jaw. Fingers on both his hands had been mangled.

Over all, Father was covered in lacerations & bleeding from dozens of superficial wounds. Most severe were injuries to his groin, where little remained of genital organs but flattened, shrunken stubs of bloody tissue, near-unrecognizable as penis & testicles; indeed, it appeared that these had been so squeezed, the insides had oozed out, in a liquid gel. His shrunken buttocks were covered in what appeared to be claw marks, stabs, & scrapings, as if a wild beast had attacked him; the anus was raw & inflamed & leaking blood & intestines. Yet, oddly, there were few burns on Father's body & few singe marks in what remained of his hair.

Failing to revive Father, Solomon ran desperately for help.

By Solomon's account, it appeared that Father had rushed to North Hall, to help patients escape from the fire, but had been forced to retreat; had fallen, injured, & dragged himself along the ground to safety, losing consciousness in the effort.

In short, Father had behaved heroically, until overcome by fire & smoke, collapsing in the grass.

This would become the account promoted by the Weir family & relatives, & subsequently reproduced in newspapers, that, discovering a fire in his research Laboratory after hours, Silas Weir rushed courageously into North Hall, in order to rescue patients; but had been overcome by flames & smoke, & only barely managed to drag himself to safety.

Indeed, this account of the heroic behavior of Silas Weir on the night of March 13, 1861, would become the official account offered by local commentators, news sources, & historians; even as rumors began to circulate that Silas Weir had set fire to North Hall himself to satisfy some *crazed, vengeful* purpose of his own having to do with a *beautiful female lunatic* who had spurned him.

My private speculation was that someone had dragged Father to safety—pointedly not wanting Silas Weir to die. His wounds were many, & some of them very cruel; yet none proved to be mortal.

Having punished the esteemed physician in a most barbaric way, & thoroughly *emasculating* him, his tormentors took particular care that he *should not die.*

In that way—(so I speculated)—Dr. Weir would have the remainder of his lifetime to contemplate his wounds, & who had executed them; more important, his (unknown) assailants would not be guilty of a capital crime, & would not be so vigorously pursued by authorities.

Needless to say, I kept this observation to myself. I may have a reputation among both the Weirs & the Cleffs for being irresponsible, unreliable, & impertinent, but none would deem me *stupid,* I am sure.

Nor was there a single person among my family or relatives to whom I felt close enough, to confide; among my Abolitionist friends & comrades, I did not care to reveal family secrets.

At this time, as Father lay in isolation, convalescing in an upstairs room of the Director's residence & waited upon by nurses from the Asylum, all of the United States was simmering to a boil, with conspiracies & dreams of revolt, mutiny. Each day, newspapers carried tales of demands for secession, on the part of the slave states; each day, demands by Abolitionists that the spread of slavery into border states be curtailed. It had been thirty years since Nat Turner's ill-fated insurrection—(long before my birth!)—yet the spirit of Nat Turner lived still, stalking the sleep of slave-owners. It had been less than two years since the most audacious of all insurrections had been undertaken, by the Christian martyr John Brown, at Harpers Ferry, West Virginia; a debacle leaving in its aftermath an acrid odor of regret, like gunpowder in the nostrils.

Of all insurrections this seemed to me the most ingenious: Captives would overcome their captor, punishing him most ignominiously, yet refraining from killing him, that he might bear the brand of their contempt through the remainder of his life; disguising their revolt amid a great fire, in such a way that their role was impossible to detect, even if they had survived.

I had no doubt, both Brigit & Gretel had been involved in this insurrection, in some way; for they were Father's most trusted nurse-assistants. But I could not believe that either, so dependent upon Silas Weir for her livelihood, & so trusted by him, would have wished to actually harm my father, bodily.

"Not Brigit. Not my angelic beloved"—this seemed a certainty to me, from which I was not likely to be nudged.

•

From this follows what can only be called the *Afterlife of Silas Aloysius Weir, M.D.*

My father continued to live for another twenty-seven years, until his death, in his seventy-seventh year, in November 1888; through all this time, he would remain Director of the New Jersey State Asylum for Female Lunatics at Trenton, but with gradually decreasing administrative responsibilities, as his younger assistant Amos Heller was elevated to the role of Acting Director; most significantly, Father's original medical research was severely curtailed after the destruction of North Hall & the (notorious) Laboratory.

It was during this less active time that professional acclaim came to Father, at first grudgingly, then in a rush of enthusiasm; as the prestigious American Association of Physicians & Surgeons inducted Silas Weir into their membership, for his "pioneering genius at the borders of medical research"; & the yet more prestigious National Society of Medical Science designated him the *Father of Modern Gyno-Psychiatry*—the first individual in the history of medical science to be so honored.

Following his death in Trenton, New Jersey, obituaries would appear in a wide variety of publications, including, most fulsomely, on the front pages of Trenton, Newark, & New Brunswick newspapers, as well as in professional journals; even Father's Cleff in-laws were impressed by a two-column obituary in *The New York Times*, praising Silas Aloysius Weir, M.D., as *pioneer-reformer, fearless seer, & humanitarian.*

In time, a statue commemorating Father would be erected near the front entrance of the Asylum grounds, replacing the statue of his predecessor, Medrick Weir; both likenesses, of a size somewhat larger than life, cast in bronze, depicting seated figures, in postures of manly dignity & sobriety, gazing into the future.

How ironic it was, in the light of such acclaim, that, following the cataclysmic fire of 1861, as everyone who knew him would declare, Silas Weir never fully recovered from his injuries, both physical & mental. *A light seemed to have gone out in his heart.*

In company, Father became ever more reticent & withdrawn; even in professional settings, where once he had behaved with the boastfulness of youth, his spirit seemed to have shrunken. Due to a gastrointestinal condition of some undefined sort, Father had to be close by a toilet at all times, which impediment greatly inconvenienced & embarrassed him, & curtailed hopes for travel he might have had—to major North American hospitals, for instance, where he had been invited to demonstrate his surgical cure of *fistula.*

It was assumed by his medical colleagues that Silas Weir chose to spend much time in the bosom of his family, even as it was assumed by his family that he chose to spend much time in his office at the Asylum!

It was a balm to my guilty heart to hear from each of my brothers & sisters that they were as uncomfortable with our father as I was; & had never felt that they knew him as anything more than a remote figure in the household, so harried & distracted by his responsibilities at the Asylum that he tended to muddle their names.

Not *my* name, however! As the firstborn son, I was always "Jonathan" to Father—with all our differences, I believed Father loved me most.

Not from Mother (who would have never spoken of such intimate matters with her children) but through relatives I would learn that, following his injuries on that cataclysmic night, Father shrank from sleeping in the same bedchamber with Mother, still less the same bed; nor would he allow Mother, or anyone, including another physician, to look upon his unclothed body. Though he was prone to severe headaches, shortness of breath, spinal & joint pain, chronic constipation & intermittent diarrhea, & much else, Father would not hear of consulting any specialist; when, having learned of his distress, his elder brother, Franklin, wrote to him proposing travel from Boston to examine him, Father responded coolly, "What Providence has granted me, that is for Providence to uphold. I would not intervene in the will of Providence."

It was Mother's belief that, as a young doctor, her husband had not time for happiness, as he was so very busy; as an older doctor, he had forgotten what happiness might be.

As it is often the case when pioneering work has been considered controversial, & a young researcher encounters widespread resistance to his discoveries, a number of years were required for Father's contributions to medical science to be tested by others. Such practical inventions as the *Weir-speculum* caught on readily, & is now in use by all gynecologists (unfairly, Father's name is not attached to the instrument); such procedures as the treatment of *fistulas* with silver wire, & the use of quinine in combating fever(s); more controversial treatments like the *Tranquility therapies* & those experiments involving the removal of female organs to treat hysteria, epilepsy, obesity, nymphomania, madness, etcetera, as well as the removal of teeth, remain issues of controversy among clinicians. (Indeed, it was often joked among Trenton medical persons that half the population of the city was *toothless*: You could identify a former Asylum patient by her sunken, collapsed lower face, for few Asylum patients were affluent enough to afford dentures.)

Similarly, Father's experiments with medications, diets, & fasting are ranked highly among some researchers, while deplored by others; Father's use of mental patients as experimental subjects is staunchly defended by some, & roundly condemned by others.

Even with his decreased responsibilities at the Asylum, Silas Weir continued to devote as many as forty hours weekly to patients, including private patients; despite his somewhat mangled hands, he persisted in performing the sort of practical gynecological surgery most requested by the guardians of female patients. Aligned with this, he produced a steady stream of articles for medical journals, as well as *Clinical Notes on Uterine Surgery* (1871) & *The Gynecologist's Handbook* (1876), both to remain in print for decades.

Yet, despite this diligence, Father was never again to be an entirely "well" person. His old robustness had vanished forever, replaced with a new diffidence, as in one who hesitates to exert himself, in anticipation of pain in joints or back. His walk, with a polished cane, was slow & calculated; the pasty-pale skin of his face appeared scarred, as if someone had scribbled on it with a sharp pen. His feathery, gray-grizzled hair grew thinly, exposing areas of scarred scalp. His mouth seemed to have shrunken, to the size of a snail.

It became an eccentricity of Father's, when greeted with the familiar *How are you?*, to narrow his eyes behind wire-rimmed glasses & reply in a nasal singsong, "Very well. And *you*?," in a way that suggested a mocking sort of mimicry.

Well-to-do women accustomed to charming their physicians encountered an enigma in Father, who seemed incapable of behaving toward them with any measure of gentlemanly gallantry. Politely he declined their invitations to social gatherings, & rarely smiled at their coquettish entreaties, as uncomprehending as a prepubescent or a monk; it was said that, in private consultations, Dr. Weir avoided gazing at women directly & touched them, when necessary, only through discreet layers of cloth. At all times, at least one nurse was in the examination room with him & the patient, standing very close as the patient was examined.

Dr. Weir is an old-fashioned gentleman!—it was widely noted, with both admiration & amusement.

True to my intrepid & impertinent manner, which has aided me, to a degree, in my career as a lawyer, as well as my penchant for not readily giving up, I would make several attempts to speak privately & frankly with my father, over a period of years.

Mother did all that she could to encourage Father to be relaxed with me, & avoid the subject of politics, but Father remained aloof, or diverted by small talk; if I inquired how he was, he would reply with the curt singsong, "Very well, Jonathan, & *you*?"

In this, I could see that Father was merely acknowledging, in this later, more subdued phase of his life, that we present to each other mere mask-selves, socially; we have little true interest in others' states of being, & hope to hide our own from them.

True, I did not ever speak sincerely to my father, or indeed to my mother, in revealing anything genuine about my state of mind; no matter how troubled I might be, my reply was invariably, "I am fine, thank you!"

And now it seemed particularly clear that Father did not trust me to maintain an air of decorum; he did not want any of his children to speak bluntly to him of matters he could not countenance.

Not once did I dare speak to him of Brigit Kinealy. Not once, of the terrible fire.

It was known of Silas Weir that he would not discuss the notorious Asylum fire of 1861, nor any of his patients from that time; if anyone alluded to these subjects, he would stiffen, & remain very still, without a word, grim-faced, sucking at his lips as if to draw them back into the small snail-mouth; then, he would excuse himself grimly and limp away.

After recovering from the worst of his injuries, Father allowed Trenton authorities to interview him, briefly. It would be his claim that the fire had been an Act of God: not arson.

Very likely, Father insisted, the fire had been started by a spark from a lantern in one of the outbuildings, falling on oily rags.

Or, the fire had been started by a flash of lightning, out of the night sky Father remembered as *heavily clouded* that evening.

He would claim that he'd been in his office in his residence, working by lamplight, perusing a text on surgery in preparation for emergency surgery in the morning, when he heard cries from North Hall, & smelled smoke, & hurried outside; saw to his astonishment that North Hall was aflame; & without giving thought to the danger, rushed to help patients evacuate the building, saving some five or six *female lunatics* before he was struck by flaming boards & choked by billowing smoke, & must have collapsed on the ground . . .

When he'd been awakened, it seemed to be a later time, & Solomon was crouching over him. It would be told to him that he'd *nearly died*, but he had no memory of the experience.

Investigators asked: Had he witnessed anyone behaving suspiciously in the vicinity of North Hall? Hospital patients, or staff?

Father shook his head, *No.* He had seen nothing suspicious—no one.

He'd been overcome by fire, he'd had no time to see anything, he insisted.

"What Providence grants us, it is for Providence to uphold. It is vain for us to wish otherwise."

No matter how authorities questioned him, Silas Weir maintained his conviction that *no individual had started the fire, the fire had been an Act of God.*

It did seem that local authorities were inclined to suspect that the fire in North Hall had been deliberately started, but lacked proof, or the testimony of witnesses. That Silas Weir insisted that *no one had started the fire, the fire was an Act of God* was a powerful counter-argument to their suspicions.

Frequently it happened, when people knew my identity, that I might be questioned in a sort of idly curious way about the Asylum fire: whether it was arson or not. Always my reply was succinct: "The Director of the Asylum has reason to believe that the fire was an 'Act of God.' That is all we can know."

In what would be the last private conversation of our lives, in the winter of 1861, I confided in Father that I had long wanted to confess to him, that I had disobeyed him the night when he'd ordered me to whip the Irish girl-nurse in that room in North Hall: "I had the whip in my hand, & there was the girl—with the white skin, & luminous eyes—but—I could not bring myself to whip her."

I spoke with an air of boyish innocence, & not contentiousness, which is a manner that has served me well as a young lawyer, arguing a case before an elder judge.

Cannily, I did not utter the name "Brigit." Still so beautiful—so special—a name to me, I feared that my voice might quaver if I had.

But hinting, to Father, that I no longer remembered the name, as if it were of no significance to me.

Hearing my words Father stiffened. A look of anguish came into the mask-like face.

As if in sheer wantonness someone had reached out to touch the man's raw, exposed heart.

"You—did not *whip her*? Not—a single stroke of the whip?"

"No, Father. I did not."

"You—lied to me?"

"Yes, Father. I lied to you."

The look of anguish was slow to drain from Father's face, & was retained in his eyes, which were filled with moisture. An awkward silence followed.

It would have been quite natural for me to continue with a heartfelt apology; yet, stubbornly, I would not apologize, for I had done nothing wrong at the time for which I should apologize.

If I had apologized, perhaps Father would have forgiven me; in a romance of the era, in which son & father were often at odds, as the generations were at odds in these troubled times, not unlike the Northern & Southern states bristling with indignation at wrongs committed by the other, certainly the son's (humble) apology would be followed by the father's (noble) forgiveness.

But this son would not *apologize;* & this father would not *forgive.*

We were in Father's office among his old things, which had not been moved about, nor even very attentively dusted, for years. Prominent on the walls were stiff-painted likenesses of distinguished scientists, inherited from Medrick Weir, as well as a large, brooding portrait of Weir himself, in a pose worthy of Rembrandt. Medrick Weir was said to be a great-uncle of my father's, of whom many strange tales were told when I was growing up on the grounds of the Asylum; it was whispered that this Director of the Asylum had been murdered by an uprising of inmates, & that his remains had been burnt in the fireplace in this very room.

Of furnishings in the room only the brass telescope had been of interest to me, as a science-minded boy, when I was very young; but when on a rare visit to Father's office I dragged the telescope to the window, to peer up at the sky at dusk, I had been unable to focus the lens, seeing only my own blinking eye reflected; & when I asked Father to help me, he had looked up irritably from his desk & said: *Son, who has time for childish games!*

Vividly now, I recalled this exchange. In retrospect wanting to correct Father: *A life with no time for childish games is no life.*

Now Father's grave, lined face suggested not irritation but melancholy. Not annoyance but resignation. I was relieved that (apparently) Father was not going to chide me or order me out of his sight.

I had to suppose that my remarks had caused him to recollect Brigit Kinealy, a memory sure to be painful to him. And perhaps he was thinking of his other nurse-assistant—the midwife from Düsseldorf—had it been Gretel?

How much younger Silas Weir had been, in those days! It was disconcerting to me to think of my ravaged father as *a youngish man,* once; who could not have failed to find Brigit Kinealy a very attractive young woman, despite being Irish, & a deaf-mute, & a lowly indentured servant.

I had to wonder: What had become of Brigit & Gretel, after the fire? Had Father ever heard from either of them? Or—of them?

I wondered: Was Father thinking of what his (unidentified) assailants had done to him, had perpetrated upon his body—with such deliberation that he should not die, but survive; that he would have no recourse except to remember, with shame & anguish, through the remainder of his life?

Or—seeing that his expression was more mournful than indignant—was he tenderly recalling something precious he had lost? Something he could not bring himself to name?

"No one must ever know, Jonathan. You must promise me."

So urgently Father spoke, I was taken aback. For I had no clear idea what he meant.

Did Father assume that I knew something that others did not? That had something to do with Brigit Kinealy, whom I *had not whipt* as bidden?

Uneasily, I tried to smile at Father, to reassure him. For he seemed to be appealing very openly to me.

Though I had no idea what he was asking quickly I murmured: "Yes, Father! Of course, I promise."

In parting, our handshake was surprisingly warm, and forceful; indeed, the only time in my life I clearly recall shaking hands with my father, all the more memorable for it being the final time.

The Pledge

O F COURSE, I searched for her.
  Weeks, months, & (six) years. To no avail.
*Vanished from the earth—*or so it seemed.

As the reader has surmised, Part V of this volume, *The Insurrection*, has been drawn in its entirety from *Lost Girl, Found: An Orphan's True Story Told by Herself* by Brigit Agnes Kinealy, a memoir published in 1868, to much acclaim, & not a little scandal; one of the first intimate accounts of the life of an indentured servant in the United States, to become something of a classic of Irish-American writings of the nineteenth century.

Such memoirs, which would appear with increasing frequency following the Civil War, to set beside popular slave-narratives of an earlier era by Sojourner Truth, Mary Prince, & William Grimes.

Since I am not qualified to render judgment as to the veracity of *Lost Girl, Found,* I have chosen not to edit any of it; but have presented excerpts verbatim from the original text, which exhibit a most idiosyncratic poetic & imagined prose, in contrast to the stiffly "formal" prose excerpted from Silas Weir's *Chronicle of a Physician's Life.*

In doing this, I am conscious of publishing material that may well offend some readers, & cannot fail to offend certain members of my family, including my mother, Theresa; from whom I would beg an apology except that, as we have learned in recent years in this tragically divided, strife-torn country, *It is best that Truth prevails at all costs.*

It was in October 1867, a full year before the publication of *Lost Girl, Found,* that I traveled from Boston (where I was living at the time, as a law-consultant for William Lloyd Garrison's *The Liberator*), to Ardmore, Pennsylvania, where, at the Ardmore Athenaeum, several young women poetesses were presenting their work, among them "Brigit Agnes Kinealy."

In time, I would come to learn Brigit's history following the Asylum fire. Here, I will quickly summarize, for the reader's information:

Soon after escaping from the conflagration on the Asylum grounds, & from the city of Trenton, Brigit & several of her sister-escapees found a safe home in Philadelphia that welcomed indentured servants & others who had escaped cruel masters; following this, Brigit was taken up by the Parrishes, a well-to-do Quaker family in Ardmore who were renowned for their "rescue missions" involving self-emancipated (i.e., runaway) Black slaves & young persons like Brigit who had been sold into servitude by older relatives, which was fully legal in the United States at this time.

In the Parrish household, Brigit was employed as a nursemaid for the family's young children & something of a caretaker, for an elderly, ailing member of the Parrish family; she was sent to a Quaker school, where she earned teaching credentials, & the skills with which to become a published poet.

Very surprising to me, in May 1867, to turn the pages of *The Stylus* & to discover a poem by "Brigit Agnes Kinealy."

The poem was titled "Joy"—obscure to my eye, & unsettling, in that it had an odd, unpoetical shape, like a broken egg, in the very center of the page; & seemed most insolently to *fail to rhyme.*

JOY

Joy there was, amid sorrow.
Amid sorrow, joy.
For sorrow-joy more
sharp to us
than mere/merest
Joy.

Several times, I read this enigmatic little poem. My first thought was that I did not like it—but, did I understand it?

But—the poem *caused me to think*.

(As it would happen, this verse would be placed as an epigraph at the very opening of *Lost Girl, Found*.)

Hearing in the pellucid near-toneless music of such speech, the barely discernible lilt of the Irish voice. Though born in America, the orphaned Irish girl had acquired something of her mother's accented English, it seemed.

To my consternation, tears spilled from my eyes.

Brigit! My love.

Of course, I wrote to Miss Brigit Agnes Kinealy immediately, at the address of *The Stylus,* & waited impatiently for days, then weeks, receiving no reply.

Again it would not be clear to me whether Brigit had received my letter(s), for I wrote several. Not wanting to persist in any way that might be unwelcome, I refrained from writing to her again, but remained vigilant, alert to see where the poetess might publish her work again—which turned out to be, in August of that year, in *The Atlantic Monthly.*

To which, naïvely yet with hope, I wrote just once again, signing my letter *With love, your friend Jonathan,* as I had in the past. But again, received no reply.

By happenstance then, a notice came to my attention in *Harper's Weekly,* in the fall of 1867, that several women poets would be reading their work, under the auspices of the Ardmore Poetry Society, in the Ardmore Athenaeum in October.

Two trains were required to travel from Boston to Philadelphia, & from Philadelphia to Ardmore, on the Main Line; but I was determined to seek out Brigit Kinealy, at least to satisfy my curiosity, that there was no hope of her loving me; or indeed, any remnant of feeling remaining between us.

The previous year, in what I considered to be my final, dogged effort, while visiting my family in Trenton, at Christmas, I dared to return to the administrative offices of the Asylum another time; thinking that a small bribe might help my cause, more than a mere impassioned plea,

I persuaded a clerk, for a cash-sum of $20, to locate for me the very document for which I had been searching, the contract that legally bound the child Brigit Kinealy to the Asylum, in servitude. Herewith, the text of this document, which cannot suggest the melancholy nature of the yellowed, much-creased & mildewed sheet of paper that had been crushed at the back of a file.

11 January 1849. For a Bargained Sum Mary Kinealy in her Owne proper person came into the Court of Magistrate T. Bedwell of Trenton, New Jersey, to Voluntarily bind her daughter Brigit Agnes an infant aged Five years old Unto the New Jersey State Asylum for Female Lunatics at Trenton, New Jersey, Untill she shall arrive to One & Twenty years of Age at which time Brigit Agnes Kinealy shall be freed from servitude & fully discharged from said Asylum unless breach of contract or other Infractions of Law extend this contract to a Future Date.

Presenting myself as an attorney in the hire of said *Brigit Agnes Kinealy,* I argued to the clerk that, as the expiration date for the contract had run its course in January 1865, eleven months before, it would be no harm if he surrendered the *nullified* contract to me, in hand; for no one was likely to seek it out, & if his office failed to surrender the contract now, much paperwork would ensue, between our offices, involving unnecessary labor for him.

"Will another twenty dollars facilitate our transaction?"—genially I inquired of the clerk, & was not at all surprised at his reply.

Making my way out of the subterranean Hall of Records, of the Asylum, with the ignominious contract in my pocket, hoping that, one day, I might present it in person to Brigit Kinealy as a contract *null & void.*

·

As soon as I sighted Brigit in the Athenaeum, a sensation of faintness came over me, & I scarcely knew where I was.

So many times in public places my heart had clenched as I glimpsed *her*—that is, someone resembling her; upon closer scrutiny, scarcely resembling the luminous Brigit of my memory at all.

So the hopeful eye plays tricks upon the craven brain. The heart responds foolishly, beating as rapidly as if the *real person* stood before us.

Seeing Brigit in the interior of the Athenaeum, at the very front of the room, I felt at once a sense of dismay, & my own folly: for (of course) Brigit was not alone as I had wished to imagine her, but with companions. Though she was immediately recognizable, I could see that Brigit was no longer the forlorn little Irish orphan whom I had befriended in her misery, & had had some part in "healing"; my bravado in securing the release of her contract from the Asylum, which contract I was carrying now on my person, seemed to me a clumsy sort of vanity.

It gladdened my heart, however—Brigit had so clearly recovered from the trauma she had endured at the Asylum, & beyond.

No one could have guessed, seeing the self-assured young woman that evening, that it had once been impossible for her to *speak & hear* as normal persons do; nor did Brigit have about her that air of scarcely disguised anxiety that had so characterized her in the past.

Still, this young woman was clearly an "albino"—with startlingly white skin, strangely transparent eyes, & pale blue veins just visible in her forehead: a most unusual-looking individual, with a beauty that would not be to all tastes, as her curious poetry was surely not to all tastes.

Clad in clothing of high quality, a long skirt & jacket of a subtle, dark-mulberry hue, a pale lavender scarf at her throat, & upon her high-held head, a smart, stylish hat with a slanted rim, that hid much of her plaited ashy-blond hair.

Ah!—in profile, I would have recognized *her*. Yet how unreal, to see my love only just a few feet from me, & oblivious of me.

I did not like it that Brigit was in the company of others, an older couple, plain-faced & stolid, & a gentleman of about thirty-five, with a close-cropped beard, whose manner with Brigit was overly solicitous & attentive, it seemed to me; a close friend, perhaps a fiancé. (I could not grasp that Brigit might be married—that possibility had never once occurred to me, & was swiftly banished now.)

Waves of emotion swept over me, in conflict. Though I was thrilled to have found Brigit Kinealy at last, I felt nonetheless a pang of loss, that the little deaf-mute orphan-girl had vanished forever: replaced by this composed-seeming stranger, whom (perhaps) I would not have dared to approach, if I did not already know her.

Painful to me, to observe Brigit in her greatly altered life. Knowing that I should remain at a distance, for her benefit if not for my own.

For I did not wish to embarrass her, among these persons with whom she had forged a new life. (Almost, one would have assumed that the older couple were Brigit's parents—somewhat ill-at-ease, & uncertain, like individuals not accustomed to society: these would turn out to be the Parrishes, of the renowned Quaker family.) For Brigit there could be no memories of me, apart from memories of my father, & the loathsome Laboratory; still more, the mysterious circumstances surrounding Brigit's disappearance from the Asylum.

I wondered that Brigit might have received the letters I had sent to her, in care of the magazines that had published her poetry: in which case, she had elected not to reply, & it would be very wrong of me to persevere, in trying to speak with her now.

Or, it might have been that, having received my letters, Brigit would not be so surprised to see Jonathan Weir among the audience at the Athenaeum.

All these thoughts, & others, swept through me, as I sat near the back of the crowded room, on the aisle, in such a position that I might gaze upon Brigit Kinealy, through the entirety of the program, that passed like a fever dream through my brain; including even Brigit's reading of her verse, the penultimate presentation of the evening, delivered in a somewhat thin voice, as in one who is not (yet) certain of herself in a public place.

Not a syllable of Brigit's poetry lodged in my brain on that occasion, as I gazed at her with a pounding heart, & a heated face; for it appeared that she was wearing the little opal ring that I had given her as a pledge; & so far as I could determine, no other ring adorned her fingers.

Not knowing what I would do next, as the program concluded, & the audience applauded with much enthusiasm.

As well-wishers crowded around the young women poets, & showed no sign of dispersing soon, I moved uncertainly into the aisle, hat in hand. In this genial company of well-to-do persons I was somewhat distinctive in that I was alone: No one knew me, nor even glanced at me, as if I were invisible.

Such awkwardness, it is painful for me to recall, still less record.

Those fraught minutes in our lives, of intense inwardness, & emotional distress, which may alter the very course of our lives, as we seem to know at the time; thus, a sensation of near-paralysis, how to act.

You must speak to her. You cannot have come so far—to retreat in silence.

You dare not. You will upset her & embarrass yourself.

Seeing at last how Brigit's gaze glided over me, then halted, & returned with a jolt—in the exquisite face a look of surprise, & almost of fright, in recognizing me.

The older couple beside Brigit took no notice as they were engaged in conversation with another party, but the male companion was aware of me at once, alert & suspicious.

Your rival! He loves her, he is possessive.

As I was not moving away, nor was I coming forward, after another awkward long moment Brigit excused herself graciously from her companions, & approached me, smiling a bright nervous smile.

Murmuring, *Hello, Jonathan!*—so softly, I could barely hear.

In turn, I greeted Brigit quietly, & offered her my hand.

Six years! So long had I rehearsed what I might say to Brigit, I found myself speechless now, as Brigit asked, in a faltering voice, how was I?—& I stumbled a reply, a flush rising in my face.

More coherently, I managed to answer that I was living now in Boston, & that my life had changed considerably since we had last seen each other.

What yearning showed in my face, I cannot imagine! But Brigit held herself poised, & maintained a calm demeanor.

In a voice that struggled to remain matter-of-fact, Brigit volunteered that she was living now in Ardmore, & employed by a local family; she had been encouraged as a poet, & had begun to publish . . . Her voice trailed off as we stood close together amid the crowd, neither looking directly at each other nor turning away.

All this while, I was aware of Brigit's companions observing us with much interest. I feared they would soon come forward, to join us.

I had not known with any certainty whether Brigit had received my letters to her, forwarded from the magazines in which her poems were published; but if so, she might well have guessed that I might make an attempt to seek her out in Ardmore, & so the sight of me could not have entirely been a surprise.

We were made awkward also by the need to address each other in formal terms, given our surroundings; as we had never done in the past, meeting in our secret place on the Asylum grounds.

As if to deflect questions I might put to her, Brigit spoke warmly of her "Quaker family"—her "new, beloved Quaker faith"—her residence in Ardmore, where she was made to feel "like one of the family." She did not speak of a fiancé, nor did she offer to introduce me to her companions.

Nervously, though politely, Brigit inquired after my family; she did not utter the name *Dr. Weir,* but I volunteered to inform her that my father was still Director of the Asylum in Trenton, though his administrative duties were less broad than previously, & he had all but ceased his experimental research.

For a moment Brigit looked as blank as a sheet of paper, as if she had gone deaf suddenly. I could not resist asking, "Did you think that my father had passed away, Brigit? In the fire?"—& when Brigit seemed still not to hear, I added, wryly, "Father is prospering, in his own way. He is being acclaimed as a 'pioneer'—he is considered a 'reformer.' He has attained his goal, the respect of the medical establishment—the title 'Father of Gyno-Psychiatry.'"

"'Gyno-Psychiatry!' What is that?" Brigit winced, as if the words pained her ears.

"It has something to do with 'psychiatry,' & something to do with 'women.'"

At this, I laughed; while Brigit remained silent, stricken. The merest suggestion of a blush had come onto the porcelain-pale face, which was looking very young now, & fragile.

I asked Brigit what had become of my father's nurse-assistant Gretel, & after some hesitation Brigit replied to me that Gretel had acquired a new name & was living now in Waltham, Massachusetts, in the employ of a physician, as a nurse & midwife.

"She has become very religious—Gretel has. She has earned a happy life."

In Brigit's eyes that brimmed with moisture I saw, or believed that I saw, a kind of anguish, of all that must remain unspoken between us.

Seeing that Brigit had been turning the little ring around her finger, not knowing what she did, I made mention of it; which was a blunder, for Brigit quickly lifted her hand before her, & stammered that she would return it to me . . . She wore it, she said, in memory of my *generosity & kindness* to her, as proof of how good a man might be in his heart, though of the *class of Masters*.

My face flushed hotly. How absurd this was!—*class of Masters*. It was hurtful to hear, that Brigit thought of me in such a way.

"You took much time, Jonathan—to teach me to read, & to write. It is entirely due to you that I can add a column of numbers, & multiply a two-digit number by a one-digit number, in my head."

This effort to be amusing, I met with a stony countenance.

"I doubt that much of that is true, Brigit. You already knew many words when I 'taught' you—you could read quite well. You had memorized pages of my father's anatomy book, as I recall."

"I—I—don't recall . . ."

". . . words like *esophagus, liver, colon* . . . You remember, you spelled them out on a sheet of paper, with crayons."

In Brigit's eyes I saw that indeed she remembered, & much else besides.

But her *will* was, she did not; & she did not want to be forced. No longer the docile indentured servant-girl, eager to defer & agree with her superiors; now a straight-backed young woman with uplifted head, determined to stand her own ground.

Impulsively then, as I had not intended to do, I said, in a lowered voice, that only Brigit might hear: "Do you remember, Brigit, we had planned to leave Trenton together?—that is, I had promised to return for you, & buy out your contract, as soon as I could."

Brigit stiffened, as if I had reached out impulsively to touch her.

"I hope I am not upsetting you, Brigit, by saying this. But—I have waited six years to say it, & it needs to be said."

In a faltering voice Brigit replied, "I—I think—I think there were false pretenses. You did not know me—your friendship with me did not include any doubt of me."

"What do you mean, 'any doubt of you'?"—this was a curious turn of phrase, which I could not comprehend.

"Doubt of my—person. My being. My—purity."

"'Purity'!" My face grew heated, for a moment I could not speak. Was Brigit alluding to something so very personal, so intimate, it could scarcely be acknowledged in private, let alone in this public space?

Seeing my astounded expression, Brigit said stiffly, "There was—there is—too much difference between us, Jonathan. You must have known, at the time. I was too young—too naïve & ignorant—to understand. Now I am with people who understand persons like myself—orphans, indentured servants. 'Masters.' All that is done to us, which we cannot prevent. Which steeps us in sin—if not our own, the sins of others, that stain us. The Parrishes have taken me in, they have 'rescued me.' As they have rescued others. They do not judge me, for God is an eternal light within us, that loves us, & does not judge."

At this, I stood confounded, trying to make sense of Brigit's words, spoken with a kind of vehemence, as if she believed that I could not possibly understand. My head felt like a bell tower in which a bell was being rung, capriciously, deafeningly.

Seeing how her words had affected me, Brigit amended: "I—I don't believe that you were serious, Jonathan. You were feeling sorry for me. You'd hoped to encourage me not to lose heart."

"Brigit, that is unfair! I was always serious, you must have known. Of course I wanted to encourage you 'not to lose heart.' I loved you—I had not the courage to tell you, exactly—I hadn't the courage to acknowledge it, myself."

Brigit winced another time, stealing a glance at me, guilty-eyed, stricken. In a childish gesture I recalled from years ago, she brought both hands to her face, as if to shield her eyes with her fingers; yet, the fingers were spread. The little opal ring, on the third finger of Brigit's right hand, glimmered faintly as if in protest.

Following this outburst, I realized that I had better leave the premises. It had been the last intention of mine, to *cause a scene,* & to upset Brigit Kinealy.

Stammering foolishly, I said good night to Brigit; I had in my hand a copy of a literary journal named *Thalia,* which had been for sale at the Athenaeum, in which all of the evening's poets were represented; & was indicating this, in some fashion to suggest, if Brigit's companions happened to be watching us, that I would read this journal soon, & was bidding farewell to Brigit, now.

My mouth seemed to be twisting in a most dangerous way, I was in terror of losing my adult poise.

Blindly I turned, to walk away. Colliding with one or two gentlemen in my path. My brain buzzed—*Is she really going to let me go? Does she really not love me?*

How naïve I had been, to bring the voided contract with me, in my coat pocket. As if I might flourish it, & quite dazzle Brigit Kinealy, & not rather shock & offend her, perhaps irrevocably.

By the time I exited through the marble portals of the Athenaeum & stepped outside into gusty air, a vise seemed to have tightened around my chest, & I could scarcely breathe.

I had engaged a room at the Ardmore Inn, for that night. I would walk there, a distance of about half a mile, clutching the literary journal like a talisman.

Yet, pausing to recover my composure. Several persons glanced at me quizzically, as if wondering if I were unwell.

"Jonathan—wait!"

There came Brigit out of the Athenaeum agitated & breathless, to catch up with me.

In the white-skinned face, a look of raw emotion, dread. The faint blue vein at her temple quivered.

"—I am sure that we weren't serious, Jonathan. We were both so young. I—don't think so . . ."

"Are you! But I *am not.*"

"You didn't really know me then—I was such a child, & in such distress—& you have no idea of me now, after so many years."

"Six years is not 'long'—in a lifetime."

"It has been a lifetime, to me."

"As to me! I have searched for you."

"Jonathan, please! You could not have been serious about—loving me—"

"No. That is not true. It was the first time in my life, that I had felt anything so 'serious.' I struck the whip against the floor, such feeling boiled over in me—you must remember."

"N-no . . ."

Though clearly *yes,* Brigit did remember.

But clearly *no,* I must not force her to remember.

Of course, it had been much earlier, that I'd struck the whip against the floor. Not when I had told her, that I loved her.

Still, it was pointless to quarrel at such a time. Like any skilled lawyer, I knew when it was strategic to retreat, or to appear to retreat.

"Brigit, I understand: I had taken advantage of your situation. You were not 'free' at the time—you had no choice."

"I—I had no choice . . ."

"Will you write to me, at least? Will we see each other again?"

"I am not sure what purpose that would serve, Jonathan. My life is different now."

"All of our lives are 'different' now. We are not children."

"I—I am in a family now. I am a Quaker. In our community there are responsibilities, expectations—"

"I greatly respect Quakers! The Quaker faith! I would happily become a Quaker myself, there is nothing left in me of cold leftovers of the Calvinist faith."

"Jonathan, please!—there is nothing amusing in this."

"I am not 'amused'—I don't mean to be 'amusing.' I have come here from Boston, purposefully to see you, & to tell you—that I have never forgotten you; & feel as strongly for you now as I had felt six years ago."

"Jonathan, please—just let me go . . ."

"I do love you, Brigit. But I will let you go." Quickly I assured Brigit in a lowered voice.

From this pledge, Brigit seemed to take heart. A light came into her face, which had been looking strained, guilty. She seemed to have forgotten entirely the notion of returning the opal ring to me.

From my fingers she took the journal *Thalia,* & with a little pencil hastily wrote several lines on the title page; thrusting it back at me, & turning quickly away, as if she feared her companions were following, & would see us together.

Grateful for this gesture, I turned away as well, & resisted the impulse to turn back. A fountain of hope soared in my heart. I had to discipline myself, not to see immediately what Brigit had written inside the journal but to wait until I was safely at the Ardmore Inn for the night.

Reader, it is true that I loved her. But I had no intention of letting her go.

ACKNOWLEDGMENTS

This is a work of fiction incorporating episodes from the lives of the historic J. Marion Sims, M.D. (1813–1883), "the Father of Modern Gynecology"; Silas Weir Mitchell, M.D. (1829–1914), "the Father of Medical Neurology"; and Henry Cotton, M.D. (1876–1933), the director of the New Jersey Lunatic Asylum from 1907 to 1930.

Several passages, scattered through the text, have been adapted from passages in Sims's *The Story of My Life* (1888). Particular thanks are due to Andrew Scull's *Madhouse: A Tragic Tale of Megalomania and Modern Medicine* (Yale University Press, 2005), a chronicle of the life and career of Henry Cotton; and Elaine Showalter's *The Female Malady: Women, Madness, and English Culture (1830–1980)* (Pantheon Books, 1985).

Chapter 2 has appeared in *Conjunctions* and excerpts from chapters 6, 7, and 9 in *Boulevard*.

Joyce Carol Oates is a recipient of the National Humanities Medal, the National Book Award, the 2019 Jerusalem Prize for Lifetime Achievement, the National Book Critics Circle Ivan Sandrof Life Achievement Award, and the Horror Writers Association Bram Stoker Award for Lifetime Achievement. She has been nominated several times for the Pulitzer Prize.

Oates has written some of the most enduring fiction of our time, including the national best sellers *We Were the Mulvaneys, Blonde, The Accursed,* and the *New York Times* best seller *The Falls,* which won the 2005 Prix Femina. In 2020 she was awarded the Cino Del Duca World Prize for Literature. She has been a member of the American Academy of Arts and Letters since 1978 and was inducted into the American Philosophical Society in 2016. She currently divides her teaching time among Princeton, New York University, and Rutgers University (New Brunswick).

A NOTE ON THE TYPE

This book was set in Minion, a typeface produced by the Adobe Corporation specifically for the Macintosh personal computer, and released in 1990. Designed by Robert Slimbach, Minion combines the classic characteristics of old-style faces with the full complement of weights required for modern typesetting.

Typeset by Scribe, Philadelphia, Pennsylvania

Printed and bound by Berryville Graphics, Berryville, Virginia

Designed by Maggie Hinders